THE DEVIL'S ANALYST

Also by Dennis Frahmann

Tales From the Loon Town Cafe

The Finnish Girl

The Devil's Analyst

A NOVEL

Dennis Frahmann

LOON TOWN BOOKS

Publisher's Note: This is a work of fiction. Names, characters, places, and incidents are a product of the author's imagination. Locales and public names are sometimes used for atmospheric purposes. Any resemblance to actual people, living or dead, or to businesses, companies, events, institutions, or locales is completely coincidental.

Book Layout © 2015 BookDesignTemplates.com

The Devil's Analyst/Dennis Frahmann. −1st ed.

Library of Congress Control Number: 2016911491

Loon Town Books
www.loontown.com

ISBN 978-0692710579

"But put forth thine hand now, and touch all that he hath, and he will curse thee to thy face."

Job 1:11

CONTENTS

In The Analyst's Office

Thank God I found you. I didn't realize how much I needed a therapist until we connected. This conflict of mine has been going on too long. I need to tell my story to someone, someone who can help me. Believe me, this will be the first of many sessions.

You're recording this, aren't you? I think it's very important to keep a record of everything I say. This situation's not that easy to understand. Sometimes I don't understand it myself. But you're a professional. You can make sense of it.

It's all about a guy named Danny. Really, he should be a nobody. There's no reason why anyone would pay one bit of attention to him. I met him a long time ago and there was something about him that made me care. He's like that, I guess. Everyone seems to like Danny Lahti—the poor little boy whose mother killed herself.

But they don't see him for the kind of person he really is. He's fooled them all. But not me. I have a mission to expose him for what he is, to make him choose one path over the other.

Remember that story about how the devil convinced God to test Job to find out the truth about the man's faith? I need to do the same with Danny. I need to test him. Maybe I'll start when he's in Wisconsin with his friends.

You see, I never wanted to be the person who made Danny face the truth. But that's my job, and I'm not afraid to do it.

PART ONE

A NEW MILLENNIUM

CHAPTER ONE

Midnight

Twenty minutes to midnight, and the ice on the frozen lake outside cracked. The loud reverberations of winter echoed through the night and invaded Danny Lahti's peace.

Danny was prepared to let time move forward in whatever incremental way it chose. At that moment . . . sitting on a sofa in an enormous room near midnight . . . huddled within a century-old hunting lodge of a long-dead lumber tycoon . . . on the shoreline of a lake nearly forgotten in the isolated woods of northern Wisconsin, Danny Lahti was not concerned about the potential for a technological apocalypse as time turned to the year 2000.

But he did feel on the brink. Something was about to happen. Things should change; they needed to change. He couldn't really say why. Danny never felt he was the introspective type. But he had always felt connected to a larger universe, one in which he received premonitions of what was to come.

The end of the century. Or maybe the start of a new millennium. It depended on the pundit. But computers only knew what they were programmed to know, and they weren't programmed to deal with changing from 1999 to 2000. Maybe early computer scientists never thought about a century starting anew. December 31, 1999 could prove an existential threat. They called it "Y2K." Who knows, maybe every generation deserved its opportunity to restart the clock.

For Danny, his past was too painful, but the future felt too uncertain. In a way, his life could be the snowdrift-covered lawns that surrounded this house. On the surface, the drifts were unblemished and glistening in the weak moonlight. But beneath their surface, under the shapeless accumulated flakes, were the remains of years of living. If Danny had the time and the tools and the energy, he could shovel his way into discovering the dead flowerbeds, the abandoned lawn furniture, and the century's worth of trails across the grounds. But who could be bothered? Eventually, the warm sun of spring would surely melt the snow. Just wait. The past would be exposed.

Danny had always been the kind of person willing to wait. When he was only twelve, his mother committed suicide and he found her dead body. He waited then, always expecting someone would eventually arrive to explain what had happened and why. When his father withdrew into a hermit-like life that barely acknowledged his adolescent son's existence, Danny still waited. Someone would surely make his father forget his dead wife and remember his child. He was still waiting.

And when Josh came into his life, promising an escape from these cold woods into the warm, loving life of the Los Angeles sun, Danny followed and waited for Josh's direction.

He waited. He always had. Perhaps he always would. It was his nature not to rebel and not to question, to try to be good and not rock the boat. A new year, a new century, a new millennium, not even "Y2K" could change that. Because Danny Lahti had never been able to find the energy to grab the reins of his own life. And he didn't intend to start now. And yet something was changing. He felt it.

The ice cracked again. Nineteen minutes to midnight.

"What are you thinking?" said the woman who stood behind Danny's sofa. Her look went beyond the large French doors on the far side of the living room, across the snow-covered fieldstone terrace, and down to the dark icy sheen of the frozen lake. She looked peaceful, just like the winter scene.

What could Danny say to his old friend Cynthia Trueheart Grant? In their high school years, she had been the bubbly cheerleader. Always an optimist, she normally made him laugh or at least smile. He wanted her energy now. In her early-thirties, she still had the perky energy of the teenage girl. They were alone in the house, since Josh and Chip had gone into town hours earlier. Chip was Cynthia's husband and owner of a local technology firm; Josh was Danny's boyfriend and a newfangled Internet mogul, and their lives were interwoven in a complicated way.

He knew Cynthia was truly interested in what he was thinking, but what could he say—that he never wanted to buy this oversized log manor that evoked far too many painful memories, yet Josh somehow convinced him that owning this grandiose property would somehow make up for his youth.

After the stock market crash in 1987, the arrogant former owner had lost the mansion to the bank and the house sat empty. Then last year Josh told Danny it was time to return to their little resort hometown of Thread, Wisconsin, buy the tycoon's foreclosed home, and restore the oversized camp to its former glory. They did it all. Dug up the old rose garden that ran amok. Trimmed the colonnade of maples that graced the long drive. Filled the chinked logs after a decade of neglect, glazed the broken windows, updated the neglected plumbing and electricity, pulled out the rotting beams of the old boat dock—the list of tasks never ended. But Josh never worried about money, just as he didn't believe in "Y2K." He swore that the current Internet boom would underwrite all their playthings. Danny didn't know enough about their finances to argue.

But he knew this place was filled with ghosts, not ectoplasmic ones, but emotional ones. No matter how tastefully the decorators had furnished the graceful rooms, they still evoked in Danny memories of the seventeen-year-old boy who once helped cater a party for the former owners. The Christmas-time decorations of that long-ago night, the expensive clothing of the cavalcade of wealthy and important guests, and the whispered joking about the oddities of the small nearby town of Thread—including the soft laughter about his oddly behaving father—this placed stored all of that.

Surely a new century would allow him to send all those ghostly echoes into exile. Forever. He could have tried to say all of that in answer to Cynthia, but instinctively he knew his friend would not want to hear these musings.

He lied instead. "I'm thinking how beautiful it is here."

Cynthia sat down and faced him, leaving a coffee table between them. The moonlit scene outside silhouetted her profile, which was still striking. "Do you really believe it's beautiful? After all, you left for Los Angeles after high school and I'm the one who stayed. But still I agree with you. Northern Wisconsin is lovely, and Chip and I are so happy the two of you restored this house. We hope you spend a lot of time here."

Another loud boom echoed. The lake ice cracked once more.

Cynthia laughed because she was so often happy, and the sound of ice was just another part of her life. "Aren't we the fools though? Spending New Year's Eve in this isolated spot? In our little hideaway when the lights of the world could go out?" She laughed again at the absurdity of the possibility.

"You know that won't happen," Danny replied.

"Remember how much fun we used to have?" Cynthia asked. "Back when you and I worked at the Loon Town Café, and Josh and Chip would come in to eat? And to woo us. That's the right word, isn't it? We were wooed. All those characters in our little town, and we thought everything was possible and everyone was wonderful."

"Well, you did."

"Because it was true. You're just too stubborn to enjoy everything you've been given. Here I am, with you, on New Year's Eve, waiting for the men we love. Isn't that worth celebrating?"

Truthfully Danny would rather have been somewhere more glamorous and crowded but Josh had insisted on flying to the camp. Danny was of two minds about spending the holidays in his home town, but Josh reminded him that the place had originally been built in the nineteenth century, as though that somehow gave the mansion more cosmic energy to welcome a new millennium.

Both Josh and Chip worked in the high tech industry, so Danny understood that "Y2K" was mostly hype and wasn't worried about the night ahead or any "Y2K" problem. In fact, he wanted not to worry about anything. The four of them were much like the favored children of myths, the ones who were blessed with a fairy-tale quality.

In such stories, Cynthia was the beloved and spoiled child who would one day marry the crown prince. Her parents, the Truehearts, owned the town's grocery store and most of the other businesses, but it was the early investment of Cynthia's father in the nearby American Seasons resort that made him truly wealthy. The local Coeur de Lattigeaux tribe, more commonly called the Lattigo, were the other major investors in the resort and Chip Grant was the tribe's leader. By marrying Chip, Cynthia rose as close to royalty as could exist in this northern kingdom.

On the other hand, Danny was the woodsman's son—the child who grew up in a household without a mother but with a father who didn't take proper care of his son no matter how much he loved him—the kind of fairy tale kid who might get lost in the woods or thrown into the witch's oven.

But like all fairy tales, Danny's life was having a happy ending. He met the attractive and charming Josh, who was blessed with the Midas touch. Danny didn't quite understand how Josh's various Internet startups worked, but clearly they did and the two of them were a wealthy couple. Josh's financial schemes paid for this camp, their Spanish-style mansion in the Los Feliz section of the Hollywood Hills, and a lifestyle of benevolent extravagance.

Out of the blue, Cynthia asked Danny, "Are you happy? I want you to be happy. Are you?"

Even as a teenager, Cynthia was always concerned about everyone's emotional well being. It was a silly question. Danny had everything.

"Of course."

"Sometimes I worry about you. I know you hated that about me even when we were teenagers. But for a while, I thought you were my Romeo in waiting. But now I know it was never meant to be because someone else was my true other half!"

Now Danny laughed. "How philosophical. Have you been reading Plato?"

Cynthia smiled but her face betrayed a small tic—a tell that appeared whenever she didn't understand one of Danny's references. She wouldn't say anything though. They were comfortable with not fully understanding each other. Beside she would prefer to think of all their fun times together, of which there had been so many.

Cynthia moved nearer the mantel of the large fieldstone fireplace. Its chimney soared to the top of the fifteen-foot ceiling of a cavernous room. The lighting was subdued. The huge first-growth timbers that framed the rooms were lost in the shadows. The ornate mantel clock chimed the quarter hour.

"Only fifteen minutes to midnight. Why aren't Josh and Chip here yet?" Cynthia glanced toward the large noble fir decorated with German blown glass ornaments and old-fashioned bubble lights. "Maybe something's gone wrong."

Danny made a scoffing sound. After dinner, their two men left for the headquarters of Lattigo Industries so Chip could check the final programming corrections for his firm's shipping and manufacturing software. It was unclear what motivated Josh to join Chip—whether Josh thought two high tech entrepreneurs should stick together, was genuinely interested, or just sought a new audience to amuse. After several days at the camp, Josh was growing restless.

"Don't worry," Danny said. "Chip always knows what he's doing. Married you, didn't he?"

Cynthia smiled again to acknowledge the compliment. "Well, I hope the two of them don't stop at the casino. It's bound to be a madhouse over there. Everyone making their last bet of the century."

Cynthia thought maybe that was why Josh had been so eager to ride along. Josh always became alive at the gambling table. He did have incredible luck, or maybe a true skill, but she felt he pushed the game too hard. Sometimes she thought he lived only in those moments. It was when he seemed most alive, his eyes flashing with amusement, his quips coming fast and furious, and his charm drawing in all those around his table. He was like a loose helium balloon in a slight breeze on a summer day at the beach, untethered and rising to the sun, happy to be bounced between hands. In those moments, Danny seemed lost in Josh's shadow.

"Do you ever think about the happiest moments in your life?" Cynthia asked. Something snapped in the flames of the fireplace, flitting shadows to dance across the room. "You know, those instances when everything comes together in a magical moment?" She really wanted to know.

Danny shook his head as though he never had such moments.

"For some reason, I'm thinking about one of those times now," said Cynthia. "Sitting here . . . it makes me nostalgic, or maybe contented."

For a moment, it looked as though Danny wanted to walk out of the room. Cynthia thought about all the bad times that might be floating through Danny's mind, so she pushed through trying to force from him his happy memories.

"Do you remember Fourth of July in 1987 in Thread? Back when everything ahead seemed so bright. Remember how all that money was flowing in to build American Seasons, and every building in town had a fresh coat of paint? Everyone was so happy. I know I was.

"And the polka band was playing in the town square. Do you recall how we all danced? God, I haven't danced a polka since then. Who even did it then, except for the old folks of Thread? But that night I wanted everyone to be on their feet. I can still picture it. How there was bunting and fresh flowers decorating every inch of town. I jumped around that dance floor with Chip, and you were with Josh. Remember? And the old cook from the Loon Town Café was dancing with Officer Campbell. Even Reverend Willy was there. And everyone was happy."

Danny pointed out the obvious, "But it didn't last. Moments like that never last."

Of course, Cynthia remembered how the euphoria of that summer proved short-lived. The 1987 stock market crashed and the Dow dropped 508 points in a single day. So many dreams tumbled that day, including the financing scheme for American Seasons. Years later, when Chip reassembled the finances that allowed his tribe to build the resort, it was significantly scaled back. Fortunes were lost that year, but, ironically, none of it affected Josh because he had already sold his parent's land to the consortium and started his first California investments.

Cynthia was not deterred by past realities. "I know it didn't last, but that doesn't matter. Don't you think special memories exist outside of time? No matter what happened before or what comes later, there remains that perfect moment . . . like a snow globe in our minds that we can always shake to see the same beautiful scene over and over."

Cynthia had no problem reconstructing the teenage self that danced the polka so long ago. She had been such a dreamer then. She knew she remained the same person, but she wondered how Danny had changed and whether the Danny that dwelled in her snow globe of nostalgia still existed. Once he had been insecure and easily frightened. Surely he had grown.

"You always were the romantic one," Danny said. "I guess that's why I like having you as my friend."

The mantel clock began the first of its twelve chimes.

"Oh, it's midnight," wailed Cynthia, "and Josh and Chip aren't here. They'll miss the best moment."

"Or maybe the worst," joked Danny. "Remember Y2K!"

The twelfth tone sounded. And everything went dark.

Blackness settled in and the music playing softly in the background vanished. The steady blowers of the furnace . . . gone. The usual drone of the large refrigerators in the kitchen—a sound so low and common that Danny seldom noticed it—seemed ominous by its absence. Danny heard only the crackle of the fireplace, the ticking of the mechanical clock, and the whispers of the wind flitting across the snow outside.

The flickering light from the flaming logs failed to reach the tall ceiling, so the shadows in the curves of the log walls grew even deeper. The glitter of the tree ornaments glinted reflections to cast a dim galaxy of lights on the walls. Beyond the French doors and the snowdrifts, moonlight still illuminated the icy lake. Far in the distance, on the opposite shore and across a dark sentinel of pine spires, Danny thought he saw a glow from the handful of streetlights that defined Thread's main square. But he couldn't be sure.

"Did it happen? Did the computers fail?"

While Danny thought a touch of fear in Cynthia's voice would be appropriate, her questions stayed calm, as though a worldwide apocalypse would be just another day.

"A tree probably fell in the woods, a leftover from last night's storm," Danny proclaimed, even though he wasn't so certain. He recalled all the predictions over the past couple of years and thought that if indeed the modern world was ending, he was glad to be with Cynthia.

The clock still ticked. The fireplace still burned. The thick walls of a century old building still protected them . . . no matter what their cell phones, Internet, and the electrical world did. Danny was hopeful that whatever occurred, it would soon be resolved.

"There's no need to worry," Danny added, mostly for his benefit. "The power will soon be back." He thought he detected a stirring in the far reaches of the shadowy room, nearer the doors to the kitchen.

Cynthia scoffed, "I'm not worried. Let's light some candles and I'll play the piano. That'll show the world!"

Sudden laughter came from the shadowy reaches. And with that, the lights flared back, the music returned, and the hum of humanity resumed.

Cynthia immediately understood what had happened and laughed. "Always joking, Josh, aren't you? Trying to frighten me into a new year? But why bother? We only have one choice . . . to leap forward."

Josh Gunderson stepped into the room. His broad smile spread across his tanned face. From the day Danny met him, Josh had always been the lively spark. Everyone liked him.

A more subdued Chip, trailing Josh by a few steps, also moved quickly into the room to enclose Cynthia in his arms and kiss her. "Happy New Year, darling."

Cynthia looked across at Danny, who seemed to be expecting a similar kiss from his lover. But Josh was still too pleased with his practical joke. As slender and trim as the first time he walked into their lives over a dozen years earlier, Josh wasn't tall or unusually good looking, yet he always seemed the largest personality in the room.

She wanted to sigh with exasperation. At times, Cynthia grew tired of playing Wendy to this band of boys who refused to grow up. Perhaps she was being unkind, but she wanted them to change. Josh, always trying to be the trickster, playing his jokes that often weren't very funny. Danny often teetered on the edge as though he were a tightrope acrobat. And although she deeply loved Chip, he was always too quick to fight the battle against the crocodiles and pirates that might lay in wait for the people of his tribe. These eternal boys were all special to her in their own ways, but it was time to move on. She should become a true mother. She didn't mean to show her exasperation, but audibly sighed.

"My idea, a little practical joke," Josh confessed. "Blame me. This place is so remote that I suggested to Chip we could stage our own little experiment to see how the world would react to a computer meltdown. But, then, Cynthia . . .well, what can I say? You're a champ. Offering to play the piano. You would have been the first to join the band on deck and serenade the sinking of the Titanic."

Cynthia wasn't embarrassed to think that's exactly what she would have done. "You boys have had your fun. But it's past midnight, and we've waited too long. Let's break out the champagne and have a toast." Cynthia raised the volume on the music. "And don't think you've escaped singing 'Auld Lang Syne.' At 1:00 a.m., we can pretend we're in Denver."

Josh said, "Let's do it. I've got a couple of bottles of a vintage Dom Perignon in the refrigerator. We can toast to a successful year and the start of an even better one." His smile seemed alive with joy, but Cynthia considered his eyes troubling, as though he was holding something back.

Cynthia also noticed that her husband Chip was evaluating Josh. He saw something too; she was sure of that.

She was equally certain that Danny saw nothing.

Josh felt the urge for fun. After most of the first bottle was drunk, he dragged Cynthia to the center of the living room to dance some drunken version of American swing.

"It's celebration time," he proclaimed.

Danny and Chip sank into facing chairs, close enough to the action to watch the dancing pair, but maintaining enough distance to avoid being dragged into the festivities. In his mind, Josh dismissed their action as typical wet blanket behavior. Tonight was a time to celebrate, and he was going to make the most of it.

At the same time, he made sure to dance near enough to overhear what the other two men were saying. He found it helpful to stay on top of everything and everyone, especially Danny.

He heard Danny ask, "Did everything go okay tonight? We expected you back sooner. We figured once midnight happened in New York without incident, you'd come home." Josh wanted to hear how Chip would respond, since he wasn't sure what Chip made of the night's activity. Most likely, he would have dismissed it as a prank.

"There was something odd," Chip said.

Josh saw worry flit across Danny's face. It was amusing how Danny so worshipped Chip Grant. As a teenager, Danny was easily swayed and, of course, the good-looking Chip seemed the hero—the Native American star who rode to the rescue of the American Seasons resort after the stock crash. Tonight, despite his quick downing of a glass of champagne, Chip seemed troubled. Maybe he noticed more than Josh thought.

"What happened?" Danny asked.

Earlier that evening, Josh had insisted on going with Chip to visit the headquarters of Lattigo Industries. It was his business and he had a job to do. It didn't matter that Chip never seemed to care that much for him even though they were in business together. Sometimes, he regretted that he had agreed to contract his own burgeoning web business to be hosted on Chip's recent expansion into server farms. But Danny had been insistent. He always trusted people from their hometown.

So if hosting this business on servers in northern Wisconsin kept Danny happy, then Josh was fine with it. Besides, he had total trust in Chip and Lattigo Industries. The guy was honest to a fault, and his company had been in the tech field since the eighties, already duplicating computer disks back when Danny was still in high school. Chip always kept this company one step ahead of technology changes. The Lattigo tribe was lucky to have someone as clever as Chip on their side.

Josh suggested dropping into the Lattigo headquarters on New Year's Eve because visiting the site always reminded Josh of what was possible. Back when Josh was a kid, his Dad's farm wasn't that far from where American Seasons now sat. (He felt a momentary twinge thinking of that farm and how his parents died.) The family homestead had been a poor expanse of weak soil, blueberry bogs, and second-growth forests, next to Indian land with no outlook for success.

Today no swamps or bogs were anywhere in sight. The land had been drained, scraped, filled, and molded until there emerged the broad building site needed for the extravagance now devoted to gambling and family fun. When Josh returned to Thread in his twenties to settle his parents' estate and first saw the original outlandish drawings depicting a giant theme park, multiple hotels, casinos and convention center, he judged the concept overkill. Still it would have been fantastic if it had actually been built. But the 1987 recession killed that pipe dream.

Instead, Chip led the successful, if hostile, takeover of the original company, kept the project alive through the financial downturn as other investors bailed, and redesigned the effort to have a gentler footprint on the natural environment. The resulting American Seasons resort was still a massive place. It attracted thousands each week, as many gamblers to the casino as families to the indoor waterpark with its pools and death-defying water slides. A broad promenade lined with spruce and white poplar separated the casino from the family hotel and its shopping center. On one end was the glass enclosed water park. On the other were the modern mid-rise office buildings of Lattigo Industries that held all of the operations of the resort, including the servers that made Josh's website run. It was there that the Lattigo programming staff had been working on its fixes to the computer problem of the millennium. Josh loved the place and all it represented.

Josh, still dancing with Cynthia, swirled in closer to eavesdrop better. Chip hadn't yet answered Danny's question, so Danny repeated it. "What happened tonight?"

"Everything was going the way we expected. For some clients, like you and Josh, your software was all written in the nineties. There wasn't much likelihood that there would be any problems. The "Y2K" issue has been recognized for at least a decade. But still we needed to consider how programs would interact with older systems. And there was the potential that local infrastructure—we are the biggest user of electricity in northern Wisconsin—might fail.

"But in reality I was there to support the troops. Long ago we identified the weak spots, programmed patches, and tested them. As New Year's Day rolled out and moved west through major city after major city, we could already see everything was fine. Josh was the one who earlier tonight convinced me we should go on site."

When he heard this, Josh smiled. He enjoyed the rush of getting out of the camp, just as he was now enjoying dancing and eavesdropping.

"So it was midnight in New York, and all our East Coast operations rolled over into the year 2000 just as they should. It was clear we could come home with a clear conscience and have a glass of champagne. Not just because of success in our computer center, but also because friends should take the time to salute the New Year together.

"That's when it occurred."

"What happened?"

Josh knew what was coming. He was quite pleased that he had been there to notice it and set the staff in action. Frankly, he enjoyed the moment of risk that occurred.

"It was an unexpected anomaly in your firm's files. Josh spotted the issue. I don't think we would have. But my guys were quickly on top of it. They isolated your servers and accounts. Something was eating up the data. It was like a snake woke up in the East Coast servers as they hit midnight, and started swallowing data like there would be no tomorrow."

"Did you stop it?" Danny asked Chip.

"We wouldn't have come home if we hadn't. Once we saw what was happening, it was easy to backtrack and find the culprit. One of our programmers isolated a computer virus programmed to go live at the turn of midnight."

"But why?" Danny asked.

"Doesn't make any sense. The virus was so easy to find and isolate, almost as though someone left it as a message. Josh dismissed it as some childish prank. But he's so cavalier. The truth is that it could have destroyed your records, and your business is nothing but information. But Josh just laughed it off."

By then, Josh and Cynthia were several feet away, but Josh had heard the entire conversation. With nothing to worry about, he continued to dance. The smile on Cynthia's face was broad.

Josh looked over and saw Danny watching, so he smiled too, to encourage Danny to join in. Danny stood up to pretend to dance, and Josh's smile grew even broader.

Tonight, after all, was a new year.

In the morning, Danny felt happy. The air was crisp and cold. Fresh snow thinly blanketed the grounds. The blue skies promised a bright new century.

Only the four friends occupied the huge house. There was no need for anyone else. The twenty-first century required no throng of servants to maintain life. Today, Danny was doing the cooking. Some circles considered him a culinary expert. In his heart, he knew that description was unwarranted. His limited skill was occasionally finding a clever way to describe food and amuse people. Just because some of those folks started reading his blog about food and dining in Los Angeles years ago didn't endow him with any real skills. It was that blog that led to a food fan magazine, or 'zine, then to a website and eventually to the company called Premios.

But Midwest holiday meals fell well within his comfort zone. In the abundant sunlight of the early afternoon, he would be ready to adorn the table with a glazed ham, mashed potatoes with raisin gravy, sweet potatoes covered with marshmallows, and a green bean casserole.

Readers of his old blog might deem such a menu outrageous, but he found such dishes as comforting as well-worn flannel sheets. He only wished that he knew how to deep-fry the doughnuts that his mother once made. Their taste would have been a perfect kickstart to a new millennium.

Josh strolled into their kitchen. He wanted it to be the showcase of the house, and it was resplendent with the latest in stainless steel appliances and a large butcher-block island. In the corner a small table was set for dinner. In their designer's notes, that space was intended primarily as a place for the caterers when they had large parties. But Danny always considered it the perfect breakfast nook, and now he noticed how Josh looked at his festive setup with dismay.

"We have a dining room, you know. We don't need to eat in here."

"The big room is too lonely."

So they ate in the kitchen. Josh never argued with Danny on things that Danny actually cared about. That's why Danny loved him. The year they first met, when Josh had returned to Thread when his parents died, the two of them started their romance. By the time summer arrived, Josh had convinced Danny that he should leave northern Wisconsin and go to college in Los Angeles. He agreed at first, but then fear took hold. Even though he stayed behind when Josh returned to the West Coast, Josh never abandoned Danny. He knew Danny just needed time, and when he was ready to venture away, Josh was there to help and to make him smile.

On that New Year's Day, with the heat and aroma of the food, and the sunlight that streamed across the tile floor, the kitchen was infused with a spirit of optimism. It infected all four of them: Cynthia and Chip, Danny and Josh. They were young. They were rich. They were friends. Everything was surely possible.

"What were you guys talking about last night?" Cynthia asked, looking at Chip and Danny.

For a moment, Danny didn't understand her question, but then realized she must be referring to what happened in the computer center. He wasn't certain he fully understood so he let Chip answer.

Chip stared at Josh for a moment before he replied. "I was telling Danny about an incident that happened with their company's files last night."

Josh set his champagne glass down with more force than required, and Danny thought it an odd reaction, especially when Josh said, "Why are you so obsessed with someone's childish prank?"

"Do you really think that's all it was?" Chip batted back.

"What else? Who would have a reason to mess with us?"

"Really. You don't think you have any enemies?"

Danny wondered what had gotten into Chip. Of course, they didn't have enemies. The very thought that people might hate them made him deeply uncomfortable. Josh and he were good people. They treated their employees well. Everyone liked them.

Josh shrugged his shoulders.

Chip wasn't willing to let it go. "Your website is full of gossip about the rich and famous. Maybe someone is carrying a grudge, and hired a hacker to go after you."

"Because of a shot of a star flashing more than she planned when she stepped out of a limo? Really?"

"Then there's the fact that you're also a successful gay couple. Lots of people don't like your lifestyle."

Danny found this offensive, but Josh just laughed. "There are a lot of gay people richer and more famous than us. We're hardly worth anyone's time or attention."

Chip was not deterred. "Last night was not random. The world's full of crazies. Think about that guy who was just caught trying to bomb LAX on New Year's Eve, the one they call the Millennium Bomber . . . "

Danny looked toward Cynthia for help. This was not the point of his holiday dinner. Cynthia, catching his glance, raised her glass.

"Enough of that," she said. "It's time for New Year's resolutions and celebrating. Now that you own this place, we'll have no excuse not to spend more time together. I resolve we do this more often."

They raised their glasses in acknowledgement, and Danny was relieved the small storm had passed. These three people were his best friends in life. Without them, life would seem empty.

Josh in his usual way played off Cynthia's peacemaking. "Cynthia, I think your resolution was far too easy to make because we all want to be together more. Don't you have a darker, more challenging resolution? Surely, you harbor some secret vice. Tell us about that."

His tone was jaunty, but Danny knew that Josh really wanted to know.

Cynthia refused to take the bait. "I don't have secrets. Chip always says I wear my heart on my sleeve, whatever that means. But I suppose there are some things I should work harder at."

"Do tell." For some reason Josh's statement made Danny laugh. Cynthia looked perturbed by that, and Danny fell quiet.

"My family. I don't spend enough time with them." Cynthia's parents, Red and Barbara Trueheart, retired to Arizona a few years earlier and Cynthia rarely visited them. Red occasionally flew north for a summer fishing excursion on his long-treasured lakes. "And it's time Chip and I got serious about starting our own family. Chip says the Lattigo tribe needs another member. So that's my resolution: to become pregnant." Chip touched her hand with an element of mock surprise.

Danny felt unexpected discomfort. Children would forever change the dynamics of their relationship.

"A grand idea," said Josh. "And if you don't know how to make that happen, I'll volunteer to take Chip aside to give him a few pointers on how all that works."

Danny stopped the banter. "What about you, Chip? What's your resolution for the new century? And don't say making babies."

"Happiness and prosperity. All around. Not enough? Okay, seriously, I need to be a better steward for my tribe. The Lattigo are wealthier than most tribes, but there are still so many problems. If Cynthia and I have a child, I want that child to be proud of his or her Lattigo heritage. Just like I want to see that pride in my people."

"What makes you the anointed one?" Josh ribbed.

Chip remained serious. "Because I forced them out of the reservation mindset and made them enter the modern world, and they made me the head of the Lattigo nation, and technically our Native American reservation is a separate nation. Ultimately, I'm only a trustee for my tribe, and I can't forget how profits impact their lives."

The sentiment stirred Danny, but Josh was quick to move on. "What about you, Danny?" he asked.

Danny hesitated because he didn't know where to begin. He needed dreams, but he didn't know how to have his own. Like Cynthia, he should be closer to his father. Even though the man still lived in Thread, Danny had yet to see him on this trip. He wasn't even sure if he wanted to. The old man probably loved him, but being near him always brought back too many memories of the mother Danny lost.

Perhaps like Cynthia, he should make a resolution about his boyfriend Josh. In the year just ended, California became the first state to create a special legal status for domestic partners. Josh lit the spark of possibility years ago when he convinced Danny to move from Thread to Los Angeles. He couldn't imagine life without Josh, so perhaps they should make their relationship official.

Danny never had a tribe like Chip. Wherever he was, whatever he did, he always felt the outsider. He never fit into the gay world, nor did he identify himself as a Wisconsinite, a second-generation Finn, or even a foodie. He was only himself and often that felt too little. When someone wrote his obituary, he was certain that none of the descriptors used would be true. Certainly, he had a wide circle of friends in Los Angeles. Many of them were people he cared deeply about, and more than a few, he hoped, returned that sentiment. But they weren't his tribe. He wanted at least one tribe into which he could disappear.

Then he thought back to his conversation with Chip the night before, and of the computer virus attack on their company. It was odd, but in the moment of the telling and again during the dinner conversation, Danny had a sense of concern. He actually cared what happened, and that was something he never would have predicted. Suddenly he knew his resolution.

"I will become more involved with our company. It is after all our future, and Josh is working hard to take it public this year. I need to pay more attention to that. In the year 2000, I will do just that."

Josh seemed startled, but quickly smiled until his grin shifted into laughter. "By God, Cynthia, I think we got pregnant first. Here's to our baby. Here's to our upcoming IPO. To Premios—may it bestow a fortune upon us."

Cynthia and Danny smiled and raised their glasses. So did Chip—but not before quick shadows of doubt and concern crossed his face.

Session Two

I admit it. I've been obsessed about Danny for years. Okay, doc, now you know my deep, dark secret. Isn't that supposed to be how this therapy thing works? I tell you everything. No barriers. No filters. Whatever. And you record it and play it back. Listen to what I say, but you can't judge, right?

So, yeah, it's fair to call Danny my obsession. Maybe even a curse. Or maybe I should think of watching him as a case study. Sort of like an experiment to see what makes someone tick.

Admittedly, it's been an experiment that's been going on a very long time. The years have been worth it, because I do more than just watch. There's something so pleasurable in manipulating him.

Oh, you think that's wrong? Okay, I'm joking. I never manipulate him. I just watch. From a safe distance.

You believe that, don't you, doc?

Of course, I could manipulate him. If I wanted to bother. I could pretty much make anyone do whatever I wanted. Even you doc.

So you asked about when this started. Danny was just a kid. I first paid attention to him after I heard how his mother offed herself. Left that poor little boy alone, to fend for himself. His dad made useless by his wife's suicide. Who knows what went on with his crazy old man?

Of course, Danny never sensed how I kept an eye out for him. I doubt that he even knew I existed. Didn't need him to know.

Poor kid. There's always been something so achingly lonely about him. He looked like the world forgot he existed, and he wasn't the kind to remind the rest of us that he was real. There's a kind of innocence in that, I guess. Maybe that's why I found him so attractive. He had something I never had. A good soul.

Not that I wanted one. A good soul, I mean. I just wanted to know what made a person like Danny tick. People like him didn't really make sense to me.

Why was he the way that he was? That's what I wanted to know.

So when I noticed his, should I call them, special qualities, I started to watch him. Just watched. At least that's all I did at first. Paid attention to what he liked. How he acted. Who his friends were. Not that he had many of those.

And I looked at what made him happy. Which wasn't often the case. But he never became bitter. He stayed innocent. Maybe there was a little darkness at his core, but that only made you want to protect him more.

You know, if Danny had lived during the Renaissance, some crazy artist would have found him and used him as a model. I don't mean an artist like Michelangelo who's creating a statue like David. Danny doesn't have that kind of strength. You couldn't imagine him slaying a giant. His strengths are more hidden.

So maybe it would have been a Botticelli bronze. Something smooth. Something vulnerable. A piece of art that made you ache with longing.

Because you want to crush it.

CHAPTER TWO

Home

Up ahead was the house. It boasted almost five thousand square feet of living space. Its four levels hugged the steep hillside. White stucco walls rose from well-landscaped lawns until they reached wooden corbels that supported the red tile roof. Bougainvillea clung to the walls and stretched around the tiled entry. It was Hollywood's version of old Spain. It was also home to Danny and Josh.

Danny was happy to be back. The airport limo rolled up the curving street, through the historic Los Feliz area neighborhood on the eastern edge of the Hollywood Hills, and into the circular driveway. This mansion was as grandiose and inappropriate to the lives of two modern men as their logging camp retreat. But unlike the Wisconsin house, this one suited Danny's romantic spirit. Here he thought he could be happy.

As the car came to a stop near the flight of stairs leading to the front door, a hefty young woman stepped out. She grinned and said with enthusiasm, "Welcome home."

Not waiting for the driver to open his door, Danny exited the car and rushed up the steps two at a time to reach her. Let the limo driver deal with unloading the suitcases, he thought. Wrapping his arms around Kenosha, he lifted her in a bear hug worthy of the north woods. "Kenosha Washington," he said, "how I've missed you."

Kenosha just waved away his good feelings. She looked pointedly at the car. "Where's that boyfriend of yours? Wouldn't think you'd take such fancy wheels unless he was along."

"Watch your tongue. That's your boss you're describing. Just so you know, Josh asked to be dropped off at the office," Danny explained. Danny felt so good to be home. Thread might have been where he was raised, but California was where he became who he was.

Sensing his feelings, Kenosha turned to the driver who was approaching the door with both men's luggage. "Just set them there. We'll get them where they belong." She turned back to Danny, effectively dismissing the hired driver.

Once again, Kenosha was acting the role of a haughty black servant, which made Danny smile since he knew his old college friend had grown up in a household in Brentwood headed by two white doctors. While nobody's servant, she seemed to have imprinted as a young girl on her black nanny and behaved as though her parents had adopted her from the depths of the South. None dared to remind her that she was really Caucasian. Even though she held a full-time job as the director of public relations for their company, she liked to housesit for them when they traveled to Wisconsin.

"I suppose Josh will expect to find me there," Kenosha said. "He's always so eager to talk about publicity. A regular press hound. But let him wait. Come inside. First thing this morning, I picked up some chocolate croissants at the bakery on Hillhurst. I knew your stomach would need more attention than Josh's business."

"You certainly know how to please me," he said. Kenosha gave him a playful swat, and he grinned. He loved having this woman as a friend, quirks and all.

Soon they were seated on the patio outside the living room's French doors. Strange, Danny thought, the way Josh and his two separate homes both had broad windows facing beautiful natural views. The terrace's balustrade looked west toward the Griffith Observatory and a hint of the Hollywood sign. On days when Los Angeles held its smog in check, there was even an ocean view. Under nearly perfect conditions, one could squint out a distant dividing line between the light blue of the sea's surface and the hazy tint of the darker sky. But on the most rare of perfect days, the view became a David Hockney painting where the sky, hills and distant sea transformed into a distinct geometry of lines. Today was not such a day.

"Anything exciting while we were gone?" Danny asked.

In the pattern of sunlight that dappled Kenosha's face some wrinkle seemed to come and go as though she recalled a disturbing fact, considered mentioning it, and changed her mind. She wasn't a good actress.

"Kenosha Jayne Washington," he liked using her full name when making a point. "I've known you since we were sophomores at USC.

You never could fool me. What happened? Did something get Kiisa? Did she get out at night and run into a coyote?"

Using the Finnish word for "cat" to name their pet seemed to amuse Josh, but the cat and its name often reminded Danny of his mother. It would have been fine with him if one of those mangy coyotes had made Kiisa a meal. Then he felt guilty for thinking such a dreadful thought.

Kenosha made a show of being offended. She knew Danny secretly hated that cat. "You'd be happy if I let Kiisa be eaten. She's only around because she showed up at your door half-dead and you're too kind-hearted to ask a vet to put her to sleep. Sorry, though, there's no missing cat. No coyote attacks. Not even a rampaging raccoon or tree rat. Although I did smell a couple of skunks."

"What then?" Danny knew there was something. Kenosha had made a half-hearted joke. It was a dead giveaway.

"This house. It gives me the creeps with all its dark corners and levels. Who needs a projector room? The place is just overkill. You know I'm accustomed to the sleek and modern."

It's true, Danny thought. Kenosha had been raised in one of those Case Study houses from the fifties. Everything was built-in with well-defined vertical and horizontal lines. Her parents couldn't abide the Spanish baroque spirit that was so popular in the early twentieth century and still infused most of these early Los Feliz estates.

In its initial days, the neighborhood had offered the height of style. The founder of the *Los Angeles Times* built a huge estate in the area, as did many celebrities during the beginning of the movie industry. Over the decades, the influential moved westward toward the favorable neighborhoods near the ocean, places like Brentwood where Kenosha was raised. A few years ago when Josh really began to make money, he wanted nothing to do with the Westside. He read in *Variety* that the popular singer Madonna had bought in the Los Feliz neighborhood and he predicted that her presence would revive the community as fashionable. As usual, he was right.

When they first saw this house, it had been a wreck. The realtor even resisted showing it. On the market for over 200 days, the estate was a probate sale. Squabbles among the heirs kept the house from even being properly cleaned and staged. But there was another reason that the real estate listing was poison.

Someone died on the premises. A once-famous director of horror movies, Augustus Cambrian, had lived long enough that the world largely forgot who he was, so when he passed away at home in quiet anonymity, no one quite realized he was dead for over a week. Eventually the smell drifted over the pool of the hot young screenwriter renovating his house next door. It was probably more the current celebrity of the writer than Cambrian's former renown that ensured the discovery of Augustus received a well-placed story in the *Los Angeles Times*.

Given California's strong disclosure laws for real estate, the history of the unfortunate corpse deterred buyers. It didn't help that the rooms were filled with memorabilia. The old man had been a packrat of the demonic and obscure. Some said he tried to preserve the relics of the early days of horror films, but to Danny, it always seemed more than that. But none of that history could explain Kenosha's current feelings. She never entered the house before the heirs had emptied it, so she couldn't have flashbacks to things she had never seen.

"It's so quiet up here," Kenosha explained, "it's easy to start imagining things."

Danny had always preferred to conjure scenes of glamour and romance. When the realtor first drove them through the gates into the circular drive, Danny was smitten. He liked the house's asymmetrical lines and the way the circular tower intersected the house's two wings at odd angles. Elaborate terra cotta cladding and tile work surrounded the door. Intricate wrought iron graced the balconies. Blooming birds of paradise lined the twenty-step staircase from the drive to the front door. The pieces fit together in an unexpected way, and convinced him that this house was where he belonged.

Stepping inside the building made his belief momentarily quaver. It smelled like a house sealed up too long with an old man's collection. A few weeks' airing by open windows had failed to dissipate an odor that seemed baked into the paint of the hand-troweled walls. Most of the director's possessions were still in place during the showing. The realtor explained that the heirs were arguing over their disposal. Although none had seen the man in years, each was convinced that his moldering collection had to be worth a fortune.

Dimness cloaked everything. It wasn't a problem of light. The windows had been washed and the old brocade draperies removed.

Rather, it was the accumulated remnants of decades. Every room was painted in a color of the past. The kitchen hadn't been touched since the sixties, and the bathrooms still sported the green and black tile of the twenties. But Danny saw a potential luster in the peg and groove floors. He knew current artisans couldn't easily duplicate the original plaster walls or the ornate bronze sconces. The staircases, fireplaces, and outdoor fountains constituted a museum showcasing early handmade tile firms: Malibu. Batchelder. Catalina. Gladding McBean. The original designer had not worried about consistency or loyalty or logic. The house pulled together whatever caught the fancy of the moment. Josh called it "a potpourri of the hodgepodge." Danny guessed it was as good a way to describe the style as any, and he liked the result.

As long as he avoided thinking about the chamber of horrors they found, Danny didn't mind the house's past. The villa's lowest level, a vast basement with few windows and just one small wooden exit to the back of the street-to-street lot, had been the director's so-called museum: a nightmare of old props from long-forgotten films; imaginary torture devices featured in one plot or another; and racks of decaying costumes. Mixed among that were genuine relics of the Dark Ages and the Spanish Inquisition. Eventually, the heirs managed to sell most of it for a good profit to one type of collector or another. None of it remained when Josh and Danny took possession. But on the first showing when Danny walked into that basement, it was all still there and it felt evil.

Josh called Danny crazy to judge a room so harshly and so Danny never told anyone how he felt, especially Kenosha. If she was spooked by the house now, it wasn't because she knew of its past.

"So what did you imagine?" he asked.

He expected to hear about the mysterious creaks and groans of an eighty-year-old house. Perhaps lights still flickered or pipes gurgled, even though Josh arranged for the entire house to be rewired and replumbed. Maybe the cat Kiisa scared her.

"I felt watched."

"What?"

"It's true. Maybe I just began to realize how alone I was at the top of these hills. It's like you're straddling the whole city up here, the way lines of street lights stretch to the horizon and you're nothing but a little point at the apex, overlooking a world beyond. But sometimes I felt the hair on the back of my neck stand up, like when someone is watching you. But I never saw anyone.

"Just forget I said anything."

Danny didn't want to be too easily influenced by her scary thoughts. "So, it was all in your imagination."

"Yeah, I guess, at least about being watched, but I did hear something. That much I know."

"Okay." He was beginning to suspect Kenosha was pulling his leg.

"Last night, something was scraping at the basement door, like it was trying to break in. No way was I going to tromp down all those stairs to the basement, so I walked out on this patio. You can look down to see the back door from up here.

"But storm clouds were heavy last night and there was no moonlight, so I couldn't be sure anything was down there, but I definitely could hear something. Down in the bushes."

Danny had an answer. "Probably a coyote. He could smell Kiisa. Everyone's always losing their pets in this neighborhood."

"You're probably right." Kenosha seemed to regret bringing up the subject.

Danny walked to the balustrade to look down into the steep backyard. He saw the small stone fence that separated the edge of their backyard, some hundred feet below, from the curling street that ran along the lot's lower edge. On the other side of the narrow street, an ornate entrance marked one of the public stairways. Because of the steep terrain of Los Feliz, the developers built public staircases to link the main avenues below with the switchbacks of the narrow streets above. At one time servants and children climbed them to move from the streetcars to their homes. Today the stairs were largely abandoned, their steps often covered with graffiti, and the landings mainly used by kids as shielded places to do drugs—but the tiers of steps beneath the overgrown shrubbery across the street directly linked Danny's hillside home to a major boulevard several hundred feet below.

Only once had Danny trudged the full set of steps. It was tiring but doable. Six separate flights totaling just over two hundred steps separated the edge of their lot from busy Los Feliz Boulevard.

And although he couldn't be certain, when he scanned the lot below, he thought he detected a clear trail of broken branches and snapped twigs that led from the top of those steps to the back door of his house. As though someone had used those stairs to try to sneak into his back yard and reach the small door below.

The entry to the scary basement.

Kenosha was right. Someone had tried to break in.

Josh watched Danny and his assistant Orleans stand in front of the window of his downtown office. From this height, they could still see and hear the clamor of Main Street below. Josh felt no need to walk over and determine what held their attention. Without doubt, a dirty bum was hassling a bag lady, or something equally down and out was in progress. Some were beginning to call this tired, forgotten corner of downtown Los Angeles the Old Bank District. While the name was grand, Josh knew no proper banker from the Westside ever frequented the neighborhood.

Which was precisely why he chose to base his company headquarters here. He leased the entire top floor of a long-forgotten oil company headquarters, where the space was cheap and the natural light was great. He liked to think his decision proved he had imagination and dared to take risks. Investors liked gutsiness and vision.

At the same time, Josh was confident the location was a sure thing. Cagey developers were everywhere, snapping up these great old buildings. In a few years, everyone would want to be in this part of downtown. But Josh liked being among the first—a pioneer. That's what he was—an innovator. So was his company—Premios. He was staking out new frontiers on the World Wide Web. Some might call him a prospector of opportunity in this Internet gold rush.

But visions of that future would have to wait. It was time to get back to the business at hand. "You two. Break away from whatever is unfolding below you, and let's talk. We have fortunes to make."

Orleans quickly moved away, but Danny continued to watch. For a moment Josh considered checking what Danny found so interesting. Even at one in the afternoon on a sunny January day, Main Street was the kind of place that could erupt into action so brutal that the police were needed. But when Orleans gave him a reassuring smile, he knew he didn't need to bother.

Josh trusted Orleans' instinct. He detected her talents the very first day he saw her at the restaurant opened by his friends Stephen and

Wally. The New Loon Town Café was on the east side of Hollywood. Even though the pair had chosen a sketchy neighborhood, Josh decided to invest in their dream. In those early days, he liked the challenge of situations that required a leap of faith. But the friends from Thread proved to know what they were doing. Everything about their business—the menu, the décor, and the buzz—was on target. That included hiring Orleans Jonas as their primary hostess.

At that point the young woman was still working on her MBA. A smart and pretty girl, she could read people at a thousand words a minute. She deciphered Josh the moment he walked through the restaurant door. She saw the swagger of a man who owned the place, which he did, at least in part. On the other hand, he liked to think he owned almost any room he entered. That wasn't a boast. Some people—and both Orleans and he were such people—could master a situation in moments. They always said the right thing, complimented the person who needed a boost, questioned the person who craved authority, and calculated the value of every response. It wasn't a surprise that a woman like Orleans immediately recognized Josh as the moneyman behind the New Loon Town Café and treated him accordingly.

Although he never mentioned it to Wally or Stephen, Josh credited Orleans as the main cause for the New Loon Town Café success. She captivated diners. When she roamed the dining room and talked to the guests, each one of them thought he or she was the most important diner that night. When she smiled at a walk-in and warned him the wait could be an hour, he still stuck around, just to be near her. Josh admired people with such talent. When Josh started his web investments and he learned Orleans had completed her MBA, he hired her away. He wanted her, and he didn't care how that impacted his friends' business. Now she was his chief financial officer, and he couldn't imagine a better one.

Danny stepped away from the window to join Josh and Orleans. He wore a troubled expression. "I wish you hadn't leased headquarters so close to skid row. No one wants to come here."

"No one needs to come to this office," Josh replied cheerfully, "they only need to visit our website. That's what we want them to do over and over again. It's new media, Danny. It's not about real estate on the ground. It's about staking territory out there. In the virtual world." He waved his arms around to suggest this mysterious realm that everyone liked to talk about.

Danny laughed. "I get it. At least that part of our business. But you know I meant it when I said my New Year's resolution was to understand Premios better. After all, it's our company, isn't it? And I shouldn't leave it all in your hands."

Josh thought the current situation was fine as it was, but didn't tell Danny that. They entered the suite's reception area, near Josh's desk, open to the floor like every other working space at the company. Orleans sat on the sofa, placed a leather-bound folio beside her, and picked up her pen to take notes. She dressed and acted as though this office were on Wall Street. Josh liked that. When he and she met with investors, she looked more like an up-and-coming banker than a start-up Internet nerd.

"What would you like to know?" she asked. "Of course, you know you still own a controlling majority of the stock. But you should be aware that we've just about used up the funding from the mezzanine stage of financing. Our monthly burn rate is significant, but then so is our rate of increase in daily impressions. More importantly, we're seeing levels of engagement go through the roof, which totally justifies the investments we've made in building the brand."

Like a traffic cop, Danny quickly held up his palm to keep her from speeding past his understanding. "You've already lost me in jargon land. Once upon a time, I wrote about local restaurants and tried to be amusing. People subscribed to my 'zine and then my blog. I never thought any of that could lead to this. I certainly never wanted to be an entrepreneur. That's Josh's thing. But . . . " Danny floundered.

After thirteen years together, Josh knew what bothered Danny, but he saw no sense in making him articulate it. There was something so endearing to see that fleeting look of panic when Danny got in water too deep.

There was no question that Josh was the entrepreneur in the family. More than that, he felt fate tapped him on the shoulder, gave him a rabbit's foot, and tossed in a four-leaf clover. He always found the right spot at the right time. When his parents died, he combined the cash from their life insurance and the proceeds from selling their farm to American Seasons. He returned to Los Angeles, made some good buys in real estate, took a chance on the New Loon Town Café, and those actions made him rich.

In another way, Danny also made him rich. He added something to his life that he could no longer imagine living without. When Josh first saw Danny that autumn in Thread, Josh had been walking into his hometown as the exotic charmer from Los Angeles. At least that's how he thought of himself. He never expected to have his self-confidence hit in the face by encountering a guy still in high school. He had never been attracted to younger men, and still wasn't. But Danny proved different. Perhaps it was because Danny was tall, when Josh was short, blonde while Josh was dark, tentative while he was supremely confident. But that approach seemed too simplistic. There was something else that made him want to be in Danny's presence and coax that smile from his troubled face. And when he thought he could return to California and leave Danny back to grow up in the cold woods of Wisconsin, he discovered it wasn't doable. He had to go back until he convinced Danny to join him on the West Coast.

It took a while, but once he convinced Danny to move west, they were happy. Eventually Danny found himself and what he wanted to be. He enrolled in the writing program at USC, then started a little 'zine called *InnerEatz* when he got the idea to write about food by hanging around Stephen and Wally's restaurant and meeting their various foodie friends. Josh was the one who suggested moving it online to be a blog. Even in the early days of the Internet, Josh sensed that someday people would scramble to find interesting content that pulled in the eyeballs. He guided Danny and helped him add the Hollywood gossip that eventually made *InnerEatz* such a hot media property that AOL America came knocking with a paycheck, because the new media giant was on a buying spree as they sought out more and more material to keep their subscribers happy.

Who could say no to a check with six zeroes? The sale put a lot of money in the bank, which in turn made it practical to buy the house in Los Feliz. Again, a move touched by serendipity. The pair closed just before the real estate market started to rebound, which meant their balance sheet bottom line soon was even bigger. The sale of *InnerEatz* also bankrolled the start of Premios. Thinking about that made Josh consider whether they shouldn't change the company name officially to premios.com. Adding ".com" to a name seemed to make a property hot in the current bull market.

Too bad that Danny was one of those people who needed everything washed in clarity. Maybe having a suicidal mother and a slightly loco father did that to him. But Josh was always happy to help Danny understand whatever he felt he needed to comprehend.

Josh jumped in. "Don't worry, Danny, Orleans and I will explain anything you need clarified. Do you want to go over the financials? The marketing plan? See the thumbnails for the new site? How about talk about the investor roadshow? Whatever you want. Just tell us."

"None of that."

"Okay."

Danny blushed by what he was about to say, "I'm worried that someone is trying to sabotage us. And I want you to take it seriously."

Orleans dropped her fountain pen, picked it up, and looked toward Josh with an expression he couldn't decipher.

"Why would you say that?" Josh asked. "Who in the world would want to harm our business? Or do you mean the two of us, you and me?"

"I mean the company. It's about what Chip told us in Wisconsin. About the computer worm that attacked our site's database."

Josh thought of it more as a Trojan horse, not a worm or a virus, but he shrugged away Danny's concern. There hadn't been any danger. "Why would you worry about that? It was just a hackers' prank. Probably not even aimed at us. Some crazy programmer released that code to create a little havoc. Besides we caught it in time. No harm done."

"Chip seemed worried."

"Chip's a worrier. Always has been. It was nothing."

Danny was wavering, but not convinced. Josh pressed on. "Okay, what else. Spill it."

Danny paused for just a moment. "Kenosha thinks someone was watching our house while we were gone."

Once he voiced a worry aloud, Danny always relaxed. Josh recognized this habit of Danny's: sharing the problem moved the responsibility to Josh.

For once, Josh wasn't going to pick it up. As some of his business friends liked to put it, one didn't let others place stray monkeys on your back, especially if those monkeys would be nothing but trouble. "I know she's your friend, but Kenosha's too imaginative. Always thinking something's going on. Remember when she claimed her house was haunted by a bloody ghost, and it turned out it was just her tom cat sitting in the bathtub and dripping blood from a urinary infection."

"Yeah, Kenosha can be imaginative. But this time I believe her. There were footprints among the shrubs at the back of our lot. Someone was back there."

Josh and Orleans exchanged such startled looks that Josh feared even Danny would see how his comments concerned them.

Danny did. "All right, you two. What's going on? Is there something wrong with our company? Do we keep some kind of data people don't want us to have?"

Cynthia had always appreciated the destructive power of cold weather, and she hated it. Her dad always warned that when temperatures dropped low enough even well protected water pipes could seize into ice and burst. But on rare January nights in northern Wisconsin, temperatures can flirt with thirty degrees or more below zero and fuel oil starts to run sluggish. Such nights can even burst human spirit. The previous night had been that kind of January night.

But now it was morning and Cynthia had other thoughts on her mind. She ignored the deep blue morning sky outside, as well as the slight chill that found its way through the triple-paned glass of their breakfast room. Cynthia had a question she wanted answered.

Both Cynthia and Chip were seated for breakfast. He was dressed for the office, wearing a well-tailored jacket and open shirt. Eggs and bacon were on their plates. Steam rose from their coffee cups. The morning's *Wall Street Journal* lay beside Chip's plate, unopened, and Chip seemed distracted. Normally by this time, he had left for his office. She also knew he hadn't slept well, and as a result she also suffered a bad night.

"You seem moody," she said. "What's wrong?"

Since New Year's Eve, something had transformed her normally calm husband into a different personality. After leaving Josh and Danny's camp late on New Year's Day, he seemed distracted. Days later, he remained edgy. She needed to understand why.

Surely, it had nothing to do with the tribe's business. The resort was filled with vacationing Midwesterners. Its enclosed water park was always the most popular when the outside air was the coldest. Somehow an arctic blast goaded kids to slip down the giant slides with greater giddiness. Maybe a rushing glance at snow-covered pines on the opposite side of the glass increased the sense of danger.

She had so many questions. "What exactly happened at the camp? Why are you worried? What haven't you told me? I've always felt you never really liked Josh."

"That's not it."

"Then tell me what is bothering you."

After a dozen years of marriage, Cynthia realized that her husband needed to run through his own complicated mental calculus of pros and cons. She would just need to wait to hear his conclusion.

"Do you remember when we talked about the computer malware we encountered during the Y2K countdown?" he finally said.

"Of course. You nearly destroyed Danny's New Year's dinner talking about it."

"I let the topic go that day, but it's still worrying me."

"Why? I don't remember Josh being concerned." Josh and her husband were two completely opposing kinds of thinkers—one was a man of emotions who made all his decisions with total ease and confidence, and the other was steeped in analysis and synthesis. No decision came quick or easy to Chip.

Still, Cynthia never doubted that Chip was the right kind of person for her. No matter what happened, she would know that every step Chip took was carefully thought through as to the risks and opportunities. Whatever the outcome, good or bad, Cynthia would never face any consequence with regrets because she would be confident that Chip's decision was the best-reasoned one that could possibly be made.

"You think more carefully than Josh. So at least tell me what you haven't told him. Because you haven't told him everything, have you?"

Chip set his napkin on the table and prepared to stand. "He wouldn't pay attention to me."

"I will, so tell me," Cynthia said, and then waited.

Chip gave the slightest nod of acknowledgement. "You win," he said. He sat down again.

"Here's what I know. While in the data center on New Year's Eve, something activated a type of malware within our software. Once alive, it began to destroy the database underlying Josh and Danny's company. Luckily we detected the problem almost immediately, stopped it, and restored the data. Nothing was lost. Everyone was happy. It was easy to say it was just a hacker's prank.

"But I can't buy such a simple explanation. It doesn't make sense. The code wasn't malicious or juvenile enough to fit a hacker's profile. There has to be some larger purpose. So I made my guys go back in and do a post mortem. And they found something more, just like I thought they would. But now it makes even less sense."

Chip stood once again and paced nervously. Stopping by the window, he stared out at the drifts. Cynthia instinctively rose to be nearer him and placed her hand on his forearm. Through the shirt's fabric she felt his tension. "What did they find?"

"It wasn't what you'd expect. The program was moving files over the net to some server farm in California, and then those files were sent back—but not before they were modified. The files were stripped out, moved, transformed, sent back, and stored in a cache. If we hadn't interrupted the process, the entire database belonging to Premios might have appeared untouched on the surface, but in reality it would have been changed. We would never have known. Only because we noticed the deletion of files at an early state did we stop the transformation."

"What was being changed?"

"We don't know Josh's business well enough to be certain, but oddly it doesn't seem as though any of the changes were significant."

"But then why make the changes?"

"Who knows? Maybe it was a test run for something. I have no idea."

Cynthia didn't know what to do with this added information. Finally she spoke.

"Well, what did Josh say when you told him?"

"I haven't told him."

"But why not?"

"You know him. He'll simply dismiss it. Especially at this point in time. He's about to go on a financial roadshow to prep the company for an initial stock offering. He doesn't want anything to interrupt that, particularly something that he's already dismissed as a random hack."

Cynthia was not about to let go. "Then tell Danny."

"Really? Danny? I know he's been your friend since high school. But he knows nothing about business or computing. He'll just follow Josh's lead."

"You can't ignore this." Cynthia said, not because it might involve a question of what was moral or right, but because she knew that Chip's mind could never let this mystery go.

"I'm not. I'm flying to California tomorrow. Don't worry. I'll find this mysterious server farm, flush out the hackers, and bring Josh the proof he needs—wrapped up in a bow. Someone is trying to destroy his business. And I'm not going to let them."

Danny walked across the office floor. Orleans was at his side. He passed Kenosha's desk. Neither Orleans nor Josh could explain their startled look when he told them about the tracks outside the basement. Danny wished he could escape Orleans' purview long enough to trade ideas with Kenosha.

Earlier that day when Kenosha drove Danny into the office after their morning coffee, they speculated as to why someone might break into the house. For some reason, Danny avoided mentioning the attack on the company's database on New Year's Eve. It wasn't that he didn't trust Kenosha; he wasn't certain he trusted his own instincts as to what mattered.

As Danny walked by her desk, Kenosha looked up and gave a quick wave. Her hand moved in a stylized motion to indicate the importance of her phone call. Whoever was on the other end, Danny was certain that Kenosha was reeling the writer into covering the story she was pitching. Like everyone at Premios, Kenosha was very good at her job.

Orleans' desk sat in the corner diagonal from Josh's. Except for the conference space bordered by slightly wavy glass in the middle of the space, the floor held no interior walls. The high ceilings were painted white; banks of massive windows stretched along every wall. This bright and noisy top floor offered no hidden corners. Josh liked to joke that Orleans and he could keep an eye on everyone. Maybe that's the way the digital world liked to work, but Danny felt he wouldn't last a day in such a madhouse.

But Josh was wrong about one thing: a person couldn't see everywhere. The translucent glass conference room in the middle interrupted the sightlines. Individually, Josh or Orleans could see only half the floor from their respective desks. Playing big brother would require them to work together. Of course, that wasn't needed. The staff held enormous freedom to work however they wished, from clocking odd hours or telecommuting from home to even spending the day on the small balcony that graced the front of the building. With a kitchen that always overflowed with catered food and a game space with foosball and Ping-Pong, the Premios office was more frat house than a place of business.

"Take a seat," Orleans said. Although she normally used a stand-up desk, she maintained a seating area with two overstuffed chairs that faced one other. "Josh asked me to walk you through the financing stages for Premios. To really understand the company, we should start with the money. If nothing else, you should understand what you own and what belongs to everyone else."

Money wasn't what interested Danny. Especially after Orleans and Josh both ignored his claim moments earlier that someone was after the company's data. He still thought the two were hiding something, even though he didn't know what questions to ask.

In Wisconsin, when Danny made his New Year's resolution, he never anticipated that the result would be Orleans walking him through a bean-counting exercise. Seeking an escape from her earnestness, he looked for Josh, hoping to catch his eye. His eyes stopped on the center conference room. With the weird wavy glass breaking up the sightlines, it was hard to be certain but it looked like Josh was in the room meeting with someone.

Suddenly nothing made sense. Even through the blur of the glass, he recognized the second person. Only one man could have that thin frame, dark hair and scruffy beard. Jesus Lopez! What was his old writing teacher from USC doing here? He didn't belong in this office. Josh would never allow it.

Lopez was a great teacher, but Danny detested him. Even when the man made Danny yearn to do more than he ever thought possible, the man scared him. He forced a life into Danny's words that startled him. It was as though Lopez transformed Danny into a god because suddenly Danny could imagine worlds into reality, but at the same time Lopez made him believe in the existence of pure evil.

As a student, Danny admired this teacher until the moment he read one of Lopez's novels. The man's books were dark and forbidding. Lopez's prose forced the reader to crawl through sickening muck and to encounter disgusting characters. After reading two of them, Danny never again saw Lopez in the same heroic light. Danny held the opinion that there was a kernel of his crazed scenes in the real Lopez— and he never wanted to meet that person.

Signing up for Jesus Lopez's creative writing course was almost an accident. While many students enrolled in the writing program at the University solely because of Lopez, Danny had a different story. He had never even heard of the writer. Only when he was enrolled and began to hear others talk about the man's charisma in the classroom did he seek a place in the man's class.

Even once he was in the class, he was at first too lazy to ferret out the man's works. Only as his reverence grew for Lopez as an instructor did Danny decide to buy a copy of the professor's first novella, *Beautifully Incomplete*, about a young man obsessed with amputees. Told in first person, the narrator was driven by a twisted love that compelled him to make the woman he loved more beautiful by amputating her legs. Sickened by the theme, Danny insisted to Josh that he would drop the class. But Josh wouldn't let him take that easy out, and reminded Danny that Jesus Lopez was considered one of the stars of the faculty.

"There has to be more to him than your first reaction," Josh maintained. "Find out what you can learn from him."

As usual, Josh was right. The following semester Danny took the advanced seminar from Lopez as well. Somehow, the teacher pulled from him unexpected observations. With Lopez as his catalyst, Danny discovered a joy in writing that nothing else in life, except for Josh, had yet given him. In some way, Lopez proved to be good for him, and so he found ways to avoid thinking about the man's fevered imaginings. He isolated the man as much as possible to his role as a teacher, avoiding any delving into his life.

Instead Danny focused on Lopez's spirit of energy. There was a forbidden essence to Lopez that attracted him like a moth to the flame. Lopez's energy and purpose seemed electric.

Spurred on by this man he both admired and detested, Danny started his 'zine and then his blog. It was the start of a life that led to this moment on the twelfth story of a 1920s building in downtown Los Angeles, where a twenty-first century business was being birthed.

Other than Jesus, only one other person in Danny's life—and it wasn't Josh—had ever sparked such a strong reaction. Danny had been sixteen, during the summer before he met Josh, when his dad arranged for him to work a summer job at a fancy resort several miles south of Thread. The staff was largely teenagers and college-age students, where everyone lived on the grounds for the summer. Breakfast and dinner were included as part of the resort fee for most guests, and Danny was a dishwasher in the hotel's kitchen.

On the first day, one of the other kitchen staff taught him how to operate the dishwasher. Oliver was tall, broad chested, Italian, and from Chicago. Since it was his second season working there, he knew his way around the resort. The man planned on attending the University of Chicago that fall.

Oliver had dark hair on his arms, and the muscles of the forearm were well defined. His fingers were long with ragged nails, but the hands made Danny think of a statue he had once seen called David. Danny, who never really noticed a man's hands before, suddenly wanted those particular fingers to touch him, and the realization scared him. Because he couldn't stop looking at the hand on that first day they worked together, Danny didn't even raise his eyes to look into Oliver's face. He could barely recall the lesson on the dishwasher's controls.

Some people had that kind of impact—Lopez, Oliver, Josh. They couldn't be forgotten.

Danny knew the shadow in the room belonged to Lopez. No matter how obscure the glass or unexpected the circumstances, such people were always immediately recognized. As Josh escorted his guest out of the Premios conference room, Danny watched, certain it was Lopez even though the conference area glass kept the guest somewhat obscured. The men exited to the elevator lobby.

Danny turned to Orleans who was pulling presentations from her files. "Why is Jesus Lopez here?" he asked.

"The novelist. That Jesus Lopez?" she replied, looking at him oddly.

"Yes. He just left that conference room with Josh."

"I don't think so. Josh was scheduled to meet with an investment banker. It must have been someone who looked similar."

Usually, Danny thought of Orleans as an expert liar. He lost too many poker games to her over the years. But at that moment he was quite certain she was lying for the second time that day—even though he couldn't think of one reason she would need to do so.

Session Three

We're still talking about Danny. I get it. If that's the subject matter that I think is so important, then that's where you want to focus. Just remember I'm the one paying the bill. We should be talking about what I think is important, not what gets you off.

So you asked what makes me so interested in the guy. I used to think I wanted to figure out if Danny was good or evil. Sure, on one hand, it's obvious he's a good guy. Some might call him a little goody two-shoes. That's what everyone thinks. But I've always wondered if that was just a mask for something deeper. Did you ever think what it would take to push a person like him over the edge and see where the true self lies? Isn't everyone a bit like Dr. Jekyll and Mr. Hyde? Think about it. Two sides to every coin. It's intriguing. At least to me.

When I think of Danny, I think of all those opposites. Good versus evil. Weak, not strong. Happy or sad. Forward instead of backward. There's a million of them. I think with Danny I just found my metaphor for all mankind. It's contradictions that make us all tick. That's my mantra.

You say I'm getting off subject? I don't think so. Can't you see how Danny is at the heart of everything I do and everything I think about? If you want to understand me, then you have to understand Danny. So play along. Do your job.

At the end of the day, I decided the best pair of words to describe Danny are just two. Hope. Despair. Which emotion wins out? Both fight deep within him.

Despair runs strong within his family. His mother killed herself when Danny was only thirteen. No one knew anything was wrong. She wasn't sick. Everyone thought she loved both her husband and son. Can you imagine the kind of despair that drives a woman to leave her only son forever without saying good-bye? No note. All she handed the kid was a mystery. Now that's despair.

Wouldn't it be a nice twist of storytelling if I could say his dad represented the opposing force of hope? But nothing is ever that simple or neat. The man's okay now, but in the years after his wife's suicide, he *rambled around like a lost soul.*

So did Danny find hope? I guess he made it for himself.

Can't you see why I find that so worthy of my attention? The kid manages to eke out a happy life from the crap dealt him—and he's fine with it. Most people want more.

But I think his hope is just a mask. I smell the despair that's still deep within him. Apply a little bit of pressure consistently . . . why, I bet he'll snap to the other side. Just like that.

Proving the paradox of Danny. That's what keeps me going.

CHAPTER THREE

Party Time

Josh hired valets for the evening gala. Because it was a big night for the company, he wanted everything to go smoothly. The red-jacketed boys were quick to take the keys from the arriving drivers, speed out of the circular drive, stash the cars, and dash back to await the next expensive car to experience.

Tonight was more than important; it was a turning point. The house would be filled with heavy hitters who might make a real difference in the forthcoming success of Premios. Josh knew you had to play the part to be the part, and, by god, Josh was determined to give an Academy Award winning performance tonight. He yearned to be a player in this world of new media, and he was sparing no expense to prove it. Appearances mattered: the lighting, the flowers, the music on the terrace, the best valet company in town—it proclaimed that Premios was a company on the rise. If you portrayed it, it would become true. After all, this was Hollywood.

The starting point was the right collection of guests. Josh hadn't hesitated to trade on the notoriety of the mansion's past to attract certain celebrity types. He added an up-and-coming sleight of hand magician from the Magic Castle to provide a close-up show. (Josh convinced him to do it for free just because the guy was so excited to be working in the old director's secret lair. It always paid to turn people on, but to do that one had to know their hot buttons.)

Some of his decisions for the evening might not turn out to be the best. For example, he let Danny convince him to hire Wally and Stephen to cater the party. Even though they were old friends and he was a part owner of their café, they had fallen off the cutting edge. If he were honest with himself, he knew the pair's small chain of restaurants was nearing its end of life and he should find a way to cut his ties. But the two chefs had a certain fan base from their low-rated show on that cooking channel—plus they would bring along their good friend, Francesca Petroff. She was the restaurant reviewer for the *Los Angeles Dispatch*, known as much for her perky and feisty persona as her prose. That was the kind of talent Premios needed to foster. Premios users wanted more than the recommendations of fellow users; they demanded the acerbic approvals of authorities. Even if Francesca wasn't yet a signed contributor to their editorial content, guests could be forgiven if they assumed otherwise. A party was like a house of cards, each person supporting another, building a buzz that made everyone think they were having a good time—whether they were or not. In the end, true feelings didn't matter. Given the right elements, everything seemed important and therefore unforgettable.

Danny just couldn't master this calculus of promotion; it would be a miracle if he could even feign interest. Josh loved the guy, but he could never understand why Danny became so obsessive over minor things. Like their flap earlier in the week over Jesus Lopez. That would have been prevented if Orleans hadn't tried to cover up Josh's meeting with Jesus. Everyone knew that Danny didn't like the professor, but Josh wanted Jesus at this party and at Premios. Jesus was like Francesca— another link in the chain of energy. Everyone understood how Jesus's writing program could be a great way to identify early new writing talent. Investors wanted to see just that kind of edgy people associated with Premios. Even better, Jesus's latest novel was being seriously shopped around Hollywood for a major picture deal. Jesus had clout and he could draw in more of the Hollywood crowd. After all, Premios wasn't just an information site about restaurants and entertainment or a referral site for reservations and shopping. Josh was shaping it into the destination for those in the know.

He needed this party to bring some of that buzz, and he was counting on Kenosha and her connections to do their magic. The game plan was simple: deliberately mingling different worlds, while engaging people that could generate gossip for the Internet crowd and the old-line press

What Danny didn't understand was that you didn't need to worry about whether you liked your guests. Earlier in the evening Danny finally bothered to review the guest list, and he had a fit. Even though he knew it was a business event and had made his recent resolution to be more involved, he hadn't bothered to prep to host the event. Danny was a Premios star too and Josh needed him to play his A-game tonight, but Josh's prediction for this evening was that Danny would try to seclude himself in the kitchen with Wally, Stephen, Francesca and the catering staff. But he would lure them out if for no other reason than Jesus wanted to talk to Danny tonight.

A new car arrived, and Josh smiled in satisfaction. It had happened—the arrival of a much-sought-after guest—Barbara Linsky, the star of his evening. Surprisingly, it was the promised presence of Francesca Petroff that had lured Linsky. Who would guess that a tired old tech guru like Linsky would be infatuated with food? It always paid to know those hidden hankerings.

Linsky was a goddess to venture capitalists and the tech press. Ever since her advisory firm, Barbara Linsky, Incorporated, started the BLINK conferences four years ago, her star had risen higher and higher. Each September, her annual conference in Boston attracted nearly two thousand of the country's most influential minds. Attendance was by invitation only, and few turned down the opportunity to attend (although their motivation might tilt more toward mingling with the influential guests than being inspired by thought-provoking lectures). People with an agenda would kill for an invitation to speak. And Barbara was here tonight, and he had all evening to work his magic.

When his primary investor Colby Endicott heard about Linsky's attendance, the man went crazy. Frankly, Josh found Colby a third-rate hanger-on when it came to the tech investment community. But he had inherited money and the right kind of friends. Knowing the money man wouldn't ask too many questions, Josh persuaded Colby early on to bring big money into Premios. Truth was, with the proceeds from the sale of *InnerEatz* to AOL, Danny and Josh could have funded the first and second stages of financing themselves. But why put their money at risk? Josh believed in letting others share that excitement.

Admittedly there was more to getting an outside investor involved than playing it safe. Over the years, Danny had given Josh a lot of himself, and that had made Josh's life fuller and more meaningful. He shouldn't risk Danny's share of money on something that was really Josh's dream. He owed Danny more than that.

God, success was so tantalizingly close. Internet companies were going public left and right at huge valuations and making their founders rich beyond sensibility. Who could say what something was worth in this new world? Maybe some claimed it was all a bubble, but bubbles could float high and far. One just had to escape the bubble before it burst.

Tonight he had gathered everything needed to fan a little hot air that would raise the Premios bubble ever so gently, ever so higher. Financiers like Colby, analysts like Barbara, celebrities like Jesus and Francesca—just tinder to his fire of expansion.

Standing on the small musician's balcony that bridged a view of the entry and the large living room, Josh realized he had removed himself too long from the main action of the party in the room below. In the original architectural plans filed with the city, the living room was labeled a ballroom. Whatever its function, tonight it was aglow with people and stemware. It was time to join them. As he reached the bottom of the steep staircase from the balcony, Orleans walked up. "Have you told Danny yet?" she wanted to know.

"About Jesus? Yes, I have. And next time he asks questions, just give him direct answers."

"That's not what I meant. Have you told him the real source of Colby Endicott's money?"

Josh shut her down with a single look. "He doesn't need to know. I'll take care of it."

Danny was so pleased to hear Francesca Petroff laugh. Frankly, it gave him goose bumps to hear such unrestrained joy. Lately she had been far too depressed, but that's why people had friends—to help one another laugh.

Even if they were secreted away in the mansion's kitchen gossiping among the din of the catering staff, Danny was happy to be with his friends. At least Stephen and Wally could claim a reason to be in the room. Technically the serving staff reported to them and all of the food came from their restaurant's kitchen. For a typical Hollywood catering job, the restaurant would have sent out a lead. Neither Wally nor Stephen would have been anywhere in sight. On the other hand, the two of them would never have been on the invitation list.

Not only were they here at his party, but they also brought Francesca with them, which Danny knew made Josh happy. But Danny was also happy. Francesca needed to get out of her house and away from depressing thoughts. What she really needed was the presence of good friends, although the music and glitter might also help.

Josh tried to explain why this party was so important, but now Danny found that he couldn't even recall the reasons. Somehow Josh saw the event as critical to taking the company public. How having a bunch of strangers drink fancy wine and eat expensive canapés could affect decision makers on Wall Street was a mystery to Danny. He regretted uttering aloud that fleeting thought about a New Year's resolution to better understand the business. He really didn't care to understand the company. All he needed were his friends.

They were important to him. Years ago, Wally had taken a chance on Danny when he gave him a job as a busboy at his restaurant in the little town of Thread. He had always looked out for Danny, and that job had led to his knowing Stephen—and in turn Francesca. Friends mattered, and they made him happy.

How could he care about the kind of people Josh invited, especially Jesus Lopez? A few days earlier, Josh finally admitted that Lopez had been in Premios' office, but Danny had no idea why Orleans first lied about it or why he had to force the information out of Josh. But he was over the incident. What did it matter how the company recruited new writers? After all, Josh would never have known Lopez if Danny hadn't enrolled in the man's writing course—and if he hadn't done that, their business probably wouldn't even exist. Truthfully, though, Danny wanted to write fiction, not offer arch reviews of restaurants or gossip about chefs. Let Francesca be the master of such work. There was a rumor that *Vanity Fair* was trying to lure her to Manhattan as their restaurant reviewer.

The party unsettled Danny. He felt a need to turn his life around. He was letting other people decide key directions for him. He had a mind of his own and he should use it. On this night his instincts told him to revel in friendship and let the party rage without him. Let Josh worry about business.

Danny and his friends were seated around a small breakfast table in a nook of the kitchen. The table held four flutes, along with a near-empty bottle of Taittinger champagne. The nook's windows overlooked the large swimming pool and a lawn terraced into the east side of the hillside lot. Below the terraces, the yard dropped steeply to the street below.

Stephen motioned to one of his waiters, "Bring us another bottle, and also one of those duck breast pizzas."

Around the table, everyone was laughing. Wally was being the indiscreet raconteur and recalling every oddball movement of any celebrity that ever came into their main restaurant in East Hollywood. He had just finished flamboyantly describing a situation involving a B-level starlet and her malfunctioning wardrobe.

Francesca wiped the tears from her eyes, "How I wish I could use a tale like that in one of my reviews, but the paper is so staid. Now, Danny, he was the lucky one when he still had his 'zine. People only read his rag to get dirt, and he could use whatever he heard." She smiled to show she wasn't serious, even though Danny knew the critique was totally true.

"But who was the one at this table hoovering up all the filth to pass it onto me?" Danny asked.

Even as he laughed in agreement, Wally held up his hands to deny it.

"It is so good to be here with my gay guys tonight," Francesca said. "For the last month, I felt like I forgot how to laugh."

For a moment, the three men were somber. They all knew about Francesca's situation. Though single, she desperately wanted to be a mother. An opportunity arose when her young cleaning girl Maria became pregnant. The girl was single, Catholic, not yet twenty-one and the father had vanished. When Francesca offered to pay Maria's expenses through birth and then adopt the child, it seemed an ideal solution for all. Those who knew Francesca were overjoyed. While the woman lived life large and her past was wild, no one doubted that she would be a fantastic mother. Wally, Stephen, Danny and Josh attended Francesca's baby shower and oohed over the sonogram showing the soon-to-be-born baby girl.

But disaster struck in an unexpected way. An INS agent arrested Maria because she was in the country illegally and working without papers. Despite the best efforts of Francesca to provide the woman with legal help, Maria was deported. Later, after the baby was born in Mexico, Maria sent a letter saying she would remain living with her parents and raise the baby in their home outside Mérida. Francesca was left with only the sonogram and a room filled with baby furniture and supplies.

Danny sometimes thought life was a pinball game. Full of chance, unexpected turns, and bumpers you couldn't avoid. He regretted the loss of Francesca's dream, but knew better than to suggest that she try adopting again or to note that at age 39 she still might get pregnant herself (even though he had toyed with the idea of offering his sperm).

One of the waiters walked into the kitchen. It was clear he was looking for the four of them. A moment later, Kenosha followed. The game was up. She walked up to Danny, "We're looking for you. Josh says you need to mingle with the rest of the guests."

"I guess that's a summons," Danny said. "But I say let Josh entertain this circus himself. "

Kenosha put on that reproving look at which she excelled. "Danny, this is a business event. You know that. Help me do my job. Be part of the party. In fact, I could use all of you out there."

Danny wanted to enjoy himself his own way, so he rebelled. "Francesca, you've been here so many times, but you've never really seen our entire house. What do you say to a tour?"

"Why not? After everything others gossip about this house, I can't pass up the chance to see it myself."

For a moment, Danny thought Josh would be pleased to know that people talked about their home. After all, the decorators had done a wonderful job, and the restoration fully showed the house's marvelous bones. Kenosha's glare grew more severe. Danny was reminded of Josh's more immediate desires and that Kenosha wasn't going to let him get away with his little rebellion.

Francesca continued, "Maybe I'm a bad guest to say so, but this house has quite the reputation among a certain Hollywood set . . . you know, those who are into the ghostly and mysterious."

"What?"

"I'm not joking. In my line of work, you hear all sorts of behind-the-scenes talk. Now, I don't know whether it was at Spago or Michael's. More likely at Musso and Frank's. It's an old-fashioned, noir kind of place. The story I heard was all about a crazy old director and his house filled with secret rooms."

"There are no secret rooms," Danny said.

Francesca just laughed. "Not that you found. Otherwise how could they be secret? Imagine what might be buried in this place! I heard everything that mattered was in the basement."

Kenosha and Danny exchanged looks. Each knew what the other was thinking. Maybe someone <u>had</u> tried to break in.

Danny heard Josh exuberantly call, "There you are! I was beginning to think you abandoned me. Left alone to swim my way through an ocean of sharks." He flashed his big smile to the surrounding circle of admirers to show that he was letting them all in on his silly jest. They might be predators, he seemed to acknowledge, but they swam together.

After Kenosha forced the four friends out of the kitchen, Francesca touched Danny just as they reached Josh, "There's someone from the paper I need to greet. It was so nice talking in the kitchen."

"Don't go yet, Francesca," Josh said. Surrounded by Linsky, Lopez and Endicott, Josh sported that happy grin of a man about to win a game. If only Danny could enjoy life as much as his boyfriend did. "I have to brag a little. Barbara just asked me to speak at her next BLINK talk." Francesca, Stephen, and Wally murmured their congratulations. Danny knew this was a major deal.

"And what would all those posers want to hear from Josh Gunderson?" Stephen asked. It was meant as a light-hearted jibe, but it annoyed Josh.

Kenosha quickly jumped in. "Barbara thinks Josh has interesting insights on how the web is changing people's decision making. She thinks that will change commerce."

"Indeed, I do," said Barbara as she slightly tipped her glass toward Josh.

Kenosha couldn't help but show a self-satisfied smile. As the public relations lead, she originally pitched the idea to Linsky. The invitation was a coup for the company and for her. The financier Colby Endicott was also smiling broadly. His investment firm, Endicott-Meyers, had bet big when they provided second round financing for Premios. No doubt he saw Linsky's invitation not only as an endorsement of the company but also as a promising indicator of a big IPO payoff. Orleans just seemed relieved, which made no sense whatsoever to Danny. Sometimes he didn't understand her. And he disliked that Jesus Lopez was hanging around this group. He didn't belong, and it chafed Danny that he still found the man attractive.

Lopez spoke, "Barbara, couldn't you extend an invitation to this minor novelist? It would be so interesting to hear what Josh might say." Now Kenosha was annoyed. She didn't want someone horning in on her triumph.

Linsky didn't care. "Don't put me on the spot, Mr. Lopez. Guest invitations are never sent before May. But don't consider yourself a minor novelist. Didn't the *New York Review of Books* just call you a major voice for the outcast society?"

Lopez beamed. Maybe some element of the former homeowner's directorial aura infected Danny, but he had flashes of being transported into a film. It wasn't the first time he felt like a trapped character in a staging directed from off-screen. In this instance it was some scene from *All About Eve*, Bette Davis, and every other arch story about social climbers, but as in all of his disorienting flashes, Danny had no clue as to what character he was playing.

Danny blamed his overactive imagination on Pete. After his mother died, his only confidante was Pete, who once owned the only movie theater in Thread. He befriended Danny, gave him small odd jobs, and occasionally convinced him to watch old movies.

Those old films introduced him to a world beyond Thread and were treasured moments. Even though finances had forced Pete to close the Thread Theater more than a decade prior to befriending Danny, he continued to own the building and the projectors still worked. Tattered publicity posters for *Cabaret* still hung in those days in the glass cases on the building's exterior, but only Danny was able to see a movie inside the building.

Because Pete loved films and couldn't let them go, he'd occasionally rent an old print to view by himself in the empty theater. He would sit on a stool in the projector's booth, watching the scenes unreel on the dingy screen, peering through the booth's small window, and letting the sound echo in the abandoned room with its missing seats and peeling paint. The theater was fading away but in the transforming light of the cinema, it didn't matter. Nothing mattered but the film.

It took only a few months of Danny doing odd jobs around Pete's house, before Pete made a daring decision to share his passion with Danny. He tentatively asked him if he'd like to see a real movie. That afternoon Pete projected a W.C. Fields flick that also starred Mae West. The two laughed together, and Danny no longer felt so forgotten. He had a friend and he had a life of imagination.

When Danny's mom was still alive, she and his dad used to talk about the movies they once saw. In Milwaukee when they first met, a theater had been their customary weekend date. After they moved back to Thread, his mother stopped working to care for Danny, and somehow Danny always knew his parents' lives changed. But when

Danny sat on a stool in the projection booth with Pete and watched the flickering shadows play across the large screen at the end of an empty room, Danny felt a lingering of his mother and life seemed bearable. He owed Pete for that.

What would his mother think of his life now? Would she approve of how he lived with a man in a mansion near Hollywood, slept in the same bedroom used by a once-famous director, and entertained famous faces that most people only knew from photos in a fan magazine? If she could have foreseen his future, would it have been enough to keep her alive?

"Premios is expanding," Josh declared.

Still encircled by Colby, Orleans and Kenosha, Josh was pimping himself to Barbara. Stephen and Wally had wandered over to the other side of the room. Danny wanted to follow, but he knew Josh expected him to stay. He owed him that.

"New York is our next big market," added Orleans. "Last year, we signed all the major restaurants, hotels, and venues on the West Coast. And we built a set of curated content with potential for national interest. It only makes sense to move East."

"Of course," said Barbara. Colby was nodding his head in full agreement.

"The idea," said Josh, "is to duplicate the same connections we provide our western customers, but in the East. Access to all the best restaurants, shopping deals to hot stores, rooms at great hotels. This is our prime mission: to be the best-connected concierge the country could ever have.

"And," he added, "you'll be surprised how we plan to accomplish that. We're scheduling a big announcement at the ABC Studios on Times Square this April. Barbara, you should come to the press conference."

"Of course, I'll be there with bells on," she replied. Kenosha clapped her hands in appreciation.

Suddenly Danny felt tired. Neither Josh nor Kenosha ever mentioned an upcoming press conference, or even plans for an East Coast expansion. Where had the money come from? He didn't pay enough attention. Even back in Thread, even with Pete, he had always been that way. Whatever happened to Pete and that crazy hat he used to wear? After that summer when the bank finally foreclosed on his theater and he lost everything, Pete's spirit crashed in upon itself.

Danny always felt a little bit responsible. Sure, he was only fourteen then, but he could have helped the guy.

Someone moved up behind him. Josh looked over, startled. When Danny turned around, he was equally surprised.

"What are you doing here?" he asked.

"I wanted to check things out in person, and talk to you guys. Hope you don't mind that I crashed your party. I told Cynthia I wanted to surprise you."

Chip Grant was in their house, uninvited, without Cynthia. From the look on Josh's face, it was clear that he was not pleased.

The next day Josh happily submitted himself to Barbara Linsky's lunchtime reign. As queen of the table at his company's New Loon Town Café event, she demanded the attention of all. Josh invited the technology guru so she could meet several people from his firm. Somehow Chip appeared as well, without an invitation and now sitting right next to Barbara. Both were engaged in a fast-paced conversation, which put Josh on edge. But he wasn't going to show it.

Like any restaurant of the moment, the place was crowded and unduly noisy. The plate glass window facing Hollywood Boulevard framed a large mechanized black bear; the taxidermist's creation continually swatted at a cartoonish diving loon fashioned out of flashing neon. The bear paw batted back and forth in a never-ending volley that brought neither satisfaction to the bear nor safety to the bird.

Josh never understood what the cafe's diorama was meant to suggest, but somehow it epitomized the hip and ironic northwoods feel of the place and gave cover for people to order bratwurst and potato pancakes instead of organic salads or free-range chicken. It also evoked memories of old beer signs from long forgotten taverns on quiet wooded lakes, which seemed to mesh nicely in the patrons' minds with the place's broad array of on-tap microbrews and ales.

The Loon Town's reasonable prices and tasty food attracted steady crowds, even as it approached its tenth anniversary, and everyone knew restaurant years were even longer than dog years. But as Josh looked around the room, he was dismayed. He saw no dining guest to excite the paparazzi, assuming any still hung outside the front door— which they did not. The absence of the famous was just another talisman of the need for Josh's money to move on.

One long-term regular walked over with excitement to tell Orleans how much he missed her as the hostess. Josh found the presumptuous guest more amusing than he knew he should. The fool. He had no idea that Orleans was now an executive at a major Internet company who could soon be worth millions. (On the other hand, it was a distraction from wondering who tipped off Chip about this lunch.)

Orleans was embarrassed by her fan, which Josh found delightful. Barbara barely noticed. Although Barbara lacked fame among ordinary folk, she would have attracted her own swarms in a different kind of place. There were those who thought she provided an inside channel to the future, or at least an advance indicator of market turns. Such folks were as unwelcome as any celebrity fans. When money was to be made, Josh knew there were always the uninvited. But when it came to Barbara, Josh and his company were in a different category. She was attracted to them. That made him glow.

While forking through the wild rice salad, Barbara was dispensing a wild garden of ideas that sprouted from her fertile mind. Josh was tiring from the sheer effort of keeping up. Kenosha had begged off attending the lunch, but he thought back to what she had told him in the office. She claimed big thinkers like Linsky blossomed only when safely separated from other well-known analysts and beyond the ears of publicists. In isolation, they grew comfortable saying whatever rose to mind. No one was there to either prune or propagate them. As a result, on this day Barbara was in full bloom.

That would have been fine, except Chip wiggled his way into the business lunch. Initially, Josh was afraid Chip would dampen the camaraderie he needed to build, but it was worse. He discovered Barbara and Chip knew each other from Chip's earlier days in New York when he worked as an investment banker before returning to his tribe. Even though he was an investor in the firm's second round financing, Chip didn't need to be around. He hoped Barbara would divert Chip from paying any more attention to Premios.

"Chip, you'd appreciate this thought I've been having lately," Barbara was about to break into a free run of thinking, "especially given your former life in New York working for hedge funds. Think about how today's markets seek to value these new Internet start-ups. But take a step back and approach it as though it were a problem in quantum mechanics. Hypothetically, can a firm's value be two things at once?"

"Like an economic version of Schrödinger's cat, I suppose," Chip suggested.

"Exactly," said Barbara. "Today's economy is as wild as any spinning electron. So here's my question. Does it act like an old-fashioned particle that we know how to explain so well? Or does it operate under rules of some newly discovered wave theory, one of those ideas that changes everything? Surely it can't be both, or can it?

"Think about it. On one hand, we value a firm based on old-fashioned ideas like profit and return. On the other, we imagine a whole new value system, and we extol the company's power to be disruptive or create radical new financial worlds. Which mindset is right? Or should we think two things at the same time?"

Chip smiled in appreciation, "Well, if we compare it to the Schrödinger's cat thought experiment, then the value will become one or the other if we actually look too closely. And if we do that, we might kill the golden goose. We wouldn't want to do that, now would we?"

Barbara laughed in appreciation.

"I thought it was a cat," said Josh, annoyed that he hadn't the slightest idea what the two of them were talking about. He was also irked that Danny seemed interested. Over a decade living together, the guy never failed to surprise him. Whenever Orleans tried to explain the financing rounds that were about to make him millions, Danny's eyes always glazed over. Now some talk about dead cats captivated him.

Barbara sensed Josh's discomfort and played the good guest. "It's simple really. We're referring to an often-discussed problem with quantum mechanics that states something might simultaneously exist in two states, acting both as a particle and a wave. Years ago a physicist named Erwin Schrödinger imagined a hypothetical sealed box that contained a cat, a bottle of poison and a source of radiation. At some point, the radiation could emit particles that would cause the poison to break open and kill the cat.

"But since the box is sealed, and you can't see inside, in a sense it can be said the cat is both alive and dead at the same time. Only if you open and inspect the box, do you ensure that it's one or another. Perhaps the same is true of quantum systems. The act of observation fixes it as one or the other. But until one looks, the cat can be thought of as both, and indeed will act as though it's in both states at the very same time. It's a dilemma of modern science."

Josh wasn't sure he followed their explanation, "That doesn't make any sense at all."

But Danny was intrigued. "It's sort of like that old riddle. If a tree falls in the woods and no one is around to hear or see it, did the tree really fall? Like do we exist only because someone sees us?"

Barbara seemed noticeably pleased but surprised by Danny's comment. "Some philosophers see it that way, but others insist that there has to be an objective reality to the world. They say there must be a reality that exists outside of a need to be observed. Now Josh would be in that camp who wants a fixed and objective reality."

Josh found Barbara's comment demeaning in some way he couldn't quite describe. Danny started to speak again.

"Maybe the answer is that things don't have to be seen by people to be real. But because God sees everything, because God sees us, that makes us real."

Even as he said this, Danny seemed troubled by his own statement.

But Barbara found it interesting. "Or perhaps something exists because you are the one who sees it. Maybe we are all God."

Barbara settled back in her chair as though she found this statement particularly satisfying.

Josh judged what a mistake this lunch was. First, Chip showed up unannounced, and now he was stuck in this boring philosophical talk. He needed to bring the conversation back to firmer ground. While he was at it, he should engineer a strategy to return Chip to Wisconsin. The last thing anyone needed was for Chip digging around the books, or worse, talking to Colby Endicott. So Josh asked the question that seemed most logical to him, "I guess I flunked. I am still not getting it. What does this dead cat have to do with the success of an Internet business?"

Barbara laughed, "Probably nothing. But to me, it seems a similar quandary. Today's investor has the dilemma that modern businesses exist in two different states of meaning. By the old rules, one of our Internet businesses would be judged worthless. Take Amazon. It's not generating any profits. Who knows when or if it ever will? On the other hand, no one dares deny that these Internet companies are truly transformational, changing the way people work and live. In the process, huge numbers of people are developing new loyalties, and shifting the patterns of their lives and behavior. Surely the economy can only follow such mass movement, resulting in a tectonic force of change. As things settle, what will it all mean to the bottom line?

"We would have to be financial detectives to know for sure, inspecting in detail every business practice and every assumption behind it. And after all that, could we even then determine which scenario is true? Any inspection process has its own associated and radioactive assumptions. You can't avoid it, but those assumptions might very well act as the catalyst that breaks open the bottle of poison that kills the cat inside the box. It is sort of a frightening Rube Goldberg construction shining in the bright lights of the financial day."

"In short, inspecting things too closely will kill the cat, and so much for our modern jobs." With that Barbara stopped talking.

"Are you telling me dot-com businesses are worthless? Are you suggesting my company is worthless?" Josh challenged. Why in hell would he ever speak at a BLINK conference if Barbara thought nonsense like that?

"I am just suggesting that we not look too close."

Session Four

You don't like me very much, do you, doc? Not that I care. I'm not paying you two hundred bucks an hour to get you to like me. I'm here to resolve my problems.

It seems to worry you though. I don't understand why. Isn't that what therapy is all about: helping people maximize their self-esteem and become the people they're meant to be? The world knows I'm meant for greatness. I just have this hurdle in my way—figuring out what to do about Danny. It's my problem, and I have to fix it.

The thing is . . . it's not just Danny. By himself, he's a big enough distraction, keeping me from my full potential. It seems like I never know what I really want to do with him. Do I want him happy? Do I want him sad? Or do I just want him to stay in his raw state?

Yeah, of course, I want him to be mine. Not anyone else's. I don't need you to tell me that. By the way, he wouldn't even need to know I'm alive. I just need to know that I control him.

Don't give me that look. We all try to control the people around us. Molding the ones we love is the American way. Turn the alcoholic into a teetotaler. Transform the conformist into a trailblazer.

Sometimes I think people only love the people they do because they want to be controlled by that person. It's so much easier than choosing your own life. And then there are those people like you. All you live for is to fuck up the lives of those around you. What God gave you that right?

Okay, I take that back. You can delete what I said from your tape if you want. I respect you.

But do you realize how hard it is to truly control the life of another? Stupid question. Of course, you do. But there are too damn many influences. That's why I don't like it when Danny makes new friends. Who knows what they will talk him into thinking or attempting.

But on the other hand, every new person opens up the door for my experiments. New people who matter to him let me inflict a little pain into his life and test him without touching him directly. Like a slow water drip form of torture.

Take that bitch Francesca Petroff. I didn't like the way she wormed her way into Danny's world, sneaking in through her friendship with those fags Wally and Stephen. One moment she was the feared restaurant critic whose bad review could destroy everything they had lived for. Next thing you know she was everyone's bosom buddy.

And I can tell Danny likes her. Something in her free spirit speaks to him. I had to squash that. It wouldn't have been long before she would've been yet another of his confidantes—the way Kenosha Washington is. That would have been unbearable. I had to find a way to make her life a little bit more miserable. Only appropriate after the way she horned into Danny's life.

The bitch was so excited about that baby, so happy that her empty bedroom would be filled with the bastard child of a wetback maid. Well, I showed her. I made certain she never achieved her little dream.

You're giving me that look again. I didn't do anything illegal. You seem overly judgmental for a therapist.

I just did my duty as a citizen. Placed that anonymous call to the government. Alerted them to an illegal alien in our midst. Had to call twice. Sweetened the pot the second time by suggesting the girl was connected to the drug trade.

Maybe she was, maybe she wasn't. But the INS finally paid attention. After that, it didn't take long and she was over the border—along with the baby in her belly. So long Francesca's longed-for daughter. Hello depression. Maybe now she'll stay out of Danny's life.

Don't mess with me when it comes to Danny. Eventually, I'll get my way.

CHAPTER FOUR

The Partner

The storm clouds that hung low over the city troubled Josh with the way their gloom obscured the hills encircling downtown Los Angeles. While the overhead lights in the Premios offices were bright, a sogginess in the air sucked out all the glow.

It was a typical wintry January day in a city that could always use more rain, but it wasn't Josh's kind of day. He much preferred a Los Angeles where the bright, unfiltered sun highlighted even the dirtiest of alleys or most untended palm trees. Subtlety and shadings had their value, but he preferred a landscape under a spotlight.

Chip's surprise visit was proving a major annoyance. The man wanted to dig into everything about the business. What did he expect from his half-million dollar stake? Didn't he realize he was a minor player? He only put in five per cent of the second round; he wasn't like Colby who provided nine and a half million, yet still had the good sense never to ask unnecessary questions.

Josh blamed only himself. Whether it was nostalgia for his days in Thread or a desire to hedge his bets, he was the one who offered the minority position to Chip. His rationale to Danny had been simple. As a successful businessperson who already ran a major tech services firm, Chip could provide practical management expertise and advice, and because of their hometown ties, Danny and he could be certain of Chip's trustworthiness. But Josh never expected Chip to actually pay attention to any aspect of Premios.

The old saw was true: be careful what you wish for. Publicly, Josh claimed that he wanted someone with the expertise to ask questions. That's how he explained it to Colby after the man questioned the need to involve Chip. Now Chip was asking questions, and they were the right questions, depending on your point of view. Josh needed to answer them sufficiently so Chip would be satisfied and depart.

Luckily, Orleans was a pro at calming investors and bankers. More than that, Orleans was a grand master of the presentation deck. She could project a slide with the full intensity of hundreds of lumens of light to blast any facts across the conference wall. She carried in her head an encyclopedia of Excel-based charts, all artfully decked in colorful formats, embellished with Premios branding elements. Whenever a slide was needed she knew exactly where it was. Revenue per employee. Costs to acquire a new subscriber. Monthly burn rates. No detail escaped capture by Orleans and her charts. Whatever Chip might ask, Josh knew Orleans would have the answer.

While Josh understood such things, they bored him, That's why he needed Orleans as a trusted right hand—someone to keep details in place and alert him to dangers ahead.

But as good as she was, on this day, Orleans wasn't sufficiently adept. Chip quickly grasped the reality hidden by details. He asked, "Are you telling me that there are no reserves remaining from the second round of financing? I can't believe that in just thirteen months you've already spent ten million dollars."

Josh could handle that. "It was a necessary investment to get where we needed to be. Success online is all about being the first to homestead valuable territory. Being the first mover, and all that."

"Where exactly did the money go?" Chip asked Orleans, not bothering to include Josh with his penetrating look. Josh pretended he wasn't insulted. But Josh noticed that Danny, sitting quietly in this meeting, sent him a worried glance, as though he thought Josh couldn't deal with Chip's question.

Orleans brought up an entirely different PowerPoint deck to explain that. Josh never expected Chip to ask this kind of question, but Orleans was prepared. She began walking through the details of a story that Josh knew by heart. In one form or another, Orleans' stacks of presentations would be shown to a dozen or more bankers. It was one of the hurdles in obtaining mezzanine funding, a series of loans that would let Premios grow to the point where an initial public stock offering could be achieved.

In one way, Barbara Linsky had been right at lunch earlier in the week. No one in the banking community understood the Internet business. Those men and women in their tailored suits just recognized something was smoking hot and that they couldn't afford to miss out on whatever that something was. They were whipped into attention by early stock offerings such as Yahoo and Amazon. Deep in their money-grubbing bones, they felt the opportunity for a quick kill. They suffered through listening to strategies about building audiences, monetizing content, creating brand equity, releasing disruptive technologies, and all the other nonsense that constructed the tenuous skeleton of every Internet company presentation. All they really understood was the potential for the emergence of fresh meat dripping with the dollar-tinged scent of new blood.

But Chip wasn't a banker. Something else motivated him, and Josh knew they should definitely not underestimate the man. Josh first met him during those heady days when a group of real estate investors contrived to launch a major casino resort near Thread. They sought to pull a good one over Chip's tribe. Instead, Chip leveraged his New York contacts and turned the tables. When everyone walked away, it was Chip and his allies who controlled the project. On the other hand, the man who originally led the American Seasons resort team spiraled into personal bankruptcy—so broke that Josh and Danny now owned the financier's former camp in Thread. Josh knew firsthand where Chip's questioning mind could lead. It was time to put a stop to it.

"Chip," Josh interrupted Orleans in the middle of her charts, "these questions are great. They really are. They're exactly the details that will interest a Lehman Brothers or Goldman Sachs when we start our investor tour.

"But what is really going on here? You didn't fly all the way to Los Angeles to talk about reports that we could have e-mailed you."

Josh stopped there and remained quiet. It was an old trick, but even smart guys like Chip couldn't abide silence for long.

Chip shifted in his chair, and Josh thought he had won. Clearly Chip was trying to decide how much he was willing to say. Mentally, Josh ran through the potential concerns. Likely Chip already processed all the facts and figures from Orleans and was correctly computing that Premios was ramping up its investments so recklessly that it could run out of money by June. The only way it could survive would be through a successful springtime initial public offering of stock, or IPO.

But a failed IPO wasn't in the cards. The market was hot. You had to bet big to win big. That was Josh's motto.

Maybe Josh was missing something. Chip could be surprisingly moralistic. The other night Josh noticed how Chip looked at Jesus Lopez with disdain. If he didn't like Lopez's novels, he also probably didn't like the methods that Premios was using to feed its blogs and contents. The truth was that sites like Premios were little more than gossip sites gussied up in new tuxedos. They thrived on secrets told by people spilling the hidden details of others. But again, that strategy didn't worry Josh. Orleans and he protected the firm by using a strong set of safeguards to distance the worst scum.

Then again maybe Chip was skeptical about the reported numbers. Premios was using pretty sophisticated approaches to boost the count of site visitors, and maybe there was a bit of exaggeration built into how they measured unique visitors or average time spent on the site. That was true of everyone in the business; every advertiser knew he had to take those numbers with a grain of salt. Besides, who even knew what accuracy was? Ultimately, this new world was all about growth and buzz.

On that topic, Colby Endicott agreed with Josh one hundred per cent. That's why the man had been so eager for his firm to be an early investor. God, he hoped Chip wasn't interested in knowing more about Colby. That might be a harder relationship to explain. Josh allowed a frown to creep across his face just by thinking about the complications.

Orleans misread Josh's facial expression and thought he was asking her to drag Chip back into the numbers. "Chip," she said, "just tell me the details you want to see, and we will pull up the right files."

"It's the files themselves," Chip said.

Orleans look confused, "What do you mean?"

Chip looked at Josh, "You know, don't you?" He didn't wait for an answer. "Someone is trying to corrupt your customer data. Ultimately, the Premios business is all about the information you collect from your users. That's how you direct advertising to the individuals most likely to be interested. That's why advertisers even care. User data is your golden goose."

Josh couldn't disagree with such a fundamental fact. "Look," he replied, "it's no secret that companies like Premios will ultimately make money from selling focused advertising. Currently, the subscription fees and sponsorships just help to keep the lights on. So, yes, in the long run, customer data is key. But who's trying to corrupt our data? What would that that even mean?"

Chip made no attempt to disguise his contempt at Josh's reply. "You know what it means. It took me a while, but I realize now that you were the one who insisted on visiting the data center with me on New

Year's Eve. You had a purpose. Somehow you knew we would find a Trojan horse in the system. That's why you detected it so quickly. You were expecting to see it and you wanted us to notice. But I'm guessing you didn't anticipate that I would ask my team to dig into it.

"Here's what I think. Someone is blackmailing you or your company. They alerted you to what their programs could do. They needed to provide a demonstration of their power. Because, as I think you know, that computer program on New Year's Eve wasn't designed to completely replace your customer user data with junk. It was just a way to prove that they could do it. So what do they want from you? Is it money? If your blackmailers were to go public with this threat, that alone would be enough to torpedo your potential stock offering. And delaying your IPO would kill your company.

"You're in deep trouble, but I can help. Tell me what's really going on. After all, I am part owner."

Josh heaved a sigh of relief, which Chip noticed, but Josh didn't care. This was so much better than he feared. Chip had no clue as to what was really going on. Thank God. Josh still had a chance to make it all work. In fact, maybe this was a good thing. Maybe he could use Chip and his connections to force Colby Endicott out.

In retrospect, bringing in Endicott and Meyers as investors had been the stupidest thing Josh ever did. Colby Endicott might appear an unsophisticated frat boy with too much money to spend, but now he was partnering with a more dangerous crowd. It took Josh a while to realize it, but he was convinced that Colby Endicott's firm was somehow laundering money and intending to take over the Premios e-commerce engine for some much larger mission.

Josh needed to discover where Colby's money came from. He knew the real partner was not Meyers. There was definitely another source of money, so much bigger than what flowed from Colby's trust fund, and it wasn't all flowing to Josh. Some of it was headed elsewhere in Los Angeles. Josh imagined all sorts of possibilities: mob money from the East Coast, Columbian or Mexican drug money, or maybe even Chinese or Middle Eastern ill-gotten gains. Whatever the money's source, the firm of Endicott Meyers existed to put it to work. They needed a respected face in the dot com world to make it happen, and unfortunately they had chosen Premios to be that front.

Josh knew only one thing for certain. He needed to be ruthless in excising this partner. He needed to do it without anyone finding out. And he needed to do it soon. While he still had a company to run.

Josh had never felt so alive.

Cynthia uneasily watched the horizon. Outside, the northern lights shifted in a jagged pattern of dancing green across the far northern skies. Alone in the house and missing Chip, Cynthia found the aura unsettling. While she knew they were a natural phenomena associated with surges of energy from the sun, somehow they seemed a harbinger of unwanted days. Even in the far northern reaches of Wisconsin, they rarely appeared, but tonight they shimmered and jerked in an ever-changing undulation.

She turned away from the north-facing window. The phone call just ended with Chip left her spooked. Days earlier, she tried to talk him out of flying to Los Angeles when she said someone else could dig into the problem because it wasn't even their issue. Now she begged him to come home and let others deal with what he had uncovered.

Chip was too principled to do that. He took ownership of issues She saw that the very first time he walked through the doors of the old Loon Town Café. She had been a waitress in Thread, and on that day business was unusually slow. His profile caught by the timeless sunlight of that long ago morning caused her to skip a breath. Remembering the moment still had impact. How was it possible to know with one look that she had encountered the one person she needed to be with for the rest of her life?

Danny was a busboy in the same restaurant that summer. Cynthia had been on a hopeless quest to light some spark of sexual connection with the brooding boy, but once she saw Chip, she began to envision a different goal. Kissing the tall, dark, and much older Native American leader from the nearby reservation became her new fantasy. Her father hated the local Indian tribe, so she couldn't mention her new-found fascination, but keeping the idea locked within her heart only made it grow faster.

From the beginning, she was attracted by the purpose and intent in Chip's every action. He had a drive that was fueled by his pride in doing the right thing for his tribe and all those he considered important. Now, she knew better than to expect that Chip would let go of any strand of an unraveling mystery. He would judge it his duty to alert Josh and Danny of perceived dangers, and she couldn't argue with such a noble intention.

Danny was trusting. He was a person who wanted to believe in others. Chip had made that observation early on, and maybe that's why both of them always tried to live up to that trust. Cynthia felt that Josh did the same. She remembered during that first season together how Josh bolstered Danny's spirit and helped him to come out of his shell. Chip judged that perhaps Josh was a good influence for Danny and they should support the relationship. Ever since, Cynthia had. But surely there were limits to how much they should do.

During the earlier phone call, Chip summarized what he had uncovered. Calling from a downtown Los Angeles hotel named the Bonaventure where Cynthia had once stayed with him, he seemed eager to pursue his investigation. In her mind, she pictured the building's clover-leaf-like arrangements of circular glass towers, its glass elevators that shot up from an enclosed atrium of fountains and pools to break through the atrium's glass roof to ride along the exterior walls of the tower all the way to the uppermost floors. From those rising elevators, if you were willing to stare out the glass, you could get a perfect view of the never-ending lines of lights that defined the Los Angeles basin.

As they talked, she pictured Chip in his room, sitting in a chair against the glass wall of one of those tower suites, his drapery open, and the bowl of lights stretching behind him. She remembered how to her the patterns of the city's lights always seemed an incomprehensible chessboard of lines.

Chip reported, "I was right to be worried. Coming here has convinced me that what happened on New Year's Eve was a deliberate hack, aimed at Josh and Danny's company, and designed to stay hidden. Only because my guys are talented did we identify the Internet address where the siphoned data was sent. With a little detective work, they found the real world street address of the server.

"I drove out there. I thought by coming to L.A. I would somehow swoop in and catch the crooks red-handed. At the least, I wanted to find out who owned the building. But so far, that hasn't happened.

"My information led me to a section of old warehouses and shoddy office buildings in the San Fernando Valley. That's north of downtown. Next door to the address was some building housing an adult porn site and video studio. But the address with our mysterious server . . . it was an empty building."

"So did you have the wrong address?" Cynthia asked.

"No, it was the right address," Chip replied. "I was just too late. They must have realized I was coming. It was obvious that a small, but working, data center had been recently removed. Likely it was just server equipment and routers, probably there only to execute this sting on Premios, and I think when they realized we might be able to track them, they packed up and moved elsewhere, leaving no clues behind."

Cynthia often thought Chip pretended to be stronger than he was. He had acquired that persona out of necessity from earlier days. Tonight reminded her of a time shortly after the tribe opened their casino at American Seasons resort when they had to fend off unwanted overtures from mobsters. Luckily Chip understood the ways power could be yielded, and he never underestimated his foes. In the end, the Lattigo kept the mob out.

"You reached an impasse," Cynthia said. "So come home."

"I'm not giving up. This week's just the start. I need to make the most out of being here. So I'm staying a little longer. Already, I dug into the public records and identified who held the leases on the office space . . . a dummy corporation, so maybe a dead end. But one thing's for sure—whoever sent this computer virus our way has gone to a lot of trouble to avoid being traced."

Cynthia wanted him home. "Chip, just hire a private detective. You have a company to run. I need you, and not to be melodramatic, but the Lattigo need you. In your office. At home."

She knew it was a low blow to play the tribal card because Chip had fierce loyalty to his community, but Cynthia found it ridiculous that he was personally taking responsibility for a mystery that didn't even bother the people directly affected. Let Josh do the worrying.

"No, I can't do that. I'm sticking around, and I'll tell you why. I had a meeting today at Premios with Josh and his CFO, Orleans. Danny was there too, which I was happy to see because I'm hoping he can put some sense into Josh.

"Not that the meeting did any good. On one hand, going through all the numbers was an eye-opener. Perhaps I should have paid more attention sooner, but I always thought of our modest investment as nothing more than a small gamble done out of friendship. Today I realized that if they successfully go public the payoff for us could be huge. But the situation is so tenuous; the company is hanging by a financial thread.

"That girl Orleans tried to paint a pretty picture, and maybe the average investor won't see through her smoke and mirrors, but the firm is nearly out of cash. There isn't the momentum or the customer base to reach the next level unless everything perfectly aligns."

"Is that what Josh says?" Cynthia demanded. Chip was always distrustful of the guy.

"Of course not. Everything out of Orleans' computer painted a rosy vision. I think Josh trusts her, but I don't. Their monthly burn rate is about to eat through everything.

"And if this hack had been successful, it would have absolutely ensured the firm's collapse. It's like a hidden rot eating away at the very foundations of their business. None of the data about their customers—what they wanted or were interested in—none of it could have been trusted. Over time, customers would have drifted away because the Premios recommendations would have become less relevant. Advertisers would jump ship when they didn't get the results expected. It would be unavoidable—a destructive circle quickly spiraling into bankruptcy."

The longer Chip spoke, the more troubled Cynthia became. She was fluent in his secret language of pauses and tone changes. Despite his outward certainty, he clearly didn't find his own explanation satisfactory. She had heard him when he was certain, like when he engineered the takeover of the American Seasons project away from the original investors, and in such moments, his confidence smoothed over every pause and blocked out any hesitation in his talk. Even his voice deepened and his diction cleared.

"You don't really believe what you're saying, do you?" she challenged.

He didn't argue.

"Nothing makes sense. There's something I'm not getting. Maybe if it were a different kind of company, at a different point in its trajectory, it would all fit together. But Premios isn't a company that is already profitable, and it doesn't really have data worth stealing. Nor does it yet have the money to fund a big blackmail payoff. Something about this reads like a long con.

"But what could it be? At first, I thought it was some weird idea for a blackmail scheme, that the whole thing was staged just so that we would discover the program. And I even thought of spite. Maybe someone is trying to make the company pay for something published on Premios. You know all the mean crap that site publishes. But who's that crazy? Besides the company is basically a reservations website mixed with reviews and gossip. What could it possibly have reported that would prompt such retribution?

"I know some people get pretty offended by stuff disclosed on the web; and maybe some celebrities would have the resources to try to go after them. But still. All I've got is conjecture, and I feel I'm missing some key angle."

"Then come home."

"Not yet, I'm staying another day or two. That's it. I promise that there are just a few more things I want to check out, and then I'll take the first flight home."

Cynthia decided to be satisfied. Already she had appealed to his loyalty to the reservation, and her only remaining card would be to call his sister Jacqueline in Paris since she could sometimes exert influence when no one else succeeded. But Cynthia feared Jacqueline would side with her brother.

Unexpectedly Chip brought up a new subject.

"Hey, honey, do you remember that weirdo who used to own the movie theater in Thread?"

"Pete Peterson," she replied.

"Yeah, him. After he lost that theater, didn't he used to project silent movies on the outside of his garage? Remember how the old ladies in town would go out and watch him. Some crazy thing like that."

Cynthia remembered. "That was Pete. He lived next door to Danny and his father. But he left town years ago, and I don't know if anyone knows what happened to him. Whatever made you think of him?'

"It's weird. When I came out of that empty office, there was someone in a car outside that porno studio across the street. And the driver was wearing one of those dumpy, broad-brimmed fisherman sun hats. You know the ones that are all round? I remember how Pete used to wear one of those hats even when he went to church. It just seemed odd, seeing that kind of headgear in L.A. and it made me think of Pete. I'm sure it's nothing, just a weird jarring of memory.

"Night, honey. I love you. See you soon."

"Someone is following me," Danny insisted a few days later. "Don't ask me how I know. I just do."

Since he was a small child, Danny always believed he was tapped into something greater than the usual five senses. While others might consider him illogical, he often felt that prickling on the neck when someone was staring, the discomfort from a ripping in the fabric of fortune, or the presentiment of a looming emotional chasm. Josh scoffed whenever Danny referenced this supposed power. Danny didn't care. He could remember still the afternoon when his mother committed suicide, how throughout his classes that day at school and during the bus ride home he dreaded what he was certain he was about to discover in his parents' bedroom. With all he had suffered in life, nothing seemed more undeserved than being given advance notice of the worse moments ahead.

"Kenosha spooked you," Josh replied. "That's all. Why would anyone follow you?"

As always, Josh was trying to keep Danny from jumping into his own terrors. Danny looked into the eyes of this man whom he loved so deeply. He knew beyond a doubt how much that love was reciprocated. But it was precisely because they shared a life together that Danny understood how Josh always sought to smooth the rough patches. It was his nature. He liked being surrounded with acquaintances who laughed easily at his jests. He attracted those who enjoyed a good time, and he floated through a world made smooth by good luck.

Josh was a creature of luck. He could never understand the dark depths of Danny's past, nor would Danny ever try to explain how his years of growing up tested him. Under the most trying of situations, Josh would somehow find a way to wrap himself with a silken chrysalis and emerge a beautiful butterfly. It was his nature. One couldn't fault him for that. In fact, Danny loved him precisely for his ability to always find such wonderment. Take the way they both suffered an unexpected loss of parents. For Josh, it had been the death of his parents in a freak incident of carbon monoxide poisoning, and Josh mourned, but quickly found a way to move on. Danny could never get past his bad moments,

When someone could float the way that Josh did, when one's toes never so much as dipped into the murkiness that sometimes entrapped Danny's soul, then there was no need for a special alert into the dangers ahead. But just because Josh didn't acknowledge such warnings didn't mean that Danny would ignore his own.

"Scoff if you like," Danny said, "but I believe someone tried to break into our house when we were gone. Kenosha didn't imagine it. I saw the broken plants in the back yard. But it's not just that. How do you explain what happened at the computer center with the computer virus."

"It wasn't a virus, more of a Trojan horse." As usual, Josh tried deflection as a strategy to end a discussion.

"Whatever you call it, you should be worried. Chip is."

"Chip has better things to do than worry about a minor incident with our computer center."

"You can't dismiss him. He's one of our investors," Danny said, "and besides it's not his money he's worried about. We're his friends. He's convinced someone's setting us up."

Josh crossed the room to sit on the sofa beside Danny. Perched atop the crest of a hill, their living room faced northward across the dark hills of Griffith Park in the Hollywood Hills, where in the distance, there was a hint of the glow of the Valley several miles away. On the opposing side, the living room opened onto a terrace that faced southward, providing a vantage point for lines of streetlights marching in darkness toward the unseen ocean. The world was theirs.

"Danny, I am here to protect you. Since the day we met, I have always been at your side. Let this worry go."

Danny wanted to, but he just couldn't.

From the day they met in Thread, Josh had never led him astray. Danny had been such a gangly, clumsy teenager that summer when he worked in the original Loon Town Café. What did a sophisticated and fun person like Josh, who was already in his mid-twenties, see in someone still in high school? But Danny knew that Josh kept returning to the café because he wanted to see him. Slowly over the summer, Josh made Danny feel like life was worth living and that joy was possible. After being betrayed by so many people in so many ways in his young life, Danny finally learned to laugh. He accepted that life was worth living.

Shortly after Josh returned to Los Angeles, the Loon Town Café in Thread closed down, and Cynthia became engaged to Chip. Everything was changing and Danny felt lost again. He couldn't leave with Josh; he had to stay. Only his father Toivo and Danny's daily treks to attend the community college in Timberton created a structure in his life, unsatisfactory as that structure was.

Later, Josh freed him from his morass when he returned to the little town in Wisconsin and made an unexpected offer. In some ways it was more of a demand, but one that Danny desperately wanted to hear. "Move to Los Angeles and live with me. Go to school there. We belong together." That's what Josh said. Danny hadn't experienced any other relationships against which he could judge whether Josh's offer was worthwhile. But his ESP worked then too. It told him that he would be a fool to pass up this chance, and so he told his father he was leaving Wisconsin, even though it shocked the old man. It was the best thing Danny ever did for himself.

With Josh's help, he reached another level in his life. Josh convinced Danny to aim for the big leagues and so he applied for college and sought a spot in the USC writing program. As much as he now found Jesus Lopez distasteful, Danny could never deny that the professor and his writing seminars opened his soul to something unexpected. At first, he barely dared to tap into the experiences that molded him but when he did, he knew he had found something extraordinary. He transformed memories and unwanted emotions into some new beast, which might be hard to contain as it snorted and tugged, but it was a beast he loved.

Because Lopez was the midwife to that transformation, Danny knew he should forgive the way Josh was now bringing the man into their business. Given the need to discover creative writers, it made sense to use Lopez's connections. Besides, whatever demons might reside in Lopez's psyche, the man clearly had the gift to burnish the gleaming possibilities of others.

Maybe that was another reason Danny admired Josh so much. Like an eagle high in the sky, Josh took in the whole terrain below. Whatever might block the way, he always seemed to know where he wanted to go, and he had always helped Danny move forward.

Josh pleaded, "So make me a promise, Danny. Let go of this worry, fear, premonition, whatever it is . . . let it go."

For Josh, Danny could do that. He could ignore the pressing black cloud that hovered in the back of his mind, because when Josh asked him to do things, they always proved worth doing.

It had been Josh's idea to start writing about the restaurant business. He pointed out how Danny had worked in restaurants as a teenager, how to this day he sometimes helped out at the New Loon Town Café, and how their friends Stephen and Wally knew all the right people in town. Put that inside knowledge to work, Josh counseled.

Which is exactly what Danny did, and he was surprised to discover that not only did he enjoy doing it but that lots of people liked reading the results. When he created his small 'zine and convinced Skylight Books in Los Feliz to stock it, he anticipated selling only a few copies. But the publication caught on; people started subscribing. Young writers even sent him material, because they saw his publication as an entry to a broader world. Sometimes he wondered how people even knew the tidbits they told him, but in the guise of industry gossip, he started repeating them. Wally once joked that he was afraid of the power that his one-time busboy was now wielding.

Josh made all of it possible. He was the one who suggested moving the 'zine online. Even as he dealt with his portfolio of real estate investments, he still found time to help Danny establish the *InnerEatz* site. He thought up new ways to engage with readers. He sought out AOL America, when he learned they were seeking new media properties to round out their subscriber offerings. He recognized how their deep pockets and almost reckless willingness to buy anything that caught their fancy could make Danny and Josh rich.

But in reality, Danny already felt rich. Once he moved in with Josh, his days of feeling poor were left behind. When they were in the small bungalow in the hills of the nearby Silver Lake neighborhood and now in the expanse of the restored mansion, he knew they could be happy.

Josh was right. He was worrying needlessly. Danny reminded himself that his mother also claimed to have inner warnings. Look where it got her: suicide before she was fifty. It was time to shove that disturbing voice into a soundproof box and lose the key.

"You're right," Danny said.

Josh chose to say nothing in reply, but it was clear he recognized the significance of the words.

Danny's cell phone rang. The ring tone was the University of Wisconsin fight song. It was Cynthia.

"Why is Cynthia calling?" he said out loud as he pressed the speaker button on his cell phone.

"What's up?" Danny asked.

Cynthia's voice was thin and uneven. She clearly had been crying and seemed on the edge of desperation.

"It's Chip," she said, "He's missing."

Session Five

What do you mean *you want to know what I've been doing? What does that matter to you? Shouldn't you focus on what I think and what goes on in my mind? What I do or don't do in the world outside this room shouldn't matter. It's my mental health I'm here to discuss. Not your morbid curiosity. And aren't you here to make me better?*

Besides I don't want to tell you too much. If I said the wrong thing, your professional ethics might make you think you had to report me to the police.

I'm just kidding, doc. I'd never do or plan anything against the law. At times, I might stretch the rules, but believe me it's always for a good cause.

Like when I drove into the Valley wearing that stupid hat. I wanted to know what Chip was up to. I can't deny that he's always been a straight shooter and that his loyalties lie with Danny.

Just like mine. The thing is that Chip doesn't know what Danny really needs. He might just stumble into something where his nose doesn't belong. I can't let that happen.

Know what I mean?

PART TWO

CLOUDS AHEAD

CHAPTER FIVE

Missing

Josh recognized reality. Things were spinning out of control. Still he saw no alternative but to continue skidding toward his destination. There was no time to worry about what was in the way. Without a counterweight, everything would spin off into its own orbit, and the thought of such an embarrassing end was unbearable.

Among the financial press, some analysts saw nothing of concern since tech stocks were still rising in the marketplace. Josh on the other hand feared that the Dow Jones had peaked. Rumors abounded that the major online medical company Healtheon was about to delay its public offering. Everyone knew that Jim Clark—the genius behind Silicon Graphics and Netscape—headed Healtheon. If a man like that was spooked, a real horror show likely lay ahead. Even the appearance of calm waters might only mask a maelstrom ahead.

An assistant knocked on the conference room door, which immediately annoyed Josh. He had provided his staff with strict instructions to not disturb Orleans and him. The two of them needed to concentrate on what was ahead. Another rap, Josh bristled, and his assistant quickly ducked into the room to say that Danny was outside and wanted to talk. Josh glared and the assistant backed out.

Calming Danny was the last thing Josh needed. After receiving Cynthia's call about Chip, Danny behaved as though the sky was falling. Ironically, Josh had the details to understand that the sky might actually be descending, but he knew the looming calamity had nothing to do with a missing friend. As Orleans finished the financial update, he assessed the outlook as far bleaker than anticipated. The firm was hemorrhaging money with no end in sight. He had to cure this problem. Danny's fears were only a distraction.

Being annoyed wasn't fair to Danny. He knew that. They were supposed to be partners in life and in business, so Danny deserved to know the true outlook for Premios. On the other hand, Danny had always left it to Josh to be the money manager, and now those patterns boxed them in. If Josh was guilty of insulating Danny from the realities of business, then Danny was responsible for wanting that. How could he give the guy a basic understanding of the real world when they were heading into a crash? Better to let him fret over a missing friend than to focus on an economic problem over which he certainly had no influence.

Josh wasn't going to worry about Chip. Over the many years of their friendship, the man consistently proved to be at the top of the game. Josh was certain that if he had time to think about it he could determine some logical explanation for the man's absence. In the meantime, Chip's disappearance made Josh happy. It provided breathing room. He didn't need some entrepreneur from Wisconsin digging into the Premios story. Convincing Chip last year to make a half-million-dollar investment in the company was going to cost him more than Josh ever expected.

A year ago, it seemed a good idea to enlist an old friend as an initial investor. Chip carried a certain reputation among the financial community, and not just those in the Midwest, because he also held clout with the Wall Street gang. After all, there weren't many Native American entrepreneurs with his kind of resume—Wall Street credibility and a thriving tribal investment fund. It never hurt to have the right people on your side.

But Chip, fabled as he was, had his negatives. Over the past few days his presence clearly illuminated that. Chip could joke with Barbara Linsky with all that stupid talk about how valuing Internet investments was like dead cats, but it just proved he didn't get the modern world. Companies like Premios would change the universe. Fortunes were going to be made. No way would Josh let a little cash flow problem stop him from being one of the winners.

Josh forced himself to focus on Orleans, who had ignored the aide's interruption and continued talking, "I recommend we cancel the investor tour."

That thought broke through Josh's reverie. "What the hell? Just take a gun and shoot me. We have to go public now, or everything is gone."

"Then you need to cancel the East Coast expansion plans. It's one or the other."

"No, not that either. We need those added cities. Without them we don't demonstrate the rapid growth that makes the numbers work."

"The numbers don't work either way. Period." Orleans glowered with a look that dared Josh to defy her. She sat across the table and said nothing more.

"That's your fucking job . . . to make the numbers work. What's the purpose of Excel and PowerPoint except to tell the story the way it needs to be told? Our concept is golden. A little time and a little more money and it'll work."

The door to the conference room opened again. Josh snapped, "I told you we're not to be disturbed. Tell Danny to go home, and I'll talk to him then."

Orleans' shocked face prompted Josh to turn around. Danny was standing in the door, not the assistant. Danny looked so ashen that Josh immediately calmed. "Hey, I'm really sorry, but Orleans and I are in the middle of some pretty heavy stuff. We have to stay focused. I can't take the time to talk about anything else."

Even though it was the truth, he doubted that would mollify Danny. The kid looked so upset. Now he had an additional problem he couldn't avoid, but he couldn't let Danny open up another can of worms.

"I just want to know if you heard anything from Chip. Cynthia says she can't stay cooped up in Wisconsin any longer and wants to fly here."

Josh suddenly felt wearier than was logical. Nothing was going his way. If Cynthia flew west then Danny would insist she stay with them, and he didn't want that, just like he didn't want Chip digging into their books and seeking explanations for details that were hard to explain. Above all, he didn't want to upset Danny.

Chip wasn't their problem. Maybe he could say the guy had a mistress, maybe that would explain what was taking up his time. To Josh, Chip always appeared a lady's man and he often wondered how loyal the guy really was to his wife. For a moment, he wanted to fling the idea out toward Cynthia, but he feared that such an allegation would only ensure Cynthia flying into town.

"I don't know why the two of you are so convinced something is wrong. It's only been two days since he went quiet."

"Josh, what are you talking about? There's email . . . and cell phones. He wouldn't just drop out of sight."

Josh didn't consider the current timeline to be an impossibility. People did that sort of thing all the time. "So has she filed a missing persons report with the police?"

"Of course, and they took her complaint seriously. They opened a case."

Josh accepted Danny's word for that, but his experience with the police suggested they wouldn't actively pursue such a situation. In his opinion, rich men often vanished for a few days, only to eventually show up, act a bit contrite, and bluster that there was never a reason to worry. They often had their reasons or affairs.

But there was no sense arguing with Danny's concern. "All right. But let's wait until tonight to help her decide. Tell Cynthia we'll call her this evening. For now Orleans and I really need to work on these finances. Can you let us get back to it?"

For a second, Danny seemed poised to argue, but with a slight nod of acquiescence he retreated. Through the wavy glass, Josh watched him walk over to Kenosha. Josh suspected she was about to get an earful about what a horrible person her boss was. He couldn't worry about that.

"Josh, do you know what happened to Chip?" Orleans asked quietly.

Josh was quite surprised. "Of course not. Why would I know anything?"

"I don't trust the guy," she said. "He almost knew too much about our business the other day. He's tenacious and sneaky. He could be testing us."

"Testing us for what?"

"You know him better than me," she replied in a way that suggested the subject was closed, but then she reopened it. "In a way I wish he were here. I'd ask him to invest another million dollars in Premios. That would improve the balance sheets and get us through the summer. It would place less pressure on the IPO."

That's what Josh liked about Orleans. She was always thinking, and he had already reached the same conclusion. They needed an additional infusion of cash—and soon. The trouble was that they couldn't go to the banks for it. Such an act would seem desperate. It needed to come from the original investors. Unfortunately added investment at this stage would dilute his holdings more than he wanted. But so what? Better to have a few million less when they went public than to be left holding an empty bag.

"I don't understand why you won't just increase your personal investment," Orleans added. "That would be the easiest approach. And the fastest."

Orleans would discover it soon enough, but he felt no need to tell her quite yet. Already the accounts of both Danny and himself were heavily overleveraged. The house, the camp, and the original seed money for Premios, to say nothing of his other interests—all of it was locked up. Money only went so far.

The single way out as he saw it was to tap the original investors. If Chip wasn't around to help, that left Endicott-Meyers. But there was one problem. He wasn't about to take more money from them until he knew two things: exactly whom he was dealing with and what they wanted from Premios.

Cynthia was angry. No one cared that Chip hadn't talked to her in days, and she couldn't understand why. He wasn't the kind of person simply to disappear or stop communicating. She longed to scream the obvious: he was in trouble; he had never done this before; and there must be a reason it was happening now. But another part of her rejected any possibility that he might in danger. A person as strong as Chip could not simply vanish.

She found herself in Chip's office. Her need to escape the house was so great and there were so few other places to go. Sitting in his office chair proved a tremendous comfort. An element of his scent clung to the leather; it was all she could do to keep herself from pushing her face into the back of that chair as though she could inhale him into her presence. She replayed his last phone call in her head. She had asked him to come home, and he promised that he would be back soon. What stopped him?

Josh and Danny were both a disappointment. Police had their procedures. It made sense that they insisted on waiting before even accepting her missing person's report. The world was bursting with runaway husbands and deadbeat dads, so why should they believe that Chip was different. They didn't know him as she did.

Chip's sister once told her a Lattigo legend about a long-ago chief named Frozen Bear. As a child Chip had adopted that same name and used it through his twenties. According to the folklore, back in the earliest days, a trickster cast a spell that froze Frozen Bear in time and separated him from his true love. But the wily Frozen Bear employed all of the creatures of the earth and water to break through the trickster's every barrier until, in triumph, Frozen Bear reached his love. He stretched out to meet her lips, kissed her, and restored time.

Surely, Chip could do the same. He was as strong as any myth. In a moment, he too might come through that door, having vanquished his foes, and their lips would meet. They would laugh together about how he overcame whatever obstacles had blocked his return. Happiness would flow again and her current despair would flow away as quickly as the melting snow in spring.

She wanted to believe such fairy tales, but she hated herself for trying to evade the obvious. Even in the myth the original Frozen Bear achieved what he did only because the Great Spirit aided him. That's why Cynthia was praying to her own god that he could make the old story come true.

She was so angry that Josh and Danny didn't share her fears. Perhaps she was unfair, but in her heart, she blamed the two of them. Chip only flew to Los Angeles to investigate their problem. They should care more about his current state, because, knowing Chip as long as they had, they also knew that he wasn't a man who could simply walk away.

How she hated the police and their questions: Was their marriage all right? Was the business doing well? What challenges were bothering Chip? There was no way she could tell them about the computer hack. She didn't know the details and she suspected Josh would deny that a problem even existed.

At the Lattigo offices everyone seemed equally unconcerned. Perhaps that was a reflection of Chip himself; he had trained them to do their job and not get distracted. With or without him, the staff continued to ensure warm water flowed in the pipes of the water park, the lights stayed bright in the casinos, and the computer servers stayed cool in the data center. The staff knew what kind of person their boss was, and so they preferred to believe he was on some deep mission—as though he were a James Bond character plotting a financial coup from afar.

She held onto the slender hope that such an explanation would appear. After all, once Chip had disappeared for a few days only to return in triumph. It was back in 1987 when he engineered the takeover of the American Seasons resort. Recently his staff reminded her of that. They were proud his victory and it had become a tribal legend.

But the situations weren't at all similar. In 1987, the two were only dating, and yet Chip had warned her of his impending absence. Now they were husband and wife; they were planning a family. No, she was certain that something terrible had happened in Los Angeles.

Only Gertie, Chip's executive assistant, understood Cynthia's anguish. Gertie, Chip's secretary since the beginning, was as much a part of Chip's life as Cynthia. They just shared alternating blocks of each day's time, and they both knew Chip was not hiding somewhere.

Cynthia's thin thread of hope was that Chip found it necessary to go undercover in his search into the computer hack. At Cynthia's request, Gertie pulled up everything she could find concerning Chip's travels and behaviors. It was a modern age—there were online credit card statements, travel records, and cell phone bills. There was no place to hide, and yet she found no clues to Chip's possible location. Maybe he stepped outside of time like the mythical Frozen Bear.

The two confirmed that Chip's credit card still held a room at the Bonaventure hotel in Los Angeles, although the hotel's manager said it appeared no one had been in the room for several days. The bed had remained neatly made for days, and the records showed his key card had not been used. The last call on his cell phone was the one made to Cynthia, while the last charge on the company credit card was for breakfast the following morning at the Pacific Dining Car, a classic 24-hour restaurant not far from the Bonaventure.

Someone knocked at the office door.

"Come in," Cynthia said.

A visibly shaken Gertie entered, holding a FedEx envelope. "This was just delivered," she said.

"What is it?"

"It's Mr. Grant's notebook." She held up a small leather bound tablet. Cynthia recognized the small pad as her husband's. Even addicted as he was to his Blackberry, Chip still jotted many key thoughts on paper, a habit he retained since the days before they married. His little book was precious; he would never let it go. In fact, their bedroom closet sheltered a file box filled with fifteen years worth of identical such notebooks.

"Who sent it?"

"There was no note, and I already called the return address. It's a Kinko's in downtown Los Angeles. They don't have any record of who sent it."

"Maybe someone found and returned it," Cynthia suggested. She took the book from Gertie without asking and flipped it open. "See how Chip put his address here and asked for its return if found."

Gertie remained concerned. "But it also notes that he would give a reward. Don't you think it's odd that someone bothered to return it and didn't give us their name? Why pass up a chance for free money?"

Cynthia was scanning the last few pages that contained writing. Chip was prone to using his notebook to record meetings and reflect on the results. She found his brief recap of the visit to the empty server building. She noted that there was nothing written about the possibility of seeing Pete Peterson lurking outside.

She turned the page to find one brief entry followed by blank pages. The last bit of writing simply said, "Oliver Meyers and Jesus Lopez, PDC, 7:00 am."

"Do you know an Oliver Meyers or Jesus Lopez?" she asked Gertie. The woman shrugged. Clearly the names meant nothing to her.

The sounds of excited people in the anteroom drew Gertie's attention, and she started to the door. Before she got to it, a man started talking excitedly to her approaching presence. "Gertie, is Mrs. Grant here? I need to talk to her."

Cynthia felt enormous relief. Chip must have contacted someone at the office. Everything would be explained. She knew the young man who walked in. His name was Andrew, and he was the firm's financial comptroller as well as a trusted member of the Lattigo tribe. Chip always said he saw great promise in Andrew. This young man was exactly the person Chip would use as an ally, but today Andrew seemed frazzled, as though he had run from the Accounting cubicles one floor below.

"What is it," she asked, trying to keep her voice from shaking with nervousness.

"Mrs. Grant, something horrible is happening. A million dollars just disappeared from our accounts."

Danny was waiting impatiently. Earlier Josh promised they would call Cynthia together when he arrived home, and an hour had passed since Josh drove up. It was already late evening in Wisconsin, and Cynthia might be going to bed soon, but Danny still wanted to talk to her this night. Time was running out. But Josh was in high spirits and keen on following his own schedule.

As soon as he walked through the door Josh asked, "Do we still have that bottle of Opus One in the wine cellar?" Danny paid little attention to what wineries or vintages were represented in the basement wine cellar. That was Josh's fascination; Danny hardly ever went into the room. He didn't even care for wine, and to him there was nothing more boring than to talk about body, tannins, legs, and the like. His dad had it right. Back in Wisconsin, people drank beer and brandy. He inherited that preference although it was a personal taste he could never acknowledge in his blog writings.

"Only you would know for sure. Unless you already drank it, anything you placed in the cellar is still down there," Danny replied. "But can't a drink wait until after we talk to Cynthia? She needs help. Nothing's changed. Chip still hasn't shown up."

Josh wasn't swayed. "Sure, sure. But first I'd like a good glass of wine. I'm feeling lucky tonight."

When Danny was at the Premios offices just before lunch, Josh and Orleans were holed up in the conference room going over the books. In his attempt to get their attention for just a few minutes, he saw Josh at his surliest. In that instant, he stopped worrying about Chip's disappearance and wondered what might be wrong with the business. Had the hackers reappeared?

But when Danny walked out and the door was shut in his face all he could perceive was their shadowy silhouettes beyond the glass. A hazy glow of multicolored line charts projected on the screen suggested a financial review. For the briefest of moments, he reconsidered his resolution to be more involved with the business and contemplated forcing himself into the room. After all, it was his company too. But instead he retreated to Kenosha's desk and his steadiest of companions, so together they could speculate about Chip. Danny might have forged a life with Josh but the man didn't really understand what motivated him.

He looked at Josh now wondering why he couldn't understand how important it was for them to reach out to Cynthia, together, as a couple. "I don't want to wait. Let's call first and then you can have the wine with dinner."

"It'll only take moment. I'll be right back."

Josh opened the door to the narrow back staircase, a leftover of the days when houses had their own routes for the servants to reach the lower floors. When Josh had an idea, it was hard to resist his enthusiasm. "You'll love this wine. A good glass of alcohol will help us focus on Cynthia. You'll see."

As the door swung shut behind Josh, Danny could hear the rapid set of footfalls of the man dashing down two flights of stairs to the lowest level. He pictured Josh walking across the theater room to the middle of the floor, opening the heavy door into the wine room that was dug into the hillside. It had been a great remodeling expense to outfit one of the old cellar storage rooms for wine, and so far Josh only stored a few cases there. But often at dinners involving a potential investor or contributor, Josh boasted about his cellar in a way that might lead one to think it was one of the best in the city. Francesca had been fooled by Josh's talk. She wanted to see it and even suggested to Danny that perhaps it could be the basis of a story about how the rich collected the best vintages. Danny carefully steered her away from the topic.

He also remembered Francesca's talk about the old director's hidden rooms in the basement. Since returning from Wisconsin, Danny avoided the basement. He didn't tell Josh, but the fact that Kenosha heard an attempted intrusion wrapped the entire bottom floor in danger. Like their camp in Wisconsin, he was beginning to find this Los Feliz mansion too big. Public and service hallways provided multiple paths between rooms that existed with no modern purpose. One could easily live day to day without ever putting a foot into most of them.

The clomps on the stair treads grew nearer. Josh swung open the door and brandished a bottle. "It was there, just like I thought."

Josh had the maniacal look of success. Sometimes, when seeing Josh in these moments of high energy, Danny recalled a book he once read in high school called *Lord of the Flies*. He pictured the leader of the boys who hunted down Piggy as a younger version of Josh. It wasn't very complimentary he knew to think of his lover caught in the excitement and frenzy of the chase, unabashedly anticipating his quarry's capture, so sometimes he tried to turn the general thought into something more wholesome—like an Indian chief with his braves about to snare a buffalo to feed the tribe. But that never rang true. Josh was a man of reckless abandon, and even though that was why Danny found him so attractive, it wasn't a feature he always liked.

"What happened today? You're a different man than this morning," Danny complained.

"I solved a problem. That's all."

Josh pulled open a drawer on the large kitchen island and pawed for a corkscrew. Quickly he scored the foil around the top of the wine bottle, removed it, and extracted the cork. He grabbed two large balloon glasses from the cupboard and proceeded to pour the wine, swirling the garnet red around the rim, as he watched the wine's heavy legs coat the glass.

"Get a whiff of that nose," he pushed a glass toward Danny. "This is gonna be great."

"What was the problem?" Danny asked. The bouquet of the wine was big.

"A technical one. You wouldn't understand. Let's call Cynthia."

Suddenly, Josh focused entirely on fulfilling Danny's request. He pulled out his cell phone, pressed the speaker button, dialed the number, and set the phone on the island. After two rings, Cynthia picked up.

"Have you heard from Chip?"

Danny found it disturbingly sad that she didn't even say hello first. Hope and desperation battled in her voice. Suddenly Danny wished Josh wasn't with him.

"No," Danny said.

While she didn't say anything to that, not even a sigh of acceptance, her silence told them everything about her state of mind.

"Have you?" he asked.

Because he didn't expect a reply, he was all the more astonished to hear her recount the unexpected appearance of Chip's notebook. Even Josh seemed surprised.

"I was hoping the book would clear up something," Cynthia explained. "But it only held one fact that I didn't already know. Chip scribbled the details for a breakfast meeting. The appointment showed two names. If he had that meeting, they must have been the last people to see him. The two were Jesus Lopez and Oliver Meyers."

A speeding car, a crash into a light pole, pianos falling from the sky, cataclysmic sinkholes opening beneath him . . . for a second Danny thought he must be dreaming, but even in his worst nightmares, he would never have joined the two men named by Cynthia.

He could understand the possibility that Chip might seek to meet Lopez. The two met at the party the night Chip arrived in Los Angeles. Still, Danny could never imagine that Chip might have found this writer intriguing enough to invite for breakfast.

Oliver Meyers was something totally different. Danny couldn't even imagine a connection between Chip and Oliver, or for that matter, Lopez and Oliver—and certainly not among all three. This could not be the same Oliver Meyers who haunted his past.

He had loved that Oliver. At least he had loved the twenty-year-old worker at the resort as much as a sixteen-year-old innocent could. When he first saw Oliver in the kitchen of that old-fashioned resort with its crazy name of White Bark Pines, Danny forgave his father for shipping him to slave at this place for the entire summer. Something about Oliver made Danny eager to be in his presence, and happy that they would be working together for the next two and a half months. Just looking at Oliver's hand seemed enough. Of course, Oliver eventually let him see more than that.

In retrospect, he realized that Oliver played on Danny's infatuation from the start. Some dewy-eyed longing probably lit up Danny's eyes in the first moment he saw Oliver instructing him on operating a dishwasher. There certainly might have been more romantic settings at the secluded resort, but it didn't take much to ignite the passion of a teenager slowly coming to grips with his true emotions. Any setting could serve.

Oliver found Danny's puppy dog admiration amusing, and he supposed it was. His bunkroom was just one door down from Oliver's in what the resort owners called the boys bunkhouse. In reality, it was just a long cabin with multiple small bedrooms. Each night, he tried to stay awake listening for the start of rhythmic breathing by Oliver next door. He liked to imagine finding the bravery to sneak into the room so he could see the man sleeping in the moonlight. Oliver always bragged that he slept in the nude. On hot, sticky summer nights, when even a top sheet felt unbearable, Danny could imagine how Oliver's muscular torso and legs must sprawl across the unused blankets. But he wouldn't let himself think too much. It made him hard and crazy.

That summer was Oliver's second season at the resort. For some reason, he decided to befriend Danny, or so Danny perceived it. As an adult, Danny now realized it was probably Oliver's job to make sure Danny could do what he was hired to do. Of all the mundane tasks, his favorite was their lunchtime runs to the dumping ground. Together, the two tossed bags of trash and kitchen scraps into the back of an old green Ford pickup until its bed was nearly overflowing with the odorous junk. Then they took off, driving out the resort's back road, and down a mile or so of shaded lane, all still on the resort's land. Finally they reached the place's small landfill. Such open dumps were probably illegal now, but back then they were almost part of the place's attraction. At night, guests would drive out the road, park, and wait until they saw black bears emerge to scavenge the grounds. The particularly adventuresome would roll down their windows and toss out marshmallows.

Each day the two of them worked together to load the truck, drive down the sun-dappled route, and toss the resort's waste into the dump. Each day under the shining sun Oliver followed another routine. He would strip off his t-shirt, claiming he didn't want his clothes to get dirty or smelly. That was fine with Danny because it allowed him to sit next to Oliver's bare and tanned torso on the entire drive to the dump, work beside his hero to throw out the cans and bags of rotting food, and then return. It didn't matter what dead raccoon carcass or pile of bad grease was thrown into the mess, because Danny could ignore it all as long as he could see the arm muscles of Oliver at work and as long as he could catch the scent of Oliver. Others might have found Oliver's sweat rank, but to Danny it was the finest of colognes.

All too soon, the truck would be empty. But then Oliver relaxed. He would sprawl across the sun-warmed metal of the Ford's hood, pull out a pack of cigarettes and smoke one cigarette before returning to the resort. He claimed the owners owed them a break, since they gave the two of them the worst job in the whole place. But it wasn't the worst job. Danny could still remember Oliver's darkened skin against the green paint job of that old Ford. In those initial days, he considered Oliver a prince and would have done anything he asked.

"There's more," Cynthia said. "Our accountants just discovered there's a million dollars missing. And it looks like Chip took it."

Danny waited. The hallway of the old red brick building on the college campus felt all too familiar. More than once as a student he sat on this uncomfortable fiberglass molded chair just outside Lopez's office. Anxiously, he would await the exit of another student so that he could have his audience with the famous writer. Today was different. Lopez wasn't the master dispensing guidance; he was the enemy that needed interrogation. Danny intended to remain focused.

Danny was still perturbed with Josh. The night before, his partner took in everything Cynthia told them and claimed not to find one element surprising.

"Surely you don't think it's possible that Chip embezzled money from his own company?" Danny demanded incredulously. They had just ended the call with Cynthia, and Josh had poured another glass of wine.

Josh shrugged. "It explains a lot. He took some money and ran. You think you know someone, Danny, but maybe Chip has his own secrets tucked away. You never know what lies beneath the surface. Life is like that frozen lake beside our camp. It looks bright and clean, but there's muck hiding in the cold below."

"You don't really believe that nonsense. Why do you always have to be so dramatic?"

Josh took another sip of his expensive Bordeaux blend. Danny recalled that it cost seventy dollars a bottle, and he found it outrageous that Josh preferred to casually drink such a wine even as the world around them fell apart. Josh, seeing Danny staring angrily at his glass, defended his actions, "The wine's already opened. Why shouldn't we drink it?"

Danny ignored that deflection. "And why would Chip meet Jesus Lopez and Oliver Meyers? How would he even know them? At the same time? The odds don't make sense."

Josh looked at him oddly, "I've never heard you mention the name Oliver Meyers."

Danny knew that was true because it was deliberate. Although Meyers deeply wronged him, he never wanted to tell Josh about the summer at the resort. Danny reluctantly acknowledged it remained a part of his life that he would not share. But he had to say something, so he quickly edited what he wanted Josh to know.

"Oliver was someone I knew when I was sixteen. This probably isn't even the same person."

Surely, the breakfast was with a different Oliver. The Oliver Meyers that wronged Danny was from Chicago, and even though their meeting was half a lifetime ago, it was unlikely the man was now in Los Angeles.

"Whatever."

Danny changed tacks. A part of him sought a fight. He didn't know why, but he felt wronged. "Why didn't you support me when I suggested that Cynthia fly out?"

Josh looked at him calmly. "The missing funds. That changes everything. Don't you see how that makes it more likely that Chip is involved in some kind of scheme? Cynthia should let the police do their job. Flying out here is a waste of her time. And ours."

"You're wrong, and I'm going to confront Lopez in the morning and find out what he knows."

"Really? You want to do that? Given the way you feel about him? Weren't you just furious when I was meeting him to make us some money? Now you want to be in his horrible presence to ask about some breakfast session?"

Of course, a meeting with Lopez was one thing that Danny would prefer to avoid, but he owed something to Cynthia. The least he could do was to find out what he could about what happened at that breakfast appointment.

So now he was at the university waiting for the man.

The door beside Danny opened. Lopez stepped out with a laughing coed. The writer, noticing Danny in the chair, took a step back, clearly startled, and Danny felt a small bit of satisfaction in showing up unannounced.

"Danny, what a surprise."

Danny stated his purpose directly, "I need to talk about Chip Grant."

Lopez gave him a quizzical look, but said goodbye to his student and motioned Danny into the office. The place was so familiar: the precisely ordered books on multiple shelves, the window framing a view of the skyscrapers two miles north in downtown Los Angeles, the thick Oriental rug, and the oak library table Lopez used as a desk. A laptop computer sat on that oak surface, next to a stack of books. They all displayed the same cover and spine, suggesting that Lopez had just unpacked a shipment of books from his publisher.

"Why were you having breakfast with Chip Grant and Oliver Meyers."

Lopez leaned back in his chair and chuckled. "Being back in my office seems to make you a bit abrupt and testy," he observed. "Are you afraid I will grade you?"

"Just answer my question."

Lopez shrugged. "Chip invited me to breakfast. We started talking at your house party that night he arrived, and he knew I worked with Premios. He said he wanted to understand the company better. I guess he was looking for an independent perspective."

"So who's Oliver Meyers?" Danny almost didn't ask the question. He feared it was the same person of his summertime nightmare, and he wasn't sure he wanted to face that.

The question clearly surprised Lopez. "What do you mean? Oliver Meyer is your investor. He's the other half of Endicott-Meyers. Surely you know that."

Everything seemed both clear and murky, as though it were possible to be two things at once. Danny knew he needed to ask more questions, but so many conflicting ideas bounced about. Why didn't Josh tell him that fact last night? And hadn't Josh claimed Colby didn't even have a partner named Meyers? Could Josh not know about Meyers? But then how did Chip know to ask him to the breakfast?

Lopez continued talking. "I suggested inviting Oliver. In fact, I mentioned it at your party. I met Oliver years ago when he was a student and I was a guest lecturer at the University of Chicago. In those days, he seemed such an attractive and interesting fellow. I always felt we were a lot alike. In fact, you can thank me for making him an investor in Premios. I introduced Colby and Oliver when Colby was starting his investment firm. I knew that Oliver has deep ties to many funding sources, and I thought they might help each other out."

While Lopez spoke, his rat-like eyes focused on Danny and seemed to strip away any pretense Danny might have to an independent life. Danny withered in that stare. He felt as though a vengeful god was testing him. There was still a chance this wasn't the same Oliver, although Lopez had just confirmed this person was also from Chicago. Danny remembered how when he first met Lopez he had been reminded of Oliver. Had some part of Oliver seeped into Lopez?

He calmed himself by maintaining that it didn't matter if this newly discovered partner was in fact the teenage love who later wronged him. He reminded himself he wasn't here to delve into his own past. He was trying to find Chip.

"What did the three of you discuss?"

Lopez glanced out the window as though he could see all the way to the Pacific Dining Car restaurant miles away. Free of Lopez's stare, Danny felt his energy become more focused. Lopez spoke slowly and low like a person trying to recall every detail.

"Really, there was nothing out of the ordinary. Chip was trying to understand the financing behind your company, and what role Oliver played in the overall Endicott-Meyers firm. Frankly, Chip had no interest in what I had to say and I found the entire breakfast meeting rather boring. Too early in the morning for me, and because we were seated in a booth near the back, I felt closed in and wanted to leave. In my opinion, that restaurant is too somber, too full of politicians and businessmen. But Chip suggested the spot. I think it was because he could walk to it from the Bonaventure. Not a very good neighborhood for walking. Of course, Chip seems the reckless type.

"But why ask all these questions? Did something happen to Chip?"

Danny's sense of danger flared. Lopez already knew something had happened, and was attempting to conceal some kind of pleasure. He was certain of it, even though Lopez's face held no sign of any such emotion. Lopez's novels dealt with dark themes, and Danny felt chilled thinking of all the possibilities that might amuse this man. Imagining those dreadful alternatives, he didn't know what to ask next.

Finally, Danny spoke, "Did you leave together?"

"As I recall breakfast ended rather abruptly. Chip had already paid the bill when he received a phone call. He answered, seemed concerned, and motioned to us that we should move along. I had the sense he thought the call would last a while. So Oliver and I both walked out. We handed our respective parking stubs to the valet. That's the last I saw of Chip.

"So why all these questions? Just ask Chip."

"He's missing," Danny said. "You may have been the last person to see him."

"Oh, I doubt that." Lopez didn't seem surprised or concerned by Danny's statement. "Sorry, but I need to head toward my next seminar."

Lopez stood.

Danny remained seated. While Chip's disappearance was disturbing enough, Danny found this reappearance of Oliver deeply rattling. He needed to talk to Josh and find out what he knew about Oliver Meyers. Maybe it was time to discuss his past. He wasn't certain what he wanted to do next.

Lopez was trying to hand him something. Danny looked up in confusion. The man was holding out a thin volume.

"My newest novel," he said.

Danny accepted the book and looked at the cover. It featured a large green pickup truck set among the trash of a country dump. Large, white sans serif letters spelled out *The Dumping Ground*.

"You might find this revealing," Lopez said with a strange smile. "I realize you're not really a fan of my themes or style, but this tale has a different feel. It's more of a coming of age story, set in the Midwest, about a young gay lad. Actually Oliver gave me the idea. Let me know what you think."

The book's physicality frightened Danny. He knew there was no need to confer with Josh about this Oliver Meyers. The book's existence confirmed what he feared. This Oliver had to be the same person from his youth in Wisconsin. There wasn't even a need to read the novel. The book jacket alone told the entire story. Oliver had stolen his life and handed it to Lopez to transform into a novel. He recognized immediately that this was his story being told, and like any Lopez novel, it was bound to be a horror.

Clutching the book as though it were a dreaded talisman, Danny fled Lopez's office. He needed to calm himself, so he sought the one place nearby that would serve that purpose. He walked the campus, crossed Exposition Boulevard, and headed toward the 1913 building that housed the Los Angeles Museum of Natural History.

The large dioramas of preserved mammals, especially those of North America, always comforted him. The Hall of Mammals was large, high ceilinged, dim, and quiet and it transported Danny to another state of mind. Even with groups of school kids clamoring about on their field trips, the exhibit hall soaked up every bit of their energy, leaving Danny with his needed sense of repose. Perhaps, it was simpler than that. Maybe he found the grace of the animals awe inspiring, which quieted him into an appreciation of the larger world.

He stood in front of the exhibit of white-tailed deer, noting the stately buck and the younger doe beside him. The leaves of the trees in the exhibit were a panoply of fall colors that reminded him of the hardwood forest bordering his father's farm. He grew up on that farm, leaving it only after his mother's funeral. But this recreation of a wooded glade was a natural reminder of a time and place when he felt secure, loved by his father and mother, and part of a happy life. It had never been quite so good since.

The North American Mammal hall opened in 1932, in time for the first Los Angeles Olympics. Danny reflected how his mother wasn't born until the following year. These preserved deer may have stood alert in quiet poses for many decades spanning multiple generations. The diorama promised an inherent stability that Danny desperately wanted. Having people pop in and out of his life was too uncomfortable.

His imagination was too vivid. Maybe at night, when no one was looking, these deer regained life. In some reality where quantum mechanics allowed for a never-ending number of alternate universes, perhaps even these animals existed in a state of being both alive and not alive. In such an unimaginable environment, perhaps neither Jesus Lopez nor Oliver Meyers would exist to torment him. He wanted that world.

A group of nine-year-olds were scrambling for optimal viewing. Surrounded, Danny realized he was standing there too long. One of the school chaperones was staring at him as though to prod him to move along. He did. After all he wasn't a product of taxidermy, nor was he captured forever in a single moment of time. He looked down at the book he carried. Whatever story Lopez may have woven, in the end it was only a piece of fiction. Whether it was derived or not from Danny's life did not matter. Only Danny and Oliver knew where the truth lay. Besides whatever story was told, it was a plot floating in a past river. As the old adage went, you could never step into the same river twice. The book didn't matter. Oliver didn't matter. Danny tried to convince himself that his logic was sound

Kids rushed forward into a new hall, eager to discover something more interesting. Danny followed. They were clustered around a display cabinet near the rotunda. As a frequent visitor to this museum, Danny knew what was inside: a giant oarfish. The strange marine creature never seemed natural—too long to be real, too rarely encountered, and too little discussed by people for the casual observer to accept its true existence. More like a serpent or sea dragon, the preserved oarfish floated in its timeless mix of yellowing resin. The display gave the specimen an unearthly aura, and allowed the preserved fish to be subjected to the laughter, stares, and gibes of the children.

Danny felt that gaze of the other again, at the back of his head, the sense that some chaperone was marking him as questionable. Not wanting to be flagged as a child predator, he knew it was time to leave, but he looked around to catch who was making him feel watched.

That's when he noticed someone across the rotunda walking rapidly into another hall. That person was wearing the same kind of blue fisherman's hat that Pete Peterson used to wear in Thread. What next? First he was reminded of Oliver, and now of Pete. His past refused to vaporize in the way that all unwanted memories should.

Danny felt chilled. The hat reminded him of a night at the resort that followed a moonlit round of skinny-dipping with Oliver. They rested on a raft floating off the sandy beach. Feeling protected by the stars and warm summer air, Danny told Oliver all about Pete—and what Pete meant to him, and in turn, what he meant to Pete.

What if Oliver had repeated that to Lopez? What if that past was recounted in the book? Danny couldn't abide such treason.

INTERLUDE

Session Six

I have a theory. Life is just a giant game board. Sort of like chess. Not so structured or unnatural as that game with all its strategies and books on famous moves. Real life is far more challenging. You have to be smarter than a chess grand master to prevail in the real world.

To answer your question before you even ask it . . . yes, I think of myself as one of those more intelligent people. You have to know it's true. You've seen me and talked to me. Don't you agree that it's an honest assessment?

But I don't operate alone. Did you really think that I did?

No, life is a team sport. Just like chess, we have to have our kings. We don't move around all that much, but when we kings move, it makes every bit of difference.

Of course, there are other players and so many pawns. Always the expendable pawns. They're needed and useful, but ultimately one can always sacrifice one's pawns. When that happens, you can't get emotional. Their demise is simply a part of the game.

The real trick is finding the right players for your team. They have to be of a similar ilk, but you never want them to be quite as smart as you. Don't believe those businessmen who claim they only hire people smarter than them. Not true. You can't trust someone smarter than you. There's always the possibility they will be operating one move ahead of you.

Admittedly, sometimes in one area or another they must be smarter. After all, you can't know everything. Even I wouldn't claim that, but then it's always been good to know your weaknesses—as well as theirs. Having a few crazies around always helps too. It makes it easier to keep everyone in check.

You want to know what all of this has to do with Danny? I'll tell you.

I play a lot of games, and he's only one of my games. Maybe in this game you can think of him as the king of the white players. Of course, he's a rather naïve player, since he doesn't even know he's playing the game. But that only makes his moves unorthodox and unexpected. It adds to the excitement. Besides, the motive of this game isn't to destroy the guy; it's to expose him for who he really is.

Why are you asking me what I mean by that? Don't you listen to anything I say? I need to know what will win out . . . hope or despair.

I have a lot of people around me and I know exactly what motivates each one of them. That's why I can play them. But I like to think Danny has something more than what I see on the surface. So what if he's an irrational obsession? There is definitely something that links the two of us as players. Bound together in some eternal, cosmic way.

I have to be certain of him before I make my final move. Call it omniscient curiosity. But once I know. Wham! It's checkmate.

CHAPTER SIX

On Tour

Josh gulped both olives; he loved a dirty martini made with Belvedere vodka. Already the staff at United Airlines Red Carpet Club at LAX was bringing his second one, and the frosted glass appeared perfectly chilled. Orleans looked at him disapprovingly. Josh didn't care; it was past two and soon they would be on the three o'clock Premium Service flight to JFK in First Class. There wasn't a better way east—other than on a private jet. But he didn't have that luxury, at least not yet.

Earlier Kenosha drove them to the airport so the three could meet in a private conference room at the airline lounge. She carried a briefcase filled with press kits that extolled the virtues of Premios. Her packs of finely honed truths, destined for the hands of multiple business reporters and bankers, were crafted to maximize the possibility of the right sort of articles and broadcast hits. To get them to this day, Orleans scheduled the investor visits and Kenosha wrangled the press. Both accomplished more than Josh thought possible, but it would be up to him to exert the final effort that would make everything pay off.

"Josh, pay attention to this," Kenosha wore her serious face. He found her willingness to don the tough woman persona amusing. He was sure it had been a hard battle to fight her way free of the wooded canyons of Brentwood.

"I know all the questions. I know all the answers. Backwards and forwards." He felt flippant. Maybe it was the cocktails.

"Do you?" she challenged. "What about this one? 'Are you concerned that one of your investors recently disappeared under suspicion of embezzlement?'"

Josh just laughed, "Kenosha, they are never going to ask that."

Kenosha was not placated. "That's beside the point. The reason we prepare a Q&A is so you're ready to respond to anything that gets thrown your way. You can't let dirt hit you in the face; you have to fling it right back."

"Kenosha's right," Orleans offered. She looked at Josh placidly, almost as though to egg him into contradicting her. He wouldn't fall for that ruse. Most of Kenosha's prepared questions were focused on finances, and while she had labored diligently to be certain he could spin out the right details to cast the perfect light on the enterprise, he had this—just like he had control over every question that might get asked. No one could rattle him.

"Reporters wouldn't know to ask such a question. No local paper has even reported Chip's disappearance, and besides, the New York press doesn't follow the *Thread Times* or whatever hick paper gets published in the back woods. The police aren't even certain any money was stolen, let alone that Chip did it. There's the possibility that it's just a computer error, or some vestige of a "Y2K" issue messing up a transaction or balance sheet. It'll take weeks before anyone figures it out, and by then, Chip will be back in the arms of all those who love him. Cynthia is a worrier. There's nothing more to it."

Josh didn't actually believe any of the nonsense he just spouted, and he would be surprised if either of these two clever women did. But it didn't matter. It sounded logical, so maybe the police would believe it.

"Just humor me," parried Kenosha. She wasn't giving up. "If it did come up, how would you answer it?"

"Ask me."

"Okay. We've heard disturbing rumors about the disappearance of Chip Grant, one of your early investors. How will that affect the planned stock offering for Premios?"

Josh smiled; this was an easy curveball. "It won't affect it at all. Mr. Grant holds less than a 2% equity stake in Premios, and is in no way actively involved in our day-to-day management or strategy. Besides, I'm not at all convinced he's even missing."

Kenosha frowned. "Don't add that last sentence. It's not in the packet because it's not relevant what you think. Circumstances may change and why let future events contradict you."

Josh shrugged. She was right, but it was a minor point.

Kenosha was still on topic. "Now, tell me again, the logic behind that two percent comment."

Just as Josh would expect her to do in an actual situation, Orleans took over. As the CFO, it was her responsibility to handle all the money questions. "Mr. Grant made a personal investment as part of the second round of funding for Premios. That round involved ten million dollars, and $500,000 came from Mr. Grant. The venture capital firm of Endicott-Meyers provided the remainder, and their total investment gave them an ownership stake of thirty-three percent of the company and giving the overall company a second round valuation of approximately thirty million dollars. Mr. Grant's half million dollars represents less than two percent of that total."

"Your answer is too long," said Kenosha.

Orleans rolled her eyes, and Josh knew that she wanted to say that one couldn't explain it more succinctly. But you could. She should have just said that Chip owned a half million dollars of a thirty million dollar company. But that was today. If this investment tour went well, Josh anticipated the IPO would raise the valuation of the company to over three hundred million.

"Okay, girls, we're overdoing this. The press kit is fine. The background provides the relevant details. I'm comfortable with the financial data. And despite your worries, Kenosha, you know I have all the Q&A well in hand.

"But, Kenosha, let me compliment you on a fantastic job. You make Orleans and me look better. Orleans, take some lessons from this whiz."

He glanced at Kenosha to see if she would press on any topic further, but she accepted the compliment and started to repack her bag. "All that's left then is to say 'good luck.' I'm looking forward to seeing my stock options make me rich."

Josh stood, offered his hand, and added, "That's what I do. I make people's dreams come true."

Kenosha left. Orleans and Josh were alone in the room, along with his glistening martini. Orleans pushed the glass away; he could see she was annoyed.

"What could I learn from that overpaid flack?" she demanded.

Josh found it amusing to stoke a little tension among the troops. "Don't worry. You know you always have to compliment some people. It's like calming a barking dog. A few pats and all is good. Besides you know that you're the one I depend on."

Orleans seemed only partially mollified. "We shouldn't be doing this tour," she said. "The timing is all wrong. The markets are unsettled. We're going to end up leaving too much cash on the table."

"You know we can't wait."

Orleans pulled out her laptop as though she was about to bring up some numbers to review. But then she unexpectedly slammed the screen down and demanded, "Where the fuck did that million dollars come from?"

"Why so angry?"

"Because I'm supposed to be your partner in this. I'm your chief financial officer. And suddenly out of the blue a million dollars gets injected into our accounts, and no one warns me. I have to rework everything in these documents."

"The pitch will look better though, won't it?"

"Again that's beside the point. You still haven't told me what's going on. I sat here all the while we met with Kenosha knowing you had something up your sleeve with that sudden infusion of cash. I'm not flying for another five hours wondering what it's all about."

Josh couldn't claim to know fully what was going on, but there was no way he would admit that to Orleans. She might be smart enough to figure out on her own what he really knew and didn't know, but that wouldn't be the same as admitting a weakness.

"Endicott-Meyers increased their level of investment." At least Josh knew that was technically true.

"Really. And what did they get for it?"

"Another five percent stake in the company."

"Did you do the math? When we go public in a few months, your five percent will be worth fifteen million or more. Are you telling me you gave up fifteen million of our money for one million now?"

He didn't like the math either. "A bird in the hand is worth two in the bush."

"What the hell does that mean?"

"You know what it means. Without an added investment from Endicott-Meyers, Premios would have sunk before we ever went public. You don't get rewarded with millions if you're in deep water clutching debris. That trade in equity was the only rational path available."

Orleans seemed to accept that, but still seemed troubled.

"What's wrong?"

"The whole presentation has to be reworked."

"Only the bankers' version," Josh replied. "Luckily we're meeting with press first, so we have plenty of time to finalize the new packets. I've already planned through what's needed."

She wasn't yet mollified.

"What else?"

She appeared deeply reluctant to voice her concern, but then she looked directly into his eyes, "It seems odd that Lattigo Industries is missing a million dollars at the same time Endicott-Meyers invests another million with us? Do you know what happened to Chip?"

"No, I do not" he replied, keeping eye contact, until Orleans relaxed.

He wasn't lying. He did not know for certain exactly what happened to Chip, but he knew enough to be unhappy. He had to get things back on track before it all unraveled.

Cynthia waved after she disembarked the plane and exited into the terminal. She was thankful to see Danny waiting for her. She had been afraid he wouldn't make it, and she felt she couldn't possibly have left the airport without him to guide her. She was neither a weak woman nor a dependent one, but the hours required to reach the West Coast had eroded her emotions bit by bit until there was barely enough resolve to hold her from failing into an all-consuming exhaustion.

Thomas, the comptroller at Lattigo Industries, had volunteered to drive her to the Timberton airport. That was where she needed to catch the short commuter flight to Minneapolis. From there she could transfer to a Northwest flight to reach Los Angeles. Only once they were in his car did she realize Thomas' hidden agenda. Troubled by Chip's situation—that's what he called it, a situation, not a disappearance—he was seeking support. But he had it backward. She was the one who needed his support, or at least an explanation for Chip's absence that she could believe.

Like most of the young men and women on the reservation, Thomas grew up protected by Chip's financial oversight. Like all the youth of the area, he worshipped her husband. Now there was a chance his hero was a villain. Unfortunately, in Thomas's face, Cynthia recognized the same tension and worries that kept her from sleeping.

"I know Chip didn't take the money," Thomas declared. "The police may think otherwise, but Chip's not that kind of person."

Of course Chip was not a scoundrel, but the Los Angeles police were leaving the case entirely in the hands of the Lattigo tribal police because they clearly considered Chip a missing embezzler.

Fortunately, the local cops were giving their fellow tribe member the benefit of doubt; moreover, they had neither the pressure nor the resources to be aggressive. That's why Cynthia convinced herself she had to go to California: to hire her own detectives and to lead the search herself. Nobody else would ensure the search was thorough.

"You're not alone," Thomas consoled her. "The IT guys have gone through our financial accounting system backwards and forwards. They're ninety-nine percent certain that the transfer of funds resulted from a computer program planted in our systems. Did Chip mention what happened on New Year's Eve?"

"He told me about the computer virus that attacked Premios."

"The guys think there's a connection. They can't prove it, but they're combing through the code, looking for something to connect both incidents."

"But how could hackers have done it?"

"There was a weakness in one of our financial routines. The payroll program uses an automatic weekly correction to adjust the final result against first estimates. It normally submits a small electronic deposit or withdrawal to make that happen. Someone hacked our program to add five zeros to that amount and to send the oversized payment to an offshore bank. The police think Chip did it himself, but that's ludicrous. We know he was searching for the hacker who infiltrated our company on New Year's Eve. To me, it seems more likely that the same people who hacked us did it.

"In any case, the money is gone. There's no way I can avoid submitting a claim with our insurers. Once I do that, we can't keep this under wraps any longer. The public will know."

After that, neither knew what to say to the other. They sped through snowy woods in quiet. At the small airport, Thomas escorted Cynthia through security and remained by her side until she was ready to board the propjet. As she was about to walk out the door to cross the icy tarmac, she consoled Thomas, "Don't worry. I will find Chip. We'll clear this up."

By the time she arrived in Los Angeles, her confidence had evaporated. Flying over the city reminded her of the enormous urban area. How could one search through such immensity? Winter storm clouds hovered off the coast, and she felt rains were about to break forth. The weather chilled the air in the terminal as Danny and she hugged.

"You'll stay with us," Danny said. "Let's get you there now before the rain arrives."

"No," she said. "Not yet. When we were about to land, I got a glimpse of the ocean. Could we walk along the beach first? Just to clear my head. Could we do that?"

When they left the airport, Danny turned west on a street bordering the facility, crested a hill and headed toward the ocean, which was grey and foaming from the offshore winds. As they passed the last of the airport runways, Cynthia noticed a series of streets curving gracefully on the sandy hills. But instead of standing houses there were only the ghostly diagrams of a former neighborhood.

"What's that?" she asked.

Danny glanced to his right. "The airport bought out an entire community that used to sit here. They tore down all the houses. I guess it was too noisy."

Cynthia wondered about the people who once lived on these shadows of former streets. What did they think at the time? Did they welcome the progress of an expanding airport? Or did they just resent the powerful who pushed them away from the ocean? How did anyone compete with the forces of progress?

Danny turned right on the busy highway that followed the ocean and then turned left into an empty parking lot. "We can walk here. It'll be noisy with the jets overhead, but we won't have much time before the rains start. Are you sure you want to do this?"

Cynthia didn't understand why it was so important to her to feel the slapping sting of cold air, but it was. No one else was on the beach. In the distance she saw unused volleyball nets. Far to the south were the towers of an industrial complex. To the north, just below the impending clouds, she could discern the outline of low mountains. "A little fresh air. That's all I need to be better."

"I understand." Danny knew it wouldn't be enough.

For several moments, they walked quietly side by side, leaving footprints in the cold, wet sand that was firm from the ebbing tide. The pounding of the waves mixed with a susurrant gasp of water being absorbed into the sand. Now and again, the roar of a departing plane punctuated through the sound of the surf. The smell of ozone made everything clearer to Cynthia. Reality was falling into place. She didn't like what it told her, but she also didn't believe in deluding herself.

"Chip is dead," she said.

"Don't say that," Danny pleaded.

"Whoever stole the money is the person who did it. We need to find Chip and we need to find that money."

Danny didn't know what to say.

"The last time I talked to Chip he mentioned that he thought he was being followed or watched. He told me he was reminded of someone back in Thread. Just because of a hat."

Danny looked at her so oddly that she wondered what he was thinking, but she continued. "He said he thought of Pete Peterson. Remember that guy? What was it that the cook at the Loon Town Café always called him?"

"Reverend Willy," Danny said.

He was flushed. Cynthia remembered how uncomfortable Danny always seemed when they were teenagers. Something else also clicked into place—how the cook Thelma always tried to protect Danny.

"Yes, that's right," said Cynthia. "Thelma did talk about him a lot. But I don't think she ever said his name when you were around. Was it because he was your neighbor? Do you even know how he got that odd name?"

"Because he went to every church service in town."

That didn't sound right to Cynthia. "Really? Wasn't it connected to his showing silent movies on his garage door and acting like doing that was as holy as a church Mass? Oh, I don't know, I just remember he was an oddball."

"I think we should be going back. I just felt some raindrops."

Cynthia felt the chill sting as well, but she didn't mind. Compared to Wisconsin, this California weather felt almost balmy. Getting wet in a sudden storm would only prove she could survive. But Danny had turned around. He was motioning her back toward the parking lot.

"But I know it wasn't Reverend Willy or Pete or whatever you want to call the man who was following Chip."

Danny slowed his pace. "Of course not, what would Pete be doing in Los Angeles?"

"Maybe looking for you," Cynthia joked.

Danny didn't laugh.

Cynthia went on, "But Pete's dead. I talked to Daddy. He told me the guy was found murdered a few years ago, and no one knows who did it."

Danny turned the switch; the gas fireplace in his bedroom flared to life. Outside, the threatening storm was gaining force. Rain-streaked windows overlooked the city below where city lights disappeared into the veil of water. In the distance, where Cynthia and he walked earlier in the day on the shores of the Pacific, nothing could be seen.

Cynthia had retreated to the guest room at the other end of the floor. Her room, like the master bedroom, occupied an entire wing and its windows faced in three directions. When she entered the room earlier in the afternoon, she went from one window to the next, locking the frames, pulling down the shades, and drawing the drapes. When she glanced over, Danny tried to hide his bewilderment at her actions, but he didn't ask what she was blocking out.

And she offered no real explanation. "I can't feel exposed," is all she said.

The storm was now in full force. It had only been impending as they first drove east from the beach. By the time they reached the house atop the hill, their car was being pelted. The rain was now assailing the tiles overhead. The Spanish-style roofs were low-pitched, and had no attic to dampen the noise. For a moment, he considered moving Cynthia to a guest room on the lower level, where she could escape the constant rain that beat from above.

Cynthia placed her suitcase on the bamboo-style luggage stand, opened it, and pulled from among her clothes a small set of speakers and Walkman. After a moment connecting the pieces, she pressed a button and low tones of classical music filled the room. "That sounds better, don't you think?"

The day slowly edged forward. Lacking energy to cook and with the weather precluding a drive to one of the restaurants in the village area below, Danny called in an order for Thai food. As he waited for the delivery boy, he made sure to turn on all the lights at the front of the mansion. Often service people claimed that they couldn't find the house, although sometimes he wondered if some lingering reputation connected to the previous owner scared people away.

But the pad thai and mee krob arrived quickly. Sitting at the marble counter of the kitchen island, with lights blazing and Cynthia's music playing, they discussed the day ahead. After Danny told Cynthia about his visit with Lopez, Cynthia wanted to visit the Pacific Dining Car restaurant to try to talk to the waiter who served Chip that day. Maybe he would remember something. She also suggested stopping by the

Premios offices to see whether Kenosha had finished her research on potential investigators. And, of course, they needed to visit the Bonaventure Hotel. Cynthia had arranged for Chip's luggage to be stored there when he failed to return to the room, and she needed to retrieve it on the chance that they could find some clue in his stuff. Left unsaid was the likelihood that the local police had already done similar things.

Danny left unvoiced his earlier conversations with Josh, who admonished against encouraging Cynthia's pursuits. "You're not a private eye," Josh snapped, "and you and Cynthia aren't in some Nancy Drew or Hardy Boys mystery. Leave the detective work to the professionals."

But how could Danny do that?

The evening ended early. Cynthia retreated to her room with the excuse that it had been a long day. Danny watched the fire within the bedroom fireplace and the rain outside the room's windows, and he brooded.

Cynthia's bringing up the name Pete Peterson troubled him and he couldn't understand why. Admittedly, for years, he avoided thinking about Pete, but then just a few days earlier he saw that hat. Of course, there was no chance that the person he glimpsed in the museum was Pete, and he was just as certain that Pete had not been outside the warehouse when Chip had been searching for the computer hackers. Pete wasn't the kind of person to stalk anyone.

Still, even though he had no reason for clinging to such a belief, he was also certain that Pete wasn't dead. He didn't care what Red Trueheart once told his daughter. If Pete had been murdered, Danny knew he would have felt the loss. Something connected them. Danny couldn't imagine a universe in which he wouldn't have been touched in some way when the man died, for if the psychic world had seen fit to forewarn him about his mother, then surely those same emanations would have alerted him to Pete's death.

Maybe he was being superstitious, but he could never be completely rational when it came to Pete. God, how he hated that some people back in Thread used to call the man Reverend Willy. That nickname turned a good man into an object of derision and the taunt had taken over so fast in town. Danny always felt responsible for that. When the man faced a fork in the road, Danny turned him down the wrong one. That choice broke Pete. But no one else knew that, and, like so many things in his life, Danny wasn't ever going to tell anyone.

The wrong path all started with watching that movie. That day was going to be the last time Pete would be able to show a film in the old Thread Theater. The bank was repossessing his building. He joked that the future would force him to screen the images against his garage door. Danny laughed because if Pete did that then he knew he would be able to watch them from his bedroom window since his house was next door to Pete's.

The film that night was an obscure silent film called *The Sad Vampire*. In the years that followed, Danny never heard anyone else ever talk about the movie, but he remembered how Pete loved it. The opening scene zoomed in on a crowded nighttime street in a Middle European city gone wild with Oktoberfest. A young man, really a boy, was lost in the revelry and unable to speak the language. Danny remembered how even the subtitles distanced the viewer by being written in German. An aristocratic man appears. The light seems to change as he sweeps the boy up and helps him to reunite with his mother.

The mother is so thankful. Her son is a violin virtuoso on tour, and the savior, supposedly a German count, soon attaches himself to both mother and son. As they travel the Continent together on the musical tour, the count appears only at night. Danny was fourteen when he watched this film with Pete, but even at that age he recognized that the story hinted at some larger tragedy than a vampire sucking the blood of a boy. The horror of the mother and of her friends grew as they began to suspect why the boy is ill, and the mother, without explanation, begins to pull back from the victim as much as from the predator.

Even now, Danny wasn't certain that the veiled ideas of this movie from the twenties had anything to do with so-called inverts (as he later learned homosexuals were sometimes called then). He only knew that Pete grew increasingly distressed by the film. When the lights were turned back on, tears were streaming from his face. Danny felt that his old protector—the man who guided him even as his own parents, each in their own way, abandoned him—wanted to say something and Danny, as young as he was, sensed that he couldn't let Pete speak, so both sat as silent as the film that just ended.

The dark rain outside the window transformed the glass into an imperfect mirror in which Danny saw his own reflection. In his image was something of Pete's emotions that night. The memory made him shudder.

Something else about that film's credits niggled in the back of his mind before suddenly bursting into his consciousness. The memory of the projected black and white lettering of the director's name seemed so clear: the credit was for Augustus Cambrian, the same man who had died in this house.

He jumped to search the bookshelves on the other side of the room. Josh had purchased some thick book about Cambrian, but Danny never read any of it. He preferred not to think about the house's past history. By now, the largely gutted and modernized mansion was their creation, not someone else's legacy. He found the title: *The Life and Work of Augustus Cambrian*. Thick and heavy, it was more a coffee table book than a traditional biography. He scanned the table of contents to find a filmography, and then turned to it. He moved his finger down the titles beginning in 1919. He didn't have far to go. The table for the year 1924 listed *The Sad Vampire*.

Danny repressed his urge to rush down the hall, wake Cynthia, and exult over this amazing coincidence. He wanted to grab the phone and call Josh in New York. But he stopped. What could he tell either of them? That he had once seen a movie directed by the man who owned this house? Cambrian's occult and horror talkies from the Thirties remained popular to this day. Probably everyone had seen at least one of his films. The coincidence would only seem amazing if Danny could explain what seeing the film with Pete had meant to him.

Danny's discovery was one of those strange things in life destined to never be more than a private memory. To quiet his emotions, he paged through the book. Several photos from the later films highlighted familiar ghouls from many a famous film. He never liked horror pictures as a boy. They gave him nightmares, even though sometimes the thrill of looking into the face of something frightening was just too alluring to resist.

When he found a chapter on this house and Cambrian's movie memorabilia collection, he stopped paging through the book, and instead quickly read the text, which provided details that largely matched what the realtor told them about the house. Over the decades, the director had amassed a major assortment of horror movie props and stills, as well as medieval instruments of torture. Danny reread one paragraph more carefully. The author claimed that Cambrian kept his most valuable items in a secret room off a basement chamber. He described an elaborate light sconce that when moved triggered the opening of the hidden door, and Danny recalled that his friend Francesca referenced a similar secret chamber a few weeks ago.

After all they had done to rebuild this house, could a hidden room still be there? Could someone be looking for it?

Josh sat alone at the table in the corner of the Charlotte Bar just off the lobby of the Millennium Hotel in Manhattan. The seat provided a perfect angle for spotting anyone entering the place. His day had been long, filled with meetings, and it wasn't over yet. The most important session of the day was still ahead, and for that he sent Orleans away.

The way he insisted she go back to her room likely prompted her to wonder if he was having an affair. But he had to get rid of her. The presentations had been grueling. Both needed more than one drink to wind down. After a long day, she talked too much and asked too many questions. And she wouldn't let any detail go. She wanted to recap every question and recall each special slide she had been forced to present. But he was tired of it all. After all the questions at Lehman Brothers, Goldman Sachs and the half dozen other executive conference rooms they had entered and exited over the past three days, he was pretty certain Orleans pulled up every single slideshow she ever created at Premios. He felt no need to repeat the performance over cocktails.

Still he questioned whether her stellar performance was enough. Kenosha had failed to think broadly enough when she created her comprehensive set of media questions and answers. Or maybe Orleans underestimated the Wall Street crowd. Whatever the truth, they had prepared for the wrong set of questions. Not one banker doubted the value in Premios's heavy burn rate; they understood the need to build up customer loyalty and a well-known brand because everyone believed in the promise of being the first mover. But bankers were an impatient lot. They badgered Josh over how long it would take to achieve dominance. Thank God the extra million dollars had been invested by Endicott-Meyers. Without that financial cushion, Orleans and Josh might have been laughed out of many of the conference rooms. But as he liked to remind Orleans, people want to believe what others believe. As long as someone was willing to pour money into this business, no banker was going to walk away—no matter how much of a rat's nest they feared existed in the bowels of the business. There was one thing Josh knew for sure: the potential to win big would always win out over the possibility of a loss.

Until it didn't. Then all of Wall Street would become a gold rush in reverse. As quick as the money guys embraced those it deemed winners, they could be even faster fleeing the potential losers. Given the recent gyrations of mainstream stocks, Wall Street was already in a tizzy with everyone questioning whether the new world of the Internet was the great hope they had convinced themselves it was. Time was running out. Any initial public offering carried with it a certain number of legal requirements that couldn't be rushed, but that didn't mean it was wise to allow the process to get delayed. In every room Josh and Orleans entered on this trip there lurked a contagious bearer of fear.

The payoff was tantalizingly close. Josh could feel it, but he knew it wasn't guaranteed. For Orleans' sake, he pretended it was. Despite her otherwise remarkable acumen, he found that she was easily lulled into complacency. Tonight he worked his magic to ensure that she would leave the bar with all qualms about the tour erased. He diverted her with misdirecting indications that he was nervously awaiting a meeting with someone special. Even when she reminded him that he had a loyal partner at home, he didn't protest or explain otherwise. Let her think he was waiting for some hot Times Square hooker.

He knew that Danny had never cheated on him. That was why he had to have this meeting tonight. It was for Danny.

Josh leaned back against the leather of the wingback chair. Few guests were left in the lobby bar. Because the hotel was just off Times Square and the theater district, Josh thought more people might show up when the shows let out. But that didn't worry him. He had chosen this specific spot because it offered dark corners. An added bonus was that his chair gave him an excellent view of 44th Street and the hotel's entrance. No one could enter without him seeing the person first. An extra moment of preparation was always useful.

"Hello, Josh,"

He looked up startled. Where had this man come from?

The man laughed. "Did I interrupt your sleuthing? Were you expecting me to come into the lobby from that street? The hotel lobby runs through to 45th Street, and I entered from the north. Hope that doesn't upset you in any way."

The man sat down opposite him without requesting permission. Josh, noticing how well trimmed and polished the man's nails were, remembered how they once were so rough. But the hands still looked strong, and the man himself was handsome in a tough sort of way. If Orleans happened to walk by and noticed the two of them talking, it would only confirm her suspicion that he was meeting with some street trade. Of course, if she noticed the quality of the Brioni suit, she might also realize the man spent more money on his clothing than a well-paid male hooker would dare.

The man motioned for the waitress. When he caught her attention, he said, "Cognac, please."

"Hello, Oliver," Josh said. This was certainly not Josh's first meeting with Oliver Meyers, although he would prefer it to be his last. That wasn't likely.

Oliver replied, "Do you have good news for me?"

Had this asshole been so smug when they first met? Josh couldn't recall. He always knew there was something about the man that he shouldn't trust. But beggars can't be choosers.

"The tour's good," he replied. "We've encountered a lot of interest in the initial offering. The stock should soar on opening day . . . as long as we get out there on time."

"That's not what I meant," Oliver said. The waitress appeared with the cognac and set it on the small table. She placed a small glass of water on a separate cocktail napkin beside the snifter. Oliver's smile promised a big tip ahead.

Josh had to admit the man had charm. Over the years, Oliver had clearly put it to good use. He had many friends, and worked a web of connections with various sorts of people, both good and bad. It was the bad ones that worried Josh.

"Really? Endicott-Meyers are the biggest investors in Premios. Why did you put in all those millions if you weren't anxious to see us go public?" Josh tried to make a joke out of it.

Oliver was having none of it. "You know why we invested."

There was just one problem with that statement. Of course Josh clearly understood the "why" of the firm's investment; he just had no insight into the "we." He only knew two things for certain. One was that the firm of Colby Endicott didn't care one bit about the source of Oliver Meyers' money and the second was that Josh knew the money certainly wasn't Oliver's.

When Colby and Oliver first showed up waving their checkbook, it had appeared too good to be true. But then the heady days of Internet investing were like that. Everyone wanted a chance at the golden ring. Still, Josh was cautious. He researched how Colby inherited his wealth; he wanted an equally solid understanding of Oliver. He dug a little and concluded that it might be mob money, but that didn't particularly bother him. Mob money turned remarkably respectable after a generation. Just look at how Joseph Kennedy transformed a rum running past into becoming the scion of an American aristocracy. Josh wasn't one to judge.

Maybe Josh's morality came from growing up in the northwoods. Generations ago, Thread and the environs had been the favored hangout for Chicago crime lords. Everyone in Thread knew how Al Capone once frequented the area. Not far from Thread, a minor resort in Manitowish Waters was called the Little Bohemia Lodge. The establishment still preserved the cabin where Dillinger had his famous shootout with the feds. Even in a small town, one grew up knowing crooks surrounded you. But crooks could be good guys . . . as long as they were on your side.

The thing was you had to know who your crooks were. Josh looked across at this well-dressed man who was a year or two younger than him. Whose man was he really?

Josh sighed, "I thought you invested to make money. And that's exactly what happens once we go public. Your nine and a half million will be worth thirty times what it is today."

"I believe it's ten and a half million now." Oliver took a sip of cognac and then held his look at Josh until he received confirmation.

"Of course."

Orleans worried over what Josh gave up by accepting a heavier investment from Endicott-Meyers. She had no idea. Josh took a sip of his martini. It had grown warm, and the glass was no longer sweating with chilled condensation. Josh knew Orleans was focused on the lost opportunity costs related to potential gains, but she worried about the wrong thing.

When Josh tried to burrow into Oliver's connections, he was shocked to find himself blocked at every turn. He was damn good at eking out hidden details, so his failure in this instance was deeply worrying. Somehow he thought Meyers' connections were more than the usual dabbling in extortion or drug smuggling. Maybe he was connected higher up the food chain, perhaps directly to Colombian or Mexican drug lords. But that at least would seem like ordinary corruption. His true fear was that Oliver was a pawn of something much larger, something global and political.

In more reflective moments, Josh acknowledged that he was prone to wild conspiracy theories, but then he knew his own story—and that made any conspiracy theory seem more plausible. At times he had behaved in some pretty devious ways, and he wasn't the only person of his type in the world. It was always safer to assume everyone had a hidden agenda and that they would be ruthless in pursuing those goals. Again, he came back to this basic question about Oliver: whose agenda was in play?

In those sleepless moments that sometimes plagued him at three or four in the morning, his thoughts would fixate on the political. There were many candidates: the Russians, the Chinese, Arab terrorists. He had to figure out which it was, or he would never devise a way to free Danny and his company of this cancer.

Oliver took another a sip of his cognac. "Naturally we wish you all the success with the public placement. If you're successful, perhaps I will start drinking Louis XIII cognac instead. But then I'm not one for ostentatious spending. Money is nice, but information is better. One can leverage the right information so much more than mere cash. Surely you know that."

Josh thought of all of the information stored within the databases at the heart of Premios. Not the listings of restaurants and hotels, or the user ratings, not even the stored credit card numbers. Rather, it was the incredible detail found in the user profiles that had been built up for their broad array of celebrity users. From the earliest days, Premios attracted the Hollywood elite, and Premios data engines captured their lives in the reservations they made, the searches they did, and the predilections of their desired purchases—all tracked by Premios to enable better and more personal recommendations.

Of course, everyone knew such data capture was private and anonymous. The terms and conditions of their unread user agreements guaranteed it. But reality seldom matched policies. Programmers were only human; they didn't always do what they promised. Information might be gathered even when it wasn't freely offered. Data might be used in ways people never intended.

"And speaking of information, how is your Premios Advisor feature coming along?"

"We can demonstrate its capabilities," Josh replied.

"And does the programming staff understand what they're building?"

"I understand it. They don't need to."

Oliver grimaced.

Josh continued. "The Advisor feature is being built in modules that will eventually link together. Each module makes logical sense to the person programming it. Only a few of us understand how it's meant to come together. And of those few, I may be the only one who really understands what can be done with it."

Now Oliver smiled. "Well, we also understand it." He stressed the word 'we.' "My colleagues have been patient. But we do have our limits, and there have been a few too many disturbing incidents lately. They need to stop. Do you understand? I trust I'm clear."

Oliver took one last gulp of his cognac, stood and exited through the 44th Street door. He didn't wait to hear whether or not Josh understood.

Josh watched him enter a town car that had been waiting. Josh understood all right. He would put a stop to the disturbing incidents. The incidents in question just might not be the ones that Oliver was talking about.

Session Seven

Everyone has secrets. *At least they think they do. And it doesn't take an expensive shrink like you to lure those tidbits out into the open.*

Early on I realized that discovering what people want to keep hidden bestows on the discoverer enormous power. The trick is to find a fast way to uncover those diamonds in the rough.

Take you, doc. You had to go to school four years to get a college degree and then how many years studying psychology and therapy? Licenses and all that, and then somehow you're allowed to know our secrets. It's not really necessary. People leave clues all the time to the very things they don't want anyone to know.

Or maybe they do want someone to know. Anyone. Just to reinforce that they matter.

Once I worked in a tony restaurant, and the owner had this idea about measuring customer satisfaction. He thought it would be great to follow up with his diners a day or two after they spent a bundle on a fancy meal. How would you rate your dinner, and would you recommend our place to your friend? Shit like that. So he had me call their homes and conduct a phone survey.

Boring stuff, except when you got a bewildered wife. 'No,' she would say, 'we didn't eat at that restaurant. My husband was working that night.' Sure he was. Working on boning some new conquest. It's amazing how often an idiot leaves a home phone number for a dinner reservation when he was setting up an affair.

That's when I realized people carelessly drop clues to their secrets all over the place. I don't know if it's from stupidity, laziness, or just not realizing the implications of a small detail. But if you could put all those details together, imagine what you might find.

Well, you don't need to imagine, do you? I guess that's what your job is all about.

Look out, doc. The Internet and the World Wide Web might just take your craft away. With computers and the net, it becomes possible to look at everything one does and keep track of all the little details, constantly sifting through them, until you find that magical leverage you can exploit. Because secrets don't stay hidden in the ether. Personal data is the real gold mine. As long as you got the data, and as long as people know they have a secret to protect, there's the opportunity to conquer the world.

But then there are the mysteries you pose to yourself. Like what makes a person tick? Like who is Danny really?

You need different tactics for problems like that.

I won't find out what I want to know about Danny by simply tracking his search history. Maybe I just need to give him the life he wanted, if only he knew that life was possible, and then snatch it away. I could do that. I could do other things. But I will find out what I need to know.

You can count on that.

CHAPTER SEVEN

Oliver

This was Danny's first visit to the Pacific Dining Car, a restaurant that had operated in the same spot since the 1920s. Danny wondered why he had never talked about the restaurant in his blog. Even though the neighborhood seemed a little sketchy, the quality of the wine list was astonishing. Who would think such a restaurant could exist and stay open around the clock? Leave it to Chip to choose a spot like this for a breakfast meeting.

Earlier that morning Cynthia appeared in the kitchen wearing her look of resolve that reminded Danny of the teenage Cynthia who took on tasks of initiating something new, like the high school prom. In those days, it always helped that her dad owned half of Thread. Nevertheless her perky grit always ensured that no mountain was unmovable. Once, Danny admired Cynthia for such determination. Today he feared it.

"I want to go to that restaurant where Chip had breakfast," Cynthia said.

"Why?" Danny told her everything that Lopez had said about that meeting. Visiting the place in person wouldn't add anything new, and could only offer a reminder that Oliver again existed in some way in Danny's life.

"Maybe the waiter who served him is there. He might know something."

"I'm sure the police already talked to him."

"You know what they would think. They already convicted my husband as a runaway embezzler. Probably convinced that he has a girl stashed away. But you know that doesn't describe Chip."

While Cynthia wore a simple dress that seemed both dignified and yet girlish, her make-up was slightly overdone which gave her an appearance of being surprised and no one would take her questions seriously. Danny recalled Josh's advice that investigations were best left to the professionals. But although Cynthia didn't look like a woman of steel, it was impossible to do anything but give in to his old friend.

Soon they were driving down Riverside, through Elysian Park and taking the backside approach to the west side of downtown Los Angeles. They turned on Sixth Street. "That's the place," he said.

At nine in the morning, several booths were still playing host to breakfast meetings between suited types. While it was unusual to see pinstripes and vests in the typical Los Angeles restaurant, this downtown eatery catered to serious financial types and appeared more Wall Street than West Coast.

Danny didn't feel comfortable in a spot that was almost the exact opposite of the New Loon Town Café. Here nobody looked hip or new media, and it definitely wasn't a hangout for the Hollywood crowd. But the smell of bacon and breakfast sausage was alluring, and Danny hoped that the excursion would at least result in a good breakfast. At his house, breakfast would have been reheated croissants.

Cynthia asked for the manager. He arrived quickly and she explained her predicament. She wondered if they could meet the waiter who was on duty when her husband had been here a week ago. The manager immediately recalled the situation.

"Sit here," said the man. "Pedro served your husband. The police talked to him a few days ago." He motioned a waiter to come over.

The middle-aged, slightly paunchy Hispanic waiter walked up. "Are you ready to order?" He shifted uncomfortably and his tone suggested he sensed something was wrong.

Cynthia smiled warmly; she was accustomed to making others feel at ease. "We'll order in a moment, but first we want to ask you a couple of questions."

"About the menu?" he replied, although he seemed to know already that it was something else.

Cynthia reached out to touch his hand. "No. It's about my husband. He disappeared and it seems the last place he may have been was this restaurant." She pulled out a photo of Chip and her. It had been taken at a Hawaiian beach on their last vacation. "It was a week ago. Do you remember him?"

He looked at her sadly. "Señora," he began as though his native language somehow made it easier to say what he had to say. "I've already told all this to the police. He was here with two men having breakfast. There was nothing out of the ordinary that day, but I remember it well because one of the three was a famous writer named

Jesus Lopez. The author often eats here."

"What about the other man?" Danny asked. He didn't know why he blurted that out.

"I did not know him, and I do not think he had been here before because he studied the menu a long time," the waiter replied. "He was about your age, maybe a little older. Dark-haired man. Good looking, I guess."

Not much to go on, Danny thought, but it sounded like it could be the Oliver Meyer of his youth. Then he thought of the book back in the bedroom, *The Dumping Ground*. Lopez could never have written that story unless he knew the same Oliver. So far, Danny had avoided reading any part of the book. There was no need, since the text on the flyleaf was enough to convince him that the novel was stolen from his own youth.

Cynthia continued to press. "Did they argue? Or did they laugh? Did it seem a business meeting?"

"As I told the police, the only thing I remember is that when I brought the bill, your husband's cell phone rang. He answered it, listened for a while, and then told the other two that the call would take a while, that he'd pay the bill and they could leave. And they did."

Realizing there was nothing to be learned, Cynthia's perkiness deflated. She accepted the unlikely nature of her quest and glumly ordered oatmeal and fresh berries. Danny asked for the special scramble with eggs, sausage, and spinach.

Danny tried to find a positive spin. "When we're done here, we could drive to the investigator's office that Kenosha suggested. She says it's someone with expertise in computer and accounting forensics. Maybe he can track the missing money."

Danny knew Cynthia was still in another space. Nothing ever remained hidden about her emotions, and no one could doubt her love for Chip or her worry. Danny sometimes wondered what others thought of Josh and him. Could they appreciate the bonds that united them?

Last night, he tried to call Josh several times, but he never answered. Danny wondered if Josh mistakenly turned off his phone or left it in the hotel room when he went to a meeting. An investment tour was stressful, and Danny didn't want to distract Josh but at the same time he felt an urgent need to confer. Normally when Josh traveled on business, they talked every evening. Missing that connection, Danny slept fitfully the entire night, haunted by a fear that whatever happened to Chip might happen to Josh. Luckily, Josh called early in the morning and apologized profusely for missing the previous night's call, explaining that it was so late by the time he realized they hadn't talked that he didn't want to risk waking Danny.

Throughout the morning call, Josh was cheerful and extraordinarily positive. Listening to his recounting of the day, Danny knew he was supposed to believe every investor was ready to jump in on the initial offering, but Danny didn't fully accept that. The day before, Kenosha reported how Orleans had fretted about the extremely challenging questions posed in nearly every financial presentation. Danny knew how Josh liked to shield him from mundane details, and he resolved again to better understand the business. Leaving it all in Josh's hands was an easy, but inappropriate, way out.

On the other hand, he suspected Chip and Cynthia lived under the same arrangement because he doubted that she knew much about the inner workings of Lattigo Industries. Neither Cynthia nor Danny was the questioning type; yet now they were trying to be private eyes. It was ludicrous, considering how ill prepared they were for the task.

Having said very little to each other, they finished breakfast. Pedro brought back Danny's credit card and leaned in. "I thought of something. You should ask the valet if he saw anything. No one ever parks on the street. In this neighborhood, especially early in the morning, people are wary about the street. Maybe he'll remember something."

They took the waiter's advice. The first guy they asked hadn't been working that day, but he brought over the other valet.

"Yeah, I remember him. Cause he walked here. No one ever does that. But then when he left, he stood by the front door for a while. I asked him if he needed a cab. But he shook his head and then this big green sedan pulled up, and like he checked out who the driver was before he opened up the door and got in. The car drove west. Last I saw of him."

Danny wondered why the car would have gone in the direction of the distant ocean when Chip's downtown hotel lay in the opposite direction. "Do you remember anything else about the car or the driver?"

"Not really, I think it was a late model Ford, but don't know for sure. The driver was wearing some kind of hat. That was kind of odd.

It wasn't no baseball cap, but then they were gone."

Another diner stepped out of the restaurant and waved his parking slip. The valet gave a look as though to say "that's all," and dashed over to pick up the ticket and find the keys. By then, the other worker was pulling up with Danny's car.

"Ready to see the private eye?" Danny asked Cynthia. The valet rushed to open the door for Cynthia, and she settled in. Danny and she both looked at one another, while Danny wondered if Cynthia had any idea who would have picked Chip up. Cynthia said nothing.

He pulled out of the parking lot to enter Sixth Street and head east toward downtown. His route took them through the new business district on Bunker Hill and then at the bottom, they turned left on Broadway, bringing them into the old center of Los Angeles. The buildings had largely been built in the 1920s and now, except for the ground floors given over to Latino merchants, stood mostly vacant. The detective's office was in the Bradbury Building, a landmark of old L.A. that was glimmering with the polish of a recent renovation.

"The police never mentioned that someone picked Chip up," Cynthia said. "I wonder who it was. And why would they drive away from Chip's hotel?"

Danny didn't answer. He focused on his rear view mirror and the late model, green sedan two cars back. It seemed to be following them.

Cynthia stared at her plate. Her search for Chip had gone nowhere and she wondered what was she was doing in this restaurant. The people who surrounded her were Danny's friends, not hers. Their so-called private room overlooked the busy floor of the New Loon Town Café. Every table below was filled and the bar was packed with an after-work, hard-drinking crowd. In the buzz, it was almost impossible to hear what anyone was saying. It would be so much quieter at home in Wisconsin.

Among these people, she only knew Danny, Wally, and Stephen—familiar faces from the old days in Thread and Lattigo. Wally's original eatery on Thread's main square failed years earlier, and it had been a decade since Stephen and Wally packed their bags to head west, after which Josh lured Danny to the coast as well. The life that Chip and she built in Wisconsin meant nothing to any of them. They did not know how hard her husband fought to preserve the tribal dream for

American Seasons and the way he wrestled with banks and governments to make it possible. He poured his heart into creating that world, not for himself, but for the tribe. Even after attending graduate school, the call of his people was too strong. They pulled him home. Over the years, Chip's obligation had become hers.

No one in this room understood that. Danny might admire Chip, even harbor a type of boyhood crush, but he hardly knew her husband. For Wally and Stephen, Chip was nothing more than a colorful figure from their past.

How could they comfort her? Or distract her? Or even camouflage her pain? Especially when she could see in their eyes that each one doubted Chip's innocence. In the back of their minds, they sheltered that small question about his honor. Of course, they would never say it, but she knew. She could feel it in every action and every look. No fancy food, elaborate drink, or insider story would disguise it.

Earlier that day in his office in the historic Bradbury Building, Samuel Denkey's eyes betrayed the same look. Regardless of his credentials as an investigator, Denkey was both a skeptical man and a poor actor. From Denkey's conference room, Danny, Cynthia, and he held a conference call with Chip's staff in Lattigo because Denkey wanted to hear their recollections first hand.

If only she could be among those staff members now instead of this alien restaurant. They knew Chip like she knew him. They knew what kind of man their boss was. No matter that their printouts and reconstructions suggested otherwise. No, she corrected herself, the kind of man Chip is. She had to keep thinking of him as alive. It was still possible to find and save him.

Denkey had been younger than she expected, not even forty. For her benefit, he quickly recapped his background. It included working for the Los Angeles Police and branching out as a computer programmer. He introduced his three associates, and they all sat around an inexpensive conference table, staring at a black speaker box as they interacted with disembodied voices from Wisconsin.

Denkey's questions were direct, simple and without emotion. What was missing? Which accounts stored the money? Where was the money sent? Was it still there? According to the computer records, who authorized the transfer? What evidence suggested their accounting system had been infected with malware? Were there any markers to connect the New Year's Eve attack on the Premios database with the impacted accounting records? Were there any common security gateways between Premios and Lattigo Industries?

The questions seemed endless. The associates all took notes on their laptops. Cynthia could feel Danny's eyes watching her from across the table. It made her want to scream. None of this was getting them anywhere. The detective was only a distraction. Just like this dinner party diverted her from what she should be doing. Just like he acted earlier at the agency, now at the restaurant Danny was continuing to stare. Worrying. It was too much.

She knew she needed to take action. She just couldn't imagine what action to take. She also couldn't conceive any way that Danny would or could help.

Danny watched Cynthia. Her eyes might be focused down and toward her food—a dish that she had not touched—but he knew she was in a different place. His suggesting this dinner had been a mistake. Why had he listened to Josh's earlier suggestion that Danny ask friends to join them in a casual meal?

On the surface, the idea carried merit. Stephen and Wally were the other two people Cynthia knew in Los Angeles, and they had such a long history together. Josh probably imagined the fun they would have reminiscing about their early life in Thread. Although a teenager at the time, Danny enjoyed working for Wally at the original Loon Town Café. He recalled with fondness all the characters in that town, and the warmth of being surrounded by loving people. He wanted to recapture that emotion tonight feeling Cynthia needed that tonic to survive her uncertainty.

But within a few minutes, he realized nostalgia easily collapsed into melancholy. He failed to consider how the happy days he wanted to evoke were the very ones that defined Cynthia's falling in love with Chip. One couldn't be discussed without the other.

And whatever made him think inviting Francesca would be a good idea? Of course he could remember his original thought—how Cynthia wanted to start a family and how important being a mother was to Francesca. Yet again his best intentions proved that he was an enormous idiot. Francesca couldn't approach discussing being a parent without being reminded how her own adoption plans had shattered. And any talk of creating babies required discussing a father, which only induced in Cynthia a painful reminder of Chip's absence.

The table of five acted lively enough. Three bottles of wine ensured that. But beneath the surface the mood was brittle and everyone realized it. Danny needed to find a way to end this. The waiter was bringing the dessert menus, and even though he loved this restaurant's cakes, it would be too much an act of courage to sit through one more course.

He waved the server away. "I hope you don't mind," Danny said to the group, "but I should drive Cynthia home. It's been a long day, and if she needs a final sweet we have a freezer full of Haagen Dazs."

No one disagreed.

"Don't worry about the bill," Stephen said. "It's our treat tonight."

"In that case," joked Francesca, "bring out the champagne. These sleepy ones can go home, and we'll have a nightcap." But it was clear she was as willing to end the evening as were Danny and Cynthia.

Cynthia stood up so quickly that Danny feared it would appear rude. "Danny's right. I'm ready to turn in for the night. But don't let my leaving end your fun. Thanks so much for a wonderful evening."

Danny had never heard a phrase uttered with so little believability. Soon they were in his car, turning onto Los Feliz Boulevard, and then going uphill on the curvy street that led to his house. He kept glancing into the rear-view mirror, even though he found the glare of headlights from behind made that painfully blinding. That driver should have dimmed them, and the brightness annoyed him because he couldn't discern if the green car from earlier in the day was again following them. Eventually, Cynthia noticed his behavior.

"Is something wrong?" she asked.

He grunted no and stopped his constant looks backward. There was nothing to see anyway, and he was probably being paranoid, but since that morning when they departed the Pacific Dining Car to head to the Bradbury Building, he felt that they were being tailed.

After leaving the detective's office, he thought he saw the same green sedan, several cars back that had been in his rear view mirror after leaving the Pacific Dining Car. When they swerved toward the onramp to the Hollywood Freeway, the auto had vanished. He couldn't even be certain it was the same vehicle as earlier in the day. In fact, it was highly unlikely that it was. Why would anyone seek to follow them?

As they turned up Westhurst Drive, the road narrowed into a

tunnel of foliage. The streetlights were now old-fashioned globes and the setting reminiscent of a former era. When he glanced once more into the rearview mirror, no car was in sight. He relaxed. Nothing to worry about.

They neared the circular drive to the mansion, and he pressed the button that opened the massive iron gate. It had been Josh's idea to add that ostentatious item. On this evening, Danny was glad it existed. The gate rolled back and he drove forward. They pulled up to the front door, and he looked down to be sure the gate was closing. Just then a dark sedan drove by, its lights off.

Danny felt a chill. Where had that car come from? Where was it going? And who was in it?

Josh was ready to leave. A car was waiting to take Orleans and him back to the airport. It was time to head west, but Orleans had yet to appear in the lobby. It was unusual for her to be late, and Josh found her delay this morning particularly annoying. Nothing on this trip was going the way he planned.

So many things justified his discomfort. His mental composure was being scratched away, as though he had stepped into a patch of poison oak and rolled in it like a crazed dog. Dawdling in the lobby only intensified his itch. Because his suitcase was already safely tucked into the trunk of the Lincoln town car, he had half a mind to let Orleans find her own way to JFK.

Orleans rushed into the lobby. "Sorry, I'm late," she said, "but it was the guy from Lehman Brothers. He wanted to clarify one of our slides. He said it contradicted something later in the pack. It turns out we didn't update one figure when we did our last minute edits. But I was able to explain the discrepancy to his satisfaction."

She seemed pleased with herself. Whatever. There were bigger concerns on his plate than one minor functionary at a third-rate investment bank.

"I predict they're on board," she said. "He's a smart guy to notice a single wrong detail in the whole pack. But we had a lot to update when we had to account for the extra million in the financing. The good news is he sees our potential. I think they're in."

The driver opened the door to the rear seat and Orleans slid in and across the seat to make room for Josh. She was well dressed for the flight home, even wearing heels. Christ, the show was over, Josh thought, but he also knew how Orleans worked. In her mind, there was always the chance that a six-hour flight back to Los Angeles might turn out to be a priceless opportunity to make a deal. You never knew who might sit next to you.

"I'm not on the same flight as you," he said. Josh could see that Orleans was surprised. The driver firmly closed the door and moved toward the front seat.

"Where to, sir?" the driver asked.

"United Airlines, JFK. Take the Midtown Tunnel," he said. Orleans was about to ask him questions, but Josh pointed toward the driver to signal Orleans to stop before she even started. She took the hint and instead unfolded her *Wall Street Journal*.

He needed quiet. Too much was going on, and everything was unfolding more rapidly that he planned. On the phone earlier, Danny was glum. Clearly, his little detective work with Cynthia wouldn't prove to be illuminating. Josh tried to tell him to leave things like that to the professionals, and that it would have been better for everyone if Cynthia had stayed at home. Josh didn't need her wandering around the City of Angels and getting in the way.

At times, Josh envied people who led simple lives. Like his parents did. They were simple farmers on a hardscrabble farm on which it was nearly impossible to make a living. But they knew what each day would bring. Get up, stoke the wood furnace, head to the barn to milk the cows, come back in for a hearty breakfast, tend the fields, mend the fences, and the routine never ended. But it was straightforward and clean . . . until it ended.

Everything must end eventually, and he reminded himself that his parents' life wasn't really such an idyllic one. Despite all that work, they still failed to keep their furnace flues clean. As a result they died from a small chimney fire, which Josh knew the townsfolk of Thread blamed on the bats that took up residence and over a summer filled his parents' chimney with guano. But Josh had a different perspective. His dad should have known better. He should have cleaned those chimneys in the fall. Both his parents died that autumn morning because his dad did not pay attention to all the details. His parents' deaths were his dad's fault. No one else's.

Josh noticed Orleans was watching him with concern, and he realized he was lightly pounding his fist against his briefcase in frustration. He stopped.

"Did something happen last night?" she asked.

It was so easy to let your guard down, to let details pass by without notice, and suddenly to find yourself caught in a morass you created. He couldn't let that kind of inattention to detail kill him the way it killed his parents. Nor could he let it take down Danny.

What was really upsetting him had nothing to do with the financial markets or the increasing fragility of their upcoming public offering. The problem was centered in Los Angeles and the person he loved. Danny told him about the car he thought was following him. Josh dismissed Danny's concerns as the result of an overactive imagination, and he counseled against Danny even mentioning it to Cynthia. It would all be better in the morning he advised. Once again, he wasn't telling Danny the truth.

Well, it was morning and he doubted very much that any of it was better. Josh knew better than to hope that Chip would reappear. He knew what kind of people had pushed their tentacles into Premios, and he feared that Chip walked right into their grasp. Their friend could have left things alone, but he had to go digging.

Josh was beginning to realize his approach seldom matched that of his partners. He had been rash and full of braggadocio when he initially convinced Colby Endicott to invest in Premios. He hadn't bothered to check out the firm or really understand the source of its money. But that was his smaller error. His true hubris was allowing a vivid imagination to paint too brilliant of an opportunity for the firm's ability to track user behavior. In a sense, nothing said at his meeting with Endicott-Meyers was untrue. In reality, all things were possible with enough money and time. But even when something was possible, it didn't mean it should happen.

Endicott-Meyers was the magic lamp that Josh rubbed until a djinn appeared—and it was an evil one, but still one that was initially quite willing to grant his wishes. Money flowed in, along with more hidden forms of support. Premios became real.

Oliver helped him recruit some pretty clever programmers. More accurately, these individuals should be called hackers. They knew how to write code to sneak into the most protected sites. But that was the thing, wasn't it? Meyers' people weren't interested in hacking the Pentagon or the Federal Reserve. No, they seemed focused on uncovering the more mundane and individual truths . . . information that would allow them to manipulate people of power . . . creating profiles of their online behavior . . . leaving behind worms that dug through personal files in their quest to feed an ever-hungrier master.

Josh chose to ride this horse, thinking he could tame it. And he could. And he would. He just needed to ensure that this beast didn't buck anyone else into oblivion.

Josh had held them off for a while, while he plotted his escape path. But he had ignored an obvious thing. He needed to know their weaknesses and secrets. He needed his own worm to penetrate the heart of those behind Endicott-Meyers. He needed to find the real masters.

Their town car was passing Flushing Park and the giant metal sculpture of a globe left over from the 1964 World's Fair. He turned to comment on it to Orleans only to discover that she had been watching him.

"What's going on now?" she asked. "Why aren't you returning to L.A. with me?"

"There are people I have to see in Chicago," he said with conviction. It was time to go on the offense.

Danny wondered what he should do about Cynthia. Even though they shared a house, they were barely speaking. Truthfully, there was little for Cynthia to investigate, and the detective needed time to work. Josh had been correct when he said she should stay in Wisconsin. Danny heard his phone ring and he picked up the mobile from the kitchen table. Cynthia looked up for a moment but then returned to reading the *Los Angeles Times*.

"Danny, come down to the office. Right now. They're here." Kenosha was slightly whispering and seemed unduly excited.

"Who's 'they'?" he asked. He hadn't the slightest idea what his friend was talking about.

"Colby Endicott and his partner, Oliver Meyers. The mythic Meyers just showed up. Can you believe it? And he wants to talk to you. I thought Josh told us that there wasn't even a Meyers, but he's here.

And he's pretty good looking."

That assessment annoyed Danny. "Don't they want Josh? Why do I need to come?"

"Because they specifically asked for you. Besides no one even knows how to reach Josh. Orleans told me that he said he was heading to Chicago, and that he ditched her at JFK. Do you know what's going on?"

Embarrassingly, he didn't. The last time they talked, Josh simply said he was stopping in Chicago, Danny never thought to ask why. He simply assumed it involved the investor tour. For that matter, he had anticipated that Orleans would be traveling with Josh.

"If Orleans is back, can't she deal with them? I don't know anything about the business." He told himself that it wouldn't be good to leave Cynthia alone in the house.

"Danny, Orleans is still on her way home. Anyway I told you they asked specifically for you . . . and Cynthia." Kenosha lowered her voice even further. "They know about Chip and the missing money. They say they want to help."

Danny dreaded asking the question he was about to pose, but he needed to know. "This may sound odd, but can you describe Oliver Meyers?"

From the shift in her tone of voice, Danny knew that Kenosha was taken aback, but she quickly replied. "Okay, and not to be flippant, but he's your type of guy, so I'd think you'd want to meet him. He's probably in his mid-thirties, your height, well built, kind of dark, dangerous and Italian looking. Very well dressed."

"What about his hands?"

"Danny, you're ridiculous. He has good hands. What do you want me to say? Get down here. I don't know what to do with them. I can't pass them along to anyone else."

"Okay."

Danny's horrible feeling of doom was back. Ever since Lopez gave him a copy of *The Dumping Ground* and had told him about Oliver Meyers, Danny sought to convince himself that there was no link between the current Meyers and the Oliver he once knew. He always knew he was deluding himself. Even though Kenosha's description fit a great many men, he was certain it would be the very same Oliver

Meyers that worked at White Bark Pines nearly two decades ago in Wisconsin—the Oliver Meyers who wronged him.

He had started to read Lopez's novel the night before. The similarities between its plot line and Danny's summer with Oliver were beyond coincidence. Only one explanation existed—Oliver provided Lopez those details. It was such a breach of their privacy that Danny didn't know what he would say or do were he to encounter Oliver.

Not everything in the novel exactly mirrored his real life. His memories were certainly richer and more detailed than those in the novel. But that would have to be the case between the memories in one's mind and a story put to paper. As happened in his real life, the novel concerned an older college-bound kid working at a summer resort and a younger boy from a nearby town. They went on their daily trash dumping detail. In the novel, the younger boy was the one who took the sexual initiative. But it hadn't been that way at all. Was that the way Oliver portrayed it, or had Lopez deliberately rewritten history in his attempt to tell a story?

In real life, the first week or so of the dump runs had all been gloriously sunny days—the kind of Wisconsin June that celebrated deeply blue skies and puffy cumulus clouds. Families from Chicago filled cabins with kids who made full use of the resort's sandy beach and its swimming raft. They also generated a lot of trash. To most, emptying those large cans filled with food scraps and used paper goods in the pickup bed might have seemed a dirty job. To Danny, it was never unpleasant as long as he was able to gaze at the shirtless Oliver. Sure, he tried to be discreet so Oliver wouldn't know he was staring. Since all the boys who worked at the resort stayed in the same bunkhouse, he didn't want to create trouble. But Oliver knew. He definitely knew.

But on a day when the blue skies went missing in action, and the smell of rain showers were stronger than the odors from the back of the truck, Oliver kept his shirt on. Danny was disappointed. Oliver's behavior was understandable of course. It was cold and wet. But whether it rained or not, the resort's kitchen never faltered in generating a steady stream of trash, and they still had to take the daily run to the dumping ground.

After they emptied all the trashcans, about the time that Oliver would normally lie back against the hood of the truck and smoke his cigarette, he instead pulled off his shirt. He complained that it was completely wet from the on-and-off showers. Bare-chested, Oliver jumped back into the cab of the truck. Danny's own clothes were equally wet but he let them cling to his shivering torso. He reentered the passenger side. Something new was in the air—not trash, not rain, but a scent that was enticing and scary at the same time.

Oliver was in no hurry to return to the resort. Instead, he pulled out his pack of cigarettes, took a stick out, and lit up. "Just because it's raining doesn't mean I'm hurrying back."

He tapped the pack to push out another cigarette to offer to Danny, who shook his head no. He had never smoked.

"You know what I like to do on a rainy day like this?" Oliver asked.

He blew some smoke in Danny's direction to force him to look in Oliver's direction. Oliver was rubbing his crotch and his pants had started to tent. Danny quickly glanced away. He could hear Oliver unzip and tug. He continued to look out the rain-swept passenger window and into the now misty wood. He remembered hoping a bear would show up so that they would have to leave. It wasn't a secret what Oliver was doing. The bunkhouse didn't have a lot of privacy. Technically, each worker had his own room, but the walls were like paper, so he knew the other boys often jacked off, some obviously not caring what others heard. As for himself, Danny wasn't innocent of this, but he always tried to be extraordinarily quiet.

"You're not even going to look at what I'm doing?" Oliver's voice had a friendly, maybe mocking, tone of laughter, challenging Danny to turn and watch.

"Nah, that's okay."

Oliver actually laughed. "Hey, you think I don't know how you're always looking at me, watching me. Just like a little puppy. I keep expecting you to sneak into my room at night and try to get a close-up look. Course, I'm a pretty heavy sleeper. For all I know, maybe you have."

Danny turned to him angrily, "I would never do that."

Oliver smiled broadly. He used one hand to tap the ash of his cigarette, but didn't stop stroking with the other. Danny had never seen another man's erect penis. Oliver seemed so much bigger than he expected.

Oliver tossed his cigarette out the open window. With his hand now free, he moved over to grasp Danny's wrist. "You should touch it," he said.

Danny wanted to protest, but he let it happen, and the hot skin felt electric.

Danny never forgot that moment—even after everything Oliver would later do.

As Danny and Cynthia drove toward the Premios office in downtown Los Angeles, Danny continued to grasp at the small hope that he would discover the person waiting was not the person he feared seeing, but as soon as they walked into the office he could see that the waiting person was Oliver. The rainy day in the Ford truck returned. Danger faced him, and he couldn't force himself to turn away. Oliver looked at Danny. He clearly recognized him, knew who he was, remembered what had happened, but still said nothing.

"Good, you made it," Kenosha said. "I was afraid you would change your mind. They're predicting such a heavy rain."

She made the introductions and ushered them into the conference room. Soon she was back with cups and a carafe of coffee. Danny felt wooden, yearning to find a way out, unable to mumble even a courtesy. He could tell that Cynthia was puzzled. Colby spoke first, "Kenosha, I think you can leave us now. This is more of a private conversation."

Kenosha paused for a moment waiting for a signal from Danny as to whether he wanted her to leave. But he wasn't helping her much. He was amazed how much Oliver still looked like the teenager back in 1985. He had thickened a bit with age, and Danny could see that his hair was already starting to recede, but he still had beautiful hands and now his nails were well manicured. Just as he found Jesus Lopez both compelling and threatening, he felt the same about seeing Oliver.

"What do you want?" Danny asked, and he knew without seeing Cynthia's expression that his tone was rude. But if they wanted to talk to him they could have come to the house. Colby knew where they lived. Better yet, they should have waited for Josh. He was the real leader of Premios.

Colby answered, "I know it's a stressful time, and although you've never met my partner . . . "

Oliver interrupted Endicott. "Actually Danny and I have met. It's been years, but we worked at the same resort for a summer. We were a bunch of kids, thinking we were living the movie *Dirty Dancing*."

Cynthia brightened, "You worked at White Bark Pines? Sometimes my parents and I drove down there for dinner. Were you a waiter? Maybe you served us?"

As he answered, Oliver kept his eyes on Danny, but Danny refused to let their eyes meet. "No, I worked in the kitchen and in the yards. I'm sure I would have remembered meeting you."

Colby seemed confused. Clearly, he had never heard of a connection between Danny and Oliver. "Well that's interesting. Of course, I know Oliver's from the Midwest and he told me once that he vacationed as a kid near Lattigo, but this is news to me. Maybe that explains why Oliver has always been so eager to help out.

"Cynthia, we heard about your missing husband and the suspicions about the missing cash. Obviously we don't know your husband well, but he is a fellow investor in Premios, and while Oliver's never met him . . ."

He stopped for a moment as a new thought percolated forward.

"Or have you?"

Oliver shook his head no.

"The whole scenario is so strange. As investors, we need to ensure that no suspicion interferes with the planned public offering of Premios. It wouldn't be fair to you or Chip to let any momentary confusion lessen the value of your investment. While we are certain there is a good explanation for what's going on, we just need to find Chip. And I'm sure you would agree.

"That's why we wanted to meet. You need to know that we're on your side. That we will do anything we can to help. All you need to do is ask."

Cynthia seemed touched. Skepticism was not a part of her make-up. Danny was convinced that these two were worried about her husband only because of their investment. They didn't really care what happened to Cynthia's husband and Danny's friend.

"We've hired a private investigator," Cynthia said.

Oliver was quick to ask, "And has he uncovered anything?"

"Not yet," she replied.

"If he does, please keep us informed."

Danny started to tune out. This conversation could have been done with a phone call. Once before Oliver had demonstrated himself as beyond untrustworthy. He suspected that something unsaid was behind the man's appearance today.

Oliver reached over to tap Danny's hand and pull him back into the conversation. "Before we go, Danny, I wanted to let you know that I am the one who insisted Colby set up this meeting. Ever since I discovered you were part of the Premios team, I wanted to see you. But I didn't feel it appropriate. Maybe I didn't dare.

"But as awful as this situation is, I couldn't let it pass by without trying to correct something horrible I once did to you.

"Danny, I want to apologize for anything I ever did to hurt you."

Session Eight

I like to take risks. That's just the kind of guy I am. But you already knew that. The thing is that when you're smart and talented, it becomes harder and harder to find risks that really excite you.

Danny's a perfect example. At first, it was fun to play with him from afar, even though that often meant I didn't get firsthand insight into how he responded. But tracking how he changed over time told me what I needed to know. There was something intriguing about molding him into that person who always sits on the edge of the fence, who can't place his feet on either side of the delicate balance between daring and fearing. But to me, neither a gung-ho daredevil nor a slobbering introvert would be very interesting.

Still there are only so many tricks you can play by yourself. Sooner or later, you have to involve others. That's when the ground becomes slippery and the chase more dangerous.

The problem is you never really know what's going on in the mind of another. Maybe you think you do, doc, given your profession and all, but I assure you: you never know what your partner in crime really wants.

So when you align yourself with new players, you have your goals and they have theirs. You can't know who's playing what game, and who thinks who's ahead.

But when the music stops playing, you just want to be sure you have a chair to sit in.

And I fear the music is about to stop.

CHAPTER EIGHT

Reckoning

Josh heard the bell from the front door. The buzzing sound disturbed him because it emitted a low buzzing as though it were about to give out. They had rewired the entire house when they put in an alarm system, including the entry system monitoring, and the elaborate system cost a fortune. Josh always wanted the best, and, for example, although they were sitting in the dining room, if they had been in the kitchen Josh could have looked at a small screen to see who was at the front door. If something were already failing, he would be making an angry call to the alarm company in the morning.

The alarm system didn't do much good if Danny and guests like Kenosha forgot to set it. Each time Danny brought up the idea that someone tampered with the cellar door, Josh wondered, but chose not to ask, if Kenosha bothered to set the alarm that evening. He knew she didn't; she never bothered. At times, he too failed to activate the continuous video monitoring, but there were occasions when he preferred it not to be active. Still he liked to imagine the look on Kenosha's face if he could have pulled up on his computer the video files for the night in question. It could have ended all discussion of any attempted entry—one way or the other. He didn't really care, because he knew it ultimately didn't matter.

"I'll get the door," he said.

He needed a reason to leave the dinner table. Francesca was dining with them in yet another useless attempt by Danny to cheer Cynthia. Earlier, arriving home from the downtown office, he heard Danny, Cynthia and Francesca making a great rumble of noise in the kitchen. When he walked into that room, it was a mess. Kettles and ingredients were everywhere. Every one of the six burners on the huge stove was flaring at their hottest settings. The industrial fan was sucking out the steam and heat with great brio. But he was happy to see Danny laughing, as were Francesca and Cynthia, so he said nothing. Besides, the kitchen smelled of slow-braised short ribs and a chocolate cake. If they had brought out a great red wine, it might not be such a bad evening. At least, that's what he hoped.

He wanted to be in a good mood. His stop in Chicago had given him the information he needed to be the victor in the fight ahead. There was just one remaining bit needed, and the person he expected at the door should be carrying that information.

Just as Josh stood up to go to the entry, Danny said in puzzlement, "Who could be at the door? Didn't you close the gate and set the alarm when you got home?"

In fact, Josh had kept the gate open because he was expecting someone. What he failed to do was alert Danny to the anticipated visitor. He knew Danny would oppose Jesus Lopez stopping by, but sometimes, he had to do things Danny didn't like just so the two of them would be safe. Besides, he couldn't understand what Danny had against his old professor. Sure, the guy was a bit out there with the creepy stuff he conjured up. But they were just stories. For a writer, Danny lacked appreciation for the power of the imagination, just like he didn't understand how nasty real life could be.

Josh decided to be blunt since it was best to get it over with. "It's Jesus, I asked him to bring something by." What passed over Danny's face surprised Josh, because it seemed something greater than anger. Maybe he had made a mistake. He was too eager to get this information; he should have waited to see Jesus in the morning.

"Don't worry," Josh continued, "I won't ask him in. We can talk in the foyer. He's just dropping off some files I need."

Cynthia was listening intently. "Is that the man who had breakfast with Chip? I'm coming with you. I want to meet him because Danny is always giving me excuses why we can't." She picked up her wine glass and stood.

"Hey, I'm always up for seeing brilliantly crazy novelists. The world has so few of them," Francesca stood as well. Josh realized she was drunk. They were well into their third bottle of Bordeaux.

Josh could see this was going in the wrong direction. He needed to get them all seated again before Danny grew too upset. Besides he had real business to discuss with Jesus that couldn't involve third parties. "Just wait here and eat dessert," he suggested, "I'll bring Jesus in for a quick hello when we're done."

"No," Cynthia said firmly. "You're just in league with Danny. You'll let this Lopez guy slip away and I won't get to ask him anything."

What could he say? He knew how to change things on the fly. It would be better if Cynthia hung on to her hopes, and maybe seeing Lopez would help. "Come along if you want."

Reluctantly Danny stood as well. He gulped the last of his glass before refilling it with the rest of the bottle. His glare warned Josh of trouble ahead. There was always trouble ahead.

Insistently, the doorbell sounded again. Something was definitely failing in the system, but Josh stepped quickly to the entry. He'd worry about the alarm system later.

The four of them entered the foyer, a two-story space where a tiled staircase curved up to a second floor landing—one way led to the musician's overlook to the large living room and the other to the hallway connecting the two main bedroom suites. A vaguely Spanish wrought-iron pendant hung from the center of the room. It cast a yellowish light over the group of four as Josh opened the door.

For a moment, Jesus Lopez appeared startled, but then broke into an infectious grin. "A welcoming party. How kind? And here I thought you just wanted to get the resumes of my most promising students. What's up?"

Josh noticed that Jesus's look lingered on Danny. Why was he trying to read him? What was up with that?

Cynthia jumped in. "I'm Chip Grant's wife. I wanted to meet you, and everyone followed me. People tell me that you're the last person who saw my husband."

Jesus looked appropriately concerned. "I'm sure many people have seen your husband since me. Perhaps he just needs a few days for himself."

Cynthia eyed the lanky writer "Is that what you really think?"

Jesus smiled sadly and simply replied, "Have faith in your husband."

Josh feared that Jesus was a matador flinging a red flag in front of an already moody Danny. Once again, he regretted his decision not asking Lopez to come to the office. "I'm sorry I asked you to come all the way out here. I'm sure you have better things to do this evening, so let me just take what you brought over, and we can plan to talk tomorrow by phone. I should go back to our guests."

It seemed a clear enough hint to all of them.

"Stop," Cynthia demanded, "I want to hear how Chip acted at breakfast."

Lopez didn't pick up on Josh's cue to leave. He answered, "Chip was calm."

Josh thought that interesting description was also an apt way to describe Jesus.

Jesus went on. "He had questions and he thought Oliver and I might have answers."

At the mention of Oliver, Danny tensed. Josh never understood why Danny so disliked his old writing teacher. After the first few classes with the man, it seemed the professor evoked a real passion in Danny. But then Danny read *Broken Beauty* and everything changed. After reading the book for himself, Josh agreed the story line was dismaying. Yet he never fully understood why Danny found it so upsetting. After all, the reviews were grudgingly positive.

Jesus seemed ready to leave, but then paused. "There is one thing I don't think I ever mentioned to Danny or the police. Being here made me think of it.

"Your husband seemed surprisingly interested in this house. At first, I thought he was engaging in idle chitchat. That's the kind of thing you do with new people—you know how one lingers on the few things held in common. Since we had both been in this house the night we met, it seemed a natural thing to discuss, and of course it is a beautiful place. Later I realized there might have been more to our conversation because Chip wanted to know something.

"He seemed to think the house harbored a secret room, and he wanted to know what I knew. I guess he thought such a thing would appeal to a writer with my reputation. Perhaps he expected to hear about dungeons or such."

Josh kept his eyes from rolling. How often would he have to listen to Jesus' made-up nonsense? Everyone knew the former owner was merely a crazy man who collected horror memorabilia. Of course a home like that would have its "secret" rooms.

Francesca perked at the mention of the hidden lairs. Her glass was empty again. "I told these guys about this very thing. The last time I was here, we were about to go on a search. Maybe Chip heard me talk about them. Know what? I want to take a look. Let's go on a search."

"Sounds good to me," Jesus said. Josh was convinced he did it merely to annoy Danny.

"If it was of interest to Chip, then I want to look," Cynthia declared.

Danny was not interested, but always wanting to be the accommodating host, he was unwilling to quash the suggestion.

Josh decided to end this nonsense. No secret rooms needed any exploration. "Come on guys, what are we going to do? Tap on all the walls? Turn the sconces? Really, don't you think if there were any dungeons or lairs, we would have discovered them during the remodel?"

"Let's at least take the tour. You know, I've never seen the lower levels and I'd like to," Francesca's words were slightly slurred. Danny looked at Josh and then agreed with Francesca's request. Josh thought he did it as some kind of payback on Josh for inviting Jesus over.

"Okay. This way," he said. There was no use fighting. They headed through the dining room and into the cluttered kitchen. Thank God, the cleaning woman would be in tomorrow. Everything was a mess. "We can take the back stairs to reach the lowest level. It was the old service basement."

He flipped the light switch, and they descended the first flight. At the first landing, they kept going. There was no reason to dally on this floor. It only contained several guest bedrooms and the old billiards room. They continued descending to the lowest level. Josh could feel the chill of the bottom floor, which was always cold even when the heat was at full blast. At this level, the exterior walls were completely concrete and two-thirds of them were buried into the hillside. Even on the sunniest of days, the space remained dim—only the south side held windows. In the remodel, Josh transformed the original collection of storage, furnace and laundry rooms into one large game room that could also serve as a screening room. The north wall was lined with bookcases, and in its center an archway opened into the wine cellar dug into the hillside—Josh's pride and joy.

Francesca stumbled out of the stairwell into the room. He couldn't let her have any more wine. As it was they would need to call her a cab or make her stay the night. Just what he wanted, another guest in the house.

The basement seemed ghostly in the moonlight filtering through the windows. Josh flipped the light switch to transform the room with a blaze of light. At the other end of the room, he noticed the curtains were flapping. The room seemed even colder than usual.

"What the hell," Josh said. Why was a window open? He strode to the moving drapery. Beneath it, the floor was littered with broken glass. The security system must have been compromised. Someone had shattered the window to break into the room. Then he remembered how he had left the system off because Jesus was coming over.

Everyone looked at Josh. Despite the wine, even Francesca recognized the implications of the flapping curtain and the glinting shards.

"So I guess it wasn't Kenosha's imagination after all," Danny declared. "Someone broke in. But for what?"

Danny was equally angry and afraid. Ever since their return from Wisconsin, Josh had minimized Kenosha's concern about a house break-in. Now the broken glass proved she was correct. Somebody was threatening their well being, but his sense of justification was balanced by a chilling premonition that things were about to turn dark.

"What's going on?" he demanded of Josh. "Why would someone break into our house? What are they looking for?"

Josh looked at him in befuddlement. "How would I know? It's probably local kids. You know they're always smoking shit on those stair streets."

"Maybe they do, but you know that's not what's happening here."

Danny didn't understand his own fervor. Maybe being near Lopez was a kind of emotional catalyst, and Danny wasn't about to back away. By some logic he felt to be true, Josh and he were clearly embroiled in someone's devious plot. He needed Josh to acknowledge it.

As a kid, a teenager, and even a young adult, Danny was always too quick to back down. Rocking the boat was never his style. He needed people around him to be happy, and he lacked the confidence to act on his own beliefs. Confronting someone he loved and accusing him of keeping secrets required a major shift. Yet he knew this man he loved was keeping something hidden because Josh should have been more surprised by the shattered glass pane, but instead it seemed he half expected it.

And Josh wore the melting look of betrayal. It was a look scarred into Danny's psyche. He had seen it as an adolescent watching the movies with Pete. And he faced it again at summer's end with Oliver so many years ago. Only that time the traitor's face was also streaked with derision. Tonight Josh was at risk of joining the camp of Pete and Oliver. Not only was he keeping something from Danny, but also he clearly knew he was in the wrong.

"You know what they're looking for, don't you!"

Danny's voice held a steeliness that as much surprised him as it comforted him. Francesca and Cynthia moved awkwardly as though to escape the scene; they only knew the weaker Danny. He was tired of letting others direct his life. It was time to be someone stronger.

Josh went on the offensive. "Who's the 'they,' Danny? We don't know who did this. We don't even know that a broken window means something."

Danny refused to accept these denials. "Okay, have it your way. Keep trying to tell me there's nothing going on. You can tell Cynthia that Chip will reappear and that money hasn't been stolen from the Lattigo Nation. You can try to convince Kenosha she's crazy, imagining someone was sneaking into our house. You can even tell me over and over that I haven't been followed. Guess what? It won't do any good. Nothing you say is true, and we all know it. And you know what else? I believe the same person and car that followed me followed Chip. Our friend came here to help us, and now he's gone. Someone breaks into our house, and you pretend it's coincidence and that everything will be all right, and I won't just go along anymore."

Cynthia caught her breath, and Danny turned to her.

"I know Cynthia. We all want to believe that Chip's okay. And none of us accept the police explanation that he's a thief. We know your husband. He's smart. He's loyal. But we have to face reality. He must have found something he wasn't supposed to. If he ran off, he would let us know he was alive. He cares too much to do any less. And it can't be a kidnapping . . . because who would have done that and why hasn't there been a ransom? He's gone."

Josh pulled Danny into a fierce hug that wasn't meant to console but to control him. He whispered for only Danny to hear, "You need to stop this. You're freaking out Cynthia. Calm down and support her. Then we can get rid of everyone, and I'll tell you what I've tried to keep hidden."

Suddenly Danny felt calm and totally sober. The danger was real; he wasn't imagining it; and he needed to be in control.

He looked over Josh's shoulder at a shaken Cynthia and his eyes tried to convey how sorry he was. Francesca was collapsed into a chair, staring at her glass. Then he saw Lopez. The man was barely holding back a self-satisfied smirk. Suddenly, everything made sense. He didn't know where the thought came from, and it hardly seemed possible. Yet from all he knew of Lopez and after reading *The Dumping Ground*, he could believe anything was possible.

He wrestled free of Josh's grasp to swing angrily at Lopez. "It's fucking Oliver, isn't it?"

Josh looked at him in amazement. "What the hell are you talking about? Oliver who?"

"Oliver Meyers! Our partner."

Now Lopez was actually smiling, and Danny was again encircled with Josh's arms. No matter how much Danny wanted to, Josh wouldn't let him hit the professor.

Lopez said, "Seriously. You think a multi-millionaire investor is behind a minor break-in."

"Why not? He's already stolen my life and handed it over to you."

"I don't know what you mean."

Lopez wasn't rattled, but Josh was upset. "Danny, what are you talking about?"

Danny felt drugged. Maybe he drank too much; yet all he could think of was that slim volume resting by his bedside. In that novel, names and locations may have been altered, but the book's spirit spun the story of Oliver's summer betrayal. Except that the story's point of view cast a light that made Danny the villain, not the victim, of that adolescent web. If Oliver would stoop so low as to betray an entire summer of memories, then who could predict what else he might do. Despite his apology to Danny just days earlier, Danny considered the possibility that Oliver blamed Danny. Maybe he wanted to get into this house to attack Danny. Maybe the only reason his company had invested in Premios was because Danny was one of the owners. The world overflowed with psychopaths, and that long ago summer surely proved that Oliver was such a person.

"Danny, breathe deeply and tell me what you mean." Josh continued to hold Danny tight, who felt comforted in Josh's arms.

As though to apologize for her personal dilemma causing such anxiety, Cynthia lightly touched Danny on his arm.

Danny took that deep breath. He needed it. He realized he needed to disclose something hidden too long from Josh. While he never planned to discuss that summer with Oliver, there was no way out now. Where to start? Not even wanting to say the man's name aloud, he nodded in Lopez's direction.

"His newest novel. It's about me. The whole thing covers a summer in my life. A summer with Oliver Meyers." He almost choked on the last sentence.

Cynthia looked away. She knew what was to come. After their brief meeting with Oliver and his unexpected apology, Danny disclosed an abbreviated version of the summer's events to Cynthia. He also told her he never wanted Josh to know.

Josh looked at him with incredulity. "Danny, this is Jesus Lopez we're talking about. Like you always say, he only writes about horrible people and horrible things. Whatever could have happened in your life that he'd find interesting?"

Danny fell quiet. Josh and he always promised to be truthful with one another, and in many ways they lived up to that commitment. In the past, Danny spoke freely about the pain and loss of his mother's suicide, and he even shared the story of the movies and Pete Peterson. In turn, Danny knew how guilt from his parents' accidental deaths years ago plagued Josh. In a way, the two of them met because of the respective tragedies, and they became the people they were only because of the sadness in their lives. But sometimes the things you weren't willing to tell anyone were the things that defined you. Some facts seemed so destructive that just a hint of them might force others to completely reexamine what they believed of you. Some truths were not worth the risk of being disclosed.

Lopez actually chuckled. "Thanks for that vote of confidence, Josh. I thought you placed higher value in my writing. But I guess not.

"As for you Danny. You were once my prize student. I had such hopes for what you could become. I tried to test you and make you strong, but you broke so easily, the way you wasted your talents with writing that silly 'zine. As a teacher, it's hard to watch someone fritter away their potential."

Danny didn't care what the man thought. "So you pay me back by letting Oliver talk you into absconding with my life."

"Really, Danny, your thinking is so narrow. Why assume it was Oliver who told me your little secret? Do you really think no one else knew what was going on?"

Danny felt unable to say anything. Why would Lopez say such a thing? No one else could have known all the details. That summer was a secret between Oliver and Danny.

Francesca stirred in her chair. It was as though Danny's outburst had sobered her up.

"Don't you think we should call the police?" she asked.

Cynthia retreated to her bedroom. The evening was all too much. She had known Danny and Josh for years and before tonight had never seen them so poised for a knockdown fight. She had no desire to be dragged into their differences. Her own problems were so huge. She glanced down at the wastebasket beside the lounge chair. The wrapping from the pregnancy kit was still there. After all this time trying to start a family, and now the test gave her the positive color that she wanted to see for so long, but she had no audience for her good news, and she feared that the small life growing inside of her could be all that remained of Chip.

Danny was right. Each of them was dancing around the precipice of truth. The only explanation for Chip's disappearance—and she should accept it—was death. If she knew for certain that Chip was gone, she could deal with it. But lingering in limbo was too tortuous.

Through the window, the empty hills of a dark Griffith Park rolled northward. At night she could see little, but she noticed a circling police helicopter about a mile away. Its spotlight remained centered on a small area. For a moment she wondered if the police were already in pursuit of some suspicious vagrant in response to Josh's incident call. That was the way life worked for Josh and Danny: one call to 911 and the Los Angeles Police Department was in full pursuit on their behalf.

On the other hand, she was forced to dig for the smallest bits of information. When she finally uncovered them, they proved unsatisfactory. Earlier in the day, her detective Samuel Denkey called from Thomas's office in Lattigo. He had flown to Wisconsin to investigate the company's accounts onsite. After examining the financials, Thomas and Denkey asked for the conference call to brief her, but it only left her with more questions.

During that entire phone meeting, she sat in the same chair that she sat in now. Throughout the detailed disclosures, she stared out the same window. In the daylight, the rain-fed hills seemed almost as green as Ireland. She longed to escape the detective's drone by losing herself in the verdant grasses. Sometimes on this visit, she watched deer in the far hills of the park. Their presence always made her think of their Wisconsin home. Something about deer had always brought a smile to Chip and her, especially in the spring when they spotted a young fawn bounding through the brush with childish joy.

Thomas began the call. "The million dollars is definitely gone," he said. "We can't trace where the funds ultimately went and there seems no way to recover any of it."

Denkey jumped in. "But I'm confident your husband didn't take the money, and I would testify to that in court. I've talked to the local police, shared my reasons and they now hold the same view."

"What's changed?" Cynthia asked.

"We've looked at the details. They simply don't support the idea of embezzlement. It's a crack team working at this computer site, as one would expect in any well-run data-hosting center. Your husband hired the best, and together we've scoured the code. The hackers were clever, but they left enough crumbs that we can piece together what happened.

"It looks like this. The hackers used a weakness in the Premios firewalls to embed their malware in the company's database. This is what happened back on New Year's Eve. By itself, that was likely a diversion to mask their real attack on the Lattigo Industries enterprise resource planning system. The hackers buried another piece of code— the one that triggered the embezzlement. We've tracked both pieces of malware back to that server farm Chip discovered in the Valley, the one that was dismantled. We're still trying to identify who rented that facility and when." Denkey paused.

Cynthia found his accounting insufficient. "I don't get it. What you describe seems a very complicated way to steal a million dollars. Why stop there? Lattigo Industries is nearly a billion dollar business. Once they did it, surely, they could have transferred more."

Thomas murmured his agreement, and Cynthia sensed he was silently urging Denkey to say more.

"Mrs. Grant, you're right. We know that we're still missing something. I guess you would call it the motive, or the payoff. This whole computer virus thing seems too complex and thought out for the amount that was taken, but at the same time too simplistic if it was intended to be a repeat job. But examining the books makes one thing perfectly clear."

"What's that?" she asked.

His reply was quick. "There's no way your husband would do this. I'm not saying that because I know anything about his character. But there's no reason for him to steal anything. Thomas gave me full access not only to the files for Lattigo Industries, but also to the books of the Lattigo Nation for which Mr. Grant is the chief. He also connected me with the manager of your personal finances. I've seen all the books, and examined them in detail. It makes no sense that anyone would steal a million dollars when you already have so much.

"As I'm sure you know, your company is financially sound. There's also no need to bolster the Lattigo Nation, which is likely one of the wealthiest Native American reservations in the country. It was among the first to offer Indian gambling. And on a personal level, Chip and you are extremely wealthy. Your personal assets are close to fifty times what went missing. If he wanted to disappear with a million dollars, there were far easier ways to accomplish it.

"In fact, recent activities show that Mr. Grant continues to be a very astute trader. Even though he long ago left his Wall Street firm, during the fall he placed major positions that anticipated the steep market decline this month. That investment alone has significantly increased your bottom line.

"Given all that, I am certain someone set him up."

Cynthia was surprised—first by Denkey's newfound confidence in Chip but also in his recounting of her family's well being. She never paid much attention to their portfolio and seldom considered how wealthy they might be. Hearing it aloud made her somewhat uncomfortable. "I guess with Premios about to go public, we'll be even richer," she joked.

Both Denkey and Thomas remained silent a beat too long. "About that," Thomas said, "the Premios stake is the only Internet investment in your family's portfolio. It's clear from your husband's notes that he evaluated the firm as having significant weaknesses. Now, this is only my own opinion, but given the current market volatility, I don't see any way Premios could successfully launch a public offering."

Thomas suddenly halted, as though he felt he had gone too far in being frank.

"That's not what Josh says," Cynthia responded. She knew Danny well enough to be certain he too thought everything was good with their company.

"It might be better not to mention our concerns to either of your hosts," Denkey warned.

"Why?"

"Premios was one of the things Mr. Grant was researching when he disappeared. I think it's prudent to keep our suspicions to ourselves. It's at least a possibility that Premios is somehow part of this."

Earlier in the day, Cynthia hadn't known what to do with that information, and she still didn't. She continued to stare out the window. The police helicopter was gone, but there was a glow emanating from that part of the hills as though there were now spotlights on the ground. She pulled the draperies closed. She wanted to retreat into safety, but she didn't know where to go.

There was a rap at the door. Danny stuck his head in, "Francesca's about to leave, and I thought you might want to say good-bye."

Cynthia would have preferred remaining cloistered in the suite, but she supposed she owed everyone the courtesy of saying good night. "Of course," she said and followed Danny through the hall, down the stairs, and into the foyer. Francesca and Josh were standing by an already opened door. That strange writer was nowhere to be seen; perhaps he had already left.

"What did the police say?" she asked Danny. They were descending the stairs. Their footsteps landing on the tiled risers echoed in the night. Francesca and Josh looked up.

"They haven't been here yet," Josh replied. She was going to mention seeing the helicopters, but then stopped herself. The sooner the farewells were given, the sooner she could retire.

As she approached the door, a police car pulled into the driveway. An officer stepped out, and he seemed startled to see a group of people framed in the doorway. The driver also exited the car.

"Well, I guess they're here now," Cynthia said to Danny.

The two men ascended the stairs together. Perhaps it was only her imagination, but Cynthia heard the thumping sounds of the helicopter returning to the area. She also thought the officers seemed unusually grim for responding to a house burglary.

The taller officer was the first to speak, "We're looking for Cynthia Grant."

Danny pointed to her, and the officer began to approach. Suddenly, hope rose within her. She was ashamed of her days of doubt. Chip had been found, and she was about to be whole again. She felt a smile trying to emerge, because they must be here with answers.

"I'm very sorry, ma'am, but we believe we have found your husband. Earlier in the evening, a hiker found a body in the park that is carrying your husband's identification and matches his description."

All hope died.

Session Nine

As Sherlock Holmes might say, "The game is afoot." Or was that from Shakespeare. I forget.

Some might think I'm losing control. I certainly never intended for anyone to die. At least that's what I tell myself. That's what I have always told myself.

But shit happens.

You have to go with the flow, and remember what it's all about.

And it's all about Danny.

I think that's all I want to say for today.

PART THREE

THE STORM BREAKS

CHAPTER NINE

Coping

Above Cynthia the sky was a clear, deep blue. Tomorrow she would leave Los Angeles, return to Wisconsin, and bury Chip. Finally released by the coroner, his body was already shipped there and his tribe was preparing a final tribute. Cynthia would arrive in time for that event. But first, she felt compelled to make a more personal final farewell, and she would remain stoic.

She needed to see the site where Chip died, and she needed to go by herself. Learning exactly where that spot was took more effort than Cynthia thought it should. Only after much prodding did the detective in charge reluctantly provide the needed details. He warned her that there was nothing left to see, except for trampled brush, and that viewing the place where Chip's body had been dumped could only evoke unhappy thoughts. She disagreed. She knew what she needed.

Her plan outraged Danny, who insisted he should go with her. He tried every approach to convince her: he maintained the park was a big and wild place—a mountain lion had recently been spotted within its hundreds of acres; she might get lost; or maybe the killer was hanging around. She didn't accept his concerns. She was a northwoods girl who could take care of herself. All she needed was time alone, and if she decided to shed a few tears at the site, then there was no need for Danny, Josh, or anyone else to be on hand. Perhaps she clung to some element of Chip's heritage, because she desperately longed to believe that Chip's spirit awaited her in that wild ravine.

She found it easy to follow the detective's detailed instructions. Because there was no way to drive to the location, he told her to park on Commonwealth and walk up that residential street. Its neatly manicured lawns and well-kept homes on that beautiful February morning reminded her that the comfortable world the neighborhood represented had vanished for her. These houses appeared inviting and warm—so unlike Danny and Josh's monstrous hulk of a mansion—and could be places where families might grow old together. She thought of the baby within her and knew that wouldn't happen for her. According to a local doctor she consulted, Cynthia would be a mother by early fall. When she found Chip's final spot, she intended to whisper that news into the wind, and if the universe were fair, it would carry the information to wherever Chip's spirit might be.

She parked her car near the end of the street not far from where an iron pipe stretched across the pavement to bar traffic from going further. Danny told her that several park roads remained closed as a result of damage from a major earthquake in the early nineties. She walked north on Commonwealth, skirted the barrier, and passed a slightly overgrown park nursery. She then turned right onto another closed road, Vista Del Valle, where it veered to the east and up the hill. The detective speculated that whoever dumped Chip's body had used a bypass through the nursery to drive up the abandoned road.

As she ascended the road, Cynthia encountered walkers, many with their dogs, each of the individuals smiling and saying good morning, but she found the good will of the early morning hikers bordering on the unbearable. Two women, each pushing their respective small child in a fashionable stroller, chatted with animation. When they noticed Cynthia, they smiled at her as if they could tell that she was soon to join their ranks.

The morning sun was warm. Her steady uphill trek was making her perspire. She stopped to catch her breath and noticed the view. In the far distance, she could see the towers of Hollywood and even further off the blue sheen of the Pacific. Nearer in on a close-by ridge was the silhouette of Danny's home, close enough that she could even see the outline of the window into her room. So close. During all her days of fear and worry, she might have seen the tops of the trees that shielded Chip's body from view. If only she had known where to look.

Near yet another sharp curve, she spotted a dirt road going off to the right. This was where the detective told her to walk. It was really more of a trail than a road, and it led into an unexpected pine forest that felt alien to these arid hills. Although the trees weren't the same type of conifers as those that surrounded her house back in Wisconsin, entering their shade felt like crossing back within the boundaries of a world that had been home. Only the tall Mexican palm stretching skyward through the evergreens disturbed her illusion.

When Danny tried to talk his way into joining this hike, he mentioned these woods were used as filming sites because they were close to the studios and felt like a northwoods setting. Even now the site seemed familiar. Perhaps she had seen the grove substituted for Wisconsin in some movie or television show. It was foolish to think this way, but somehow it seemed appropriate that Chip's final journey in this world transported him through such woods, and that perhaps these trees prepared his spirit to enter its next stage of being. She could only hope.

The police speculated that Chip's murderer drove his car all the way into these woods, parked in the clearing that sported a few picnic tables, and then dragged Chip's body through the woods before rolling it downhill into a deep ravine filled with poison oak. There was another possibility. The dumping spot wasn't far from the end of a residential street that abutted the park and ended with a small gate allowing pedestrian access to the park. But the police deemed that entry unlikely since the houses on the steep hilly street sat right on the street. The killer would have recognized how easily the residents could have seen him if he had parked there.

In all probability, Cynthia was now following the same path taken by her husband's killer, but it didn't help her accept or understand what had occurred. She knew the police speculated on why the murderer would dump a body so close to the park's edge. Often bodies were found deep in the park according to the lead detective, but he suggested that the killer had been in a hurry since he hadn't even bothered to bury the body.

She reached the spot and stood on a knoll above the ravine. Based on the pattern of broken brush, the police determined the killer sent the body rolling downhill from this location. Cynthia could see the ground at the base of the ravine trampled from the police investigation, but she judged it too steep for her to scramble down. Besides there was no need. If Chip were still here in some ethereal way, he would certainly sense her presence. She sat in the shade of a twisted California oak, using a low horizontal branch as her bench. In the shade of the trees, she appreciated the fact that it was still a California winter. A light breeze chilled her, but she was calm.

"Goodbye, Chip," she whispered.

In the wind that rustled through the trees, she yearned to feel the light brush of his touch—but she was too realistic to expect it.

"I loved you," she said, this time more loudly. "We were meant for each other. From the moment I saw you, I knew. We should have had so many years together as family. I didn't get to tell you that I'm pregnant, but I hope you know, wherever you are, that there now exists a combined part of both of us. You will live on."

In a rush, her emotions overwhelmed her. She could no longer play the widow controlling her sorrow. She sank to the ground and her tears were soon followed by sobs. It was too much. Life had promised her so much more and now it was all gone.

Something rustled behind her. For a moment she thought Danny had followed her, so she turned around in anger, but all she saw was a young buck stepping into the dappled sunlight, and it reminded her of the Lattigo legend of Frozen Bear and the myth that he transformed himself into many different creatures to return to his true love. Suddenly she knew that she would never be truly alone. She dried her tears.

"Goodbye, Chip. I will always remember you," she whispered again. The deer ran off.

It was time to leave, but Cynthia was reluctant to return to the house. Danny and Josh would be there, and they always had their unending questions. She didn't want to talk. Instead she returned to the nearby path and rather than retrace her path, she turned downhill, venturing onto new routes.

The path was narrow, steep, and muddy from recent rains. But she could hear the murmur of running water. Soon she found herself alongside a seasonal flow of water. Everything was lushly green, and there were frogs croaking in the small pools of the stream. She didn't know where she was headed exactly, or how long this detour might take in getting her back to her car, but she knew she had a map of the neighborhood in her bag and wasn't worried. This setting removed her from the urban stress of Los Angeles, and that was where she wanted to be.

Eventually, her rivulet broadened into something that could actually be called a small stream, and her muddy path joined up with a gravel road. The stream cascaded through a set of baby rapids and then dropped some ten feet in a small waterfall beside the road. The water was picking up speed.

Ahead she spotted another long pipe gate closing off this park road from the actual city street just beyond. The real world waited, and it couldn't be escaped. She walked through the gate and onto the street pavement. Beside her the stream broadened as it flowed beneath a wooden bridge that formed the driveway to a sleek modern house of the fifties. Cynthia always thought of Los Angeles as a desert, and yet on this street some lucky person lived with his own little river.

Perhaps all things were possible. One fact was certain. It was time to leave Los Angeles. She would not give up searching for Chip's killers, even if the police did. Someone robbed Chip and her company; someone framed Chip; and someone killed him. She wouldn't rest until she knew who that someone was.

She walked a bit further. The stream was gone. She realized it must have been diverted into underground culverts to be hidden from life and the sun. Cities destroyed nature. This city destroyed her husband. But she would overcome it and she would honor Chip.

And she would do it without the help of Danny or Josh.

Today everything annoyed Josh: the polished concrete floors, the exposed ceilings, the rows of workstations, and the perky kids pounding away at their computers. Josh was sick of Premios and everything it stood for. Yet at the same time, the company remained his obsession. Last week, the Fed raised the discount rate; the Dow Jones continued to flounder; and their bankers asked too many questions. He needed to stay focused, but there was always the matter of Chip.

Danny considered him heartless. Josh knew that, but he also knew that nothing would bring their friend back to life, so all he could do was take steps to ensure that their future didn't include the same early demise. And he had to concentrate to make that happen. Old friendships would only muddy the waters.

"Josh, I need your attention," said Orleans. She was sitting across from him in their glassed-in conference room. In front of her were stacked several folders of financial statements and projections.

Was it time to share his idea he wondered. He needed to present the concept in the right way to avoid Orleans perceiving his end game. The girl was clever with sensing out insights about motivations, but she was hobbled by not knowing that Endicott-Meyers invested in Premios to grab the power of Project Big Stick.

Josh knew his project name didn't make a lot of sense, but code names for computer endeavors seldom did. Some firms liked to wrap their dreams in names of animals or national parks. He happened to have a liking for Teddy Roosevelt. There was something alluring about the concept of speaking softly and carrying a big stick, plus the long ago president also cut a swaggering figure. Of course, Josh would never allow Orleans to learn about Big Stick. Not one of those charts in her stacks of folders carried a hint of that name. Others of his projects were there. It was safe for her to know about them, since she wouldn't get into trouble if she pulled up the status of Project Dakota or San Juan. Project Dakota simply allowed the parsing of stored data about Premios users to detect preferences—all to ensure the firm's customers would be presented with the most meaningful content. Nor would it be a problem if she also had slides, or even a dedicated folder, on Project San Juan. It was an artful way to deposit digital tracking bits on the devices that accessed Premios. Again, it was just to enable an efficient user experience, and Josh had outsourced it to an independent programming team in Chennai, India. Orleans could even know about something called Project Rough Rider. After all, everyone expected it to be an industry-leading approach at streamlining the quick transmission of mass amounts of data. A company like Premios had a lot of projects and as far as Orleans needed to know they were all on track.

But only Josh, Oliver Meyers, and that crazy genius of a programmer in Poland knew how these three projects were ultimately intended to mesh together and create Big Stick. Unfortunately, that integration wasn't on schedule, and Oliver Meyers wasn't happy. And Oliver didn't even know the full extent of the delays.

The problem wasn't the delay in Big Stick; the problem was Oliver Meyers, who knew too much and was too demanding. The original concept for Big Stick had been simple and benign. In those initial meetings with Meyer, Josh allowed himself to get carried away with possibilities. He deliberately fanned the idea that Big Stick could first spy on people's personal information stored on their computers and captured from their interactions with the Internet and then process the resulting mounds of data in ways that would be meaningful and useful. Josh thought his exaggeration was a way to ensure financing. Everyone did the grand talk. Big ideas could be patented and sold to others. Josh was good at weaving a dream and lighting up possibilities that day—too good because he prepared a bonfire of potential that now blazed in Oliver's mind once he detected the potential for more than actionable data. He saw the opportunity for fraud, theft, and blackmail.

That brought in his hidden money and embedded Oliver's hook deep into Premios. And Josh had swallowed so willingly. What a fool.

Yes, Oliver knew too much, and that kept Josh from wriggling free. But information worked both ways. When he stopped in Chicago back in January, Josh uncovered what he needed to know. He deciphered sufficient details about Oliver's backers that they could never afford for him to make these facts public. The trick was to use his newfound knowledge to escape their grasp—and not get killed in the process.

All of this went though Josh's mind as he considered again how to initiate the necessary conversation with Orleans. Finally, he just blurted, "I think Chip's death has given us an opportunity."

Startled, Orleans replied, "An opportunity for what?"

'To change course," he replied.

A new direction was exactly what was needed. When all of this started, he could never have predicted Chip's murder, but he placed that crime's responsibility squarely on Oliver. How perfect it would be if the death of his friend created a path to fling Oliver and his cohorts completely away from Danny and his orbit.

Since the discovery of Chip's body, Danny had changed. Josh couldn't quite describe the transformation, but his boyfriend's spirit had been tempered into some stronger stuff. Cynthia played no role in that metamorphosis. It was clear she blamed both Danny and Josh in some way for Chip's death, and even seemed suspicious of them. Now that the police acknowledged there was little in the way of active leads, she at last decided to return home. After she undertook her final hike through Griffith Park to find the spot where Chip's body had been left, she would be gone. He considered her quest romantic but foolish. In the end, he didn't care, as long as it ensured her departure.

Danny and he needed time alone. Things were fraying. Danny was too focused on trying to break through Cynthia's silence instead of tending to home fires. Danny worried that the always emotional woman he loved had simply shut down in grief. Josh had little choice but to suffer through it since he could never let Danny know what was really happening. It had been a mistake to keep Danny from hearing about Oliver Meyers. Even though it was never discussed and Danny might not realize it, Josh had long known enough of Danny's past to understand why Danny wouldn't want Oliver around. Yet he allowed the intrusion of the guy, and then even perpetuated the idea that there wasn't a partner named Meyers.

In the conference room, Orleans was perplexed by Josh's desire to change course. She opened one of her folders as though to return to her planned agenda. "I see only one possible course," she said. "If we want a successful IPO, we need to answer these questions we're getting from Merrill Lynch."

Josh plunged forward. "Listen to me, Orleans. We could tack in a new direction, even as we continue to shoot for the IPO." Orleans' eyes widened at the mere questioning of the initial public offering of stock.

"Chip was on our board of directors," he continued. "His death creates an opening. He needs to be replaced."

Orleans agreed with that. "Yes, of course, but remember that Endicott-Meyers is the largest shareholder, especially after you gave them extra shares for the added million dollars. Won't they see it as their prerogative to select that director?"

"But does it have to be that way?" he asked.

Orleans answered, "Given Cynthia's share as Chip's heir and the share that you and Danny own of Premios, the majority of the company is technically yours. But you can't buck the desires of your primary investors, especially not before going public. You need them on board. Besides, why does it matter?"

Josh chose not to answer that. "I was thinking of someone so influential and so well respected that they could never say no. We would need someone who would add to the prestige of the company."

"And who would that be?"

"Barbara Linsky."

The idea came to him in the middle of the previous night. Danny was sleeping restlessly, tossing and turning, which in turn kept Josh awake. At two in the morning, his mind went into overdrive. Part of him wanted to get out of bed, put on a robe, and go to work in the office, but he feared such actions would only rouse Danny.

That's when he thought of Barbara and that strange luncheon discussion about Schrödinger's cat. Something about how things could be two things at once, and you only knew which it was once you looked. That's when he thought that maybe the company could be theirs, and also not theirs—but in either case, definitely not belonging to Endicott-Meyers and definitely not to Oliver Meyers and his backers

Barbara Linsky was the perfect conduit for achieving this paradox. Her brilliance and her insights into the Internet economy were undeniable. She ran a small investment firm and sat on other boards. She knew every investor and every up-and-comer in the industry. Why couldn't they convince her to be a director for Premios? It was a perfect way out. Barbara was a strong-willed person who would always do what was best for the company. And in this economy maybe that would be a route different than the one originally envisioned.

Orleans remained silent. "Well, what do you think?" Josh asked.

"I agree. She would be a great addition to the board. If you could convince Linsky to do it, no one could object. But why would she? People must ask for her participation all the time. Remember how you didn't want Chip snooping around the details . . . what about her? She could be even worse."

"Leave those worries to me. I want the board to have a strong and independent voice."

Orleans closed her folders. For a moment, the only sound in the room was the office buzz that filtered through the glass. She watched Josh. He knew that she was trying to figure out his motives. He just sat quietly. He didn't need to provide any clues.

Finally, she gave up. "So, tell me. Why do you need someone like Linsky on the Board?

"Because I'll need her vote when we sell the company."

Danny yearned for a friendly voice. Cynthia was on her Griffith Park quest. He contemplated going into the Premios office but at that moment he couldn't face being around Josh. Instead he suggested that Kenosha meet him for lunch.

Because she claimed she couldn't be out of the office for long, they agreed to meet in a restaurant around the corner from Premios. Pete's Café was a popular place with good burgers and a sense of history; the walls were lined with old photos of the area; and the basement restrooms with their tiled walls and floors seemed transported straight from some Eastern city with a long dusty history. Pete's had the added advantage of being one of the few places in the sketchy neighborhood where Danny was willing to linger.

He arrived first, ordered a café au lait, and thought about his planned discussion with Kenosha. Adrift in currents that seemed to lack direction, he felt as though he had no shelter, no ability to navigate, and was burning under the glare of horrible events.

An emotional wall separated Cynthia and him, and there seemed no way to break through her suffering. Initially when he sat with her as she met with the police, he thought she welcomed his help. The small town police from the Lattigo reservation, perhaps biased by their admiration for the tribal leader, operated with the premise that Chip was a victim. On the other hand, the L.A. cops always dismissed the theory that Chip was framed for the disappearing funds. Each day the case seemed to drop in the LAPD's priority. Although they never said so, they seemed convinced that Chip had stolen the money and that some unknown accomplice killed him. Both teams accepted the coroner's report that Chip had been drugged, smothered, and rolled dead into a secluded ravine. The killer made no attempt either to hide Chip's identity or cover his grave, nor did they take his expensive watch or his wallet. The scene suggested a cold, calculating killer who seemed little concerned with when or how the dead body would be discovered.

But as the police visits went on, Cynthia shut Danny out. She said she preferred to meet with her investigator alone. Samuel Denkey's office was only a few blocks from this restaurant, and Danny was tempted after his lunch with Kenosha to drop in on the guy. He suspected the detective might have his own theories. Cynthia had every right to keep the investigation private, but shutting him out felt like a betrayal. They had been friends since high school.

He wanted to lean on Josh, but Josh wasn't there. He was all consumed with the future of Premios. Still trying to be more involved, Danny asked Orleans to walk him through the roadmap for the planned public offering in late April; he sat down with the marketing staff to approve the planned advertising campaign designed for increased traffic and engagement on the site; and he even made what he thought were constructive suggestions on honing the message.

Most challenging for him, after agreeing to help assemble a broader team of writers, he sat around a long mahogany table with Lopez and potential writer interns. Danny understood the site needed fresh voices and compelling content because interesting material drove the numbers, and Danny recognized that Lopez's program attracted some of the most talented young writers in the country. He had once been one of them. As he reviewed their samples and listened to their story pitches, he welcomed the real strength they could bring to the writing bench. But he hated that finding these writers required him to work with Lopez.

Lopez was part of every interview, but generally so were Josh and Kenosha. On the Premios organization chart, Danny was the editor in chief and the vice president for content. It was his 'zine and blog that gave credibility in the early days of the site so he accepted his responsibility to guide editorial direction. That's what Josh told him, although Danny suspected it was only Josh's approach to keeping Danny involved.

Still he tried to do his job. For hours he sat in the same room as Lopez, conferred with him after each candidate's interview, compared notes on writing style and attitude, and negotiated compromises on overall rankings. Throughout it all, Danny pushed back the unsettling suspicion that Lopez knew not only the details of his teenage past, but also spent hours, days . . . maybe months working through those details until his fecund imagination could transform it into the fantasies that marched forth as the sentences and paragraphs of *The Dumping Ground*. Somehow, Lopez meshed facts and imaginings into a character named Gary—an alternative version of the real Danny, a creative character that was manipulative and uncaring, rather than a betrayed teenage boy. It wasn't Danny, but others would think that it was, and Danny detested that possibility.

As they interviewed potential new staff writers, Danny watched their faces for clues. Had they read Lopez's latest book and did they know it was based on Danny? And he wondered about Lopez's motivations. Why did he recast Danny's character in such an unflattering light? What did Lopez actually think of him? Did he see Danny as the unlikeable cad who was at the center of *The Dumping Ground*? It was painful to admit, but Danny realized he was hurt more by how unsavory the novel's main protagonist was than by the way his very private life had been appropriated without permission. Lopez must hate him.

Kenosha walked briskly past the outside sidewalk patio tables and headed toward the corner door. Danny stood to wave. She walked over and sat.

"Thanks for coming," he said.

"Happy to," she replied. "Besides I needed to clear my mind. Josh and Orleans have been holed up in the conference room all morning. Plotting their next move forward."

"I know," Danny acknowledged. "It's a hectic time for them. Lots of things underway to ensure a positive IPO. But Josh is so upbeat. Says we're going to make millions on opening day."

Kenosha grimaced.

"What?" Danny demanded.

"I hope Josh is right. I have a lot riding on this too. All my options and everything. It'd be great if the company ended up north of three hundred million in valuation like Josh promises. After all, a couple of months ago when Webvan went public it was valued at eight billion dollars—and that's for an online grocery store. Who believes anyone is really going to buy a gallon of milk and fresh berries online?"

Danny didn't understand Kenosha's pessimism. "If anything, what you're saying is that Josh is thinking too low. He told me the Goldman Sachs folks think we should reach at least five hundred million. They claim Premios is a whole new paradigm for leisure communications."

Kenosha sighed, "Yeah, I know. After all I am the communication director. But we're seeing all these companies going public this quarter: pets.com, e-greeting. There must be a hundred. Did you know that last year there were nearly eight hundred venture capital firms pumping money into start-ups? But with the Dow down and the Fed changing the discount rate, the financial climate is changing. And if you don't believe me, look at what happened to pets.com when it went public this week. It was priced at $11 a share, but by the end of the day it was down to $7½."

"Is that bad?" Danny asked.

"Of course it is. People who bought that stock on the first day lost millions. Right out of the box. It's got to make people stop and think."

"I suppose," Danny acknowledged, "but Josh doesn't seem worried."

The truth was that Danny didn't know what Josh thought. Since Chip's disappearance, he felt Josh slipping away. The problem wasn't the sex, which remained intense but erratic; rather, it was the quiet moments of really speaking with one another. Now Josh was always in another place. Danny wanted the full Josh back.

"You place Josh on too high a pedestal," Kenosha said.

"Why do you say that?"

"Maybe we should order," she murmured.

Danny didn't like that Kenosha seemed suddenly more interested in the menu than their conversation. He was having none of it. "No, you brought this up. What are you trying to tell me about Josh?"

She set the menu down and fully met his gaze. It was as though they started a stare contest, and he flinched first. Only then did she speak.

"Okay. Here's the deal. I've known you almost since the day you arrived in Los Angeles. And I've known Josh just as long. You and I . . . we have a connection. With Josh, not so much. So maybe that colors what I've got to say."

"Kenosha, you've never held back on anything. Hey, where's your fake inner city swagger? Just spill it."

"All right. Here goes. You worship Josh. You always have. It's kind of sweet, really. And I guess he worships you as well. I get it.

"But it like you wear blinders. You filter everything about Josh through some screen of goodness. I know you love how people are so attracted to him. He's the kind of guy everyone wants at a party. You bask in his energy."

"But," Danny prompted, "it feels like there's a big 'but' coming."

"But . . . you never notice the ways that Josh is calculating and manipulative, even cruel."

"That's not Josh. We've been together fourteen years. I know. Can you give me one example?"

Kenosha looked away and signaled the waiter. "Let's skip this and order."

The waiter walked over, but Danny motioned him away. "No, tell me. If you're right about this, shouldn't I know? You're like family, Kenosha. You can tell me anything. You owe me the truth."

She sighed again and gave in. "Here's one example. That's all you get, and then we're going to order. Okay? So you know Aaron, the gay kid in accounting." Danny nodded his head. "He's a shy guy, but paranoid about AIDS, just super concerned. Still, he's really sweet. Josh knows that, but even so he set him up with a waiter from the New Loon Town Café."

"That's good. Isn't it?"

"The waiter was HIV positive. Josh knew it, but he didn't tell Aaron."

"Why would he do something like that?"

"Because he thought it was funny, and he wanted to see how Aaron would react when he found out." Kenosha leaned back against her chair, folded her arms, and rested her case.

Danny didn't know how to respond, so he motioned the waiter back. At least, they could eat. It would keep him from thinking.

Session Ten

I'm not the only one. That's the important thing to remember. Whenever I do something, there are always others at my side

You know what attracts people to me? I'm like a mirror that reflects back whatever they want to see. People don't want mirrors that tell the truth. They want the mirror to project the image that they think they are, their imaginary soul. Not their real essence.

Remember that myth about Narcissus? He was such a beauty that when he happened to glance at his own reflection in a quiet pool he fell in love with the beautiful person before him. But he never realized he was looking at himself.

To me, what's interesting about a true Narcissus is that they're not in love with themselves. No, they're in the love with the ideal. It's just that their vision of what is perfection happens to be themselves.

And you know in the Greek story, no one ever said Narcissus was ugly. In fact, quite the opposite, he was the most handsome person around. So what was wrong with falling in love with yourself? Shouldn't you love the very best?

I know what you're thinking. You're just figuring out a way to help me realize that I'm a narcissist. Not at all, doc. I'm the other one in the story.

What? You don't know? I thought analysts were supposed to know all these archetypes. The story involves more than Narcissus. The original Greek tale says a spirit of divine retribution attracted Narcissus to the water, so that he could be smitten by his own reflection.

That's who I am. I am that divine retribution and my name is Nemesis . . . just like in the myth.

I exist to be everyone's Nemesis. I can be the god who makes everyone look into a mirror and see the beauty and joy that they imagine is possible. I want to know what attracts them and then I can turn it on them. Francesca wanted nothing more than to be a mother; and I gutted her dream. Chip Grant saw himself as a great leader of his people, and I made certain the world at large learned he was nothing more than a common crook.

That's what I do. I make people face reality. That's all that Nemesis ever did. He makes people realize what they truly love, and then breaks their illusions. Nemesis shatters the mirrors and forces people to recognize truth. Nemesis is the ultimate truth seeker.

You and I share that, don't we? We value the truth.

Do you recall how the myth of Narcissus ends?

No? Let me tell you. Nemesis tempted the beautiful Narcissus to the water's edge, and when Narcissus realizes he could never achieve what he sees shimmering in the water below, he deliberately falls in and drowns himself. Narcissus destroys all that he is. He knows he can't be both what he really is and what he seeks to be.

Remember that lesson. The only way to escape Nemesis is death.

CHAPTER TEN

Shifting Sands

Josh exited the subway at Union Station, walked to the far end of the platform, rode multiple flights of escalators, and then entered the heart of the last great railroad station built in America. Its grand space always inspired him even as it reminded him of hardboiled detective novels. As new arrivals buzzed around him, he reflected on how the recent building of the Metro subway and the revival of the commuter trains gave this *grande dame* some spurts of liveliness. But he kept walking. He had an appointment to keep.

He exited the door to cross Alameda Street and reach the Plaza that fronted Olvera Street, the original heart of historic Los Angeles. On a sunny day in late February the place was bustling with tourists searching for colorful piñatas, cheap leather goods, and a strong margarita.

On a bench beneath the towering fig tree across from the Mexican consulate, he sat and waited. Soon a good-looking man dressed in shorts and a golf shirt, wearing a digital camera hanging from a strap around his neck, sat beside Josh.

"Bit cloak and dagger, don't you think?" said Josh drolly.

Oliver Meyers responded, "You're the one who insisted we meet in public. So if we have to be visible, we do it my way."

"Whatever. Anyway, it's all good. I just don't want people in my office knowing that we're meeting."

On the far side of the plaza, the bells at the Catholic church began to toll the hour. "What's so important anyway that we needed to talk?" asked Josh.

Josh had better things to do than meet with this guy, but Oliver had been so insistent on the phone that they needed a discussion. Oliver wasn't the real power anyway. Along with Colby Endicott, he was just the front for far more dangerous people. Josh didn't know why be bothered, but Josh knew a little bit about who Oliver's people were, so he felt he had the upper hand.

Oliver never took his eyes from the entrance to the paseo of small souvenir shops and restaurants that made up the heart of this tourist attraction. It was as though he expected some menace to emerge. He sighed and complained, "We aren't seeing much progress."

Josh said nothing. He wasn't about to offer an opinion on how things were going.

Oliver continued, "Big Stick isn't carrying its weight, and that's not good. So far, we supported you in every way you asked. Don't think we're doing it for the pleasure of your company. We're expecting results."

"I provided the first demonstration. Like you asked."

"And that was months ago. What's been happening since? You demanded an extra million to keep going, and we found it. Don't you think it's time to start repaying? You know why we invested in you."

Josh just sighed. This man was so tiresome.

Josh gained no energy from any of the bustle around him—not the steady stream of visitors to the consulate across the plaza, nor the tourists heading to the small firefighting museum, and not even the ones taking pictures of themselves with the burro wrapped in serapes. Josh was reminded that this corner of the United States once belonged to the Spanish empire and then the Republic of Mexico. Everybody was always fighting over territory. The battles continued to this day, but he also had territory to protect. Premios was not going to be ruled by Meyers' gang.

Looking back over his interactions with Endicott and Meyers, Josh couldn't finger exactly the moment when he first should have resisted. It was easy to say now that the best solution would have been to avoid Endicott-Meyers from the start. But at first bringing in Colby seemed an easy solution. A frequent patron of the New Loon Town Café, Colby was drinking buddies with Josh, who in turn thought he knew and understood the addition of Oliver. The two men were a known quantity, and they were so eager to invest. Only a fool could resist taking as much as they wanted to give. Besides Danny and his money had other places to be. Who could argue with the wisdom of leveraging other people's money when it came to building one's own dreams?

There were troublesome indicators from the start. Oliver kept drilling him about data mining, and then he put him in touch with the hacker in Poland. That was the first major red flag. Things only went downhill from there. Josh liked to think he was always the one in control, but an independent analysis would likely show he was manipulated throughout. It would be hard to say for certain who even dreamed up Project Big Stick.

Clearly he should have shucked free the moment Endicott-Meyers couldn't account for the source of the money they were investing. But now things were different because Josh had pinpointed whose money they were really spending—and because Oliver didn't know that Josh knew this, Josh felt in the driver's seat.

After Oliver insisted his people needed to see Project Rough Rider at work, Josh's first proof was the New Year stunt. There was no great trick to the rapid transmission of huge blocks of bits; the art was to sneak that data out without anyone knowing it was gone, and even better replacing it with something corrupted with hidden gizmos. Oliver forced Josh to use a real world lab but Josh didn't dare to do his first major experiment with anything other than his own company. If the transfer hadn't worked, it might have set off too many questions. That's why Josh insisted on accompanying Chip that evening to the data center. Josh knew when and what to look for. Part of the test was to determine how a dedicated data center staff would respond, and part of his plan to make sure the demonstration didn't go too far.

The demonstration passed with flying colors. The short-term server, which Oliver's people set up in the Valley, received the anticipated data. Once everyone saw what they wanted to see, they dismantled that office. But by that point Josh was in too deep. He had failed to plan his escape quickly enough.

Oliver spoke, "It's time to take the next step with Big Stick." His voice was calm. He pointed his camera to frame a shot of the front facade of Union Station. It clicked, but Josh knew the photo taking was only a prop. "My team wants to see the next level of demonstration."

Josh chose to change the subject. "Your guys are too focused on the original objective. Events change. If you stay myopic, you'll let a fortune slip away. When we started who would have guessed the market would be so hot. You're going to make tens of millions on this deal. Make sure that IPO goes off without a hitch before you try anything with Big Stick."

Oliver couldn't bother to keep the condescension out of his voice. "It's not up for negotiation, Josh. You don't understand what we're about. The goal isn't a few million dollars. It's about something much bigger."

Internally Josh smirked. He had a pretty good idea what the real goal was. One didn't need to be a genius to extrapolate the potential of Big Stick.

Oliver kept talking. "The only reason we care if your firm thrives is because we need you to finish this project. If that goal requires your company going public and making you a few million, well, we'll consider that your payoff. It's not what motivates us. Remember you got what you claimed you needed—that extra million. Now it's delivery time."

Josh considered Oliver's statement an artful rewriting of history. Josh originated the idea behind Project San Juan on how to burrow in and take control of a client's system. He suggested they unleash it on Lattigo Industries and embezzle the million dollars and transfer it through the Cayman Islands into Endicott-Meyers accounts so that they could in turn invest it in Premios. It was the perfect solution: it provided the extra investment at no cost to Meyers' people and it should have forced Chip to head home and deal with all the signs that were pointing to his own crime. Unfortunately timing forced a different course.

Oliver was droning on. "We also need to see the full power of Dakota in action. We need to know that this software program is as powerful at mining personal data as you say it is.

"Soon," Josh replied. "It will happen soon."

"Soon better be within thirty days. We expect to receive a portfolio of details on your customers that proves interesting."

"Just call it what it is. Blackmail."

"Call it what you want. Just deliver the facts. If your tools are collecting all this data you claim and your algorithms are so strong at connecting the dots, it shouldn't be hard—no one cares if you've got a big haystack and very few needles. Identify those needles."

"Don't worry, we can find them."

"Good. Then do it."

"And when we do . . . what then?" Josh needed to understand

Oliver's end game.

"Then we assemble all of your programs into Big Stick and put it to work. Wasn't that always your idea?"

The concept was alluring, but knowing where such software integration might lead and given Oliver's partners, Josh feared such a step would result in his being executed for treason. He needed a new kind of big stick that would be just his.

"Before you go Oliver, I need one other thing."

Oliver was already standing. Having delivered his message he was eager to be on his way. "What's that?"

"With Chip dead, we need to elect a new director to the board."

"We already have a name."

"Whoever it is, no. Your goals won't work if this company doesn't have a successful IPO. The market's getting touchy. We need someone on the board who speaks to stability and vision. We need some one the bankers respect."

"And I suppose you have a suggestion." Oliver was nervous. Josh found that amusing.

"Barbara Linsky."

Oliver was eager to leave. "Then go for it," he snapped.

With that, Oliver was walking into the crowded paseo, just another Southern California tourist blending with the others. Josh watched the man slip through the crowd between the shops. He smiled.

"I got you now," he thought.

The air smelled clean. It always did whenever a strong rain rinsed the soot from the Los Angeles air. With the skies so clear, the hills to the north appeared close enough to touch. In the distance, the San Gabriel Mountains reflected the March sunlight and the snow on Mt. Baldy shone brightly. Sitting on the terrace of the twelfth floor offices of Premios, Danny was fulfilling his promise to Josh. For days Danny put off driving to the office to review and approve the final slate of the proposed new writers. He waited for a day when Josh was traveling, because lately he had started to find ways to avoid Josh. Kenosha's story of Josh's cruelty with the kid in accounting had wormed its way into his trust.

Even with Josh away, Danny chose to sit outside in the chilly air. He found it to be a neutral space. Kenosha brought him a large cup of coffee and a stack of folders. She reminded him that he could more easily read everything on his laptop, but he preferred the tactile reinforcement of dragging a yellow highlighter across paper or using a red pen to slash at poorly written prose.

But today Danny couldn't concentrate. Even though the Premios employees deferred to his presence by not heading outside to smoke or gossip, office noise still surrounded him. All the daily sounds of business reminded him of Josh, who had created everything inside— and thinking of Josh only retrieved reflections on Kenosha's tale.

The moment she told him about Josh's prank, Kenosha tried to pull her story back. She looked as though she tattled on a favorite brother. It was too late. Long ago, Danny learned that once words were spoken they became uncontrollable living creatures.

Of course, he knew that every person had multiple facets. He also acknowledged that the personality Josh displayed toward him might not be the same for others. But Josh had always seemed loving, fun, and kind. Danny cast himself back to the wintry day when Josh first kissed him. Danny was just seventeen and so wary of the world, but along with Cynthia and Wally from the café, they took a trip to skate on the frozen flowage where Josh and Danny sped along the windswept ice, while the other two warmed themselves beside the bonfire on the shore. A hard freeze, combined with a winter of little snow, transformed the long stretch of the flowage into a natural ice track. The two boys made the most of it.

Danny still remembered the freedom of that day. It was the first-time joy of being with someone who made him feel alive. The low winter sun and even lower winter temperatures couldn't detract from that high. When the two boys stumbled and fell entwined on the ice, Josh leaned down and kissed him without warning. Danny wanted to sing with joy.

When had Josh ever been cruel? As Danny peered toward the northern horizon, his mind retraced how the skating day ended. That was the afternoon Cynthia's crazy teenage admirer—that rich Van Elkind kid—tracked her to the frozen flowage. The guy had been more than a little off, thinking he was destined to love Cynthia, but the misfit also loved to hang around Josh. Danny tried to remember just how Josh treated that unwanted admirer. Josh had been nice to the boy, hadn't he?

The door from the office space opened, and he looked up, surprised to see Kenosha walk out with Barbara Linsky. Carrying a tray with a pot and two cups, Kenosha said, "Barbara stopped by unexpectedly. I thought the two of you might want to talk."

"I hope you don't mind," Linsky said, "but I was speaking to a users forum at the convention center, and I had some time before my flight east. It was my spur of the moment idea to stop by."

"No, that's fine," Danny replied. He didn't have the slightest idea what he could possibly discuss with this industry guru. "Kenosha, why don't you stay?"

He intended his words to be a friendly command, but Kenosha squirmed away. "I'm on a tight deadline," she said and the door closed behind her.

"Don't worry," Linsky said. "I'm not here to grill you. But, as I'm sure Josh told you, he's asked me to join the board of directors for Premios. He needs someone to replace the opening left by the unfortunate death of your friend Chip Grant."

In fact, Josh had not mentioned that to Danny, and he wondered if Kenosha knew. Maybe that explained why she was so eager to avoid joining this conversation.

Linsky pretended not to notice any confusion on Danny's part. "I haven't said yes yet. As I told your partner, I don't enter into such relationships easily. I asked Josh for a lot of background on what you guys are doing. It's impressive stuff. I was hoping to catch Josh and learn a bit more."

"Josh will be back tomorrow, and I'm sure he'll regret missing you."

Barbara reached over to take the coffee pot and she poured herself a cup. "Refill?" she asked pointing to Danny's foam cup. He shook his head no. He hoped it would signal Linsky to leave but she settled in.

"It doesn't really matter. If it had been essential to talk to Josh, I would have called ahead. There's something refreshing in the unexpected visit. You get a real sense of the spirit of an enterprise when there's no opportunity to build up the false front.

"As I said, I haven't decided yet whether or not I will accept Josh's invitation. Without a doubt this firm offers a lot that's interesting, and I can see its potential. I always have—otherwise I would never have extended my conference speaking invitation to Josh. But I find your choice to partner with a venture capital firm like Endicott-Meyers disturbing. Frankly, the company is a lightweight and has little to offer. You'd be better off without them."

On that point, Danny certainly agreed . . . although he suspected Barbara and he didn't share the same rationale. "So when will you decide?" he asked. It seemed the polite thing to ask.

"Probably on the flight home. There's plenty of time to run through the strengths and weaknesses. Josh has provided me with a great deal of company private data, even made me sign a non-disclosure agreement. One would almost think he didn't trust me. That's a joke, Danny, I know your lawyers would have insisted upon it."

Danny smiled weakly. He wondered why she was hanging around. He couldn't imagine what she could learn from him.

"I am very impressed by some of the firm's underlying technologies. Josh is very clever to focus development in his little scrum teams. It speaks to his unique long-term vision, and is likely to result in a core basket of valuable patents. Particularly interesting to me is the work one of your teams is doing around the concept of a personal online advisor. Of course, places like Amazon already track a user's browsing and purchase history to suggest new book titles, but this vision is so much more encompassing about both lifestyles and life choices. I can see how it could be the backbone of an entire new class of services. Assuming the patent is granted, licensing fees to other tech firms alone could be a major source of revenue. Quite intriguing."

Danny didn't have the slightest idea what the woman was talking about. Despite constantly restating his desire to become more involved, he never dove into any of the firm's strategies. He vaguely recalled some presentation from Orleans about projects with weird code names like Dakota and Rough Rider. He had no idea what any of those names represented.

"On the other hand, some of the other developments underway seem quite off-mission, and I don't understand why your company funds them. For example, take this project to speed up the mass transmission of big sets of data. Great concept with a well thought out approach, and if successful, highly valuable. Easily patentable. But really . . . it's the foundation for a totally different company. Frankly, if I do become one of your directors, I will likely encourage Josh to cancel the project. Perhaps he wouldn't want me on the board after all.

"Oh, how I have rambled on, and it does appear little of this is of interest to you." Linsky set her coffee cup down, but it seemed she had found out what she sought. Danny wondered what it might be.

Danny took advantage of her motion to stand up. "Thank you for coming, and I'll be sure to tell Josh how interested you are in the company's projects."

That was likely to be another of Danny's failed promises, because he doubted he would recall the conversation well enough to report it.

Linsky stood as well. "Do tell Josh one thing for me. Let him know that after reading his brief, I totally agree that in this unsettled financial climate, a sensible next step could be to sell or merge this company. It could be so much more stable than going public. I like people who think in a contrarian way."

Danny quickly looked away. He couldn't let her see how startled he was.

He walked with her through the office, to the front door of the suite, and stayed by her side until the elevator arrived. He watched as the doors closed, not because he was being polite, but because he needed the time to process her bombshell. Josh never once mentioned selling the company.

Cynthia lounged in the hot desert sun, idly watching a hummingbird as it darted about the large century plant in her father's garden. Typical of the homes in this Scottsdale subdivision, the backyard was a mixture of desert plants and lacy-leafed mesquite trees, which filtered the sunlight but never completely provided shade. On a March morning, the air felt a bit nippy, but pleasant. Her parents bought this sprawling adobe-style home as their winter getaway. What she would never comprehend is why her father decided to live in the desert year-round, since it seemed almost torturous that someone like Red Trueheart, lover of ice fishing and raised in the cool winds of northern Wisconsin, would subject himself to the stifling dry heat of an Arizonan summer.

Her mother no longer put up with it. Even in the temperate spring, she found excuses to spend time in their small condo on Chicago's lakeshore. While she claimed her decorating business demanded it, Cynthia and her father both knew there were no real clients for her mother. For Barbara Trueheart, being an interior decorator was at best a money-eating hobby and at worst a self-delusion.

But Cynthia engaged in her own evasions. Reclining in a lounge chair, gazing over the Sonoran desert just beyond the house's back wall, and staring at the mountains to the north was Cynthia's route to avoiding reality. Retreating to her parents' home as a spoiled child let her escape the demands of the real world.

These days she was always fleeing. She raced from Los Angeles, Danny, and Josh because they were too painful a reminder of Chip's murder. For a few days after Chip's funeral and memorial service, she forced herself to appear steady in Lattigo. She felt she owed that to the tribe, and to his sister Jackie who had flown home from Paris. The service had been heartfelt but far too long. The community's grief was real and too palpable for her to bear, so she moved on. She told no one about her pregnancy, not even Jackie. Whatever they might say in response would just seem wrong. And she didn't know where she could go next.

She bore Wisconsin as long as she could but the days were too cold and the nights too long. Each moment was too silent and too filled with memories. The house, the town, the business, and every tree and snow bank only reflected her grief. So she sought escape in Arizona with her father.

Certainly she was a miserable companion but her father loved her too much to say so. He was an active guy. He wanted to be on the golf courses, hitting balls with his pals, or taking trips into the mountains to go fishing or hunting or whatever he did to keep his retired days active. But since he loved her, he stayed at home and puttered while she sat in the sun and tried to read or at least to avoid thinking.

In the darkened interior she could hear the phone ringing. Her father appeared at the sliding glass doors, opened them, and handed her the cordless phone. "It's your detective," he said before heading back into the cool of the living room.

She should have stopped Denkey's investigation. No one, including the police, expected to make any progress in Chip's case. Allowing Denkey and his team to continue the pursuit was simply throwing money to the wind.

"Hello, Samuel," she said.

"You didn't call yesterday as planned," Denkey remonstrated. He was a stickler for detail, but there was no reason to talk when the man never reported anything new.

"Something has turned up," he said. "It probably means nothing, but I wanted you to know. You need to decide if we should take it further."

She felt a flutter of hope, and tried to pull the emotion back. Two months ago, she held her final conversation with Chip, and a month ago the police appeared in Los Feliz to report his body's discovery. Among all those days, weeks, and months, her hopes and fears cascaded atop one another in waves of emotions. Now at last she found a quiet place, as though she were on a gentle stream slowly flowing down a deep valley. She just wanted to lay back, let her face turn toward the distant sky, and float between the featureless walls that defined her despair. What she didn't want to do was drop her feet into the muck of the stream below. She wasn't about to fight for the strength to stand upright, and there was no way to fathom the energy required to scale those walls. Yet, maybe . . .

Denkey, knowing none of this, continued to talk. "One of the new people on the team, Patricia, came up with this. When we didn't find many calls on Chip's cell phone records during his last two days, she wondered if he suspected his phone was bugged. She postulated that he might have picked up a cheap cell phone. There seemed no way to track that avenue, especially if he bought it with cash. But Patricia's a detail person and she wanted to canvass the cellular phone places near the Bonaventure Hotel. She hoped to hit on someone who remembered him."

"Did she find someone?" Cynthia asked, knowing the answer had to be yes, otherwise why was he calling?

"Not really," Denkey replied, "but when she was in the Bonaventure, she checked out every level in that massive lobby and noticed a bank of pay phones by the elevators closest to Chip's room. She checked to see if they were still working. Most places these days have had the pay phones torn out or they've fallen out of service. Everyone's using their cell phones, especially in an expensive business hotel like the Bonaventure.

"That's when she noticed some graffiti by one of the phones . . . she recognized it as the logo for American Seasons, and she thought, 'What if Chip used a pay phone to reach people? What if he was here doodling as he talked?'

"To make a long story short, we secured the records for the calls made and received by that phone for the days just before Chip's disappearance. Pay phones don't get used a lot, so it wasn't hard to identify if any of the calls might have been Chip's."

Cynthia felt as though her feet were beginning to drop down into the mud, and even though she wanted to remain floating aimlessly, she knew she couldn't.

"And were they?" she asked.

"We think so, at least two of them. One was to Arnold Twin Feathers. He heads the Tringush tribe here in Southern California. They're the biggest Native American casino operators on the West Coast—certainly someone that Chip would know, given that both the Lattigo and the Tringush are leaders in Indian gaming."

"And the other?" she asked.

"He called your father."

The float was over and Cynthia was standing upright, already scanning the walls for an escape path. She needed to scramble out and understand this.

Denkey was quiet for a moment as he waited for a reaction. Finally he asked, "We haven't followed up with either person. Do you want us to?"

"No," she replied. "I'll talk to Daddy myself."

Red Trueheart looked at his daughter with dismay. "Cynthia," he started, "I wasn't trying to keep anything from you. Chip and I talked all the time. If he had said anything out of the ordinary that day, I would have told you. But it was just our usual talk."

"Daddy, you probably were one of the last people who spoke to Chip. When exactly was this call and what did he say?"

"It was nothing, baby. The kind of call he and I had all the time. I didn't bring it up because frankly it never occurred to me that it was important. Besides once he was gone, I didn't want to remind you of what you lost."

"Daddy, can't you see that I would need to know?"

Red went to the sofa and motioned his daughter to sit next to him. "Listen, I loved your husband. I know I was a prejudiced fool back when you two first started dating. I thought he was too old for you, and I didn't want my little girl having anything to do with Indians.

"Well, I was wrong . . . on every account. That whole mess with the start of American Seasons. Everyone knows that Chip saved the day. He did, you know, and I figured out how he did it for all the right reasons. Just like I realized he truly loved you."

Cynthia was still. Even in death her husband amazed her. She never realized there had been any bond between her dad and her husband. For the first time, she wondered guiltily how her father was dealing with Chip's murder. Maybe he hurt as much as she did. She reached out to take his hand. "Daddy, I never knew you two even talked. But was there a reason that he called that morning?"

"I don't think so. It was early, but I always get up at five, so I didn't find it odd that he would call before breakfast. He knew I'd be up and about. But Arizona's an hour ahead of L.A., so I guess it was even earlier for him. I remember he mentioned he was going to a breakfast meeting, but he didn't say anything more about that. We just chatted about the usual stuff, like how my golf game was going and whether I'd visit the two of you in January. He promised that we could go ice fishing on Big Sapphire Lake. That was about it.

"I miss him, Cynthia, I really do, and I know that he didn't do any of those things that some people say he did. He was a good man."

Cynthia felt tears forming at the corner of her eye. It was the first time she and her father were talking about Chip. "I have to tell you something, Daddy," she said. "I'm pregnant."

"I know that, baby. I recognize the signs from when your Mum had you. It makes me happy. You won't be alone."

They sat there for a few moments without talking, and the silence strengthened Cynthia. Finally, she said, "I don't know what to do next."

"Baby, you're not one to do things alone. You always needed friends around you. I think you've got to rejoin the world, and it should start with Danny. You would have married him back in high school if he had been interested. You were goofy in love, teenage-style."

She smiled, with tears drying. "I do miss him," she admitted.

"Then you should call him."

As Cynthia stood, her dad stifled a small groan. "What?" asked Cynthia.

"Nothing really, just that I remembered how Chip did say something odd right at the end of the call. We were talking about ice fishing, like I said, and about fishing in general back in Thread and Lattigo. Somehow that weird hat Pete Peterson always wore came up and Chip asked me if I was really certain that Pete was dead."

Danny weighed ten pounds less than he did at the end of the last century—and that was less than three months ago. Maybe if his New Year's resolution had been to slim down instead of understanding the business better, he would weigh just as much but actually comprehend Premios better. But he knew resolutions didn't work that way, although in a way, it was the business that drove his weight loss. Trying to cope with the company that linked Josh to him and led to this new obsession with trekking the hundreds of stairs that linked their backyard to Los Feliz Boulevard.

He first walked the flights of stairs the day after the break-in and the police's report of the discovery of Chip's body. Feeling hopeless and unneeded, he hungered to do something that felt relevant. Checking out the stair street provided that purpose. He reasoned that if someone broke into their basement, then they probably left by the series of steps. Perhaps if he carefully walked the stairs in both directions, he might find a clue.

Unless a used condom or an abandoned cigarette lighter was the key to unlocking all the turmoil, Danny's search that day was in vain. But he did learn something. Descending and then climbing up several hundred steps proved to be both exhausting and freeing. On the way down, while trying to be observant and looking for potential clues, his mind kept wandering. As he contemplated lives glimpsed in the houses bordering the stairs, he was tempted to knock on their doors to see if any of them had suffered burglaries. But his issues began to dissolve into the background.

On the route back up, something else took over. The hundreds of steps became his massive Stairmaster, and he simply became focused on placing one foot higher than the last, until he discovered he was in a Zen-like state. He exited the last flight of stairs feeling calm and able to go on.

As a result, walking the route became his daily routine; sometimes he even did it twice, jogging up and down once, and then walking the second time more slowly. After a month of this behavior, Danny was in far better shape than before, and he found it easier to fall into a state of reflection.

Once, maybe, talking to Josh would have provided that easy calm, but now Josh was one of the things he had to consider. So much was going on in his life, and he couldn't fit all the pieces together. Someone launched a cyber attack on Premios, and yet Josh was never worried by it. Someone, maybe the same person, electronically lifted a million dollars from Chip's firm and made it look as though Chip did it. When Chip tried to investigate, he was murdered. And someone broke into the house, violating all sense of personal safety. All these things couldn't be a random coincidence. Surely, they must be connected. But what could be the link? And why did none of it upset Josh?

When he tried to discuss it with Josh, Josh declared the items unrelated. Josh suggested the break-in was nothing more than neighborhood hooligans or maybe tramps from the park looking for something to hock for their next fix. Josh also doubted that Chip's murder was in any way connected to the computer virus that hit Premios. Danny couldn't believe Josh's worldview . . . because one simple story from Kenosha capsized his long-held trust in Josh.

Perhaps if they could really talk about Danny's concerns, things would be different. The problem was that Josh was obsessed with business. Danny understood that the markets were wobbly and realized that could imperil the launch plans. But he couldn't understand . . . or Josh wouldn't tell him . . . why the public offering itself was so important. The two of them were rich from the sale of their first company, to say nothing of Josh's many investments in real estate as well as the New Loon Town Café. They could survive any downturn. The idea for Premios was sound, and as a couple, they should be willing to take a risk. Instead, Josh viewed the whole thing as a giant gamble in Vegas that he was determined to win. But Danny knew they weren't playing roulette or craps.

Unless Josh wasn't telling him everything. It was amazing how much Kenosha's story about Josh and the kid in accounting shook Danny's belief in the man he loved. Climbing the concrete steps every day only pounded deeper cracks into his faith in Josh.

Danny knew he owed the guy the benefit of the doubt. How could Danny even be sure that Kenosha's tale was true? He never questioned Josh, nor did he ask anyone in the office. But he knew it wouldn't make a difference. Sometimes, things just rang true.

Deep water often sloshed about behind the dikes Danny built to protect his life, and he always avoided peering over the edge. He wanted Josh to be a certain kind of person, but the slow trickle of doubt had started. Danny's solitary hikes gave him too many opportunities to rethink fifteen years of life. What once seemed Josh's exuberance now seemed a cutting remark. When once he welcomed

Josh's willingness to shield him from difficult times, Danny now questioned what he wasn't being told.

Danny had also acquired a second newfound obsession—the literary works of Jesus Lopez. Danny drove to the big bookstore near the Cinerama Dome in Hollywood and scoured the stacks to find everything by Lopez. When that yielded insufficient results, he went online to order the rest from Amazon.com. He found a few out-of-print titles in used bookstores. While Lopez never was a best seller, he was prolific. An entire shelf in Danny's library was now dedicated to Lopez.

In some way Danny realized *The Dumping Ground* was the most uplifting and hopeful of Lopez's books. At least it didn't deal with dismemberment or murder, just the raping of the soul. Because of that, Danny couldn't understand what prompted Lopez to write it.

As he climbed from one landing of the stair street to the next, Danny tried to recall the details of his first meetings with Lopez. In the past he always got caught on the ways Lopez reminded him of Oliver. But today, he turned it around and wondered what Lopez thought of him. From this different lens, Danny realized that Lopez had been unusually interested in him as a student. In retrospect it seemed suspicious. Danny's writing was never strong enough to justify such an immediate and intense interest.

Danny had read *The Dumping Ground* three times. He probably knew the book as well as Lopez's editor. It was as though Lopez had read his mind. The end of the book focused on the guilt that the lead character felt over how he once treated his neighbor. Danny knew that exact feeling, but he had never talked about it with anyone in his life, nor could he remember touching upon such themes in any of his own class writings. Did he just wear his experiences in a way that any half-talented person could decipher?

Lopez's book read so true, as though he had been the therapist to whom Danny disclosed the guilt he harbored for mistreating Pete Peterson. Maybe Danny should have been angry about Pete's behavior toward him, but that wasn't how it worked. When the former theater owner began to spiral into his own form of madness, Danny blamed himself. Because Danny and his dad lived next to Pete, Danny had to watch what happened. From his bedroom window, he couldn't avoid knowing that Pete played those old silent movies on the garage door after dark. Danny knew how townspeople came to think of Pete as one of the town kooks, never understanding that his projecting of films was a form of contrition, never knowing that Pete was seeking absolution from Danny, and never understanding what the movies really meant.

But in those days Danny could never give Pete the forgiveness that the man sought. Instead, he would draw the curtains and pull the shades until he was certain the last flickering lights of projector were gone and the town onlookers had backed their cars away. Then he might sneak a peek through the window, and whenever he did, Pete would still be outside, standing in the darkness, watching for that glimmer of light from Danny's window, seeking some sign of grace.

There was nothing that Pete needed forgiveness for, but this realization came too late for Danny to act upon.

He needed to pull his life together. He needed to understand what every person currently in his life was seeking . . . before everything proved too late again. His mother was gone; he didn't talk to his father; and he betrayed the one adult friend he had as a child. Was he to blame for it all?

He exited the stairs and crossed the narrow street. His house loomed above. He leaped across the low stone wall and walked to the back door. After so many walks, there was now a trodden path through the otherwise natural landscape of the steep lot. He used a key to open the door, heard the buzzer of the alarm, and pressed the keypad installed by Josh after the break in.

The phone was ringing. He rushed forward and picked it up.

"Danny is that you?"

It was Cynthia.

"I need you. I want your help."

Session Eleven

Before you can look in the mirror, you have to open your eyes. I feel like Danny is about to open his eyes. I think he really wants to know what he will see.

Don't you think that's exciting? I do. It's what I've been working for all along, and that's been a long journey. I had to make some tough decisions, and not always easy ones, but you gotta do what you gotta do.

I don't know how you do it, doc. Day after day, patient after patient. Of course, I don't suppose most of your patients are as interesting and noteworthy as I find Danny. It's probably hard to even stay awake while some of them yammer.

Do you have that problem with me? Do I keep you awake? Or do I just repeat myself?

I don't think so. I'm not here to waste your time. I told you from the start what this was all about.

I need Danny to make a choice. Between hope and despair. It's as simple as that. It's the only way I will ever know who he really is.

CHAPTER ELEVEN

Dossier

Exiting the plane at Phoenix Sky Harbor, Danny scanned the waiting crowd. Cynthia promised to meet him at the gate, and he was eager to see her again.

When she requested he join her in Phoenix, he immediately said yes. Instinctively, he knew it was necessary even though Josh totaled up many reasons that a jaunt to Arizona would be a waste of Danny's time. Once he might have found Josh compelling, but Danny was no longer allowing Josh to tell him what was appropriate and what wasn't, so he mentally weighed each statement and he judged Josh's overall argument lightweight.

Cynthia was standing alone and still, even as the crowd coursed by her as though she were a stone dividing the current. She appeared tanned and relaxed. A few weeks in the sun with her father had released the visible lines of tension. A smile broke through her composure. He walked over. She looked good, comfortable in the casual clothes common to the tennis-loving, sun-seeking upper class of Scottsdale.

"Thank you so much for coming." Cynthia hugged him tight, and he felt forgiven, not that he had done anything wrong.

"Thank you for calling," is all he replied.

Leaving the airport, they headed north toward the hills above Scottsdale. Danny avoided the topic of Chip; he didn't want to risk losing Cynthia's good cheer. Instead, he allowed her to chatter about her parents and their life in the desert. In her gossip, there was a dash of the Cynthia he knew long ago, but there was also something different. He said little, feigning interest in Red's golf game and Barbara's frequent stays in Chicago. It was good to simply soak in the energetic aura of the once familiar Cynthia persona. She was coming back.

In the dim confines of the house, sitting around the dining room table, Cynthia placed a large folder in front of them. He sensed a change in mood that happened without warning. The familiar and emotional Cynthia seemed replaced by a straightforward woman—not the calm one in the airport but rather the one that had been happy to see him leave Los Angeles.

Cynthia didn't mince words. "I waited to tell you this because we needed to be together as I wanted to see your reactions first hand. I've learned something about Chip."

Later, Danny reflected that her words would have prompted most people to consider the negative possibilities—Chip always plotted to run off, or he schemed the disappearing of funds, or some other dark disclosure. But Danny assumed it was something positive—maybe they discovered that Chip left a letter or the detective discovered a clear clue to the killer's identity. Danny's ESP failed to work for him that afternoon. He never considered a third possibility in which Cynthia's detective uncovered something implicating him.

"What did you find out?" he asked.

"Chip talked to Daddy the morning he disappeared," she replied.

"About what?"

"Daddy considered it nothing. Just their usual stuff. I didn't know but apparently Chip talked to Daddy all the time. That morning, Chip brought up a topic out of the blue."

She stopped there and repositioned herself to have a clear view of Danny. But she didn't say anything, so finally Danny asked, "Well, what was discussed?"

"Chip asked if Pete Peterson was really dead."

"Why would Chip want to know that?" he managed to ask.

Cynthia shrugged. "I thought you might know," she said. Danny couldn't decipher the look on her face.

Cynthia's stare was intrusive, unforgiving, demanding, and without merit.

Danny wanted to escape that gaze even though he knew that she understood nothing about Pete and him. Well maybe she did but in any case the past had nothing to do with present. He tried to mimic her calm, but he couldn't control what he felt. His face flushed, his eyelids fluttered, and he felt a need to gasp for air. That was ridiculous. He was overreacting. She wouldn't see anything odd in him. He was who he was. She didn't need to know that Pete's name could have such impact on him after all these years.

Everyone knew that Pete was dead, and Danny couldn't even imagine why Chip might have asked his question, but the funny thing was that Danny often wondered whether the man was still alive. He knew better. Even his father had told him about Pete's funeral. Or was he imagining that story? It didn't seem possible though that his adolescent guide was really dead, because Danny should have felt a shift in his universe the day Pete died. That's how Danny's life always worked: the universe nudged him along. But in this case he never felt an iota of loss.

Danny owed Pete so much. Even now, years later, he felt a need to protect him. Without Pete's presence, Danny knew he might have killed himself during his troubled adolescent years. After his mother's suicide, he felt so abandoned and life held no promise. His father was as lost as Danny was, but as a fourteen-year-old boy, Danny didn't realize that. He only knew that he existed alone. After his mother failed to care enough to explain why she took that overdose of pills, he had nothing to hold on to. There was no suicide note. All Danny ever discovered was a packet of letters and clippings, none of which made sense to him and which he burned in frustration. He couldn't forgive his mother's silence. Even in those times when he felt that the answer to his pain was to emulate his mother's actions, he vowed he would leave behind a detailed letter—not because he would care whether his father really knew what drove Danny's act, but because he would want to be certain that he could force his father to weep over the son he lost.

Only Pete kept Danny sane. He paid attention to him; he listened to him; and he showed him that there was more to life than grief. Their unusual friendship started with Danny doing odd jobs for the guy next door, then eating snacks on the man's front porch, and eventually watching old movies in Pete's abandoned theater. Pete selected those movies with such care. Eventually Danny realized each film was meant as a pathway for Danny to crawl forth from his deep emotional sinkhole.

In some ways, it worked. Pete was there at every step. Danny counted on the older man and looked forward to seeing him every day. He filled a role that Danny's father never did. But even when the friendship started, Danny sensed unmentionable undercurrents. He saw the sad longing in Pete's eyes, and the way Pete would flinch but then accept Danny's hugs. It gave Danny power. He knew he had something that Pete hungered for, and it gave Danny the importance that he longed for. Over the course of two summers as Danny grew into his own body and his own longings, Danny's mind blossomed into a pretty clear understanding of Pete's emotions.

Danny learned to sneak up to the very edge of forcing Pete's feelings to become overt, but never to go too far. It was exciting not only because it was dangerous, but also because it reinforced his power over a much older man. In a way, it was an exhilarating ride on a roller coaster of his design. Whatever insult or careless taunt he flung toward Pete, the man had to accept it—no matter how painful. Danny would see the strained smile emerge on Pete's face, knowing it masked some deeper emotion, and Danny would revel in his ride into the victory lap. This guy wouldn't leave him; this guy wouldn't down a bottle of pills; this guy wouldn't disappear forever. He was Danny's.

By his fifteenth summer, Danny grew more and more creative in devising ways to test the boundaries. After spending an afternoon swimming at the beach at Promontory Point, Danny would jump on his bike, cycle toward home, stop at Pete's house for lemonade or cookies, lean back against the faded pillows of the glider on Pete's porch, and laugh at his own jokes. Danny could still remember the muted colors of those pillows and the look on Pete's face as he tried to keep from staring at Danny's long legs downy with blonde hair or his smooth chest.

Danny never gave a thought as to what would happen when he pushed Pete too hard. Maybe he didn't foresee that Pete was a man with limits, and maybe he didn't think he would care if one day he prompted Pete to take the lure he dangled.

Of course, it eventually happened—one afternoon in mid-August when Danny was still fifteen. The week before, he read a Mary Renault novel about the ancient Greeks. Completing the novel made him feel cocky about his understanding of Pete. But Danny didn't really understand, and moreover he hadn't a clue about himself. One afternoon after swimming he arrived at Pete's house, still wet, but also sweaty from his rapid pedaling. He jumped off his bike, sat on the glider next to Pete, and pushed his near naked body against the older man. He flexed his arms and said, "You should feel my muscles."

It was true. That summer, he was developing into a man and for the first time could feel the strength of a lean body within. But the provocation was too much. Pete suddenly leaned over to kiss Danny on the lips.

Even though he had been pressing his bare skin against the man, Danny pulled back sharply in shock and fear. Pete realized immediately that he had fallen over the edge. He too pulled away, and muttered, "I'm sorry."

But Danny wasn't content with that. He pushed Pete off the swing, stood, and shouted, "You filthy pervert." His voice bellowed unimpeded by sense or care that his voice might carry next door to where his father was already home. It was amplified as much by guilt and shame as fear. There was certainly no surprise.

"What the hell do you think you're doing?" he cried.

He dashed down the steps, jumped onto his bike, and pedaled to the safety of his own yard. He rushed up the stairs to his bedroom. His father didn't even bother to ask what was wrong, and perhaps he didn't even notice. Once safe in his own space, Danny snuck to the window that overlooked Pete's house. He saw Pete sitting on the porch glider with his head in his hands. He knew the man was sobbing, and he wanted to go back and comfort him, but he wouldn't. He couldn't.

That was the start of Pete's decline. He had always been a loner and a bit odd in the eyes of people in Thread, but on that afternoon he snapped. That very first evening he showed a movie on his garage door. No one but Pete (and Danny peering from his upstairs window) was there to watch. Danny knew the film was intended for him as an overture of forgiveness. But he couldn't give Pete what he wanted. It would have been admitting too much.

In the weeks that followed, Pete continued projecting the movies. Eventually people noticed. Pete started attending one church, then another, and then all of them. It was an atonement that no god would acknowledge. Townspeople began to whisper. Inspired by Pete's churchgoing habits, someone started calling him Reverend Willy. No one knew why, but the name stuck. Somehow it seemed to go with his showing movies on his garage door. Maybe the locals were curious, maybe they were mean, or maybe they just wanted to see a movie. The nearest drive-in theater was sixty miles away. By summer's end, there started to be a nightly audience for Pete. And Pete played to their desire for oddity by behaving more and more strangely. But Danny knew every frame of every film was meant for him. Pete was only trying to proclaim that he was willing to do whatever it took to be forgiven and to be Danny's friend again.

But Danny never gave in. It would have been easier to fly to the moon than to provide that forgiveness. Instead, as the year went on, Danny came to realize he had destroyed a third parent, and it reinforced his fear that he may also have been the catalyst for his mother's suicide. Surely, Danny would have grown lonelier and stranger—if not for that summer at the Loon Town Café, the summer when he truly became friends with Cynthia, the year when he met and fell in love with Josh.

Cynthia knew none of this. Neither did Chip. Once on a particularly bad evening after a full bottle of wine, Danny told Josh the barest outline of the story, but even from Josh he held back the details. He knew that the full story reflected an unforgivable flaw in him.

Cynthia waited for his answer, and finally Danny spoke, "I can't imagine why Chip would wonder that. Did he even know Pete?"

"I think it was because of the guy he saw wearing Pete's hat," Cynthia replied. And Danny recalled the car that followed them weeks earlier after their visit to the Pacific Dining Car.

Cynthia continued to watch Danny as though she thought he might say something more. But he didn't and she decided to move on. "The detectives have sent me copies of everything. I terminated the investigation, but I thought we should look through everything and wanted to do that with you. Maybe together we can see something that they didn't because we know Chip better."

She pushed the folder toward Danny. He opened it and laid out elements of the report. It included photos of those who had been interviewed, and Danny set the photos of Jesus Lopez and Oliver Meyers to the side.

"When they found out that Chip talked to my father that last day, they also learned he made one other call," Cynthia added. "It was to Arnold Twin Feathers who runs the Tringush Casino. I plan to visit him, and ask him what Chip wanted. His casino is right outside Palm Springs, so if we drove back to Los Angeles we could stop on the way."

Danny wondered why Cynthia wasn't willing to pay the agency to do that, but perhaps she required a different path toward closure. He agreed. He looked up when he heard Red Trueheart walk into the room. He stood to shake the man's hand; it had been a long time.

Red walked around the table but stopped in his tracks to stare at the photos on the table. He pointed at the glossy image of Oliver Meyers, and his face was as red as Danny had ever seen it. He demanded to know, "Why the hell do you have a photo of that punk?"

"That kid is one of the worst human beings I've ever known."

Josh felt secure. He always did in the serene quiet of his personal study. No one was allowed in this room—not Orleans and certainly not Danny. In fact, neither even knew it existed. He needed a place where he could reflect alone. In this room lined with shelves, Josh had no need to wear a mask or worry about what others thought. This spot with its large desk and comfortable chairs was a getaway where he could focus on what was needed. This was his sanctuary.

Everything was spiraling out of control. His plans had been simple. The potential for millions was straightforward. Nothing was particularly challenging. He was only repeating proven formulas from his past. When he received his parents' life insurance money, he found a way to transform it into a small real estate fortune. Their untimely death provided the start he needed. When others were afraid to invest, he saw the potential in Wally and Stephen's restaurant ideas. He understood that Los Angeles was primed for a touch of the friendly Midwest. He didn't care that his friends' only previous experience was a failed café in a tiny hamlet in the middle of nowhere. He was prepared to take the leap of faith that they could conceive of a venue that would become the lively Los Angeles place to be seen. By luring Danny west, he helped the kid unleash his real talents. No one else would nurture Danny's little germ of a food blog into something real. Josh knew how to make money flow. He could motivate all the little industrious ants to pile dollar atop dollar until a true mountain emerged.

Now everything was threatened. No wonder he needed time to himself in this room. Only one person was to blame—Oliver Meyers. Without Josh, that guy would still be a nobody. He owed Josh everything, but he wasn't repaying him. Instead Oliver was about to stab him in the back even though Josh was the one who helped him time after time.

But Oliver Meyers had a surprise coming. And there was no way he could duck when Josh's attack hit him straight between the eyes.

Josh never found it challenging to keep on top of everything that was going on in his life. After all, he wasn't just anybody. Of course, Josh had people he trusted, and he had Project Big Stick. Luckily, only he knew how far along the secret activity really was. It was remarkable the ways it could already poke into the hidden crannies of the World Wide Web. Oliver might think his secret backers could protect him, but truly there was no place for Oliver to hide. For the moment, Josh would let the guy savor his delusion that no one knew of his partners and that Oliver held the winning hand. Oliver would discover soon enough that it was damn hard to win when the other side always saw your cards.

Feeling satisfied with the tricks up his sleeve, Josh wanted to dance a little jig around his desk. It was so energizing to know you were going to win. Oliver and his people thought they controlled Josh and Premios, but it was the other way around. That prick Oliver tried to threaten Josh at the New York hotel with hints of his backers. Someday Josh would thank him for that because it gave him the impetus to do what he needed to.

A quick stop in Chicago on his way back from New York, a cab ride downtown, an unannounced visit to the Endicott-Meyers offices, and a slight distraction to the receptionist—that's all it took. When he sent the receptionist off on a meaningless errand, it was easy to plant a prototype of Big Stick into the assistant's computer. A firm trying to manipulate data capture should have given more thought to constructing its own firewalls.

Thanks to the installation of Big Stick, Josh could sit back and wait for the relevant facts to trickle in. Unable to trust anyone else with this mission, Josh didn't always know how to synthesize the data he snared. That didn't matter. One thing clearly emerged: Colby Endicott was a dupe with no idea who his partners really were or what they were up to. It was too bad Josh couldn't involve Orleans in a review of his purloined information. She would have made quick work of the bank transfers and what Josh suspected was an extended case of money laundering and why they seemed to be paying for kids in pilot school. But in the end it did not matter. He could decipher the disbursements enough to recognize immediately the name Ahmed Ressam. That discovery was like being dealt a royal flush.

Ressam was the Millennium Bomber. The FBI arrested him on December 14, 1999 when he entered the United States with components for building a bomb. Reportedly, he planned to bomb the Los Angeles International Airport on New Year's Eve, but the plot was foiled when a border guard found the explosives in Ressam's car. Ressam was currently in federal custody awaiting trial.

In the Endicott-Meyers financial books, the accounting trail was carefully hidden but that was the beauty of Big Stick. It let you detect the patterns no one else could see. It was clear to Josh that the funding for Ressam's plot flowed through Endicott-Meyers. When he first suspected the investment firm was a cover for something more nefarious, he thought of mob or drug money. Now he realized his provincial worldview gave him blinders. In reality Oliver was linked to Arab terrorists—a detail he thought Federal authorities would find quite interesting.

But at the moment there was no need to involve the Feds. His information was too valuable for that and anyway it might be hard to explain how he obtained it. Rather, he considered his new knowledge a "Get Out Of Jail" card and he intended to play it at the right point to destroy Oliver and release Premios.

Unfortunately Josh also needed to deal with so many other loose ends. There were the bankers and investment houses growing more and more antsy over the prospects for Premios' public offering. While Josh didn't care what happened with the wobbly market, he needed to keep the bankers calm until he could get rid of Meyers. His long-term plan called for a private sale or merger with an existing firm seeking a high tech media investment. He just had to find the right buyer. That's why he connived to get Barbara Linsky named to the Board.

But Linsky was proving to be a challenge with the way she kept asking the same penetrating questions that Chip did, but at least Josh had learned how to deflect such inquiries. All it took to distract Barbara was to toss around the potential of one of his special projects. That kept her from finding out about Big Stick and it avoided his needing to take more drastic actions.

But Big Stick had its own problems. His guy in Poland was slowing down. The programmer kept hitting the same roadblocks that prevented everything from merging together. If Josh proved successful at ousting Oliver and his people, then that would only be a minor concern because Josh would have all the time in the world to finish Big Stick . . .

. . . as long as he successfully sold the company . . . and soon. He needed cash. He had grown too cocky with his personal real estate investments. His portfolio was over-leveraged with mortgage atop mortgage. One strong gust of wind and everything would tumble down. He couldn't let Danny know that they were living in a financial house of straw.

And then there was Danny. No wonder he needed to hole up in this secret office. Any lesser person would go insane from everything he needed to juggle—but he just had to remind himself that it was all for Danny. Since Chip's death, Danny was always moping and the house burglary didn't help. He was obsessed with Chip's murder, and he tried to talk him out of flying to Cynthia's side. Now he seemed to be pushing Josh away, and he didn't understand that. It was almost as though Danny didn't trust him.

That would all have to wait. His first priority was excising Endicott-Meyers. He had the instrument to force them out. Barbara Linsky would help him find a buyer. A private sale would make the current market turmoil meaningless and provide the cash needed to right his financial empire. And Danny need never know.

It was doable. He could make it happen.

He glanced over at the shelves on the opposite side of the wall, and he shuddered at what he saw. That damn hat. Why the hell was he holding on to that damn fisherman's hat?

Cynthia looked at her father in surprise. How could he be aware of Oliver Meyers and what prompted his extreme reaction? Quite pale, Danny seemed equally taken aback.

Danny was the first to react. "How do you know Oliver?" he asked.

"God, who would ever have thought I'd have to look at that mug again? Why the hell do you have a picture of him, Cynthia? Did he have something to do with Chip?"

"'He may have been one of the last people to see Chip alive," she responded. "At least, he's the last person we know about. But how do you know him?"

"What did he want with Chip?"

Danny jumped in, "He's a partner in the investment company behind Josh's and my company. Chip asked to meet him." Cynthia could see Danny fidgeting, as though he wanted to turn the photo over. She sensed Danny knew more about Meyers than he had ever said.

"Daddy, what do you know about this man?"

Red didn't answer immediately. Instead he gazed at Danny as though trying to decipher some puzzle. When he finally spoke, his words were directed at Danny. "I can't believe you would have anything to do with an asshole like Oliver. Pete Peterson treated you like his own son. What would he think?"

Danny reddened, but said nothing. Clearly her father's comment hurt Danny but it did little to explain the situation.

"Daddy, you still haven't told us anything."

Red pulled out a chair and slumped in it. "I never liked bullies," he said, "Can't abide them, and won't put up with them. Never would."

"Okay, Daddy, but what's that got to do with Oliver Meyers?"

"Baby, I can't believe you don't remember him. His family rented Grandpa's place on Big Sapphire Lake that one summer. Well, maybe you were only twelve or thirteen. I don't recall exactly when it was, but this kid was already sixteen or seventeen, so I guess you wouldn't have hung out together. Funny how someone gets older and still looks the same. Recognized him right away."

"What did he do?" Cynthia found it frustrating that her father wouldn't get to the point.

Red looked over at Danny as though seeking permission to tell the story, but Danny was pointedly looking off into the distance. "Okay, the kid ran with a bunch of punk summer kids, all from Chicago, with nothing better to do than to cause trouble. Somehow I guess they found out about Pete."

"Found out what?" Cynthia demanded.

"You know, that he was that way, gay, you know. But Thread isn't the kind of town that cared much about what people did or thought in their private lives. Remember some of those crazy coots that used to hang around that café you worked in? Everyone got along. Or at least they looked the other way."

Cynthia noticed her father wasn't looking any longer in the

direction of Danny, in fact, just the opposite and she wondered what he meant earlier about how Danny should care about Pete Peterson. All she could really remember about the guy was the way he showed movies every night on his garage door.

"Did they do something to Pete?"

"Harassed him. Taunted him. Sent him threatening notes. Who knows what all? I just know they made his life a living hell. No good reason for it. He never did anything to anyone. Not that I know of anyway. But then one night they actually beat Pete up and I had to intervene. Took the town cop with me and told the kid's parents that their lease was up and that I didn't want their family in Grandpa's house anymore. There was no fight; the summer was nearly over. They packed up and headed down to Chicago. Didn't want to take the risk that their kid would face assault and battery charges."

"Daddy, you never told me this."

"You were just a kid. You didn't need to know about how low people can act."

"Pete never mentioned anything to me," Danny said. His voice was shaky and Cynthia thought she saw a tear on his cheek. Why did this upset him so? She loved the guy, but he had his secrets.

"Don't suppose he ever wanted you to know. Never told him what I did."

"Daddy, Chip talked about Pete the last time we were together."

"I know, baby, but like I told you then, he couldn't have seen him. Pete's dead."

"Do you know that for sure, Mr. Trueheart?"

Cynthia wondered why Danny sounded both hopeful and demanding when he asked. Somehow, Danny seemed different since his arrival in Phoenix. In a way he was unlike the friend she had known so long. He had become harder. She thought that was a good thing.

"Pretty sure," Red replied. "After you left for L.A., that right wing, Moral Majority district attorney up in Lantern County took it in her mind to go after Pete. She always wanted to find something on him. Not sure what happened exactly, but whatever the deal, he pled guilty to something and got labeled a sex offender. That's when he left town. He ended up here in Phoenix, living on the streets. Ran into him a few times after we bought the winter place. But he always looked away. Never acknowledged knowing me.

"Then I didn't see him for a while and when I asked the guy at the minimart he hung around, I was told he got killed. A couple of years ago by now. Don't think the case was ever solved."

Danny fidgeted. He had insisted they find Pete's grave before driving west and interviewing the chief at the Tringush casino in California. But Red Trueheart had no idea where the homeless man was buried, and there seemed no one to ask.

Cynthia suggested asking her detective Samuel Denkey to make a few calls into the Phoenix Police Department. Her man was diligent. A few hours later he called back with the name of a detective who was willing to meet with them; he had been the person handling Pete's murder.

They drove downtown, found the block-size headquarters of the department—a concrete bunker that looked straight out of the seventies, its few narrow windows facing a street sparse with trees. Sitting inside an unadorned conference room with plastic chairs and a beat-up Formica-topped table, they waited for Detective Hernandez. He was running a few minutes late.

"Why is Pete so important to you?" Cynthia wanted to know.

Danny wasn't certain of the answer, but he knew that he never properly ended things with Pete. Being in the city where the man died, Danny thought the least he could do was locate the appropriate cemetery, stand silently for a few moments over the grave, and reflect on what he should have said years earlier. Somehow, Danny was certain Cynthia would understand that impulse. Hadn't she insisted on tramping through Griffith Park just to see the spot where Chip's body was found? Nevertheless, he resisted answering her question. It would take too much to explain.

Hernandez entered the room. He carried a thin folder. After giving the two of them a cursory nod, he sat down.

"Used to work with Denkey when I was in L.A. County. Good guy," he said, "but there's not much to tell you about this Pete Peterson case. Why you interested?"

By the way he opened the folder, fanned the few sheets and looked ready to talk, the guy didn't look like he cared about the answer. Danny answered anyway.

"We grew up where Pete used to live, and we wanted to find out where he was buried."

"'Fraid I can't help you with that. It would have saved us all some time if Denkey had mentioned that was your goal."

Cynthia took offense at the man's somewhat cavalier attitude. "Why can't you tell us? It seems a simple request."

"Because Pete Peterson ain't buried, at least no place that we know about. We never recovered a body."

Danny was confused. "I thought he was murdered. How can there not be a body?"

Hernandez grudgingly acknowledged that the question was sensible. "Here's the thing. Your guy was a registered sex offender. Kinda surprised anyone is interested in him, especially after all this time. But we always knew where he was. He was good at following the rules.

"He tended to hang out past the airport toward Tempe, slept somewhere near the Salt River Wash, panhandled up Scottsdale Road sometimes. Hung around with the same group of homeless people.

"Two years ago, one of those homeless people reported that this Pete Peterson had been murdered during one of our monsoonal rains, and we were told Peterson was arguing with someone under the bridge. The witness said a knife fight broke out, and that Peterson was stabbed multiple times. According to this guy, the assailant kicked Peterson's body down into the river. In heavy rains, flash floods deluge these dry gulches.

"The thing is there was blood under the bridge, a lot of it, and it matched Peterson's DNA, but no body ever turned up. Who knows how far downstream his body got carried. Probably got covered with debris, buried in the flood plain. Someday a new rain maybe will wash him out.

"But believe me, your friend's dead. Eyewitness, the blood, and no one's seen him since."

"But did you look for his body?"

"For a pervert drifter? Get real. We have better things to do."

With that, the detective pushed the papers back into the folder, stood up and said, "Sorry you came down here for nothing."

He walked out of the room. Cynthia reached over to console Danny. Perhaps she wanted to show her concern that now he could never make his final good-byes. But Danny was thinking not at all about lost opportunities.

No, what he was thinking was far simpler. Pete wasn't dead. He was alive and still trying to take care of him.

The freeway was strangely monotonous. Danny estimated it would take less than seven hours to arrive at the Tringush casino east of Palm Springs. The time driving would offer Cynthia and him a chance to make sense of all that they had learned.

"It's weird," Danny started, "the way that Oliver Meyers seems to be at the center of it all. Chip meets him for breakfast and he disappears. Chip asks about Pete Peterson that same day, and your dad tells us that Oliver used to torment him. This guy's my business partner, and I didn't even know it."

Cynthia was driving, and she kept her eyes on the road, even though the divided freeway had little traffic. Danny thought maybe she didn't want to look at him, but he couldn't imagine why. Did she blame him in some way? Did she think that Josh and his business connection to Oliver is what brought the guy into her life? Did she somehow know that he had a deeper connection with Oliver?

Finally she spoke, "It doesn't make any sense. It's as though everything tells us that this Oliver had something to do with Chip's killing. But why?"

"Chip was trying to better understand our business. Maybe he found out something."

"Something worth killing over? Come on, Danny, what could that possibly be?"

Danny wasn't about to dismiss the possibility. "I don't know. But look at everything that's happened? Someone was behind a cyber attack on our business. Someone tried to break into my house. Someone stole money from Lattigo Industries. It must all be connected. Somehow."

"But why Oliver?"

Because Danny knew Oliver in a way that Cynthia didn't, he was willing to believe the man was capable of any act. Once Oliver had been his god, but no more. For a few weeks on that summer job at the resort when Danny thought himself in heaven, he had simply fallen into the mix of infatuation swirled with a teenage discovery of sex. But in those long summer days it seemed so much more. Nobody ever waited more fervently than Danny to take kitchen refuse to the dump. Each afternoon provided another chance to relax with a shirtless Oliver in the sunny clearing of the resort's dumping ground.

Even now after so many years, the smell of trash evoked in Danny a thrill of anticipation. Rotting lettuce held the same power as some expensive cologne filled with the rarest of scents. The memories were powerful, like those afternoons combining the lingering odor of trash and the close-up smell of Oliver's sweat and sex.

Their afternoon activities became routine so fast. Oliver reeled him in with all the expertise of a master fisherman, playing on both Danny's trepidation and his anticipation, until Danny was flopping around the truck like a fresh trout. The moment Oliver first pulled Danny's hand over to touch him was the point that firmly hooked Danny.

"Danny, are you listening?" Now Cynthia was looking at him and demanding a response. "Do you know how Oliver could be connected to all of this?"

Danny understood he should tell Cynthia about his past with Oliver. All he really had to do was hand her Lopez's novel. *The Dumping Ground* was practically a day-by-day diary of Oliver and Danny's teenage affair. But the book's accuracy extended only to what they did and the progress of events as the summer went on—the steady escalation from touching to kissing to oral sex to the day that Danny was bent over the tailgate of the truck, his nose inches from stink of the trash, his virginity being pounded away. Lopez captured all of those transgressions.

But the novel never got close to how Danny actually felt. He was actually happy for those few weeks. He smiled all the time and laughed easily at the stupid jokes of the resort's chef. He felt protected and wanted, and a little guilty that he had been so mean to Pete Peterson the summer before. At last he understood what love was, what caring was, and what it meant to be understood so completely by another person. In those stolen minutes from work as Danny lay on the ground staring up at the cumulus Wisconsin clouds above, as he watched Oliver's handsome face bob above him, as he felt the man inside him, he knew life could never be better.

But he was wrong.

There was no point in telling Cynthia any of his history. It was in the past. It had nothing to do with the present. Maybe it said something about Oliver's character, but it wouldn't explain his motivation. People didn't kill and steal over a teenage case of puppy love—especially when they were the one who committed the wrong.

Cynthia abandoned the topic of Oliver Meyers, and then drove for several miles without speaking. When they passed the sign welcoming them to California, Cynthia looked over, "What did my dad mean when he said something about Pete Peterson being special to you?"

Danny crept carefully into his answer. "Pete was good to me at a bad point in my life. You remember when my mom committed suicide how Dad moved us closer to town? Pete lived next door. I was just turning fourteen, but he gave me odd jobs, kept me busy, and used to show me movies in his old theater. That was before he lost the building to the bank."

"I always thought the theater closed years before that."

"It did, but he still had the projectors inside, and sometimes he'd fire it up to let me see old films. I once told him how my mom said she and Dad fell in love by going to the movies and he understood how watching old movies somehow made Mom seem alive again, at least for a little while. He tried to help me deal with what she did. I guess he loved me. At least more than my Dad did."

"It sounds like Pete tried to be your protector."

"I guess."

Cynthia was chewing her lip, a habit she displayed as a teenager when she debated saying something aloud. "Remember how Chip told me he saw someone with a hat like Pete's? What if it was actually Pete's hat? What if it was Pete?"

Even though he had already wondered the same thing, Danny felt a need to scoff. "But he's dead."

"We don't know that. Not for sure. Maybe he just disappeared after that fight. Maybe he's still alive, still trying to protect you. Maybe he's watching out for you."

They could hear a 747 jet coming in low, heading west for the runways at LAX. Oliver glanced skyward as though to confirm the plane was sufficiently far away not to land on them. The man looked uncomfortable, which was fine with Josh.

"Last time, you said I was acting like we were in a spy movie," Oliver complained. "How hard did you search to find a meeting spot to do me one better?"

"What can I say? I like this place." Josh glanced around the hilly scrublands near the airport and into the cracked bowl of the abandoned Baldwin Hills reservoir. In 1963, the dam on the far end of this bowl failed and tons of water rushed down the hillsides, through the residential neighborhood below, killing five and destroying nearly 300 homes. He thought it a properly apocalyptic setting for the conversation they needed to have. Plus he liked the imagery of being so close to the flight path for the international airport.

"You know this whole neighborhood is black," Oliver complained. "Two white guys stand out like a sore thumb."

"Then I guess you can't kill me, can you? Everyone would notice."

Josh wasn't concerned about violence. The cracked reservoir was now part of the Kenneth Hahn Recreation Area, a popular place for jogging and a great vantage point for spectacular views of downtown Los Angeles. On the other hand it wasn't a frequently visited park. While most of the users were likely residents of the now upper-middle-class African American neighborhoods that surrounded the park's woods and grasslands, there were never many people about. In reality, the site wouldn't be a bad place to kill someone. Some sixty years earlier someone dumped the cut-up body of a woman somewhere down below and the press called that victim the Black Dahlia. As Josh recalled, the case was never solved.

Josh thought he would just take his sweet time. It was a picture-perfect day. No smog anywhere. Across the basin and flats of Los Angeles, he could easily read the letters of the Hollywood sign in the hills to the north. To the northeast were the skyscrapers of the downtown area with the First Interstate tower projecting high into the sky. In the distance, Mt. Baldy and the surrounding mountains were covered with snow. Everything seemed clear.

Finally, Josh spoke, "Here's what I want.

"Premios is not going public. The market is too weak. Instead, Barbara Linsky is going to help us find a buyer. We'll sell or merge, and in the process, Endicott-Meyers will get its money back with a nice profit. You and Colby will drop off the Board, and the Big Stick project will remain unfinished. We'll all go our separate ways. Live happily ever after."

"Who the fuck do you think you're dealing with? I'm not that im-pressionable teenager you met back in Thread. Josh, you're in deep water here, and my friends take their games quite seriously."

Oliver kept his voice low and controlled, but his hands were trembling with suppressed rage. Or maybe it was fear. Josh didn't really care. Let Oliver worry about what his superiors might do to him when he brought Josh's message back.

"What makes you think we would ever agree to your asinine plan?"

Another plane flew by. LAX was a busy airport, and jets were landing every minute or so, all circling to come in from the west, all getting a perfect bulls-eye view of the Baldwin Hills and the spot where Josh stood with Oliver.

Josh reached into his jacket to pull out a folded-up section of that morning's *Los Angeles Times.* "See that story?"

The headline was focused on the potential trial of Ahmed Ressam, the Millennium Bomber and the government claim that there would be over one hundred witnesses. The guy was certain to be found guilty.

"What's that?" Oliver attempted to appear nonchalant, but Josh could see he was shaken. His hands were no longer trembling with anger, but beads of sweat were breaking out on his forehead.

"I wouldn't want to say aloud why you should be concerned, but you know Big Stick is what it is. A big stick. And whoever controls the big stick can beat the one who doesn't yet have it." Josh allowed himself a smirk.

Josh enjoyed going on. "Let's just say that I have reason to believe the government doesn't know about every witness that it should call for this trial. Maybe it doesn't know about all the friends and acquaintances that Ressam has in the United States. Maybe it doesn't know how the money reaches those people. Or its strange projects here in Los Angeles and Arizona. Don't you think the Feds would like to know all of that?"

Oliver stood still, his gaze pointed, a slight flush now entering his cheek. "Are you seriously trying to threaten us?"

"I'm just showing some of the cards in my hand." Josh wasn't concerned with body language. The small lizards in the park might be eager to puff their bodies up and do grandiose pushups in the sun, attempting to prove to the world that they were in control, but they shouldn't be so cocky. Any hawk could come down and snatch them up for lunch.

"Don't forget your card deck also contains Danny."

The little vermin. Did Oliver really think he could win with a ploy like that?

Oliver continued, "I know what he means to you. I've known your lover a long time. What good is winning your little game if you don't have him?"

"He's not part of this round."

"Isn't he? Didn't you tell me once that all's fair in love and war? This is it, isn't it? Both love and war, I mean, all wrapped together. What could be fairer?" Oliver's face was clearing. He thought he was ahead, but Josh knew he wasn't.

Josh handed the newspaper to Oliver. "Take that story to your bosses. And don't try threatening me. I'm the one who calls the shots.

"Tell your guys it's over. What I'm offering is not a bad deal. At the moment, we hold each other in check, because we can both destroy the other. Take the deal. I get to go on with my life and my business. You get to go on to foster new plots. I don't care what you and your friends do, and you needn't care what I do. Really, it's simple. We both know too many secrets about each other. If either side goes down, both sides go down.

"But consider your role, Oliver. You're only incidental to your friends, and remember I share at least one thing with your masters. Neither of us cares if you live. So be a good puppy. Do what you're told."

Arnold Twin Feathers was impatient, and Cynthia took an immediate dislike to the man. She didn't like his Tringush casino either. Standing fifteen stories high, alone in the middle of an empty desert, its structure pointed skyward as an insult to the heavens. The cars in its parking lot mostly sported license plate holders from dealerships in southern California, but the din inside was an echo of Las Vegas.

Perhaps her judgment was unduly harsh. After all, the Lattigo Nation operated a similarly large casino, and it was just as filled with slot machines, poker tables, roulette wheels, and the like. In Lattigo, there was the same sense of smoke in the air and stale booze in the carpets. But in Cynthia's mind, the American Seasons Resort and Casino glistened with a fairyland touch as the kingdom her husband created. It attracted families with its northwoods-themed attractions and its glass-enclosed water slides. Plus she always knew that Chip truly sought to do the best for his tribe. She doubted if Twin Feathers was so noble.

"I don't have much time," he said. He didn't offer them any refreshments. "I've got to meet with my auditors in fifteen minutes. Besides I don't know what I could tell you. Of course, I'm sorry to hear of your loss. Your husband was well regarded in our community."

Cynthia didn't believe a word of it. His words were just social tripe. She could tell that Danny didn't care for him either. But they were here, and she would ask her questions.

Twin Feathers didn't bother to feign interest in what was asked. "Yeah, your husband called me one night back in January. I didn't realize it was just before he disappeared. Didn't really see anything in the local papers, just heard the gossip that he had taken off with the tribe's funds. Didn't seem like that kind of guy, but then you never know."

Cynthia forced herself to stay calm. "Do you remember why he called or what you talked about?" she asked.

"It wasn't special. We occasionally conferred in the past. Bunch of us rely on each other to vet people we encounter. There's a lot of mob money trying to sneak into our casinos. I guess they think we're a bunch of idiots who won't mind being taken over by gangsters. They discover soon enough that's not the case."

"Did he ask about anyone specifically in this call?"

"Yeah."

Cynthia was irritated. Didn't her husband and this guy share some common blood as Native Americans? Why was he so unhelpful? "Who was that?"

"He asked about this firm called Endicott-Meyers." Twin Feathers noticed how Danny and Cynthia exchanged looks, "but I'm guessing you already knew about them."

Danny spoke first, "What did you tell him?"

"As far as I knew the firm was clean. That's all I told him. The name had never come up with any of my contacts."

Like a balloon slowly deflating, Cynthia shrank. She didn't know what she had expected or wanted to hear, but it wasn't this.

Twin Feathers stood. He looked at both of them slowly. "I got this meeting to go to, like I said, but I told Chip I thought the firm was clean. But I also told him I had heard things about one of the investors, the one named Oliver Meyers. Word on the street is that he's in bed with all sorts of unsavory types, like the kind of guys willing to fuck with anybody that shows a wad of cash. Foreign types is what I hear. Crazy types.

"I wouldn't let a guy with friends like that near my tribe with a ten-foot pole. Take a word of advice. Neither should you."

INTERLUDE

Session Twelve

I have this theory about life. It's not what you do; it's who you know.

Come on, doc, why didn't you laugh? You don't really think that's how I view the world, do you? I don't give a damn who you know. Ultimately it's only what you do that matters. Every person controls his own destiny.

All of this stuff about God and the devil that people like to talk about. It doesn't mean a thing. There's no God playing roulette with your life, just like He's not out there pre-arranging your destiny.

And there's no devil either—making you do things you didn't want to do.

So if it's not worth knowing God or the devil, because ultimately they hold no power over you, then who would be worth knowing?

That's a trick question. You just got to know one person. Who's that you ask? Yourself. And don't think it's possible to be whatever you want to be. At some point you are simply who you are. And you got to know what that is.

If that wasn't the case, why would people need a doc like you? You help people discover themselves right?

So tell people to look into themselves. That's what I say. See yourself for what you truly are. You can't let it scare you. You can't fall in love with what you think you see, or what you want to see. And you certainly can't change what's really there.

But if you know who you really are, then the sky's the limit. Anything is possible, because you're a super hero, able to do what you need to do to get where you want to be.

Which brings me to my central question. If you really love someone, if you really want them to be able to do whatever they want to do, then could you possibly do anything greater for them than to force themselves to look honestly in the mirror and determine what kind of person they really are?

Sometimes you try to make me think I'm the devil tempting Danny with evil. And if it's not that, then you want me to think I'm playing God and trying to control Danny's life.

You know that it's not either of those things.

The fact is that I just love Danny and I need him to face his personal reality, no matter what it takes.

It's just so damn hard making him choose a side.

But I will.

CHAPTER TWELVE

The Lair

Back in New York, Josh mentally prepared to walk on stage for Barbara Linsky's spring session. Within the hotel atop Grand Central Station, some six hundred nerds and technocrats crowded the ballroom at the Grand Hyatt. They were just the tip of the crowd that followed Barbara Linsky with slavish attention. Barbara viewed this morning's speech as the dry run for her planned inclusion of Josh at the September BLINK conference in Boston. He couldn't afford to let her down.

But he couldn't focus on the speech ahead. Too much was going on related to his need to wrestle Premios away from Endicott-Meyers. Although the jailed terrorist in Los Angeles was key to his approach, Josh was afraid that Ressam might seek a plea bargain, which could weaken his negotiating leverage with Oliver and his friends. On the other hand, he reminded himself that his hand was strong and the planned trial showed how serious the US government took Islamic terrorism.

The real problem was Barbara. So far she had failed to lure a suitable buyer to the table. Even though his real goal was to cut out Endicott-Meyers with a private sale, he also had to keep the IPO option open. Balancing it all was driving him crazy, especially given the gyrations on the exchanges. Already this week the NASDAQ had dropped hundreds of points as though determined to follow the same selloff that haunted the overall Dow.

Everywhere things were falling apart.

But first things first. It was Friday, the fourteenth of April and he was scheduled to preview the wondrous ideas of Premios to the New York investment elite. Barbara expected him to wow her followers with his innovative thoughts on how the network could become one's personal advisor.

"You ready?" Barbara asked. Smartly dressed, she appeared calm and relaxed. She allotted Josh the opening Friday spot, and he knew that was a huge honor. But for a moment he doubted himself. Maybe he wasn't a visionary.

"Of course," he replied.

She gave the cue to her assistant and the floor director. The show was ready to start. From behind the stage set, Josh could see only the back of the giant screens. Behind him, the rear-screen equipment began projecting the opening video. Even from backstage, he could feel the swell of music pounding in the room. On the other side of the screen, floor lights dimmed. Spotlights swirled the room in time to the staccato bump of the music. An unseen person standing somewhere behind him in the production space used his voice of god to project over the ballroom's speakers, "Please welcome to the stage America's most forward thinker and visionary, Miss Barbara Linsky . . . and her special guest for this morning's session . . . the CEO and founder of Premios.com, Mr. Josh Gunderson."

Applause thundered, and he felt alive. In front of him, the assistant pulled back the stage curtains. Barbara walked out, and then Josh stepped into the bright light. The stage lights blinded him to the rows and rows of people that he knew were sitting in the room; all that was clear were the arrows marked in tape on the stage risers and beyond them the shimmering confidence monitors already displaying the opening words of his scripted remarks, poised and ready to roll. The clapping rolled down through the hall to merge with the excitement of the music and the beating of his heart. It would all be okay.

Barbara was off and running. "Welcome, everyone, to our third annual Spring BLINK, a time and place where we encounter the brightest and the newest thinkers in America. For me, it is always such a great honor and privilege to be your guide. I am the lucky one who gets to roam the entrepreneurial byways of this great country to find the first signals of innovations that will transform tomorrow. And I get to introduce it to you.

"Our speaker this morning is one of those game changers. His company will surely prove to be one of the important dot-com innovators of this first decade of the twenty-first century. But I didn't find this person in the Silicon Valley or in Manhattan's Digital Gulch. Josh Gunderson is proof that many of the next new things of the Internet age will be found in the most unexpected places . . . in this case, downtown Los Angeles. There among the abandoned building of last century's commercial district, creative minds are at work.

"On the surface, Premios.com might seem nothing more than a content site for lifestyle information. In other hands, that might be the case. But as you are about to discover, this unpretentious West Coast firm is rethinking what it means to serve your customers, and what it takes to help them find what they are looking for.

"Welcome to BLINK. Josh, let's get started."

And Josh knew it would be all right. Each question was planned. The demonstrations were in the can. The relevant charts and illustrations were cued. Backstage, the operator of the teleprompter was trained to follow his cadence. All that was required to be added to the mix was his light-hearted wit. Barbara tossed the first easy ball question, and he lobbed it back with all the self-deprecating charm that was planned. Light laughter rippled through the room.

It was going well. But then he noticed it. Something was off. Truthfully, Barbara realized it first. She was tuned in to the behavior of a typical BLINK talk, and he could see her shift in her chair as the audience reaction came a beat too late. Even he felt it. It was as though half the room had tuned out. As the talk went on, the sensation intensified. At times, he was convinced Barbara was no longer listening to him, but to the quiescent interest of the crowd. An earpiece allowed the event director to talk to her directly, and he wondered if a story was being whispered into Barbara's ear that was being kept from him.

The shifting audience reaction threw Josh off his game. He felt as though his zipper was open, and no one would tell him. Although he couldn't see the audience, his ears detected what was happening. As the forty-five minute session went on, he became obsessed with trying to track the number of people standing up and hurrying out. He attempted to peer through the blinding lights to focus on the doors in the back, pretending to connect with the audience but actually trying to monitor his suspicions. He was right. Each person who snuck out unleashed a brief flash of light as the rear doors opened and closed. The flashes grew more frequent.

His big debut and no one was paying any attention. He wanted them back. They didn't know what they were missing. For a moment, he thought about tactics to grab them and ensure they stayed planted in their seats. Maybe if he disclosed everything that Premios was doing, they'd return to their places. Imagine Barbara's face if he spilled the beans about Project Big Stick. What would the front row thick with reporters from *Wired, Red Herring, Business 2.0* and others write about Barbara if they learned of her protégé's conspiracies?

He squelched that thought. He wasn't about to commit career suicide. He had to ignore whatever was going on with the audience. Just get through what had been rehearsed. After all, he would still need Barbara after this morning. The investment houses and bankers still needed to believe in the company.

Finally, it was over. The closing applause was a weak echo of the earlier greeting. The mild clapping pissed him off. As soon as they were behind the curtains, he handed his head mike to the tech rep and he turned on Barbara.

"What the hell was going on out there?"

"NASDAQ is crashing," she replied "Already down hundreds of points."

"What are you talking about?" he asked, but no one cared what he thought.

Barbara was already in conference with her executive assistant. "How many attendees are left? Do you think we can get them back in the room after the break?"

"I don't know," the woman replied. "They're all jittery. The index just keeps dropping, and you know how much it fell already this week. It's plummeted again this morning. People are losing their shirts. The lucky ones want to lock in whatever profits they already have. The rest . . . well, they're dealing with margin calls. They have to come up with more cash. Today, no one is going to be interested in the trends of tomorrow. They've got to survive the morning."

Barbara walked off with this assistant and didn't even bother to say goodbye. Josh was left abandoned among the back stage crew and the banks of computer monitors—each one displaying the respective title slide of the speakers' presentations still to come. A few staff huddled around the table with stale Danish and over-boiled coffee. They weren't interested in him either, and he felt scared.

The day didn't get better. By four p.m., Josh needed a drink. During the day, the Dow dropped more than six hundred points, over five percent of its value. Percentage-wise, the S&P was down even more. But the real measure of his life—the index for high tech stocks, the NASDAQ—fell over nine percent. That represented a loss of over twenty-five percent for the week, and a vaporization of billions of dollars in value since its peak just a month earlier.

In such conditions, what company could possibly go public? In a market gone crazy, who would want to risk buying Premios? Josh was fucked.

Cynthia still remained in Los Angeles. Each day since driving back with Danny from Phoenix the previous month, she promised herself that she would soon return to Wisconsin. But she was deluding herself. She wasn't ready to go back. After a few days of staying again with Josh and Danny, she found living under such conditions suffocating and asked her old friend Wally to help her find a week-to-week rental near the beach in Santa Monica.

Being physically separated from Danny actually made it easier for the two of them to spend more time together. They met in neutral places, favoring the New Loon Town Café. Sometimes hanging around in Wally and Stephen's restaurant, Cynthia felt almost as though she were a teenager again. For a few moments, she could imagine her existence before that first moment when Chip walked into the Thread café.

Everyone wanted to know why she didn't go home. But thinking of sitting alone in a Wisconsin house in April seemed too cold and bleak. There were phones to answer the questions that came from people back there, and she had friends who could check on her home. Just that morning, she talked to the office staff at Lattigo Industries, who reported it snowed again. Why was it snowing on April 14?

As long as she remained in this city, she could cling to the hope, however slight it might be, that one day she would uncover the truth behind her husband's murder. No one else cared. The L.A. cops pretty much closed down their case the month before, and the tribal police were ill equipped to investigate further. Wondering about Chip was solely her chore. More than once she paid a visit to the spot where Chip's body was found. She never told Danny about those hikes into the canyon woods. He might find it too macabre.

She also never mentioned how she drove to the university to interview Professor Jesus Lopez. Even though Danny studied under the man, he bristled so at the mention of the man's name. Cynthia didn't care. The fact was that Lopez was one of the last people to see her husband alive. Why wouldn't she want to talk to him? Plus he knew Oliver Meyers, and she felt certain there was something still she needed to learn about Meyers.

Her visit to the campus failed to help her better understand either her husband or his final meeting. Most of the time with Lopez was spent talking about Danny. She was surprised how warmly Lopez thought of Danny. Unexpectedly, he handed her a slim volume when she left. It was Lopez's latest novel, *The Dumping Ground*, and when she started reading it that evening—alone in her rented condo and watching the sun set over the Santa Monica Bay—she recognized that the protagonist of the story was likely modeled after Danny. This disturbed her because she wondered how much of the plot was also taken from his life. The mere fact that Lopez knew this story, which Danny had only ever hinted to her, even more deeply bothered her. Why would Danny tell a mere acquaintance such details? By the time she finished the book, she decided she would throw it away and never let Danny know she read it.

She remained haunted by one passage, and wondered how much of it might be truly the story of Danny:

> *As the years passed, each of the men would think of the other and of the blissful summer afternoons when love and innocence still seemed possible, of the lingering moments when a physical brush of the lips or caress of the hands was not just a stolen pleasure but a moment for possibility. For the lost child grown into a sullen man, those fragments of the past were always tinged with a bitterness that poisoned the memory. For the older mentor who knew he had fallen into a love which frightened him with its unexpected nature that became a catalyst to committing unbearable cruelty, there was always the lingering hope that the past could be repaired, that second and third acts of even teenage love were possible, and that one horrible but foolish act wouldn't assign two lives into the dumping ground of decay.*

Thinking about that passage almost made Cynthia fear seeing Danny. Even though she knew the book was fiction, she couldn't help but wonder if there weren't some truth to it and that thought caused her to question so much of what she knew about her friend.

Danny asked to meet Cynthia at the Premios offices. She balked because that wasn't neutral ground, but eventually gave in. Now as she sat in the glassed-in conference room, she was annoyed that Danny had not arrived before her—and she had even been deliberately late. Already, she suffered through five minutes of catching up with Kenosha who eventually left Cynthia alone with her cup of coffee. Cynthia told herself she should feel more at home in these offices. After all, she owned a percentage of the company. Chip's death didn't change the fact he was an original investor and now that made her one.

Danny walked in, trailed by Orleans, and while he tried to signal to Cynthia his apologies at being late, Orleans was demanding his attention.

"Danny, we need to talk. It can't wait."

"Whatever it is, it can wait," Danny replied. "I only stopped by to pick up Cynthia so we could walk over to the Temporary Contemporary art museum in Little Tokyo. I've held up Cynthia long enough. We need to go."

"You can't go. Josh has disappeared again. I can't find him, and I need a decision made. Time is running out."

Danny just stared at his company's chief financial officer. He clearly had no idea what concerned her. Cynthia thought that she should leave the room.

"Okay, just tell me."

"No. Not with Cynthia here. It's about the business and is highly confidential."

Danny didn't care. "Cynthia is a major investor," he countered.

"It also concerns your personal funds."

That didn't faze Danny. "Cynthia is one of my closest and oldest friends. Just tell me, so we can get on our way."

Cynthia stood up. "I think I should go."

"No," Danny insisted. "Please sit and take a moment. If this is so important, then maybe I'll need your help. Let's hear it together." He turned toward Orleans. "You've got the floor."

The woman gave in. She brushed some loose hair back behind her ear. "Financially, things are critical. You have to make a decision."

"Why aren't you talking to Josh? I know he's at that BLINK conference in Manhattan, but he's got his Blackberry. Just call him. Send him an email."

"I just told you I tried and he hasn't answered. No one at the conference knows where he is. He disappeared as soon as his talk ended earlier this morning, and he checked out of the Hyatt. The market's crashing around us, and the bankers are getting nervous."

"Okay," Danny said but he was mentally checking out. Cynthia was reminded of the high school boy he once was.

Orleans didn't notice. She had a message to deliver. "We're out of cash. We may not be able to make payroll."

Danny just looked at her. "How can that be? Endicott-Meyers invested an extra million back in January, and I know our subscription rates have been going up every month since then. We can't be low on funds."

"Danny, believe me when I tell you our run rate has burned through all the reserves. If we had gone public by now, which was our plan, that step would have provided ample new financing. But we haven't been able to do that."

Danny was still unconcerned. "I don't know a lot about the books, but why don't Josh and I put more of our money into the company to tide it over? Josh always tells me he wants other people to take the risk, but, hey, we're rich, aren't we? If there's a rough patch, Josh and I can afford taking the other investors through it."

Cynthia watched Orleans, and thought how she had never before seen this woman so unsure and unable to speak.

"Danny," Orleans finally determined what to say. "You know that I'm not only the CFO for Premios, but that I also head finances for Josh's personal company including all of his real estate holdings."

"That's really Josh's thing, not mine. But, yeah, I know you're his right hand man, woman, whatever."

Orleans was slowly finding her ground. "When I said earlier that the bankers are calling, it's not the potential investors in Premios, it's the guys holding the mortgages on all of Josh's other holdings. Everything he owns, everything you own, is mortgaged to the hilt—and then some. Josh's stake in Premios is without a doubt the most important part of his collateral. In the bankers' eyes, the rout on Wall Street is pretty much reducing that stake to the value of a piece of shit. They're threatening to call the loans. All of them. And there's no cash."

While Cynthia was sitting in the room, it was clear she no longer mattered to Orleans. The woman was locked onto Danny whose face was ashen. He struggled to appear unsurprised, but Cynthia could tell he was deeply shocked. Orleans clearly realized the same, and began to backpedal on the harsh disclosures. "Are you aware of other resources you could tap?" she asked.

"What about the house in Los Feliz? The camp in Wisconsin? Each is worth millions. Can't we tap into them?"

Orleans had the decency to look to the ground. "Already done."

"Okay," Danny's voice was halting. "What about my proceeds from the sale of my blog InnerEatz. When we sold that to AOL, we invested my share in a bunch of mutual funds. We can use that, can't we?"

"Danny, you gave Josh full power of attorney over those investment accounts. They've already been emptied. I am sorry that I have to tell you this, but Josh has faced several reversals in his real estate developments. Everything hinges on the success of Premios. And this company has just been flushed down the drain."

Danny slumped into the chair next to Cynthia. She grasped his hand, but he didn't seem to care or even notice.

"Is everything gone?" he whispered.

"What are you doing here?" demanded Oliver. He was standing on the high stoop of a newly built townhouse not far from Chicago's McCormick Center. The street was stately but rather barren—the kind of in-town development mostly occupied by the young and newly rich. He quickly glanced in both directions to see who might be watching. But it wasn't the kind of street to attract nosy neighbors.

"Aren't you going to invite me in?" Josh asked.

A brisk spring wind was blowing off the lake. The patch of daffodils in the small bed by the bottom step didn't seem to be doing well in the chill. Josh understood how they felt. He wanted out of the weather.

Oliver stepped aside and motioned him to enter. Josh walked in, unbuttoned his coat, threw it on a chair in the foyer, and strolled into the living room where he promptly sat. He smiled because he didn't care whether Oliver wanted him there or not. He knew what had to be done.

"We've had our offices and computers scanned," Oliver said, knowing that Josh would understand what he meant. "We found the malware left behind from your last visit. It's gone now, so your snooping days are over. You should behave more carefully. My colleagues aren't happy."

"Who can be happy in times like these?" Josh asked rhetorically.

There was something exhilarating when you reached the point of no return. There would be no safe harbor ahead unless he created it.

Everything was so monitored these days. It was getting harder and harder to avoid scrutiny, he thought. Credit card records could be tracked. Video cameras were becoming more and more common in public spaces. But there were still ways around all of that. That's why he boarded Amtrak's Broadway Limited the night before to take a sleeper into Chicago from Manhattan. No one paid attention to anyone's identification when you took the train, especially when you paid with cash. He saw no reason to make it easy for anyone to discover his unannounced stop in this Lincoln Park neighborhood.

The real trick was to stay off the computer and the network. You thought you were alone, but you weren't. Oliver should have known that, but people were so quick to forget unpleasant truths. Of course, few held the tools that Josh did to focus on people of interest. Josh supposed the government did, but he wasn't likely to be of interest to them, and he meant to keep it that way.

Josh was feeling himself again, the man in control, although it took a while to get his bearings back after stepping off the stage at the BLINK conference. Barbara abandoned him like a dead weight. The panic in the hotel was infectious. Over the past few weeks, reality had a nasty way of stripping away any illusions one had about the economy. On the overnight train ride, he fell into a nightmarish slumber where he relived over and over a conversation that Barbara and Chip once had about some cat and whether it was dead or alive. In the clarity of the morning, there wasn't a question in his mind. This dot-com cat was dead, and that rather limited Josh's options.

He hadn't been quick enough. The demands of Oliver and his pals kept him from dipping into the IPO sea soon enough. Their focus on proving the viability of Project Big Stick ate up his cash and delayed his real business. Josh wasn't a miracle worker. He tried everything he knew to keep things afloat while he found a way to toss the bad guys overboard. He wanted to do it without swamping them all. It didn't work, but he didn't intend to drown in his own mistakes.

A safe passage was still possible. The problem was that for a while it seemed so unclear exactly what his bearings should be.

Throughout yesterday and all during the night, his Blackberry buzzed incessantly with Orleans' calls and e-mails. Finally, he turned the device off. He wasn't going to pick up a call no matter how many times she tried, nor was he going to look at her written pleas. They would only be a distraction.

Josh wasn't an idiot. He understood every way in which he had allowed himself to become overextended. He knew how much of his world was built like a house of cards. One wrong burst of air and it would all be sent tumbling. Yesterday, he was pretty certain, that gust occurred. But could he keep Danny from finding out? Could he reset the playing field before Danny discovered the ways in which Josh had betrayed him? The opportunity was narrow, but there was a glimmer of an exit.

In the townhouse, Oliver failed to find Josh's flippancy amusing. "Don't you see it's over?" Oliver asked with a tone that clearly conveyed that he considered it over.

"You tried to get rid of us, but we're not playing your game. You see, you're playing ours. If we don't step in with more cash, Premios won't survive and neither will your personal finances.

"Admittedly Colby Endicott is rather a fool. I whispered a few things in his ear yesterday about Danny and your net worth. After all, Josh, you're not the only one who does his homework. We learned how much you owe, and to whom you owe it. That information is all it took with Colby. He's easily spooked, and I suspect he called some of the bankers he knew. He probably expressed his concerns. Have you been getting calls from your bankers, Josh?"

"I don't know," Josh answered honestly. "I turned off my Blackberry. There's a reason they call it a Crackberry. You can become so addicted."

He was looking forward to what he was about to tell Oliver, because he knew all too well what Oliver was—a man who lacked any sense of discretion or honor. Perhaps Oliver thought Josh would never stumble across Lopez's most recent novel, but Josh had seen it on Danny's shelves. He read the book, and he knew that Lopez could only have gotten some of the details in that story from Oliver. Of course, there were some elements missing or wrong. But that didn't really change his assessment. For reasons that didn't really matter now, the man in front of him had wronged Danny once long ago, did it a second time by misleading Jesus Lopez, and now was attempting a third. Josh would not feel guilty about what he had to do.

Oliver was smirking. "It's over, Josh. You lost. I know you like to think you're the emperor of the world, always outthinking the rest of us, always one step ahead. But you're just a man."

"I'm sure that's true," Josh replied. "We all have our weaknesses. Yours is that you don't maintain a very strategic view. And for an asshole at heart, you're also remarkably trusting of the people that you think are on your side. After all this time, you never learned that in every game, you always have to play alone. There's no one on your side but you."

"Whatever." Oliver was slowly stepping backward into the hall, as though he would cross over into the den. Josh had visited this townhouse before, and knew that was where Oliver kept a gun. But that didn't worry Josh. He wanted Oliver to have that gun.

"Your team demanded a demonstration of Big Stick," Josh continued speaking as though he had all the time in the world. He imagined how he might talk about these topics the next time he spoke at a BLINK conference. Admittedly, he would have to do some careful editing, recast the story into a different setting, but still he could envision how what was about to happen could be transformed into an amusing anecdote.

"You may think you erased our software, but you didn't. Actually, the last few weeks have turned out better than I thought they would. Our guy in Poland, who you so helpfully introduced, has programmed for me an incredibly effective money laundering capability. What we did with Chip and Lattigo was child's play compared with our most recent feats. It's too bad your guys weren't the mafia needing to find a better tool for hiding money. I think we could have been really good at it, and everyone would have been happier."

Oliver looked confused. "What are you talking about?"

Then Oliver gained confidence as he continued. "You never really understood anything you know. Because you've always been fascinated by holding information over other people, you assume that's what we want. Such a fool, Josh. Focused always on the wrong thing. Big Stick lets us disrupt the modern world, screwing up databases and manipulating financial records. Cyber terrorism. That's what this game is really about."

Josh laughed at the ridiculous nature of Oliver's rant. The man never understood the people he was playing with or the limits and possibilities of the technology they sought. It didn't matter now.

Throughout Josh's harangue, Oliver continued to inch slowly backward from the living room across the foyer and into his den. Josh obligingly followed, happy to pretend he didn't notice what Oliver was doing. He acknowledged that he was acting a bit like a James Bond villain, making sure Oliver knew what was about to happen, but that was part of the pleasure of the plan.

"I'm afraid your guys in Beirut or Tehran or wherever they call home will never get to fully enjoy their plot. In fact, I think they will have a bit of a surprise tomorrow morning because I can confidently predict that they will discover that about $50 million in their secret accounts has vaporized. Do you think it will take them long to follow the paper trail through the offshore accounts? Sad to say but it will look quite clear that all their money was headed in your direction." Josh smiled.

"Funny thing, though, I am also quite certain the final destination of that cash will never be determined. What choice will they have but to conclude you thought you were a bit too clever, and I am sure they would find ingenious ways to try to make you talk. A bit of advice: it's never good to steal from terrorist gangs, especially when you work for them."

"They know that I would never dare to double cross them. They'll know it was you."

"Will they? Perhaps. It will only be a coincidence that Premios attracts a surprising number of new advertisers in the coming weeks, and then that the firm just keeps growing with its unexpected business success. Believe it or not, revenue is going to save my little Internet company. But how will that have anything to do with your missing funds? That will be your problem. Not mine."

Oliver was finally behind his desk. Like most of the furnishings in the house, it sported a very contemporary look. Josh would be disappointed to see it covered in blood.

"You see, your guys know that I know all about them, and they also understand how you were the weak link. We may have a little bit of a Mexican standoff at the moment, but as I see it, neither side will need you to reach an appropriate and stable understanding. In fact you're just in the way."

Oliver quickly opened the desk drawer. "You've been an asshole since the day I met you." he snarled and pulled out his handgun.

Josh only thought, "That certainly took long enough."

Monday morning and Danny hadn't heard from Josh all weekend. He didn't pick up Danny's calls; he didn't respond to email messages. Because the circumstances seemed too much like what happened with Chip, Danny barely slept all weekend. One minute Josh was there, and the next he had vanished

Danny paced through the mansion late into the night, and was up again before the sun rose. There was no way he could sleep, and yet he was unwilling to reach out to anyone he knew. Cynthia needed no reminders of what she had lost. Kenosha and Orleans were trying to put out fires at the company, and he knew that they already doubted him when he said he couldn't reach Josh. There were others. Francesca would dash over in a moment if he called. Certainly, Wally and Stephen would drop everything at their café if he asked for their help. But what could any of them do?

Once again he had to trust his instincts. Somehow he was certain that Josh was alive and staying hidden for his own reasons. Perhaps he just wasn't willing to face the possibility that a cruel cosmos was pulling yet another person from his life, but Danny was sick and tired of the way fate toyed with him. So many people in his life had failed to stand by his side. His mother committed suicide for reasons he never learned. His father drifted into loneliness. Pete wanted too much and Oliver betrayed him. Perhaps, it was Danny who caused it all.

He glanced over and noticed the spine of Lopez's book. Even his teacher was a traitor. He surely understood the implications of publishing *The Dumping Ground*, but Danny wondered if Lopez knew how far his story wandered from the truth.

In those days at the resort, Danny would have done anything for Oliver and Oliver surely knew it. Maybe Oliver pushed him down a path of sexual maturity faster than would otherwise have occurred, but he willingly trod that road. He was excited to experiment and a sixteen-year-old boy had a lot of energy. While Oliver was only a few years older, that time should have brought him maturity, not cruelty.

Could Oliver's actions have been described as anything but cruelty?

The boys' bunkhouse was set well back from the rest of the lodge. It was always in the shadows of the tall pine trees that surrounded it, and the air inside had the odor of rotting wood, leaking roofs, and too many boys. All the male staff—the kitchen kids, the yard crew, the bellhops, and the marina guys—lived during the summer in that long cabin. It had been moved to the resort from a long-abandoned lumber camp. Oliver, as the oldest of the crew, carried authority and influence. The rest were just kids, impressionable, horny, and often drunk late at night. Were any of them still haunted by that night the way Danny was?

He was the youngest worker that summer, but already six feet tall, scrawny, and shy. Looking back, Danny knew he certainly wasn't the most handsome or the most adventuresome of kids. On the other side of the resort, the comparable working girls' cabin was filled with waitresses and room maids who swooned over Oliver. He could have had any of them. The few hundred yards that separated the two dormitories didn't stop other boys and girls from spending nights together. The distance certainly wouldn't have been a barrier to Oliver.

Instead, he chose Danny and that could only have been the man's innate cruelty. No other explanation made sense, but Lopez omitted that cruelty from his fictional retelling of that summer. Lopez portrayed Danny as the precocious Lolita pursuing the reticent Oliver when it had been the exact opposite. Danny suspected Oliver knew from the very first moment where he intended to lead the summer sequence of events—to the night of Danny's abasement on the moldy decrepit sofa.

Everything about that night was set up. It had to be. There was no other explanation for why all of the other boys would have crept in quietly into the cabin's common room on a night with no moon, reassembling at midnight after Danny drank too many brandies and was laying naked against that crusty sofa giving head to a fully clothed Oliver. Oliver, the exhibitionist, always found a reason to discard his clothing. But not that night . . . when the lights suddenly blazed on and a naked Danny was sprawled on a sofa with Oliver in his mouth, when he was surrounded by a circle of coworkers laughing at him, when he looked up at Oliver sneering.

"I love this little cocksucker," Oliver chortled. "You should all give him a try." Danny still blazed red just thinking of how he wanted to sink into the ground and disappear forever. But he was caught.

If he could have, he would have killed Oliver that night.

But he never told anyone the details. And yet the newest book by this prizewinning novelist detailed a virtually identical scene. Only Oliver could have made it happen.

The doorbell rang. Danny broke out of his unpleasant reverie. When he reached the foyer, he opened the door to find Kenosha. She walked in without waiting. "We have to talk," she said.

He motioned his friend to follow him back into the kitchen. "I told you already I don't know where Josh is," he jumped in. He figured Orleans and Kenosha thought he was still holding out. "He hasn't been in contact all weekend, and I'm starting to worry this is a repeat of Chip."

"No, it's not," she replied sternly. "Josh just called me. Actually, he only left a cryptic message that said I had to help you find the secret room."

That made no sense to Danny. There was no secret room, and why wouldn't Josh call him if he had a message to deliver. "That's all he said?"

"That's it. Everything's falling to pieces at work. People can tell that money's running out, and I think some of those programming rats are abandoning ship. We need Josh. I don't know what kind of sick game he's playing, and I'm in no mood to go along, so just tell me about this secret room."

"There isn't one."

"Really? I don't believe you. Don't you remember how Francesca told us her tales of this place? That old director loved that kind of shit. If he built a hidden room, it has to be on the bottom level. That's where people tried to break in."

"I tell you. There's no such room. I don't know what Josh meant."

Kenosha stood there, grim and determined, and Danny wasn't in a mood to fight her, because she had confirmed what he already felt. Josh was alive somewhere, but then he wondered.

"How can you be sure the message was from Josh?"

"Because the voice sounded like his. Because the call came from his number. Because no one else would have sent it." She softened a bit, perhaps because she could see how little sleep Danny had had. "Tell you what. Let's just go to the bottom level and look. If there is a room, there has to be a switch or knob or something that opens the door."

Soft morning light was filtering through the lower windows, which provided a view over the back of the lot, the street, and the arched entrance to the stairs across the street. Kenosha looked at the room appraisingly.

"If there's a hidden space down here it has to be on the back side, and built into the hill, like the wine cellar is. The rest of the space is accounted for. So if there's a way in, it's probably on these shelves at the back of the room, or from inside the wine cellar itself."

"If there is such a space . . . " Danny was having none of it. Josh would have told him if such a room had been uncovered during the remodeling, because Josh was no Nancy Drew character who had to hide away.

"I'm going to start in the wine cellar," Kenosha said. "You never go in there, and we know that space was all rebuilt during the renovation." She walked in. Danny stood behind.

"Are you coming or not? Josh asked me to help. There must be a reason."

He followed. Kenosha was methodical. Assuming the entrance wouldn't likely be along the back wall, which was already deep into the hillside, she instead examined the two adjoining walls.

"What are you looking for?" Danny asked.

"If there's a door, it's probably not where the wall is covered in stacks of wine bottles." She pointed to a sidewall with a small built-in bar for tasting. "That seems the most likely spot."

She stooped under the bar and examined it for a while, then pushed on one side, which caused it to slip upward into a vertical position. She stood. She looked at Danny as though waiting for a signal to proceed. He nodded his head okay, and she pushed against the wall. The space behind the bar smoothly swung open, carrying the bar shelf with it.

As the door opened, lights automatically came on in the space beyond. They peered into a good-sized room, maybe twelve by sixteen. It was filled with bookcases, a desk, and two easy chairs. A thick Oriental carpet lay on the floor.

"Welcome to the secret lair," Kenosha said. But there was neither humor nor satisfaction in her voice.

The Final Session

Sooner or later, it was going to be time to rip the Band-Aid off. Now is that time.

Sorry I have to phone this session in, doc, but I can't be in your office right now. But I know you'll understand. Just like you get why I'm always interfering in Danny's life, trying to test him, and to see what he will do. Maybe the final test is to let him know me for who I really am. I think he deserves that.

Nothing to say about my latest confession, doc? Well, I got a lot to say.

I can't know for sure why I started all this. I hardly knew the kid when his mother died. Back then I was in high school and he was still in middle school. Needless to say, we didn't hang out together.

But I could see there was such a dogged air about him, and I could tell even then that he was gay. It made me notice Danny, watch him, and somehow I became fascinated. I could have protected him, but I liked the power of being in control. It filled some inner need for me to know that I had facts no one else had.

Danny's father didn't pay attention to his boy. I don't think the guy had the slightest clue to the way Pete Peterson was invading his son's life. You know, Pete was a crummy guy. Took advantage of young boys. Believe me, I know. But there was something about Danny that changed Pete and made him want to be a better person. It didn't make sense to me that Danny could somehow do that and still escape Pete's grasp. It was Danny's innocence that turned Pete into that crazy kook showing movies on his garage door.

But that was the year when I began to think Danny was really something special. He held some kind of grace that I didn't understand. But then I thought, maybe he just needs more testing.

I discovered he was working at the same summer resort as Oliver—little mean Oliver. What a prick that one was. A few years before, I learned how easy it was to manipulate him when his family vacationed for the summer down the road. I gave him the idea to harass Pete. Oliver was always ready *to try something new as long as it would let him fit in. It made him feel important to create a gang of summer kids that targeted an old fag. Oliver never was good for much else.*

Of course, Oliver loved my suggestion to taunt Danny. I just wanted to know if the kid would act out his true sexuality. Oliver got carried away. Maybe he even cared too much. Caring does that to you. But if I had known what Oliver planned, I would have snuck into the back of that cabin that night so I could have seen firsthand Danny's expression when he discovered that he had been betrayed by the one he loved. That would have told me so much.

Trouble is none of these tests were ever satisfactory. They never told me what I wanted to know. I wasn't trying to answer a question; I had a goal. I wanted Danny to fall into despair. Everyone falls into despair, but yet the kid always hung on. He kept landing on the side of hope. I can't abide that. It gives a lie to everything I believe.

That's why I finally needed to make that call to Kenosha. That's why I prompted the search for my secret room. Danny needs the final test.

And Danny can take it only when he finally knows the truth about Josh Gunderson.

Doc, I think we're about done here.

PART FOUR

DISCOVERY

CHAPTER THIRTEEN

Secrets

Danny stepped into Josh's hidden room, which was pleasant, almost comforting, with its upholstered furniture, warm lighting, and wooden textures. A bit of Josh remained in the room—a familiar mixture of Calvin Klein cologne mixed with Josh's slightly woody and musky body odor. Even as the hint of fragrance elicited a momentary worry about Josh's whereabouts, Danny felt awash in an unwanted wave of betrayal.

How many more times would he have to handle the gut-wrenching experience of realizing that the people who meant so much to him were so willing to hurt him? Did they even know they were doing it? He tried to block out one disturbing possibility: did his actions encourage such extreme acts?

Kenosha asked, "You really didn't know this room existed?"

Danny had almost forgotten she was with him. She circled the room, taking everything in, mentally conducting an inventory, and trying to take charge. Danny had to forgive her for as it was her nature, but luckily she knew enough to avoid direct eye contact.

"Not a clue." His voice quavered. He was so close to crying. An unbearable truth crept into his mind. Josh wanted him to find this room. Why else did he leave Kenosha the message? And if that was the case, there must be a reason for making the room known. There seemed only one possibility. Danny couldn't voice it to Kenosha, but he feared this disclosure was Josh's way of saying good-bye. Maybe Josh had foreseen that, like Chip, he couldn't come back from wherever he was.

"Maybe he meant this place to be a safe room," Kenosha ventured. "You know that's the latest thing among the rich. In case you need a place to escape during a home invasion." Danny didn't respond. "Or a fallout shelter."

Kenosha was grasping at straws. There was only one explanation for why Josh needed to have this room—to keep secrets from Danny. And now Josh was forcing Danny to look for those secrets.

Danny hated secrets. He recalled the quiet bedroom in Thread the day his mother took her overdose of pills. That afternoon, as he exited the school bus and walked up the driveway, kicking through the falling leaves of autumn, he sensed something was wrong, but he was cursed. Always aware when danger lurked, but never able to do anything about it.

The house was so quiet. And cold. No one had started a fire in the wood furnace of the old farmhouse. The fall winds pulled every bit of heat through the poorly insulated walls. He remembered how clean the place smelled. But that was wrong. On a Friday afternoon, the aromas of his mother's weekend baking should have spilled from the kitchen to take over every inch of his home, but instead of cinnamon and fried dough, which were the constant accompaniments to her Friday donut making, only remnants of Lysol and Pledge lingered. Everything was in its place, neat and correct—except for the Friday bakery smell of normalcy.

It was all horribly wrong. In the housekeeping order, he found an auger that everything in his life was about to tumble into disorder. Danny didn't even call out for his mother. It was as though he already knew she couldn't answer. There was a closed door to the bedroom. She could have been sleeping. She might have had a headache. Anything was still possible in that moment before he looked.

But his stomach, if not his brain, knew that wasn't the case. When he walked into the room, he found her cold body on a properly made bed, an empty bottle by the bedside, in a scene serenaded by the slow mechanistic ticking of the windup alarm clock. After all these years, Danny still felt guilty that he didn't rush to phone for an ambulance. There might have been a chance his mother was still alive. But he didn't even allow for the fantasy of that possibility. His advance warning had left him only the energy to sink to the floor and to wait.

A dead mother in a cold room. An empty room chilled by a missing partner. They turned out to be not at all that much different.

Danny collapsed into one of the overstuffed chairs. It felt broken-in. Josh must have used it often. Kenosha came over to sit on the arm. Luckily the chair was stout and easily took the weight. "Danny," she began, "what should we do now?"

Kenosha's question suggested that there could be a joint action ahead, but it was an empty possibility because the weight of the moment fell fully on him. "I think," Danny stated, and then stopped. He couldn't continue for a moment. "This room must always have been here. There was a reference to it in a book about Augustus Cambrian. The author described a room like this where Cambrian stored special props. Probably Josh discovered it during the renovation and decided to keep it."

His statement was meant to defend the action of Josh, but even he judged the room damnable. He avoided Kenosha's eyes as much as she avoided his.

"But why didn't he tell you?"

People never told him anything. They just did what they wanted.

"You know Josh. Always dramatic. I'm sure he thought it was fun to have his own little hideaway."

Kenosha had the grace to avoid commenting. Maybe it was good that Josh chose to tell him about the room through a message to Kenosha. If Danny had received the phone call directly, he would have dismissed the entreaty as nonsense. Or, worse, he would have sought out the room alone, and he couldn't have survived that discovery.

So melodramatic. Hadn't he survived his mother's suicide and the fact that she didn't leave her son any message of explanation? After her funeral, he tore through his childhood home, convinced that she left a message somewhere and that he would find some note that had been overlooked. All he ever found was an unexpected envelope of trivia in a trunk of old keepsakes.

The packet was filled with a handful of clippings and photos. Some were in Finnish, and none answered his questions. Later in life, he often wondered about the source of that envelope. As a child, he frequently rummaged in that trunk and he was certain the envelope had not been there in the weeks before his mother's death. But it did little good to wonder any more about the envelope and its contents since he destroyed any possibility of ever learning what the mementos meant. In anger, he burned everything he found that day. He flung them, one by one, into the wood furnace and watched as every bit flamed up to disappear as smoke. It took less than a minute. The moment the items were gone, he wanted each and every one back.

All he kept was a single photo. It was of his mother and him as a baby. It also showed an old friend of his mother's named Pauline. For some reason, he treasured that photo and still kept it in his wallet. Once he tried to talk about the picture with his father, but the man refused to say anything other than the snapshot was taken just before Danny's first Christmas. Feeling an urge to look at it again, he took it out and wondered what it meant.

"What's that?" Kenosha wanted to know.

"Just a snapshot of me as a baby, with my mom and one of her friends."

"You look like your mother," Kenosha said, "That's the Finnish blood, I think. You even resemble that other woman. She must have been a relative."

"I don't think so." He changed subjects. "I could never accept the way my mother committed suicide without leaving any message. I feel the same way finding this room. I can't explain it. There are so many things I should worry about, like why Josh hasn't called, or where he is. But I can't get past wondering why he wanted me to find this room. What's in here? What does he want me to know?"

Kenosha had an answer. She always did. "Danny, think about it. He is trying to tell you something. That's so Josh."

Danny wasn't listening. Since being a small child, he always tried to do the right thing. He believed in behaving and following the rules, because that's what good people were supposed to do. He had been blessed. He had acquired a small bit of fame as a blogger and that was followed by plenty of money. His friends were many and loyal, and he always felt that Josh let him achieve more than he could ever have done by himself.

Yet throughout his life everything was taken away from him—his mother, his father's attention, his pillars of strength, and his innocence—so much. And the pattern just seemed to continue. Based on Orleans's gloomy predictions, everything they had including their houses could soon be repossessed. And now he faced this ultimate loss—learning that his own lover could not be trusted.

"I don't care," Danny said. "It's already too much."

"Danny, listen to me. Maybe you aren't the joking, jovial guy at the party, but at your core, you don't know how to give up. Don't do it now. Let's look around. Isn't it better to know the full truth? We need to find whatever Josh hid in this room."

Danny looked around the room wondering where to begin. The first object that caught his attention was the large mannequin in a corner. Walking over, he saw that the figure was in a doctor's uniform and that its monstrous head was some kind of latex movie mask.

"I think that's left over from Cambrian's horror movie collection," Kenosha said. "I recognize the face. The character was in one of those early 1930s movies. Some film about a mad psychiatrist."

"Gives me the creeps," Danny replied.

The room was lined with rows of shelves, many holding archival filing boxes. He couldn't imagine what would be in them. In all likelihood, these were nothing more than the records of Josh's various real estate investments but he knew he would have to examine them in detail. Then he noticed it: a tattered blue fishing hat. Seeing it scared him, but still he walked directly over to the shelf, picked up the hat, and inspected it closely.

"I know this hat," he said.

"Okay," Kenosha said tentatively.

Danny realized she didn't know that someone wearing a hat like this had been following him, or that Chip reported such a person tailing him.

"So what about it?" she asked.

"Chip and I both thought someone was watching us, and we both remembered the person wearing a hat like this. Someone we knew years ago in Thread named Pete always had this same kind of hat. That's why we noticed it."

"You think Josh was following you and wearing this hat?" she asked.

"Maybe," Danny replied, "but that's not what bothers me."

"What does?" Kenosha sounded perplexed.

"This hat doesn't just look like Pete's. It **is** Pete's hat—the very one he used to wear all the time. I recognize it. But Pete's dead. Murdered years ago. How could Josh have his hat?"

Memories. Betrayals. Danny could not let his life be defined by what others did. At some point, the world he inhabited was the world he decided upon. He deeply admired those people who could respond to any downfall with a smile, and he wanted to be that kind of person.

But it was so hard. Early yesterday, Kenosha and he completed their quick inventory of the room. Afterwards he insisted Kenosha go home. He had discovered far too much already, and he didn't want her around as he surely learned more. He wouldn't listen to any of her arguments for staying, no matter how valid they might be. Being forced to see that Josh hid something so massive was like tumbling down the many flights of the stair streets that tiered the hills of their neighborhood. One couldn't suffer such unexpected trauma and still stand up. The bruises were there; they were severe; and having someone next to him didn't make them hurt less. While it might be true that the call that Josh made to Kenosha proved he was still alive, that was just another black-and-blue hurt, and, maybe, it was the most painful of all. Danny hoped that Josh might contact him directly at any moment, but having Kenosha at his side would only keep him from saying what must be said.

Instead of the security of being surrounded by people, Danny longed for the comfort of routine. He wanted rote actions, lists, and the pleasure of falling into what he knew learning experts called executive motor routines—to let his body take over and complete actions without any thought, like it did with the beating of the heart, the breathing of the lungs, or the crying of his eyes. If Danny had been a runner, he might have dashed into the trails of the nearby park and jogged for hours along the crests and canyons of its scrub-covered hills. Perhaps he should have taken to the routine of his stairs, descending to the boulevard below and then struggling back up, over and over until he dropped in exhaustion. But instinctively he knew that wouldn't suffice.

Instead, Danny transformed into his mother, who had often been a compulsive cleaner and organizer. In one way, the only thing she left behind on the day of her death was an immaculate house, which over time Danny learned was its own form of confession.

He walked out of the secret room, left its door ajar, and returned to his home's more familiar spaces. He pulled out the cleaning supplies and started on the top floor, dusting every room, vacuuming every floor, and placing every item in its proper location. Between the weekly housekeeper and Danny's own behavior, the house was seldom disorderly. As a result, his manic cleaning could only last so long. It wasn't many hours until he found his way back to the basement level.

The shadows were deep, as the sun had lowered behind the trees near the bottom of the lot. The lamp from inside the secret office cast its cascade of light through the wine cellar and drew a rectangle of light across the darkened game room, like a yellow carpet of illumination to draw him back in.

The wine cellar's air conditioning, designed to keep every precious bottle at the right temperature, fought with the warm air issuing from the hidden den, and created a slight breeze, like a spring day struggling to fight the winter. Danny shivered, but nevertheless walked in.

Outside the room, the house phone rang. Likely Kenosha once more. Throughout the day, she tried his cell phone, but he always ignored it. Now she was trying the landline. He still wouldn't answer. He needed solitude.

Amazing how much one room could embody another person's spirit. If Danny saw a picture of this office, positioned with other individuals' work spaces in some decorator's lineup of potential culprits, there would have been no question that this belonged to Josh. The color of the paint, the placement of the furniture, and the casual disorder on the shelves—it all spoke of Josh.

Something in this room had to make sense of all the bizarre, unsettling incidents of the previous weeks. Others had tried to find this room. He was convinced there was no other explanation for the attempted break-ins, despite Josh's lying to him and telling him nobody was targeting them. One couldn't ignore reality. That was the thing about entering the room . . . the space was more than just the physical representation of a betrayal. Its physicality broke through his consciousness like the tip of the iceberg thrusting above a sea of lies. But beneath that, like the frozen bulk that could ram a ship and sink it, there were the sudden questions of a lifetime.

But if he allowed himself to sink low enough beneath the turbulence, he could sense the bottom and the beckoning of some type of calm. If there was nothing left in the house for him to clean, there still remained a multitude of unknown items to inventory. Whatever it took, he would account for everything in this room. That listing would fashion something meaningful. Josh made this happen when he called Kenosha. Josh forced him to look for this room, to find its entrance, and to discover things Danny didn't want to know. He wouldn't betray Josh now by turning back.

Pete's hat still sat on the desk where Danny had placed it after proclaiming that this was the actual hat once worn by Pete. Danny had seen it in Pete's house so many times, and had even jokingly donned it more than once. The hat might now be dirty and fraying, but it was the same color, size, and shape. And Danny's initials were inked on the inside brim just where Danny had written them. He remembered the day he did it. He had saved much of his earnings from doing chores for Pete to give the man something back, and he wanted to ensure that Pete would think about him. Pete's eyes watered with joy when he accepted the gift and that gave Danny a small taste of his power over the man.

Putting the hat on himself, Danny expected to feel something cosmic. Instead he only questioned how Josh came to possess Pete's hat.

All his life Danny kept lists. There were lists of books he owned, experiences he had, futures he envisioned, and people who mattered. Sometimes he ran through those tallies in his head, and recalled why and when each entry was inscribed on the roster. The harshest of those accountings identified those who harmed him: his mother, his father, Pete, Oliver, all the boys at the resort. Today, he was adding Josh to that list.

He began his inventory in one corner of the room—the one with the horror figure in the doctor's coat. He planned to work completely around the space by going counterclockwise. He placed a pad of paper on the desk on which to write a short description of each item encountered—whether a photograph, a book, a knickknack, or whatever. There was no rationale for such a list other than to pull order out of disorder.

By the time he completed a full circle of the room, leaving only the desk and its contents, Danny felt he had learned nothing. While everything seemed to speak of Josh, most of the items were little more than decorations chosen for an image. Taken together, they shimmered with only a mere suggestion of Josh. None of the book titles had anything to do with Josh's interests. Only a few personal photos were on the wall: a picture of Josh's parents' farm back in Thread and another of the house where Danny once lived. Oddly, there was even a framed postcard of the resort where Danny first met Oliver. But there were no framed certificates, newspaper clippings, or photos of Josh with others. Nothing in the room spoke of the man's accomplishments.

It was time to tackle the desk. Danny was worried over what he might find, such as a drawer containing some disgusting cache of pornography, but as he opened the bottom file drawers, all he found were business files. He pulled out the first hanging folder, which contained within it another series of folders, each labeled with titles like 'Project Rough Rider' and 'Project Big Stick.' Sitting down in the large leather chair, he spread the folders across the leather-topped desk to read them.

Hours later, and still only a third of the way through, Danny was bewildered. He couldn't follow everything he read, but it was clear that a number of projects were being hidden from everyone at Premios, including Orleans and the investors. As near as he could tell, the real purpose of Premios was a scam. Josh was setting the stage to abscond with personal information from the users of the site so that the data might be manipulated in various ways for illegal purposes.

Josh was a crook.

There was no other way to put it. The entire company existed only to hide a double strategy. To be certain he would have to read through everything. Already Danny wondered about the real story connecting several events over the past several months: the hacking of Premios on New Year's Eve, the embezzlement of funds from Lattigo, and the murder of Chip Grant. Was it possible that Josh was involved with all these crimes? Not only involved, but the ringleader? And was someone else connected? Was that who attempted the home burglary?

Once again, the phone was ringing. Danny decided to answer it. He had gone as far as he could by himself, and he knew he could no longer deal with his discoveries alone. He stepped out of the vault, across the wine cellar and back into the game room. He picked up the phone, and then walked back to Josh's space.

"Danny, is that you?" It wasn't Kenosha, but Orleans.

"Yes."

She was frantic. "I have to talk to Josh. I'm certain you know where he is, or how to get in contact with him. I need him now. It can't wait."

Danny wondered how much Orleans might suspect about what he had just uncovered in the files. Would he dare tell her? "I don't know where Josh is. What's so important?"

"It's happened again," she said. "Another investor is dead. Oliver Meyers was murdered in his townhouse in Chicago. The police say it's a robbery gone bad. But I don't believe that. Someone is targeting us.

Somebody is out to destroy Premios."

But Danny wasn't listening. By accident he had just pulled an unexpected latch in the desk and opened up a secret drawer. Inside were an automated tape machine and a stack of cassettes.

The Ferris wheel on the Santa Monica Pier stopped moving. From her bench on the palisades high above the beach and hundreds of yards from the amusement pier, Cynthia couldn't discern if there were people stuck in the cars. All she could see was a wharf crowded with people and the breaking waves of the surf that hit the sandy beach below.

"Thanks for agreeing to meet me," said Jesus Lopez. He sat next to her on the bench, and he was right on time.

She didn't bother to look over, and she wasn't quite sure why she had agreed to meet, but he had been so insistent. After multiple emails and more than one phone message, she finally suggested they meet in a public park in mid-afternoon. It wasn't that she felt a need to be cautious, or that she was unwilling to drive across town to his college campus. Instead she wanted to stay close to shore, to see and hear the ocean. A distant horizon combined with the constant beating of waves kept her fears at bay. Whatever Lopez had to say—and she held little hope that it would be positive—she was certain she could deal with it better if facing the sea.

"Why did you need to see me?" she asked. "If you know something, why wouldn't you go to Danny?"

"Because I don't trust him."

For the first time she looked look over. Lopez was gaunter than she remembered him.

"That's funny. Danny doesn't trust you either."

"Do you know that Oliver Meyers is dead?" he asked. "They found him murdered in his townhouse in Chicago last week."

That was old news to Cynthia. Colby Endicott called her the day he found out. Terrified, he tried to convince her that someone was killing off the funders of Premios. Cynthia found Colby's ravings tedious. Oliver's murder was clearly a case of a burglary gone wrong. All of Oliver's best contemporary art pieces had been taken from the walls. Despite that, she did ask Denkey to investigate the coincidence of another death, but he reported that the Chicago police agreed that it pointed toward thieves.

"And I suppose you know that Josh Gunderson is missing?" Cynthia batted that question back. She was hoping that she might actually learn something, since Danny refused to talk about Josh's whereabouts. What little Cynthia knew was from information relayed by Orleans. Things were insane; maybe Lopez was right. Not for the first time, Cynthia decided to quit her short-term lease and head back to the Midwest. She truly was alone on the West Coast.

Looking out over Santa Monica Bay with its many sailboats, Lopez sat quietly and didn't respond for a long beat. With the sun still high overhead, the water sparkled. Cynthia wondered again what was on his mind. Finally, he spoke.

"Of course, I know about Josh's disappearance. And Colby told me that he tried to warn you, but you dismissed him. Can't you see there's a pattern? It began with your husband. Then Oliver. Now Josh. Everyone connected with this firm disappears. I submitted my resignation. I want nothing to do with that company."

Ignoring the last part of Lopez's statement, Cynthia instead focused on his insinuation. "Do you think Josh is dead?" she asked calmly, not that she cared if he was or not, because being part of Danny and Josh's life was too much a burden to carry, and she needed to drop them all.

"I don't know, but these events can't be coincidental. You remain an investor, inheriting your husband's share. You should be concerned. You could be next."

Cynthia was unwilling to buy into conspiracy theory. "It's a random set of coincidences. Is that why you wanted to meet me? To warn me away? Are you working as Colby's surrogate? Trying to scare me so I flee back home to Wisconsin?"

Lopez looked shocked. "It's not about you. It's about Danny."

Suddenly, Cynthia was fed up. This man had no right to be concerned about her old friend. "You want to talk about Danny. Okay, here you go. Why write a book based on his teenage experiences? And without his knowledge. Don't you know how it's eating him alive? I can't even pretend to say that I know the details of what happened to him that summer. But one thing is certain: he's happy that Oliver is dead—because Danny blames him for the book, and he blames you too. You turned his life into a horror story. He'd probably be happy to see you dead as well."

"And you wonder why I said I don't trust him."

Cynthia felt as though he goaded her into that outburst, and she wanted to wipe away his smug smile. It was simply too much. She had read *The Dumping Ground* out of curiosity. While she acknowledged that it was well written, it also proved quite moving. In some ways she couldn't help but think of Danny as she read every scene. When they first worked together as teenagers, she always considered Danny brittle, and she treated him gently because she valued that delicacy. But the novel forced her to think that maybe Danny was tougher than she realized. Maybe an element of steel was hidden in his tall lanky frame.

Cynthia thought carefully about what to say to Lopez. "To me, you're the one who's not to be trusted. You chose to write that book. Why shouldn't Danny hate you for it? What were you thinking?"

"It wasn't my idea." Lopez almost whispered those words. Cynthia wasn't certain she had heard correctly because the afternoon breeze was starting to blow in from the sea.

"Not your idea. Then whose?"

He chose not to answer. "I told you I've severed my relationship with Premios," he said without prompting. "I don't think it's the right place for me or my students to be working. It's not a healthy environment. I've also encouraged Colby to dump his investment before it's too late."

Back in Lattigo, Cynthia's financial team was recommending the same. They calculated the odds of the company surviving the year as less than ten percent. She felt no loyalty to the firm, but she doubted there was anyone likely to want to buy her shares.

In ten minutes, she could walk to her condo and watch the ocean from her balcony. She could sink back into the blank canvas of a sea view. She decided to make a joke of it, and quickly find a way to escape this conversation. "I hope you're not suggesting I buy Oliver's stake."

"Everything Danny touches get corrupted," Jesus said "It's taken me too long to realize that."

That line of thinking was ridiculous. Of course it would be cathartic to blame Danny for everything: for Chip flying west to investigate the firm, for all the steps that led to his murder, for her being alone, and for everything that she did not like. But there was no proof of that and it belied years of friendship.

She swiveled back to the book conversation that Lopez dodged.

"You said it wasn't your idea to write about Danny's summer. Then whose idea was it?"

"Josh's, of course. It was at the dinner meeting when I thought I was introducing Josh and Oliver to one another. Well, I soon realized they had known each other for years. They started talking about the summer when Oliver and Danny worked together."

"Josh talked about that?"

"Completely," Lopez replied. "He joked about how hard Danny fell for Oliver and how Oliver misused his infatuation. The conversation clearly made Oliver quite uncomfortable. To defuse the situation, I joked that I thought it sounded like the kind of twisted love story I'd write. Oliver was horrified at the suggestion and demanded I never follow through.

"But weeks later when Josh stopped by, he encouraged me to pursue the idea. He claimed that it would be good to force Danny to face the reality of that summer. He maintained that whatever happened, Danny needed to learn to talk about it. People get mistreated all the time, he said, and they just need to get over it.

"What can I say? I was intrigued by the idea. Once planted, the seeds germinated, so I took Josh up on his offer. He proved to be a man of his word, and provided the background, even reviewed the draft early on. It's as much his story as mine."

Cynthia vowed she would never let Danny find out. While she truly believed that Danny loved Josh, she often questioned if the reverse were true. A dangerous idea flittered through her mind—what if Danny discovered the genesis of *The Dumping Ground* and murdered Josh in anger? Maybe Josh wasn't missing, but dead.

Lopez seemed compelled to seek some sort of absolution. "I tried to present the hidden side of a person like Danny in the novel because I think these quiet types are capable of anything. Danny is smart and wily. He's also fiercely protective. I think there is every possibility that he is the monster within Premios. That's why I'm encouraging you to leave.

"Can't you see now why I didn't want to talk to Danny?"

Cynthia felt soiled by even entertaining the possibilities of his claims. It was such utter nonsense. Only a man who wrote novels with themes and plots as horrible as Lopez's could conceive such lunacy. But once stated, the idea burrowed into her mind like a parasitical worm, and she feared she wouldn't be able to purge it.

Lopez stood up to leave. "Tell me, Cynthia, how well do you know your old friend Danny? Do you know that it was his suggestion to Chip that he meet with me that morning? And although I have no evidence to support this idea, I've always had the distinct impression that Chip was expecting Danny to pick him up that morning."

CHAPTER FOURTEEN

The Beginnings

Josh missed Dr. Van Psycho, the mannequin that he kept in the corner of his secret office. The figure always made it easier for him to begin his taped self-reflections. He could never have bared his soul to a real doctor, but he trusted his imagined movie psychoanalyst. While he never actually saw the Augustus Cambrian movie that featured the character, when the renovation crew discovered the hidden chamber that still contained a few of the old movie artifacts including the Van Psycho pieces, he found it oddly exciting and it gave him the idea. Apparently Cambrian sold off most of whatever else he stored in the room over the years, and Josh arranged to sell at a private auction what little remained, but something about the Van Psycho model with its deformed and scarred face spoke to him, and he kept it. Over time the piece almost became a companion. But his therapy sessions were over.

Josh found it an easy decision to restore Cambrian's hideaway. He never thought twice whether he should inform Danny about the spot. Josh liked keeping hidden aces up his sleeve. One never knew when the going might get tough. As time went on what surprised him was how much an old movie prop could pull on him. Growing up as a single child, Josh knew his parents never appreciated his special nature, and he learned to keep a lot of his thoughts to himself, so it felt good to have someone finally who could listen and not judge. Josh never wanted to be judged. Who was good enough to do that? But he liked telling his story.

From a small child on, Josh always felt different. He wasn't like other kids in school or for that matter like his parents. Other people always felt such a need to consider the feelings of those around them. He never understood that. What did it matter whether you were liked or disliked? What mattered was the game.

What Josh found enormously beguiling was testing the limits. He had a special knack for it. From an early age, he discovered the art of amusing others. No matter the situation, he could be funny when he wanted, charming as needed, even appearing as the perfectly behaved child when it was useful. Such skills came in handy when meeting new people. By the time he was in primary school, he sensed that Ma and Pa saw through his act. They stepped around his behaviors gingerly, almost afraid of what he might do, but they were never worried about what he might say to others. Every word he uttered was always appropriate. But in their eyes, his overall behavior was another matter. At first he didn't care, but sometimes some of the teachers at school started to show that same look as his parents. He hated that look.

Maybe that's when he first started testing people. He wanted to know how far he could push them in the direction he wanted before they rebelled. Often he didn't even care about where he pushed them. It was enough to get the ball rolling and see what it might smash. Usually, people never caught on to his manipulations. They just weren't that smart.

His games made life worthwhile. The truth was that there wasn't much that was interesting on their worn-out farm sitting at the edge of the swamp. Pa tried dairy farming but the land wasn't rich enough to host sufficient milk cows to make it worthwhile. Besides that, the twice daily milkings made for a damn hard life. As he got older, Josh realized that his father wasn't particularly fond of hard work. At one point, the man raised enough money to dig out and flood some of his low grounds as cranberry bogs. But that didn't turn out very well either. The freeze got the first crop. The second year, the market was glutted and the prices were low. The family survived only because Ma always worked in town and Pa knew how to be tight with money. When it came to avoiding dispensing cash, he had a powerful ability; the man just never learned to apply himself to earning it. Josh wouldn't begrudge his old man for that. At least he always kept the life insurance up.

Most years there weren't many chores for Josh to do. It left a lot of free time to amuse himself. He didn't care much for reading and there weren't any other kids within walking distance, so early on he experimented with his parents, pushing them to see what he could make them do and how they might react.

He probably started this behavior as a toddler, but Josh treasured a vivid memory of what he considered his first deliberate provocation. Ma loved her fresh raspberries. There was a thick bramble of the berries planted just past the clotheslines back by the wood patch.

Come mid-summer the bracts would be thick with ripening fruit. Josh liked berries almost as much as Ma, especially when she used them to make a custard pie. It was his favorite dessert.

He was only six or seven that summer when Ma came home after a long day working at the hardware store in Thread. Josh no longer recalled where Pa might have been, maybe working back in the woods or out fishing. It was getting late in summer, and the raspberries were nearing the end of the run. But when Ma reached home a little after five there were still several sunlit hours ahead. She asked Josh to head out to the patch and pick whatever berries remained. In exchange, she promised him his pie. She equipped her boy with a plastic bucket and then headed into the kitchen to start preparations for supper. Josh still remembered how tired she looked that night, having worked all day, but yet determined to make a meal for her men that included a special pie.

Under the clouds of that afternoon, he wondered what it would take to break her. It was a strange thought for a little kid. Even all these years later, Josh looked back on his former self with a sense of pride at that early precociousness. He went to the berry patch and worked hard picking those raspberries. Ignoring the thorns pricking and scratching his hands, he found every last one of them. His filled his bucket; it was enough for a pie as well as plenty left to fill several bowls with fresh berries and thick cream for their morning breakfast.

Ma came out of the house to check on his progress. "How's the berries coming along?" she asked.

"Fine," he yelled back.

Then he walked toward her slowly—presenting the bucket before him, looking down with pride at that luscious fruit, and inhaling the beautiful smell of overripe fruit. Ma was smiling. He remembered that.

Just as he reached the gravel driveway to cross over to the kitchen door, he made a grand show of tripping. Anyone could tell he did it on purpose, and he insured that he flung that bucket in such a way that all the berries tumbled out into the gravel. He fell to the ground, rolled across the fallen fruit, crushed their red stain into his clean clothes, and destroying any chance for a pie that night.

And he stood up and smiled. Grinned, really.

So Josh didn't get pie that night, but he got to see the look on his mother's face. That was almost as good. Ma had an expression of horror and fear . . . and resignation . . . and love. Even knowing what happened in that moment on the driveway, she still pretended to love him. She rushed forward to be sure he wasn't hurt, checking if he had any knee scrapes that required an application of stinging Mercurochrome.

Josh felt satisfied. The afternoon stunt was better than eating a slice or two of raspberry custard pie, and it scratched his itch to see where he could lead people, what he could make them do, and how they would respond. He didn't repeat such tricks often, not because he couldn't nor because he thought there was anything wrong with his actions. But he was easily bored and he needed to continually find interesting new problems to solve. There was no satisfaction in doing the same thing over and over. It became harder and harder to invent satisfying and worthwhile new challenges.

As the growing up years went by, an uneasy truce took hold in the Gunderson household. When they thought he wasn't paying attention, both Ma and Pa looked at Josh with suspicion, but what they never realized was that he was also always watching them. In his presence, they carefully skirted betraying any hint about what troubled them. At times he considered secreting a tape recorder in their bedroom, because he suspected that only in the twilight hours, alone in their bedroom, did they dare to whisper to one another their true thoughts about their son. But he never took that step. It was more intriguing to imagine what they might be saying than to know for certain. In the uncertainty he could think of them as both innocent and guilty. If he actually bugged the place, he would know for sure.

At school, he mostly worked his charms to make life easy. He was a good student, and if asked, the other kids would have said that they liked him. But none of them hung out with Josh. Maybe the other kids sensed that he didn't really care about them.

At least the smart ones figured that out. There was a dim boy named Clarence who wasn't quite so clever. About the time Josh was entering puberty, Clarence decided he wanted to be friends with Josh. Clarence, who had been held back in classes a couple of years, was already fifteen when he entered eighth grade, but mentally he was younger than Josh. Not having other friends, Josh let him hang around. They made an odd couple, but since Ma and Pa pretended not to notice that Clarence came by every afternoon, it didn't really matter. At the small school in Thread, Josh avoided paying any public attention to Clarence, but Clarence didn't seem to mind. Since they weren't in the same classes and Clarence lacked the ability to recognize how he was being ignored, everything was good.

After school hours, they built a fort of hay bales in the loft of the barn. Pa pretty much ignored the little hay that was left in the upper reaches of the barn since they no longer had cows to feed. The hay fort was theirs alone. By his age, Clarence should have long given up playing cowboys and Indians in the haymow, but he still loved it. Then Josh introduced the dim boy to other kinds of games. They were ones that Josh found more interesting.

Just getting the first signs of pubic hair, Josh found his changing body especially fascinating, and it wasn't long before he convinced Clarence to drop his trousers so he could inspect what that older boy looked like. Clarence had thick black hair around a long cock, and Josh wanted to touch it. So he did. Not long after he introduced Clarence into the art of jacking off. It was amazing that the boy hadn't learned already, but he was slow, and once he did it, Clarence loved it. Their afternoons in the privacy of the hay bale fort became an adolescent frenzy of masturbation.

Over time, Josh began to consider the on-going hand jobs tedious, but he put up with it since the mutual activity turned Clarence into a virtual slave, letting Josh be the slave master. While he found that role interesting, it eventually became a burden because it always required Josh to monitor Clarence and keep him from ever discussing their activities in front of others. The kid was too slow to comprehend that some things couldn't be talked about.

As autumn turned into winter, this afternoon play went on. When the weather grew colder, the boys branched out into smoking cigarettes and sipping whiskey. Josh had filched the drink from Pa's limited alcohol cabinet. The barn's temperature was too cold for getting naked anyway, although Clarence had a strong sex urge and was always ready for whatever Josh suggested. As hints of spring emerged, Josh came up with a different idea.

On a trip to Duluth with his Ma, he pilfered a copy of *The Joy of Sex* from a bookstore they visited. The book gave him a lot of ideas, especially when he read about this thing called auto-asphyxiation in which a person cuts off the flow of blood to his brain just as he's about to climax sexually. He tried it once, and found the experience intense. He thought it would be a hoot to convince Clarence to give it a try.

Later he contemplated whether he should have been more careful in how he described the act. The kid didn't always grasp all the implications or dangers of an action. But truthfully by spring Josh was finding Clarence tiresome, and he was ready to move on, and so he held no qualms in urging Clarence to try this new thing. He just counseled him to be sure to do it in secrecy, somewhere back in the woods where no one would possibly see him. He also said it would be better if Clarence tried it without Josh around since that would heighten the sense of danger and the reward of the thrill.

On a Saturday night when the senior play was about to open in the Thread high school gymnasium, the alarm was sounded in town to pull together the volunteer fire department. That annoyed Josh since it interfered with his evening's plans. In a rather weak version of *The Music Man*, Josh was about to play the role of Harold Hill, con man par excellence. Josh was always good in any stage production, since he had the knack of assuming the right emotions. People were naturally drawn to him, and he liked to think he could display a certain light in his eyes.

But the alarm canceled the opening night. Clarence was missing and his mom was frantic. Divorced, raising the boy alone, and trying to do the best of a difficult job, she became frantic when he wasn't home by mealtime. Everyone in town knew about Clarence's limited abilities, so it wasn't difficult for the only policeman in town to believe the boy was lost and to convince dozens to join him for a search of the local woods. So many people signed up, including several students from the cast that the high school drama teacher had no choice but to postpone the play.

No one found Clarence that night. In fact, they only found his body a week later, after it had been desecrated by scavenging crows and coyotes. While the evidence wasn't all that clear, the coroner ruled that the boy had hung himself. He declared it a suicide, although Clarence's mom refused to believe that her son could take such an act. She said he was always so happy.

As for Josh, he was pleased to have his afternoons free once again.

That was the first time Josh's experiments went too far, although at the time Josh didn't think of it that way. In his opinion, every person controlled his own fate. While Josh might set in motion certain actions, it was up to the other individual to respond however he might. Josh certainly never lost any sleep over Clarence's death.

Just like Josh never worried about the way parents died. As the years went on, Josh found Ma and Pa more and more troublesome. They were sitting atop all that life insurance, and he could use that money if they were to die since Josh's attempted career in Hollywood was going nowhere. The charms he displayed in the small pond of Thread, Wisconsin didn't work as well in a major city. He hadn't counted on there being so many other people just like him. He also went a little crazy with playing up the gay thing. He blamed that on Thread. It had been so much fun in Thread to let a little mascara and flamboyance needle people, but in Hollywood, mere appearance didn't have the same power.

As he floundered trying to find himself, he met a guy who had made a fortune flipping houses. Josh thought to himself that he could do the same. While his father might not have been very successful, Pa did succeed at drilling into Josh's mind basic economic principles. All Josh needed to get started was a small grubstake.

So when on a summer visit to his parents Josh discovered that their chimney was clogged, he decided not to warn them. He figured Ma wouldn't even think about such matters and that Pa, lazy as he was, would never get around to cleaning the chimney himself or calling someone out. Thinking of that untapped life insurance, Josh decided to wait and see what would happen when his Pa turned the furnace back on in the fall. To minimize heating bills, his father kept the house well insulated so if the chimney clogged and carbon monoxide backed up, it wouldn't take much to suffocate the old folks.

He reasoned his parents never really did anything for him, and he was pretty certain they would have preferred if he hadn't bothered to even come home for a visit. What was it to him if something should happen? It would be their own fault. It was Pa's responsibility to maintain the old house better.

When Officer Campbell called from Thread to inform him of the tragedy, Josh was of course appropriately surprised, even after Campbell tiptoed around his disclosure so gingerly that it took all of Josh's skill not to blurt it out first. Of course, he returned to Thread for the funeral. A good son had to do that.

And he was glad that he did. He had only been expecting to receive the life insurance. The farm was worthless. But then he discovered someone was buying up land in the area. While he had no idea it was part of a plan to build a major new resort, it didn't matter whether he knew that or not. He was still able to negotiate a great price. That extra cash really let him transform his financial life.

The trip also had other benefits. When attending the funeral and standing by his parents graves for a tedious reading by the fussy old minister, he delighted in sporting glitter on his eyelashes just to see whether the old reverend could sputter his way through the ceremony. Then he noticed how his appearance attracted the attention of a local hunk named Tony Masters. Everyone other than Tony had their eyes down to contemplate his parents' sad passing. But Tony was looking at Josh with interest, and Josh liked flirting with the hunky husband of the town nurse. He hoped it could lead to a pretty hot night, and make his hometown visit even more memorable.

But Josh happened to glance away from Tony and that's when he saw Danny. Danny wasn't looking down at the ground like any good Christian should have been doing. Rather he was spying on Tony and Danny as they gave each other the eye.

That's when his old obsession reignited. A few years earlier, he had wondered about Danny's purity of soul for a short period following the suicide of the boy's mother, but Josh thought he had been able to escape that interest after the previous summer's escapade when he convinced Oliver to play his trick on Danny. He figured he had learned what he wanted to know. But now he was suddenly jabbed with an intuition that Danny had survived that experience too easily. What had Josh really learned about Danny? Somehow the question of what constituted the true Danny became even more important. He had to find out everything about the kid.

But this time he decided to be more careful about how he approached gaining that information. He could take his time. It would be his best experiment to date. It was a long game ahead.

CHAPTER FIFTEEN

Firmer Ground

Colby Endicott had demanded the meeting, and he was waiting in the conference room for Danny. Danny was instead sitting in Josh's office chair, feeling unsettled and unwilling to confront the next steps needed. A dampened sense of disorder had lowered the buzz of the office. When once the floor hummed with the energy of dozens of excited young men and women, each thinking they were about to create a new world that would endow them with riches, the remaining staff now hunkered close to their desks. They worked with a beaten air, wondering if their jobs and the company would survive to the next paycheck.

Nearly a month had passed since Josh vanished and Oliver had been found murdered. Colby and Danny needed to talk, but Danny had put it off as long as possible. No one in authority wanted to connect all the fallen pieces—Josh, Chip, and Oliver. Missing funds. Why should they? Nothing suggested that Oliver had died in anything other than a burglary gone wrong. No fingerprints on the scene linked Oliver's murder to anyone; his own gun had been turned against him when he tried to stop a thief. Each crime was a broken shard with no matching edge to another. Different police departments. Different stories. Danny felt everything was dangerously entwined, and he suspected Colby thought the same but only Danny had access to the full details of what was hidden in the files and tapes of Josh's secret room. But that extra knowledge gave him no insight as to what to do next.

He walked toward the conference room where Orleans was keeping Colby distracted with a review of the company's financials. Although Orleans was upbeat about the firm's future, Danny doubted a positive spreadsheet would diminish Colby's concerns.

He entered the room. Colby looked a decade older. His hair needed cutting and his clothes were wrinkled. The pallor in his cheeks contradicted the beautiful spring weather outside. He smiled weakly at Danny, but his face held no joy and only sought comfort. Danny thought of the cats on the old farm where he grew up. If they lived long enough, such animals reached the point where they seemed to realize their time was over. On the sounding of their internal alarm, they would display one final bout of friendliness, rubbing their arched backs insistently once more against everyone's legs in a final farewell before walking off in a last trek into the woods. Danny never knew where they went. But they seemed to understand there was a place waiting for their death. And he always appreciated that sad, last rub. And they never looked back once they started that stroll.

There was that scent of end times about Colby Endicott. Danny didn't want to be in the room with him.

"Have you heard from Josh?" Colby demanded.

Knowing that Danny didn't like to talk about Josh, Orleans quickly jumped in and answered. "The last communication we received was two weeks ago after he executed a durable power of attorney and sent it to my attention by express mail. It came from a notary public near the Miami airport. We tracked that guy down, who said he had never seen Josh before that day. According to him, Josh didn't say anything about what he was doing or why. He simply provided his driver's license, stamped his fingerprint on the register, and signed the documents. We had the fingerprint checked. It was Josh's. Since this happened in Miami, I think he may have fled to Latin America, but if he did he used a fake passport. In short, we have not seen Josh."

Danny listened passively to Orleans' speculation. He didn't believe it. Josh was still nearby, watching, waiting, and plotting. He knew it. He had listened to the tapes. All of them. Josh would never let him go.

Colby feared someone was trying to kill the investors in Premios, and because he assumed Josh was motivated by that same emotion, Colby believed he had fled to safety, a step that Colby desperately wanted to take if only he knew where that zone of safety might be. So he demanded to know, "Why did Josh disappear?"

For Danny, the acceptance had been slow and painful achieved, but he finally realized that he never really knew Josh. Maybe decades of experience together and the slow accretion of daily details should have made Josh's character clear, but it took the metaphorical bomb dropped into Danny's life to knock down the obscuring trees of life and open up the dangerous vistas that he never realized existed.

But that wasn't quite right. The situation was more like the first time he returned to Thread after residing in Los Angeles for several years. Upon his return, the house he grew up in seemed so small, and the stores around Thread's town square so barren. Without being able to see them each day, the elements that once defined his life had melded into something different. The trees in the forest no longer seemed so tall, the clouds in the deep blue sky of summer appeared alien, and the shadows they pulled across the lake water below were chilly and dark. Everything was different and yet remained entirely the same. A Wisconsin summer in a small town was eternal. It was he who had changed. He grew comfortable existing under different kinds of light and shadow. The familiar elements of his youth were transformed into a foreign place, not because they had shifted, but because the man he once had been was now transformed by new experiences.

So too had Danny lost the Josh he loved. It was more than discovering the man's secrets. Once he might have laughed about his lover shielding a private hideaway. Everyone kept secrets. Good lord, he harbored enough of his own, each hidden away and never expressed to Josh. In all likelihood, that room meant less to Josh than Danny's tortured childhood memories meant to him. But then Danny discovered all the details squirreled away within the folders and he listened to Josh bare his soul on those inexplicable tapes. Facts that once learned could never be ignored.

Neither Orleans nor Danny answered Colby's rhetorical question, so Colby gave a response that they already knew he held. "We've stumbled into something evil. I don't understand it, and maybe that's all for the better. But Chip and Oliver were murdered because of something about this firm. And Josh is hiding to avoid the same fate. I know the police laugh at me. I can tell. But I don't think you can laugh so easily. But I don't know for sure. Maybe Josh let you in on the truth. Maybe you know what was unleashed. Maybe he figured out how to protect you."

Danny was certain Josh had done just the opposite. After so many years, Josh ripped off his mask and forced Danny to stare at the man's true appearance. Colby wasn't the one in danger. It was Danny. At any moment, the snare would be drawn tight.

Neither Orleans nor Danny had any idea where Josh was, nor did Danny have any faith in anything Josh told him these past few months. For all of Josh's talk about the dangers of Premios going under and their entire lives at risk of bankruptcy, such a view had proved to be highly melodramatic. While the company might have missed the window for a big successful public launch, the outlook for Premios currently appeared bright.

Somehow Josh made that happen. At least that's what Orleans claimed.

Maybe that was the trap intended to lure Danny in. Within days of Josh's talk at the New York BLINK conference and from his hidden location, Josh arranged a sale of one of his major pieces of land. The real estate deal arrived neatly wrapped up in a folder with a real bow accompanied by a transfer of several million dollars into the couple's bank account. It came with instructions to invest the money back into Premios. Orleans was shocked. Josh never mentioned trying to sell that particular block of land, nor was she aware that a real estate company was assembling a major block of land for a new plant in the inland empire. Danny remembered how well Josh had negotiated the sale of his parents' marshy farmland years ago to the Lattigo when they were secretly buying up the land needed for the American Seasons resort. Josh knew how the world worked.

Colby understood how the firm's financial footing was stronger, but he didn't care. He sputtered out what he had come to say, "Endicott-Meyers wants to sever our relationship with Premios. We don't believe there's a future in your business model."

Orleans and Danny exchanged looks. She had warned Danny to expect this ultimatum. Colby had been hinting at it for days.

"That doesn't make sense," she countered. "Have you even looked at what's been happening over the past month? We've turned the corner. Look at the growth in unique visitors and their levels of engagement. Advertisers are noticing. The aggregators have started to sign up and they're bringing in big name brands. Revenue is way up. With the added investments that Josh and Danny placed in the firm, our projections look great. We'll weather this storm in the market and be in a great position to go public when the timing is better. We might even be profitable by the end of the year."

Colby pushed away the folders. Normally, Danny would have found this behavior odd, but he knew no amount of capitalistic voyeurism was sufficient to make Colby grab the bait.

"I've been looking around," Colby said, "and talking to friends on Madison Avenue. I know people at Razorfish and the other big digital agencies. None of us believe what you're seeing is anything more than a statistical blip. It's time to pull the plug."

Silently Danny cheered Colby on. It was time to end it. He should follow that advice himself. If he ever saw Josh again, he would make clear that their life together was over, including that part called Premios. It had come to an end. Danny should never have looked at all those papers or listened to those tapes. Josh didn't love him. Yet for some reason, Danny felt obligated to continue to protect Josh by holding on to the files.

How had he never seen the true Josh? He thought back over a relationship filled with memories: the first time Josh kissed him when they went skating on that frozen flowage; the evening they first had sex in his parent's house the night before the sale was finalized; the way Josh convinced him to pack up and move west and their first nights together in that tiny duplex in the Silverlake neighborhood. His mental scrapbook, once filled with beautiful moments, was dissolving into a brownish swirl of muck.

Colby was still talking. "We don't care what you do, but I intend to stay alive. Find a candidate to buy out the Endicott-Meyers stake. We're done."

"Where will we find an investor? You have to give us time," said Orleans.

"Don't give me that. I've talked to Barbara Linsky. Josh asked her to find a buyer months ago. We've known for months that he wanted us out. Well, now we're granting Josh his wish. Make it happen."

Cynthia toyed with her food. The pork medallions with potato pancakes and freshly made applesauce looked delicious. It was one of Wally's favorite recipes, first perfected at his original Loon Town Café back in Thread and long retained in the Los Angeles incarnation. When she was a waitress, she always encouraged patrons to order the dish. She chose it today thinking that its taste would somehow comfort her. But she had no appetite.

"So you're really going back to Wisconsin?" Wally asked. He was developing a serious paunch and his hair displayed a healthy dose of grey. Both Stephen and Wally were at the table. She was the one who suggested a last lunch together. She touched her own stomach to remind herself of why she was leaving. Already starting to show, she wanted to ensure that Chip's daughter, their child, would be born on tribal land. Her return had been delayed too long. Lingering in Los Angeles had taught her nothing and gave her no comfort.

"Do you have any theories?" Stephen asked. "I mean about what ties all this craziness together."

"What do you mean?" she replied, although she knew exactly his intent. When she was a child, Cynthia seldom wondered how pieces fit together or why things happened the way they did. While everyone and everything fascinated her, she never felt a need to understand the connections beneath the surface but accepted everything as it was thanks to her boundless optimism. Recent events took more than Chip from her. They had also absconded with her joy.

Stephen's question was typical of him, as the logical and serious one in this couple. Before he met Danny, Stephen ran the Van Elkind estate as their local majordomo. Stephen seldom smiled, but he noticed everything.

"There's such a pattern of wrong-doing," Stephen pointed out. "The police stay in their own little circles of responsibilities. Maybe they don't want to see the linkages. But it's obvious. All these crimes must be related to Premios and Josh. You and Chip invested in Premios, and your company is embezzled and Chip is killed. Someone breaks into Danny's house. A major investor in Premios is found murdered in a household break-in back in Chicago. And Josh conveniently disappears. Has anyone heard from him?"

"No. I talked to Danny yesterday," Cynthia replied, "to tell him that I was leaving tomorrow. He said there's been no recent sign of Josh, but I have trouble getting him to say anything more."

Even over the phone she could tell that Danny had hardened. At the same time she worried that she was allowing Jesus Lopez's conversation at the park to influence her. No matter what Lopez insinuated, whatever connected all of these incidents, Danny was not at the heart of it. It was Josh.

"But Kenosha told me that no one has seen Josh since he was in New York to speak at the BLINK conference. Still they know he's alive. Apparently he arranged the sale of some property and signed over responsibility to Danny for all his legal affairs. That's the last anyone at

Premios has heard from him. I'm hoping he's fled to protect Danny."

"You really think he would do that?" asked Wally.

"He loves him. Of course he would." It's what they expected her to say, but Cynthia knew that Wally was really wondering if Josh was capable of causing all the damage. They all wanted to believe the man would do anything for Danny, but they feared they were entirely wrong in their assessment of the man.

Wally took a sip of his wine. He motioned toward Cynthia's largely uneaten food. "You should finish that. We put it back on the menu today just for you."

Cynthia wasn't going to let his motherly talk distract her. "Josh and Danny have been together since 1987. I know they love each other."

"I have no doubt that Danny loves Josh," Wally said. He looked toward Stephen as though seeking affirmation, but his partner maintained his usual quiet stance. Wally sighed. "The thing is I've always distrusted Josh."

"Really. I've never heard this before."

"Remember that fall in Thread when he showed up after his parents died in that freak accident of carbon monoxide poisoning? He was so flamboyant and sought to be the center of attention wherever he went." Wally shuddered as though recalling some memory he didn't care to disclose. "He tried to win over everyone, even that creepy Van Elkind kid who used to torment you. Remember how he fanned that kid's obsessions?"

Cynthia never liked to dwell on the unpleasant parts of her past. Once distasteful things were concluded she preferred to tuck them away in the recesses of her memory. The Van Elkind boy was a drug-addled, obsessed teenager, a kid that in the end she felt sorry for, like she usually did for everyone, especially after his grandmother, the matron and his guardian at the Van Elkind camp, died and he became so desolate.

Wally continued, "I always thought Josh egged on half of what that kid did. He really knew how to push the kid's buttons. Weird in a way. And then after all these years, Josh actually goes out and buys the abandoned estate that once belonged to the kid's family. What's with that? Why would he want to go back there? I know that you and Chip still live in the area, but Danny and Josh never talked about northern Wisconsin. So suddenly, he drops a million or more buying a derelict mansion and restoring it. It never made sense to me."

"Chip and I were happy when they made the purchase. We liked having them back in our lives."

Neither Stephen nor Wally said anything. She knew what they were thinking: if Josh hadn't bought the old camp, then maybe he would never have talked Chip into investing in Premios, and Chip might still be alive. She rubbed her stomach reflexively as though that might bring forth a genie to grant that different existence. But truthfully, both Chip and she were happy to see the two men back in the area. Chip welcomed having someone restore the old mansion. While the American Seasons complex generally propped up property prices around the lakes, few folks wanted the enormous places that were once the getaways of millionaires from Milwaukee and Chicago and the abandoned place was becoming an eyesore. Chip always considered it a good omen to have the estate shiny once again.

When she joined her two friends in one of their first walk-throughs of the abandoned place, she was enthralled. An interior decorator from Los Angeles, who had flown out to take on the restoration job, was also on hand. (That irked Cynthia's mother, since she thought she deserved to be first in line for the design job, having once done work for the Van Elkind family.) But Josh bragged about wanting the finest, and the designer was excited about the camp's potential. All the work was the very best.

The house had stood empty for years. While its thick log walls and double-paned windows certainly protected the interior, evidence of mice was throughout and there were raccoons in the attic. The few pieces of furniture that had been abandoned in the place were dusty and deteriorating. All in all, the place exuded a spooky air. Danny seemed subdued as though the house was haunted, but Josh was ebullient. He flung out ideas to the designer with the abandon of a kitten in catnip, gleefully rolling in his own imagination.

Stephen signaled for a server to clear the table. He recognized that Cynthia would not eat any more of her dish. "A black coffee for me," he said to the server and then gestured for the others at the table to place their orders.

"I'm fine," Cynthia said. She knew what was coming. Stephen always felt most at home with a coffee in hand. He wanted to add something.

Once his cup arrived, he took time swirling one sugar cube into its blackness. "I find I have to agree with Wally," he said. "There is something troubling about Josh. Life is only about him."

"What do you mean?" Cynthia asked.

"There came a point when we really didn't want him involved with our restaurants any more. Certainly, he's charming, feckless in a way, and always filled with grand ideas. I don't deny that he's smart and clever. But he achieves all of that with a price. He's remarkably manipulative. You hardly know that he's doing it, and it's even harder to explain what he's done. But he leaves behind a trail of bad feelings and disorder. He always gets what he want, although I must admit that usually I was never quite certain what it was he wanted."

Cynthia wanted to shout at both of these men for their silence, but she bit her tongue, because she knew the reason. That was the laconic Wisconsin way. They never said anything. Just as Chip never mentioned to Danny how he distrusted Josh's integrity. As a younger man, Chip was easily angered and quick to take offense at perceived slights. It took a great deal of personal constraint for him to tamp down that part of his personality. His first encounters with Josh had been testy, and Chip always feared that he never released his early resentments and so he gave Josh the benefit of the doubt. Everyone was always willing to forgive Josh for actions that might doom others.

But Cynthia never felt those vibes. The few times that Chip and she discussed his assessment of Josh, she quickly dismissed his concerns. All that mattered to her was that Danny was happy.

"I know that Josh wasn't always the most sincere," she said, "but did you ever see him do anything that would make you believe he's capable of such horrible events?"

"I could list many things," Stephen said, "but everything I would tell you would seem superficial. It would also make me look petty."

Wally nodded his head in agreement.

Stephen continued, "But here's one example of what I mean. Josh was always good at talking to our customers. He has a knack for knowing what people want to hear, and he gives them what they want. But I always felt his customer interactions were a ploy to prompt our guests to open up and disclose something that they might otherwise keep hidden. He liked to collect secrets."

"He never forgot anything," Wally added.

"And it wasn't just that he remembered it all. He looked for ways to use it maliciously. We had this well-connected Hollywood producer who frequently dined with us. Most of the time his companion wasn't his wife, and we assumed he was sleeping with most of the young women who ate at his table. But a restaurant booth is like a church confessional. What happens in them stays there.

"Josh knew that. But one night—it was still in our early days when Josh worked as a host—he walked over to the man's table. It was on a night when he was actually eating with his wife. Josh made a point of welcoming the man, and then dropped a comment about he hoped to see him back with his beautiful daughter again. Because the wife was quick to assume that the dinner had been with some fling, she straightened her back and her face flared with anger. The husband's mood darkened, and Josh immediately backtracked about confusing the man with another guest. But the damage was done. I saw Josh's face when he turned to walk back to the reservations desk. It bore a look of triumph. He deliberately provoked that discord. Of course, I couldn't prove it, and there was no rational reason why he would want to do it, especially since we never saw that particular man again. And he had been a big spender. But I think Josh did it just for the pleasure of doing it." Stephen wrapped his story with the finality of a lawyer's summation.

"He did it because he's twisted," Wally added.

"Even if all that is true, and I'm sure it is, isn't it quite a leap to what we're imagining? Are you saying Josh set in motion a plot to kill both a good friend and a major investor? Why?" Cynthia wanted someone to blame for her loss, and Josh could be that person, but it had to make sense.

Neither man could offer her that explanation.

But as she looked around the table, one nagging thought troubled Cynthia and she had to express it. "How is it possible that Danny didn't see this?"

The hidden room was comforting. Danny could understand why Josh liked it and now often wondered, because he was a sound sleeper, if there had been nights when his lover would get out of bed, walk down the several flights of stairs, and work in this room. Although Danny couldn't ever recall not being able to find Josh in the house, it was clear the room had been often used.

Now Danny spent too much time in the hideaway, and he didn't understand why. Night after night, year after year, he slept next to a man who kept so many secrets. They rose together, took turns showering, drank coffee, read the paper, went to work, watched television, made love, and kissed each other good night—all without ever really knowing one other. Josh could have asked him anything, and Danny would have answered as truthfully as possible. But not Josh. Instead, this man obsessed over plots and goals.

Just outside the wine cellar, the game room held a large fireplace with a showplace of a hearth that sported an enormous mantel. Outfitted with gas logs, the fireplace required only one flick of the finger on a switch and the flames would burst forth. Danny was tempted to sweep everything off the shelves and out of the desk drawers . . . and carry everything out, set the fire blazing, and toss each piece onto the flames. One by one, the ashes could float up the flue and out into the night breezes. But Danny had learned his lesson decades earlier. Eliminating the possibility of knowing didn't keep one from wondering and reliving what might have been.

It was painful but he had forced himself to face the room. During the course of the past few weeks, he read through every document. Upon completion, he wasn't certain he had made the right decision. He wasn't even certain he understood Josh one bit better than before he had started. But Danny had learned he stood alone.

The truth was he preferred the Josh that shimmered in his happy memories captured in the photo albums upstairs and in the stories that friends would repeat. That Josh was gone, not just because he was missing for two months and not because he left behind the tools that made it moot whether he was dead, alive, in Los Angeles, or lounging in some remote South American jungle . . . no, it was because everything he was meant to be had been torn away and Josh had been the one to rip it off.

Why? That was the question. What had he hoped to accomplish? Somehow, Danny knew that Josh's stunt was meant as a test and he was certain he would fail it.

Back in 1988, on the first weekend that Danny spent in Los Angeles, Josh woke him up one morning to say they were taking a hike. Grabbing a basket containing a thermos of coffee, cups, a bottle of champagne and fresh croissants, Josh drove them a few miles from their tiny home and parked near the Griffith Observatory. Danny expected their destination would be the broad terraces and roofs of that iconic building that promised an expansive view of the city. Instead Josh said, "Follow me."

It was a brisk January morning coming after several days of winter rain. All dirt had been washed away, leaving nothing in the air to obscure the cleansing sun. In the unclouded Los Angeles light, every twig and grass blade appeared distinct and sharp. The hills stretched upward in a brilliant green. A variety of birds twittered in the bushes. The two started to walk up a dirt path, which was damp and packed solid by the recent rains. Since it was early in the morning, there were only a few cars parked nearby and Danny could see just a handful of other hikers on the paths—mostly a few solitary walkers with their dogs. Up ahead was the crest of a high hill, and the path they were on seemed to lead toward its peak.

"Is that where we're going?" Danny asked.

"Yes," Josh said, "we're hiking to the top of Mount Hollywood, because I want to show you your new world."

He pulled out the thermos and two cups, poured some coffee and handed Danny a filled cup. "Take a look," he said as he moved his arm to encompass the scene in front of them. Straight ahead was the copper dome of the observatory. Beyond and below stretched the streets and avenues of Los Angeles marching in straight lines toward the sea. "That hill in the distance," he said, "is Palos Verdes and off to the side you can make out the towers of downtown Long Beach. We're lucky that this morning is so clear. Look at it all."

And Danny discerned each of those locations, but in his imagination, he also envisioned trips back in time and across the ocean. Josh went on, "And in that direction is Hollywood. We can catch a good view of the famous sign from here. And over there are Beverly Hills and Westwood, and where you see the line of deeper blue that's the ocean. In that direction, you're looking at Santa Monica. I'll take you there one day and we'll ride the Ferris wheel on the pier so we can see even further. We'll stare beyond the horizon."

It seemed magical, this landscape of fabled names. "Now turn in that direction." Josh commanded.

And Danny turned toward the east, where the early morning sun was still low and reflected off the tall towers of downtown Los Angeles. "That tall building under construction is Library Tower.

When it opens it will be seventy-three stories high, the tallest building west of the Mississippi and the tallest building in the world topped with a helicopter pad. Wouldn't it be something to fly and land there?"

The towns of Thread and Lattigo seemed a distant memory. He made the right decision to move here and live with Josh. "When we get to the top of the mountain," Josh promised, "we'll open the champagne and the world will all be clear. Let's go."

They began to walk, crossing the remnants of some old bridge, and then moving upward in a series of switchbacks, each offering new and interesting views. At one point, they passed an oasis of plantings, benches, and tables. There was a water trough, maybe for horses or dogs, and Danny remembered that honeybees were crawling on its edge to get to the water. "They call that Dante's View. Some old guy comes up every day to water and tend it." In giving his tour and providing commentary, Josh was happier than Danny had ever seen him.

They rounded another bend, which opened up a view of the other side of the peak and hills. An entirely different cityscape spread before them. "There's the Valley," Josh said. "But no champagne yet."

Danny remembered how he started to tire, but Josh encouraged him to maintain a steady pace. Eventually they neared the top of the mountain where there was a viewing platform. "That's where we're headed," Josh said.

Once there, he removed the champagne bottle and two plastic cups. "We need to keep this hidden," he said. "No alcohol allowed in public parks." But he poured them each a glass.

"Look around," he commanded.

In every direction, the world spread out in its glory. The Hollywood Hills and Santa Monica Mountains marched toward the west. To the east, the San Gabriel Mountains reached high into the sky with snow-peaked tops that defined the distance. The Los Angeles basin, the San Gabriel Valley, the San Fernando Valley, the ribbon of the concrete-controlled Los Angeles River, the distant plains of Orange County, the millions of people, the ships on the Pacific, and the industry of an entire world lay before them. It was awe-inspiring.

Josh smiled. "We don't need a helicopter to reach the top of a building to see the world. We did it ourselves by using our own two feet. There's no better view than this from anywhere. Welcome to Los Angeles. Thank you for coming."

Josh tipped his glass and touched its plastic lip against Danny's. They took a sip and then Josh leaned forward to kiss Danny's lips. "I love you," he said.

Danny held back his tears. This was all that he had ever wanted—to be loved and to belong. The world was indeed a wondrous place, and he would revel in it from this day forward.

Josh made a grand gesture to encompass the 360-degree view. "It's all ours," he said. "But it only became complete today. With you."

Was any of it true? Then or today?

Danny was afraid that he would never know for sure.

Barbara Linsky was not happy. "Why show me these files?" she asked.

Danny had lured Orleans and her to Josh's office hidden away on the bottom level of the mansion. He needed other people to know some of what he had discovered. Danny was looking at them both, wondering what they made of the various notes about the business. He was still keeping the recordings his secret.

As always, Orleans seemed fully in control. But Danny had known her a long time. Flickers of emotion passed through her eyes, and she was displaying the nervous flipping of errant strands of hair and the clasping of her hands. She was not happy. He wondered what upset her the most: the hidden projects, the secret room, or the growing awareness that she knew so little about her boss.

"These files could destroy everything that I've been working on, and you don't want that to happen," Barbara went on. "The sale with the Mexican media firm Actuades is so close. But give them the slightest whiff of scandal and they'll rush back to Mexico City. No matter how much they want a new media toehold in the United States, they won't put up with this."

Danny no longer cared what Barbara Linsky wanted to see or not. The fact was that after Colby's surprise resignation she had been named Chairman of the Board and the person in that role needed to know about Josh's secret projects.

Danny had spent a lot of time reviewing these files and trying to make sense of them. They frightened him, not just because they proved how little he knew Josh, but also because they demonstrated

Premios' role in planning an enormous crime.

"We have to do something," Danny said. He was calm. He accepted the weight of Josh's transgressions. "It's all clearly laid out in these flowcharts and planning documents. Josh was acting illegally, the way he commissioned various programming projects that on the surface seemed related to a distinct part of the business model, but were all building blocks for this person or team in Poland to assemble into 'Project Big Stick.'"

Danny wanted to be clear, concise, and thorough. He had spent too many hours trying to make sense of it all and he needed these two women to understand what seemed so clear.

"Once complete, Big Stick was intended to be an automated way to insert malware into the computers of clients of Premios, suck back data from those clients—things like personal information, credit card data, and even work files—transfer that data into an off-site repository where the algorithms supposedly intended for making recommendations based on personal preferences would instead sift through mountains of information and detect usable data. In other words, they could access details to allow them to use funds, blackmail clients, and manipulate public interest.

"The crazy thing is—even from reading all of this—I can't tell if Josh even had a clear goal for how to use this stolen material. Sometimes I don't even think it was all his idea, that maybe somebody else was forcing him to do these horrible things."

There he had said it. After a week of devouring and cross-referencing every file in the room, Danny had voiced the only explanation he could generate that might make sense of it all and still redeem Josh. The man might have his secrets, but at the same time, he had an inherent goodness, and if their years together were not an entire fiction, then Danny couldn't let all those memories be transformed into lies. And the only way he could see to forgive Josh's behavior was if Josh had been coerced or blackmailed.

"You're grasping at straws," Orleans said tiredly.

"What do you mean?" he demanded.

Orleans stood up, walked toward the desk, and dropped the folder she had been reviewing. It landed atop a stack of well-thumbed documents. Small colored tags were attached to various pages where Danny had jotted notes or observations.

"You refuse to see your boyfriend for who he really is."

Linsky didn't say anything, but she observed both closely. Danny had no idea what the famed financial analyst thought of any of this.

Finally Danny said, "I've known Josh longer than either of you."

Enigmatically Linsky replied, "Time can be its own mask."

"You love the man. I get that," said Orleans. "But people wear different masks for different people. When Josh was with you, he always played the thoughtful, kind, and amusing person you wanted him to be. But when he was around other people, he became other things. Maybe he's not the person you most want him to be.

"When I first met him at the New Loon Town Café, he truly bowled me over . . . the way he read people so easily and always seemed to know what to say to win their attention. I envied that skill and I wanted it. I loved seeing him show me what was possible. In so many ways, Josh pushed me to be better."

Danny didn't understand what point she was trying to make. "That's what I love about him too."

"But there's another side. He loves knowing things that other people want hidden. When I first started as the restaurant's hostess and getting to know the frequent guests, Josh would often ask to have a drink together near the end of service. We would sit at the bar, and he'd order me a glass of champagne and ask about the night. He'd wait to hear whatever little bits of gossip I picked up, especially when it involved a guest with a public persona. Who were they with? What did they order? How did they behave? For the longest time, I was flattered by Josh's attention. But gradually, I realized he was using me to find out what was going on. Fine, I thought, he's the boss. That's his prerogative. But he loved my stories too much, and he never forgot a detail."

"So why did you go to work for him when we started Premios?" Danny demanded.

"Because he believed in me. He pushed me to get my MBA, and he listened. I knew I was talented and smart, and he saw that in me. Just like he saw your talents. Without him, do you think you would have accomplished nearly half of what you've done? He pushed you into writing. Don't you realize how he fed you the best of his gossip so you could add flavor and scandal to your early blogs? That's what drew readers, more than your descriptions about food or wine. He wanted you to succeed and he ensured it happened. Josh makes people bloom."

Linsky interrupted. "We're running out of time, and while this is all very nice to hear, frankly, I don't give a damn whether the man was a crook or a saint. He left us a problem and we have to deal with it.

"Nothing more is to be sent to the man in Poland. There's no reason to debate this, because we simply must sever our relationship with him immediately. And in a very quiet way. I can't stress that enough. And, Danny, destroy these files. And we will march forward as though they never existed."

"Why?" Danny asked.

"I really don't care what motivated Josh to engineer this fiasco, whether someone forced him, or he's some mad evil genius. It doesn't matter. Bottom line, this is a crime scene, and Josh was about to break the law, or maybe he already did, but we're stopping it in its tracks, minimizing the damage and getting out."

"Maybe we should inform the authorities," ventured Orleans.

"If you want to kiss Premios and your stock options good-bye, go ahead. And don't involve an attorney. We need to maximize deniability. At this point, the sale to Actuades is virtually a done deal, as long as we keep the product from getting tainted. Make any of this public and Actuades will walk. Keep quiet, and we all pick up a few million as we let Premios go its own way."

Orleans was not so easily deterred. Danny suspected she saw Josh's disappearance as giving her a chance to become the CEO of Premios, but that potential wouldn't last long with new owners. She argued her case. "Things have turned around. Revenues are up. Premios could survive without a sale. We should stay private."

Linsky scoffed. "You're the CFO. You know that's not true. The company needs to be fed a significantly bigger investment if there's any chance of growing it into what it wants to be. That was the whole purpose of an early IPO. To get the investment funds you need. The piddling advertising that's shown up isn't going to last, and even if it did, it's insufficient to monetize the site. There are a lot of challenges for long-term viability. Only the kind of cash this Mexican media company offers Premios gives it a chance to weather the storm. As long as this shit's around, that won't happen."

They all looked at the pile of paper on the desk. Danny thought about how much work he had done trying to make sense of it all. In a way the documents were his only remaining link to the still-missing Josh. "So what are you recommending?"

"We end it." Her tone was no-nonsense. "You said you have the contact information for the overseas programmer. Send him his final payment and say it's finished. Burn these files. But only Big Stick has to go. There's nothing at Premios to suggest the various projects are connected, so if we let the legitimate ones go forward, they can benefit Premios; I might even invite one of you to speak about the preference engine at next year's BLINK. It's good tactics to deploy the smaller truths to hide larger disasters."

"What happens when Josh reappears?" Josh asked.

Orleans murmured in response, "If he reappears."

Danny turned on her. "Why do you say that? Do you think he's dead?"

Orleans was not cowed. "Seriously, Danny, wouldn't it be better if he were? Harsh as that sounds. And remember what's happened to Chip and Oliver. Somehow their deaths have to be connected to this. Maybe you're right, and maybe Josh is a pawn of something bigger. But we don't need to know. We don't want to know. If he was being used, Josh has probably already been killed. On the other hand, if he was the ringleader . . . well, then, we can only hope he's realized his evil and killed himself, or at least disappeared forever. Look. He knew something was coming. He planned for it by setting up the durable power of attorney and selling that property."

Danny wouldn't give up hope, as much as he vacillated between hating Josh and wanting him back. "And maybe he's just waiting."

Linsky commented on that. "Maybe. But I hope not."

But Danny thought otherwise.

He was the only one in the room who had listened to the final recording that Danny phoned in as part of his therapy tapes. The message was simple and direct.

"Danny, I know you found these, and now you know the real me. And you may be calling me the devil, but don't think it's over yet. I still have to figure out just who you are."

CHAPTER SIXTEEN

In Hiding

Josh was bored. He never planned to spend so much time hiding out at the Wisconsin camp. Before he confronted Oliver, Josh hadn't even planned out his follow-on steps. But maybe he always knew where he needed to go. After all, he used a fake identity and credit card to rent a van to head toward Oliver's townhouse. After that messy event, the choice seemed clear. He simply drove north toward Thread, stopping at a grocery warehouse west of Green Bay to fill the van with everything he needed. He told himself the escape north was a short-term solution until he determined his long-term game. While he had solved one problem in protecting Danny's future, he still grappled with an unquenchable thirst that would only be sated once he tapped into Danny's true nature.

Once he was in Thread, Josh avoided venturing outside the camp. He didn't even go near the lake because a fisherman offshore might spot him. For the same reason, he abandoned the main rooms of the house. Their expansive windows of glass were too exposed. Instead, he holed up in the upper floors where heavy drapes could black out any evening lights. He knew it was too early to be discovered.

Determining the next step was unclear. It would be easy to simply flee as a fugitive since a great deal of money awaited him in his hidden accounts. From the money stolen from the Arabs, he used just enough to give Premios and Danny breathing room. After all, Danny had to survive, because Josh wasn't done with him yet. But the bigger question was whether Josh was done with the life he had always led. Was he willing to go into hiding with an assumed identity, always looking over his shoulder? Or was there still some way out?

For some reason, the conversation held months earlier with Chip and Barbara still obsessed him. It was the talk about the physicist and his damn cat. It irked him that he didn't understand what they were discussing that day at lunch. It was amazing how they seemed so confident spouting their gibberish. While locked up in this old camp, he found time to read more about the Schrödinger's cat problem, and he didn't think Chip or Barbara were so clever. The way he read it was this scientist posed his famous problem only to make clear how absurd the contention was that some element could be both one thing and not that thing at the same time. It certainly didn't require a viewer to look into the box to force it into being one state or the other. Things were what they were. It was the observer who didn't understand the true situation.

In some metaphysical way Josh supposed that when he knocked on Oliver's door and surprised him in Chicago there was some truth to the contention that in that afternoon moment Oliver was both dead and alive. For those few seconds of the confrontation, Oliver thought he was alive and Josh thought of him as dead. But the reverse was probably equally true. No doubt, Oliver, knowing about his hidden gun, also believed that Josh would soon be dead, and that Oliver would survive. So perhaps Josh had also been in that nether state, neither one thing nor the other, but both at the same time. Actually he too should have considered his condition that way. He didn't control what would happen in Oliver's home office, and it might have gone the other way. Instead of grabbing the gun away from Oliver and firing, Oliver might have triggered the first shot and left Josh lying dead in a pool of blood on Oliver's fine Oriental carpet.

And what if that had happened? Would it really have made any difference? Yes, Josh would have been gone. But Josh didn't believe in gods or devils, so he held no fears of dropping into hell. Life would simply have been over, and he would have known nothing. Truthfully, he was more than a little tired of his games—especially since nothing ever seemed to force Danny into that existential choice between hope and despair.

Maybe some of these scientists were right. Something could exist in two states at the same time. But if so, Josh still felt so impotent because no matter how hard he tried to examine the question, he couldn't force matters. What was that scientific idea called again? A quantum superposition. Why couldn't he cause Danny to collapse into one ethical state or another?

No person was needed to catalyze Josh's entry into his current state of being. It happened early on and the result never bothered him. He didn't care that his mother didn't get her raspberry pie or that Clarence ended up hanging lifeless in the woods, that Danny was humiliated in front of all his coworkers, or that his parents suffocated in their beds from carbon monoxide poisoning.

Why should any of those things disturb his sleep? He didn't actually tie the noose or force bats to dwell in the chimney. He didn't agree to suck Oliver's cock. Everyone else made his or her individual fatal choices. Josh simply let people thrive and fall based on their own decisions.

That's what he told himself, but there was one time that he had trouble believing his own stories. He still didn't understand why. What happened with Tony Masters, that good-looking husband of the town nurse in Thread, never sat right with Josh—even though Josh didn't make the guy stare at him that wintry afternoon of his parents' burial nor did Josh ask Tony to hang around and laugh with him that afternoon at the meal served by the Ladies' Aid in the basement of the Lutheran Church. Plenty of people mourned his parents at that reception and few stayed to listen to Josh's jokes and stories of Los Angeles. Tony made the choice to do that.

From the moment he saw Tony staring across the open grave, Josh knew that the man was infatuated. He also recognized that the man didn't seem to realize it. Several rounds of drinks later in the evening at the local tavern, even as Tony failed to wake up to his attraction, only made the connection clearer to Josh. It wasn't the first time Josh had encountered deeply closeted gays, the kind of men who managed to get married, have kids, and think they were living the All-American life, only to discover at some point that they hungered for something different. Tony was one of those lost souls, and after downing all those boilermakers, he was more than willing to head back to Josh's old farm to fulfill a hunger he usually ignored, and once there, Josh knew full well the moves to make.

And he made every one of them. It wasn't hard at all. The guy had probably never cheated on his wife, but suddenly he was stretched out naked on the deathbed of two of the town's upright citizens having his cock sucked by the town fag. Tony didn't let himself think about any of it, not until after the final climax. Then instead of lighting up a cigarette, he let his mind stew in the details of what he had done.

For Josh, Tony's moment of self-awareness was the best part of the night. It was better than porn to watch Tony's realizations bubble through his drunken state. He grew quiet and more flushed. Then he hurried to find his strewn-about clothes, never looking Josh in the eyes, or uttering anything other than an animal-like mumble.

That night turned out pretty amazing. Josh should have headed back to Los Angeles to wait for the payout from Ma and Pa's life insurance. But instead, hearing about how someone seemed to be buying up the old farms in the area, he decided to hang around and find out more. Every time he ran into Tony at the Piggly Wiggly, or the Wink o'the North Bar, or the Loon Town Café, it was an added little bonus to see the handsome local blush and scurry away. Except for those times Tony compulsively hung back.

Then came the day which no one else in town could explain— except for Josh, who was not willing to share his theories with anyone. Tony left his house to drive north on Highway 17. When he saw a convoy of motorcycles coming south, for some reason that everyone else debated but no one comprehended, he veered straight into the cyclists, killing not only himself but many of them. The enormous accident was the talk of Thread for weeks.

Josh did not go to Tony Masters' funeral. After it, he avoided even being in the same place as Tony's widow. For some reason he couldn't fathom, he felt guilt. There was no basis for his emotion. He never suggested that Tony kill himself. He didn't ask the guy to drive north, or arrange for others to be riding toward him. Compared to his other crimes, in this case Josh was truly innocent. And yet for the first time, it somehow seemed his fault, which bothered him in ways he couldn't explain.

No one saw the acts in which Tony and Josh reveled—except for Tony, but that was enough to transform not only Tony but also Josh. That winter in Thread, Josh began to watch Danny with a different set of eyes. He wanted to believe in the boy's goodness and the possibility that someone might actually be different. Being near someone who was so opposite of Josh might pull him back toward the middle, or so he hoped. In some ways, he wasn't even aware of what was happening because he just thought he had an itch to test Danny and to fuck up others. But something new had clicked into place.

Danny's and his lives had become entangled; there was no other word for it. From that moment forward, Josh anticipated that no matter where he might be, Danny's actions would somehow affect him. The two of them were linked in an inexplicable way. So he needed to understand the boy if only to understand himself.

Josh told himself that he was remaining in Thread merely to sell the farm for the best possible price. But he could have used a realtor for that. Danny was his motivation. Josh fell in love with the possibility that Danny's presence would make Josh a better person. Even when a moment of clarity rushed over Josh, and he forced himself to move back to the West Coast, the break wasn't totally successful. Without Danny he felt incomplete. After little more than a year, he fully gave in and convinced Danny Lahti to leave Thread and move in with him. By that point, Josh felt he had become a more moral person, and there would be no more dead Tony Masters on his conscience.

But then maybe Danny wasn't such a spirit of goodness. His presence didn't balance out Josh's own nature. Or perhaps Josh didn't really have a conscience after all, and he had merely been acting in a different sort of play for a few years, trying on a different role, a part for which he was not suited. He fell back into testing people and seeking their motivating secrets, always hoping that eventually Danny would anchor him from drifting too far.

But there always remained the old dilemma. How could Danny be a strong anchor if under the right circumstances Danny's moral certitude could be switched? For Josh, the nagging question of Danny's true character bloomed again.

When Josh confronted Oliver in Chicago, every element of Josh's complicated relationship with Danny inhabited that room. Ghosts of past actions and plots rattled about the baseboards and corners. So long ago, Josh influenced Oliver to entice Danny into a sexual trap just for the fun of it. Maybe in the end it wasn't so different than what Josh did with Tony. Through Oliver, Josh forced Danny to confront his own desires and to see those urges reflected through the mockery of his coworkers. But it didn't really work to turn Danny bad. His goodness persevered.

Josh should have abandoned Oliver. But he was like a pair of well-worn shoes—always comfortable to slip on when an errand needed doing, like egging Oliver into harassing Pete Peterson in Thread. When he went looking for first stage funders for Premios, there were so many potential sources, yet when Jesus Lopez casually mentioned knowing Oliver and Colby, it was a revelation. Josh had lost track of

Oliver and hadn't known of his present role as a venture capitalist. Rediscovering Oliver was the impetus for Josh creating the most elaborate test yet for Danny.

The plan evolved as time went on, as all good things in life did. It was like drafting a novel and not knowing how it might end. He courted Endicott and Meyers, and delighted in that first meeting when Oliver realized it was Josh who ran this potential investment, at the same time deliberately keeping Oliver's presence hidden from Danny. Josh thought that someday his subterfuge would pay off. And it might have. He had high hopes for purposely dangling the story of Oliver and Danny in front of Jesus. When the writer bit, just as predicted from the writer's jaded interests, Josh was once again the master.

But he failed to foresee that Oliver wasn't his alone. Even as he began to worry about the source of Oliver's money, Josh never considered the possibility of Arab terrorists. But then there were the danger signs, and that's when Josh had to improvise, losing control of his usual carefully planned tests. By the time Josh knocked on Oliver's townhouse door, Josh couldn't really say exactly what he was thinking or planning to do.

Maybe that's why the more he read about this Schrödinger's cat, the more Josh thought it confounding. Because he was beginning to accept that on that day in Chicago, he was in two alternate possibilities at the same time. He wanted to kill Oliver to see how his death would force Danny into yet another test of faith, but he also wanted to kill Oliver to protect Danny and their relationship by ridding them of something rotten. Both hopes were true. Only an observer taking an action— Oliver with his gun—could push Josh from one side to the other.

But which side did he land on? Why did he use Oliver's own gun to kill him? In one of these readings about quantum superpositions, he ran across the idea of multiple universes—and the concept that at every instant the cosmos split into new alternatives, one in which the cat lived and one in which the cat died. Over the years, Josh had set in motion so many potential realities: One in which Clarence still lived and was beloved by his aged mother. One where Danny was never humiliated and became a totally different personality. Another where Josh could go home to see his parents at Christmas. And still one in which he allowed no information to be hacked on New Year's Eve. And yet another where Pete continued to inhabit his camp beneath the bridge and still wore his hat to ward off the monsoon rains.

This was a set of possibilities he could not explore. He was not a quantum physicist dealing with the strange paradoxes of entanglement and superpositioning. He would not contemplate all of the alternative universes that might coexist and thrive. He was not willing to consider the possibility that he was the outside observer. It could not be his destructive actions that forced this continual branching of good and evil.

Besides, he wasn't alone. He had his allies, people like Jesus Lopez, who were always so eager to follow up on Josh's suggestions, even when they weren't aware of their being manipulated. With Lopez, the man's novels reflected his character. It's what attracted Josh and why Josh thought it would be funny when he loaned Pete's hat for some of Jesus's recent errands. He could always count on Jesus to say or do whatever Josh requested.

But he wasn't going to let himself relive decisions and choices involving Pete and Danny and Jesus. There was too much time on his hands in the old camp. He had to stop thinking and start doing. He needed to design the ultimate experiment. It was time to stop skirting around the core matter. Until he knew Danny—fully and completely— Josh could never know who and what he was, nor could he be truly independent again. He needed to understand his own soul.

In this box with the poison ready to pour out, there were two cats, and their names were Danny and Josh. Which was dead? Which was alive?

CHAPTER SEVENTEEN

Whirlwind

Storm clouds darkened the horizon. With rains and winds rushing in from the Plains States, the air promised the kind of summer storm that prompted tornados to dance through the woods as they toppled trees in mad patterns and skipped across lakes.

There were many places Danny might want to be. The camp was not one of them. Life marched on—and at the moment it appeared that the way forward no longer required Josh. Actuades had completed its purchase of Premios, placing the company inside an international media conglomerate and making it part of Danny's past. Orleans landed at a Silicon Valley investment firm, a position likely achieved with the help of Barbara Linsky. Before leaving southern California, Orleans put order to Danny's finances by liquidating Josh's various real estate investments, refinancing both the camp and the mansion with proceeds from the sale of Premios, and consolidating various trusts. She counseled Danny to put one or the other of his homes on the market, telling Danny he wasn't as rich as Josh always claimed.

Still Danny felt financially, if not emotionally, secure, and was surprised to discover that he was happy to have Josh continue to remain missing. Wherever Josh had gone or whatever he had done, Danny felt he no longer needed the man—who seemed to have planned his exit well, covered his tracks carefully, and left behind no sign of ever intending to reappear.

But then Cynthia called.

A worker from Lattigo Industries had been fishing in front of the Wisconsin camp. He saw someone lurking in the windows of the upper floor and alerted Cynthia out of concern for the widow of his dead boss. She requested a home check by the local police, who reported that the house, although now empty, had recently been occupied. Both she and the police thought the same thing: Josh Gunderson had been using the place as a hideaway.

Danny hated the call when it came.

"Danny, I don't want to have to tell you this but I think Josh is here in Wisconsin," Cynthia said, "or at least he was here. Maybe you should come back."

"And do what?" he asked. He really meant it. What good would it do for him to examine the hulking log mansion on the lake? What would he look for? Another hidden room? So what if there were empty TV dinner trays or slept-in sheets? By seeing the signs in person, what would he learn that he didn't already know? He did not need to reinforce the reality that he never really knew Josh and that the man was not trustworthy. He wanted Josh to flee to another country and be gone forever, because he was happy without him.

It was best to be cautious. Josh was a patient spider weaving a web, but if Danny didn't fly into the trap, he couldn't be caught. Already he had followed Barbara's advice and burned every one of Josh's files concerning Project Big Stick. That included all of the written notes about the suspected funders of Endicott-Meyers. Danny never told anyone, not even Barbara, about Josh's documented case for where Oliver's money was derived. He also destroyed the tapes but only after torturing himself by listening a second time. They provided the strongest reason for Danny to resist returning to Wisconsin, because they fully convinced him of Josh's insanity.

Cynthia had no patience for Danny's reluctance to come home but he had avoided telling her anything of what was revealed by the tapes. Danny knew that Cynthia was trapped by her vision of what she would do were she to discover a sign that Chip was still alive, but he knew there was nothing similar about their two situations. She lost a beautiful lover; he uncovered a crazed man.

In the end Danny was too much a son of the Midwest to ignore the call to be responsible, so he returned. The lake house was much as he expected. The kitchen was stocked with easy-to-heat canned goods and the freezer contained a variety of one-serving meals. Dirty dishes remained in the sink, as though the squatter had quickly vacated the place. One of the upper-floor bedrooms looked well lived-in. Dirty towels were scattered on the floor of the attached bathroom. At the same time, the dust was thick throughout the major public rooms of the ground floor, and there was little indication of any recent activity. Apparently the camp had only been a way station on Josh's overall journey.

After going through every room in the mansion and the servants quarters that were built over the old stables now converted into garages, Danny felt certain Josh was gone forever. Sitting on the stone terrace outside the living room and gazing toward the dock and boathouse, he contemplated seeking freedom by prepping the suspended powerboat in that building. He could motor it out on the flowage and away from the house. Almost twenty miles in length, the flowage had been formed years ago when the Coeur de Lattigeaux River was dammed to generate power. Channels from the resulting flowage offered connections to many of the true lakes, including this one, Clearwater Lake. Danny could speed for miles across these waters and let his thoughts go where they might. Maybe he could decide whether to reach out to his father and try to reconcile He could take his old man fishing. He hadn't ever invited his father to see the place after its refurbishment. For too long, they had acted as though they lived in different universes. Maybe together they could visit his mother's grave. That was at least one thing that still connected them. It wasn't too late.

Danny looked across the lake and watched the dark skies that were transforming the water below into a black mirror. The rising wind was driving the water frothy with whitecaps as the front edge of the rain raced toward him. He headed back into the house because it wouldn't be long until the storm hit. Inside, he turned on lights, placed a CD in the player, lit the fireplace, poured himself a glass of wine, and sat by the fire. Maybe he should call Cynthia. Instead he stared toward the lake and decided to wait out the storm.

That's when he saw it—the dark funnel shape descending from the clouds, skirting the opposite edge of the lake, heading northeast toward the border of Wisconsin and upper Michigan, and ripping the forest apart. Outside, the roar of the wind grew monstrous, and rain pelted the window until it completely obscured what lay beyond. It was foolish to sit in the living room near so many enormous panes of glass, as though he was tempting the churning tornado to shift direction and slam into the camp. Danny didn't move.

The lights flickered and then went out. Danny reasoned the funnel touched the transmission lines that went from Thread toward the power plant in Timberton. If the twister had pulled up the lines, trees were also likely downed across them and it might be hours before the power would come back on. In the distance across the lakes, as the rain abated, he could see a glow rising from the American Seasons complex.

Apparently, the resort still had its power. But he was alone in a dark house.

In the quiet dimness of the swirl of the stormy twilight, he heard a creak and then a voice.

"Reminds one of New Year's Eve, doesn't it?" said a familiar voice. Josh.

"Were you looking for me?" he asked. "I had to move out when someone sent the cops to check on the place. But I couldn't leave entirely. I figured eventually you would show up. Wanted to be here when you did. And now here you are."

Danny said nothing.

"I know you found my room in Los Feliz," Josh said. "Did you like what you found?"

Danny wondered if he was safe, but if not, where could he flee? Could he get to the car? If only he had already placed that boat in the water. Even in this storm, he would rather be on the lake than in this room with Josh.

Josh seemed not to care. "I just need you to know something. There's one thing left to discover, and that's why I'm here. Everything I've ever done is for you. You believe that, don't you? I wanted to give you everything you could ever want. A career. Money. Friends. A lover."

Danny felt unreasonable hope.

"Know why? Because if you didn't have everything, I couldn't take it away." And Josh laughed.

Hope vanished. "Who are you?" he asked.

"I am your nemesis," and Josh laughed again.

Danny remembered some Greek myth about Nemesis and Narcissus. He seemed to recall that it didn't end well. "Do you think you can break me? Are you hoping I will commit suicide? Is that what you want?"

As Josh sat on the chair across from Danny, he looked at him in a way that Danny once would have considered an expression of love, but now he wondered what it really meant. Josh smiled sadly, "Don't you think suicide is best left to your mother?"

"Don't bring my mom into this." Danny almost shouted, surprised at how much it stung to hear his mother mentioned.

"What do they say? 'Like mother, like son.' Genes run deep."

Danny wanted no more of this. "I can't believe that I never knew who you really were. Maybe if none of this happened, I never would have. But you would never have let that happen, would you? You made sure I discovered the real you, didn't you? So now I know what you are: a killer."

Josh didn't protest. "My goal isn't to make you know who I am. It's just the opposite. I want to make sure you know who you are. I need you to look into the mirror and see yourself for who you really are. Listen up. This is who you are: Your mother's son. Pete's special boy. Oliver's plaything. You're a fraud."

"Shut up! This is about you. Not me. You're the crazy one . . . the criminal . . . the terrorist. I read your notes and listened to your tapes."

"Funny the words you chose. Terrorist. Killer."

Danny suddenly felt wary. Something had shifted and he remembered how he feared the house was a giant trap, but he couldn't keep himself from asking, "What do you mean?"

From the way Josh leaned back against the chair, Danny knew that he wanted to be asked that very question. Josh pointed toward the goblet that Danny had set on the coffee table. "I'm getting a glass of that wine. My story might take a while."

Again, Danny debated fleeing. Could he outrace Josh in this rain and make it somewhere safe? Why hadn't he invited Cynthia over?

"Do you still carry around that picture of you as a baby with your mother?" Without thinking, Danny nodded his head to indicate yes. "Remember that other woman? The one you said was your mother's friend?" Again without wanting to, he agreed.

"Her name was Pauline Newmann. You probably knew that. Did you know that she grew up in the same town as your mom, and that she was her dearest friend? Did your dad ever tell you that?"

Josh knew that Danny's dad never talked about the past, especially not when it came to his dead wife.

"I bet he never said a word about how Pauline died, did he? Let me tell you the unhappy story. She was blown up on Christmas Eve in 1968 when a terrorist bombed a building at Bremen College where she worked, the same place your mother worked. An anti-war protest, and she was the one who died. Not a politician. Not an army general. No, your mother's friend. At Bremen College in Milwaukee where your parents lived in 1968, the year you were born."

Danny felt uncertain. He should know about Pauline. He still carried a photo of his mother and her but he had just been born then. Maybe his dad had mentioned it. Danny felt shaky, reminded of the day he discovered his mother was dead.

"I bet no one ever told you about your mom's role in that. Did you ever hear that she was part of the anti-Vietnam War group that claimed responsibility for the bombing? The FBI always thought she was the one who set it in motion, but they could never prove it. But she was. She was the one responsible for killing her best friend. Maybe that's why she committed suicide. Maybe she just felt guilty."

"You don't know that," Danny's voice had sunk to a whisper. It couldn't be true, but yet somehow he felt Josh was telling the truth.

"Yes, I can know it," Josh replied. "You know how I like to check things out. A while back, I filed a Freedom of Information Act request on your mother's files. I just wanted to know your past. That's how I discovered there's a lot you don't know about your roots. Maybe it's time.

"I always thought that you and I were somehow entangled in a way that meant for our lives to be connected. Even if I wanted to exist without you, I couldn't. But here's the problem: I can't exist <u>with</u> you either—at least not until we both know who you are and what really defines you. I can't rest until I know your true colors. Because you are my reality, and I am yours.

"So are you your mother's son? And if so, how will you react to the truth? I've always wanted to tear away everything until we face ourselves in abject nakedness, unable to hide behind anything but our essence."

Josh walked over to one of the bookshelves and pulled out a book. Behind it, there was a folder that he had apparently hidden. "You can't guess how much I have been looking forward to this day."

He handed over the file.

"Sometimes, it seems you can look at yourself and not change. Maybe that mirror has no power on you. But can you look at your mother and still not escape your past? Let's find out."

And then Josh said something odd. "I think the cat is finally dead. And it's time for me to go. Forever."

And he walked toward the entry, into the darkness, and exited into the storm.

CHAPTER EIGHTEEN

Josh

The confrontation wasn't satisfying. Handing over the synopsis of files on Danny's mother should have provided great satisfaction, but he felt nothing. No, worse than that, he felt guilty, a feeling he never liked.

Testing Danny was proving disappointing, and it was becoming an issue. Just in case it was ever needed, years ago, Josh planned a detailed escape route. To do so, he created more than one false identity and scouted out various countries with non-extradition treaties. He always thought such foresight might prove handy—one never knew when old crimes might come back to haunt one. Even though he somewhat exaggerated the level of grand larceny he perpetrated on Oliver's gang of Arab friends, Josh had siphoned more than a few million dollars of their funding that had been secreted away in European banks. Some of that purloined cash was used to give Premios and Danny breathing room, but the rest was in a safe place for Josh's future use. He saw no reason to feel guilty about the financial hack. In some ways, it was downright patriotic. Who knew what Oliver's gang planned to do with that money? Let them think their own colleague made off with it, just in time to get murdered in a home burglary. Even if these guys suspected Josh was behind the loss of money, they weren't going to find him.

As long as he got out of the country.

But he still needed to complete things with Danny. That wasn't happening. By now he had offered Danny both the carrot and the stick. Over the years, he showered Danny with all the blessings of a good life. He helped engineer Danny's fame as a blogger. And he bestowed wealth. Such things didn't come easily, but Josh was always willing to pull whatever levers of influence were needed to grease the skids. He gave the kid everything, but Danny never abused his new powers. It was inexplicable. So much for the carrot.

He had no alternative but to use the stick and take things away.

Doing so would surely nudge Danny into his baser nature until he would collapse into the despair that Josh was certain ran deep inside everyone. Destroying Danny's image of him was a small price to pay and Josh had paid it; yet Josh still didn't see the change he wanted. It wasn't fair.

He had only one card left to play—Danny's mother—and he was lucky to have it. Since Josh truly believed that some horrid truth lay behind every action of every person, he had often thought there had to be a reason the woman killed herself. Maybe that speculation gave him the idea to go digging, or perhaps someone in town referenced the woman's past. Whatever, once he decided one day to seek out more, never expecting anything to come of it, he found it easy enough to submit Freedom of Information requests to the various federal agencies. Soon he had several folders on Lempi, her parents and even her husband Toivo—Danny's father. Josh figured that all those odd Finnish names would make it easy to scope out forgotten facts.

His requests had been a lark, but then he hit the jackpot. While there was nothing about Danny's father, it was another situation with Danny's grandmother, Marja Makinen. Turns out the government tried to deport her during the Fifties and the Red Scare era. They didn't succeed.

But there was an even bigger surprise. It was Lempi, Danny's mother. She had her own skeletons, including a suspected radical past. Although several major passages in the documents were redacted, the FBI files clearly documented their unproven suspicions about a never-solved bombing and those details were enough to fill Josh with an anticipatory rush of joy. Even Danny couldn't withstand this revelation. His mother's death haunted Danny, but it was a haunting of longing and love, not fear. What would he do with the truth?

Josh never considered leaving those files in his hidden room. It would have been like displaying a thermonuclear bomb in an open field. No, Josh had held onto his secret for more than two years, never expecting to use it. But times changed. Turned out that Danny was tougher than he thought.

There was no alternative but to deploy his one remaining tool, and Josh was certain the unveiling would have the greatest impact in the backwoods of Thread. That was his only reason for hiding out in the camp. He needed to disclose reality in the setting where it had been forgotten. Unfortunately, over the past few months, Danny never acted as Josh anticipated. As far as Josh could tell, Danny never even checked if Josh was sequestered at the lake house. Finally, Josh deliberately made himself visible to fishermen off shore so that sooner or later, word would get back to Danny.

Maybe he was losing his touch. Josh always thought he could with equal skill read people and manipulate them. That's why he was so quick to hire Orleans, expecting to mentor her until she could apply her skill at reading people and be a companion in his machinations. Sometimes it was lonely trying to play god with people's lives. But Orleans hadn't lived up to her potential. Unfortunately by the time her backbone of morality became clear, he had grown too dependent on her financial acumen. Orleans had to stay, but not in the role he had planned.

Jesus Lopez was another acolyte who offered great potential. Discovering Lopez's novels was an almost sexually charged event. Josh delighted in this amoral author who thrived on chaos and evil. Josh even suggested to Danny that he enroll in Lopez's seminar, not because he thought the man would be a good teacher, but because he wanted to meet the guy.

It worked. They hit it off. Jesus even dragged Josh into some darker sexual escapades that wouldn't normally have intrigued him, but proved to be a form of brotherly bonding. Josh had been ecstatic when he stumbled over the amazing coincidence that Jesus and Oliver knew each other from their days together at a university in Chicago, and he played that opportunity for everything that it was worth.

Whatever Josh asked Jesus to do, he was always downright eager to follow through. That included trailing Chip, especially when Josh made up some cock-and-bull story about why Jesus should wear that old fisherman's hat on the stakeout. Josh still didn't understand why he added such a stupid detail. Sometimes, Josh thought a part of him wanted to be caught. In the end, the hat didn't matter. Jesus saw Chip check out the buildings. As Josh hoped, Jesus shared the news about Chip's investigation with Oliver. Admittedly Josh failed to anticipate that Oliver would call in reinforcements to deal with Chip. But that didn't matter. Josh didn't own any responsibility for what happened to Chip. Plausible deniability. He only helped people get to where they wanted to be.

It was too bad about the break-ins at the Los Feliz house. Life had its coincidences, and Josh was sure the attempted burglaries were just the actions of local kids. At first the occurrences greatly angered him, but then he realize how much the actions spooked Danny, and that proved good for his test.

But Josh still had to get Danny to reach that point of personal self-discovery. Someday Danny would understand and appreciate that Josh wasn't being vindictive. He was doing this out of love. He really was. But he couldn't take these actions directly. He wasn't a murderer. He only helped things along. Turning the gun on Oliver was an anomaly. Just like stabbing Pete wasn't really Josh's nature.

Josh didn't want another anomaly. He wanted Danny to make his own choices.

CHAPTER NINETEEN

The Flowage

"**You need to call** the police," Cynthia was firm.

From across the dinner table, Danny replied equally adamant, "I can't."

They were at a crossroads and blocked. On one hand, Danny could choose what Cynthia considered the only logical path to follow even though it would betray Josh. On the other hand, he might choose the alternative of staying silent, which each knew should never be taken, even if it might protect the man that Danny once thought he loved but now didn't trust. Both choices were untenable, and Cynthia could understand why Danny just floated between the two, unable to moor on either. After Chip's murder, she felt a similar sense of being lost. But at some point, you needed to drop your feet to the bottom, stand up and start walking in one direction or the other.

The night before, the tornado left a streak of fallen trees in its wake. While the storm caused no damage to the American Seasons resort, downed trees continued to block several back roads between Lattigo and Thread. Safely driving the country lanes from Danny's camp to reach the resort was still impossible. When Danny called that morning to rage about Josh, Cynthia encouraged him to take his motorboat through the flowage to reach the American Seasons marina. With its powerful engine, the trip would take less than half an hour. She wanted them to meet in person, sooner rather than later. She wished that he had called the night before, and didn't like imagining him brooding alone in the huge house with Josh in the vicinity

Danny resisted her recommendation, partly because the boat remained stored in the boathouse. Cynthia persevered until he finally broke down and said yes. Still she questioned if he would really follow through. At mid-morning, he called and changed the timing to an early dinner. He claimed he was having trouble lowering the boat into the water. She prepped herself for the possibility of a no-show. But eventually he appeared and now he sat opposite her at Harvest

Landing Restaurant, arriving at five, just as he said he would. Located outside on a screened deck, the dining room overlooked the marina and a lake that shimmered brightly in the afternoon sun. In mid-June, the sun wouldn't set for hours this far north. It provided plenty of time for talk, while still ensuring Danny could motor home in daylight.

The trouble was they weren't really talking. Instead, Danny stared out at the docks below and his enormous boat; it was almost a cabin cruiser and not at all well suited to the waters of the flowage and interconnected lakes. Cynthia suspected the purchase had been Josh's since he always sought out whatever was the biggest and flashiest.

Finally, she spoke, "Tell me what you're thinking." He had already described the surprise appearance of Josh during the storm as well as the unexpected files he handed over. She wasn't certain what upset Danny the most—Josh's reappearance or the biography of Danny's mother.

Maybe it was a mistake trying to connect with Danny. Days ago when one of the men in the office mentioned that he saw lights at the camp, which all the locals still called the Van Elkind place, she immediately thought it had to be Josh. She debated whether to alert Danny, but finally decided it was her responsibility as a friend.

Over these past few years, she grew to dislike the hulking lake house. As a child, she was never allowed to visit the estate but because her parents, who occasionally interacted with the Van Elkinds, often told glamorous tales of the place, she endowed it with an almost mystical elegance. Her childish imaginings made it a gateway to the kind of world she daydreamed she might eventually inhabit. But when she joined Josh and Danny on their first walk-through, reality gave a different interpretation. Years of standing empty through harsh Wisconsin winters resulted in a downbeaten look. The layout was spacious, the views incredible, and the lake frontage and acres of surrounding virgin forest inspiring. But for some reason the overall setting was not the fairy-tale place she once imagined. Maybe being married to a Native American whose tribe was robbed of these lands made her focus on what had been lost when the original lumber barons ruthlessly clear-cut entire counties. In this case, the man only left pristine the one area he wanted for his own summer home. She preferred to imagine the original landscape still inhabited, haunted really, by the native spirits who once lived in these woods. Such a setting deserved a fate other than being Josh's trophy.

Because Josh liked the house so much, it didn't surprise her that he might use it as a hideaway. What she didn't understand was why she encouraged Danny to fly out and check for himself. The police had already visited and deemed the place empty again. She shouldn't have meddled, just like she probably should not have suggested this meal. What could she possibly advise Danny? Each of them was in over their heads. Why did she want to know what Danny was thinking, when she didn't even understand her own thoughts or motivation?

"My heart lifted when I realized Josh was in the room with me," Danny blushed as he admitted that fact. "I longed for an explanation that I could believe. I wanted it all resolved."

"That's all that I've wanted since the day I first walked into his secret room in Los Feliz. I need a story that makes sense of it all. Without it, I can't believe in him, and then how can I possibly believe in myself?"

Cynthia saw no value in hiking down that path. "Listen, Josh is a psychopath. He occupies a space beyond the behaviors that make the rest of us human. Don't try to make sense of him. Just because he took you in doesn't say anything about you. We all believed him. We've all known him for years."

Danny returned to staring at the lake, and his voice was disconnected as though Cynthia had dissolved into the summer breeze. "But you didn't kiss this man every day, wait for him, and miss him. You didn't wake up in the middle of the night, and fall back asleep with the comfort of hearing him breathe, knowing that he was beside you, that he held your back. Discovering all of this . . . it's like he stripped me bare and has left me nothing."

"He's changed nothing about who you are," she insisted.

"Hasn't he?"

Danny looked down at his steak frites. He hadn't touched them. The glass of red wine remained full.

Cynthia knew she needed to ask about Danny's mom. "You haven't said anything about the information he left you on your mother. When we talked on the phone this morning, you seemed very disturbed by it. What exactly did he tell you?"

"You'd be upset too," he snapped. "To learn that your mother had an FBI file, that she was suspected of bombing a university building in an explosion that killed her best friend. I always thought I somehow disappointed my mom, but now I have to look at her as a murderer. I used to worry that I had too much of my mother inside me and that one day I would try to kill myself. Now . . . I never knew her. How can I share anything of my life with her? Maybe suicide wasn't good enough for her."

Cynthia was shocked. She vaguely remembered Lempi Makinen, a woman she never found the least bit interesting, certainly not a person with a history. "Maybe your father . . ."

He cut her off. "I can't discuss this with him. He still loves her. He worships her memory, and he's never even really accepted her death. For a while I thought he was starting over, but then he fell back. I always wanted him to be there for me, not her, but she held on to him even after she died. How do you compete with a memory?

"That's why it was so easy for me to leave Thread. I couldn't live any longer with my father and the way he was living in the past. I needed to abandon him and her. But now it feels like she's reaching back, pulling me down into her darkness. I don't know how to resist."

"Maybe it's time to reconnect with your dad," Cynthia said. "Maybe he knows more about what Josh uncovered. You don't even know any of this is true. It could all be lies. You can't trust Josh."

Danny seemed to be thinking about some memory, as though it now made sense, and Cynthia wanted to ask him what that was. But she felt she was already on the border of having gone too far. Instead she asked, "What are you going to do?"

"I think I will go home and burn those files. Then I can pretend that I never saw them. I'm good at burning things." He knew Cynthia was unaware of what he had destroyed back in California. "And while I'm tossing the past into the fire, I should burn every picture of Josh.

"But, no, I have to keep one. I need to give one to the police. They need to know what I know. They need to understand Josh."

As the sun sank toward the horizon, and against his better judgment, Danny joined Cynthia in ordering a full bottle of merlot. He knew a glass or two would mean nothing to her. She could always stay in the hotel adjacent to the restaurant and marina. After all, the resort was partially hers, and even if she drove home, her house was only minutes away. On the other hand, Danny would need to maneuver several miles through the flowage, motor through the channel to Clearwater Lake and then speed across the broad lake to reach the dock at his camp. He didn't want to undertake the journey in the darkness, and twilight was rapidly approaching. He needed his wits.

Nevertheless, he was the one who ended up drinking most of the wine. Cynthia only toyed with her glass and he remembered that she was pregnant and shouldn't drink.

As he walked from the restaurant to the marina, he felt a bit unsteady. The light wind shimmered its way through the quaking leaves of the white birch trees that lined the brick path to the wooden docks. Everything was taking on a golden hue in the lingering light. Even as the ripples of lapping waves along the shore grew more iridescent, the deeper waters toward the center of the flowage darkened. Evening birds called out to proclaim the boundaries of their territories. Around his ear, Danny heard the whir of encroaching mosquitoes. Not many here, so close to the resort, which sprayed its grounds, but Danny knew that out on the water the insects would hover as a heavy, hungry, buzzing cloud. Lacking any insect repellant, his trip home would be filled with bites.

His comforting relationship with Cynthia lulled him into lingering too long. A room filled with happy tourists, a friendly waiter, and a good glass of wine momentarily gave the world a mask that made it appear sane once more. For a moment, the jumble of facts and emotions that defined his life receded as unimportant.

But under the growing onslaught of evening insects, reality reasserted itself. Danny hurried toward his boat and clambered into it. He needed to get home. At twenty-four feet in length, this boat was among the biggest in its class; its powerful motor could make good speed. Originally Josh chose it because it was fast enough for water skiing but still provided the set-up for fishing. Danny was glad to have the craft tonight. It would bring him home before dark.

He unknotted the mooring line, pulled it into the boat, and stood at the steering wheel. As he began to maneuver his way past the end of the floating dock, someone ran down the planks and leaped from the end of the pier to land on the boat's prow. His unsteady body crouched in front of the windshield and blocked Danny's view into the lake.

The person looked up and laughed. It was Josh.

Before Danny could yell for him to get off, Josh scrambled over the windshield, landed on the floor of the craft and pushed Danny from the controls. Josh yanked up on the speed control, revved the engine, and turned the boat so it sped past the docks into the open water. No other boats were in the way. Before long the two were alone in a boat on the water, speeding toward the center of the flowage, away from the marina and resort, heading into the depths of the woods.

"Don't worry. I'll get you home," Josh said, "but I needed one more chance to talk. You owe me at least that, don't you?"

"I owe you nothing," Danny replied.

Had Josh been watching him and Cynthia all afternoon, just waiting for his return to the boat? Soon they would be too far from shore for anyone to see them but Danny hoped that Cynthia had remained at the table, watched him board his boat and saw Josh boatnap him. Would she call the police? Didn't the tribe maintain some kind of watercraft patrol to handle all the vacationing fishermen and water-skiers at this end of the flowage? Maybe her alarm was already sending someone on the way.

"You owe me everything," Josh replied. "I gave you everything you have and I can take it all back. Whenever I want."

"Then take back my mother's file and everything I learned," Danny spat.

"That I can't do," Josh responded. "But the material things. The fame. The fortune. Those are the things I can take back. But these other things. The mental images. The emotions. They're more like computer viruses that infect your mind. They'll just grow and turn until they fulfill their mission. Everything has its purpose, you know. You just have to wait to find out what it is. I've been waiting a very long time for that to happen."

Danny's fears were true. Josh was mad. In some crazy way, everything Danny discovered over the past weeks truly reflected the yearnings and imaginings of this man. He wondered if he could survive the night. On the horizon, the first star of the night popped into view and he made a promise. If he lived to morning, he would do everything possible to ensure that the proper authorities arrested Josh.

Without offering explanation, Josh suddenly stepped away from the controls and sat on one of the back seats. The boat was still going forward full speed. Danny rushed toward the controls to slow the speed. With its many shallow spots, the flowage often hid copses of dead trees just below the surface. Hitting one could sink a boat and he didn't intend to drown out here in the inky waters of the night.

Josh pulled open one of the fishing compartments built into the boat. He seemed to be searching for something among the tackle. Danny didn't even realize the boat was equipped with lures and sinkers suitable for fishing muskie or northern pike.

"What are you doing," he asked. Danny slowed down the boat and kept one eye out for unexplained ripples that might mark danger below the surface. The other remained focused on Josh.

Josh looked up with a self-satisfied smile. He pulled a large folding utility knife from one of the tackle box trays. "I thought this was here," he said and unfolded the blade. Even in the fading light, its gleaming stainless steel edge managed to reflect back some of the fleeting molten sky.

The knife worried Danny. He could kill the motor, Danny thought, and just let the boat drift in the weak currents of the flowage. Or he could increase speed and race toward the safety of land. Neither choice was appealing. He didn't remember the shore well enough to know where to run aground and seek sanctuary. Much of the shore was swamp. The firmer ground usually sported summer homes, which were frequently unused. If he could make it to the channel and into the first lake in the chain, then he could reach the year-round home of the high school principal in Thread and escape Josh and his knife by dropping off the boat and swimming to that man's house. The principal was always at home.

"Did you ever go fishing?" Josh asked. He didn't seem concerned about what Danny might be plotting. "With some fish, you just have to be patient, let the bait float down and just do its job. Are you that kind of fish Danny? What does it take to land you? I really want to know. You never bit at anything I sent your way. Do I just need to be more patient?

"Now your mother—I thought telling her story would be enough to make you bite. You've always blamed yourself for her suicide. It was written all over your face whenever you mentioned her. But I never thought you held any responsibility, and now I've blessed you with that freedom. But will you take it? Face it. Your mother was no saint, so no matter what she did, she was the one who chose death. She had reason to despair and none of it had anything to do with you. Don't hold it on yourself. You've been living a lie."

Danny agreed. His life was a lie, but it was one that became a falsehood due to Josh's existence. Not his mother. He realized he didn't care what she did or why. This was his life, and he wouldn't be pushed into one path or the other just to satisfy a whim of Josh. He needed to understand one thing.

"Why research my mother and why show me the findings?"

Josh was playing with the knife, tossing it back and forth between his hands. The opened tackle box contained large lures, designed to catch the region's biggest fighting fish, the muskie. Danny always considered the hooks on such lures to be dangerous.

"I needed to know," Josh said, "That's all it's ever been. Not about your mother, but about you. What kind of person are you really? I've always felt that you've been too afraid to peel back the layers of your true emotions. But bottom line, you're no better than me. You need to know it. You never dared to get away with anything. You're stuck in the normal, never grasping for more. But until you realize that you and I aren't so different, I can't help you."

Danny felt there was one more thing he needed to ask. And then he would act. While he still had time.

The sound of the rushing engine drowned out normal evening sounds, and the boat's speed kept the mosquitoes at bay. They were heading toward a distant shore, but it wouldn't take that long to run aground. Josh simply watched Danny, awaiting his move, measuring some trait that only he seemed to detect. Then Josh sighed.

"Maybe I'm wrong. Perhaps you're filled with grace, blessed by God and able to move on. But I don't think so. You know Pete always worried about you."

Danny had been planning to rush Josh to knock him overboard, but those words derailed his plotting. The last thing he had expected was a mention of Pete. "What do you know about Pete's worries?"

"Quite a bit actually. A few years ago when I felt that I just wasn't able to understand you the way that I wanted to, I tracked Pete down. You know everyone in town knew about the two of you. They know that you're the one who pushed Pete over the edge with desire. Made him crazy. But I wanted to hear from him first-hand how it happened. I heard he was still around, so I tracked him down in Phoenix. Met up with him under a freeway overpass on one of those crazy monsoon rainy nights in the desert."

Danny knew he had to do it. Push the guy overboard. It was either Josh or him. Only one of them could make it to shore.

Josh laughed. "You're so transparent. Thinking about rushing me, aren't you? That's what Pete thought too that night. I think he planned to push me into the flood channel. But I had a knife that night too. He tried, but I guess you know how that ended. Did you find his hat in my secret room?"

A calm descended on Danny. Maybe, he realized this was his final night. Alone in the middle of a lake, caught in the light that was rapidly vanishing into the night, standing face to face with the man he had always thought he loved, trying to keep balanced on a moving boat.

"Did you ever love me?" Danny asked.

"What is love?" Josh responded.

Danny could always define love. It was loyalty and the willingness to wait for however long it might take for the right thing to occur. It was dedication to a person, taking the steps that honor required— while never forgetting the person you honored. It was focus and perseverance. It was all the stories that had populated his mind while growing up in Thread—tales of Indian chiefs and French voyageurs, of copper miners and poor farmers, of those individual people who saw in another person the opportunity to achieve their own self-realization. It was Josh.

And then it clearly wasn't.

"Maybe love is just the way we get tumbled together, or maybe there is no love greater than the person who will sacrifice everything for you and your future," said Josh. Danny had no idea what he meant, but it infuriated him.

Josh toyed with the utility knife, held out his palm, and lightly drew the tip of the blade across his skin until blood seeped out. Some drops fell on the floor of the boat. "We could become blood brothers," he said. Danny didn't know what to make of the look in Josh's eyes.

"Your turn," Josh commanded, pointing the knife toward Danny. "Let's make a pact, mingle our blood together, and forget everything in the past. We will look only toward the future."

Still facing Josh, Danny pushed upward on the lever that would drive the boat into full throttle. The entrance to the channel was only a few hundred yards more. The boat's red and green running lights on the edge of the boat were growing more visible. The moon wouldn't rise for hours, but several stars were already shining down. A loon sounded in the distance. The motor still roared, and the wake rushed behind them.

Josh took a step closer and then he lunged. The knife pierced Danny's chest and was quickly withdrawn. Surprised but not frightened, Danny tapped an unexpected reservoir of strength. He rushed forward, butted his head into Josh's chest and knocked the knife loose from Josh's hand. It clanked as it hit the boat's floor, but the sound was lost in the roar of Danny's pent-up anger. He continued to push into Josh, who lost his footing and began to tumble backward. Danny skidded to a stop as Josh fell backward. For a moment he was perched precariously on the rear corner of the boat. He looked up toward Danny with a startled look, which transformed into a smug smile of satisfaction as though some long-held belief had at last been confirmed. The boat continued to rush forward. It hit some submerged object. The entire boat bucked.

And Josh lost balance.

He fell overboard. Energy from the displacement propelled the boat forward and helped it leap over the submerged obstacle. It continued to rush forward.

Blood was seeping from Danny's chest wound, and he had trouble concentrating. He needed to stop the boat. He needed to search for Josh. He needed to . . .

. . . and Danny blacked out.

CHAPTER TWENTY

Aftermath

The hospital room felt sterile. Sitting in the chair beside the bed, Cynthia watched her friend, listened to the sounds of the instruments registering his heartbeat and blood pressure, noted the slow drip in the various tubes, and waited for Danny to wake.

Earlier the doctor said, "He should fully recover. The knife wound was never life threatening, but Mr. Lahti likely felt faint from the shock, blacked out and fell, and then suffered a concussion from hitting the deck. When he does wake up, the mosquito bites resulting from floating all night on a boat in the middle of the lake might just be the worst of it. So don't worry."

But Cynthia did. She blamed herself for not calling the authorities immediately the night before. Because she accidentally left her credit card behind, she returned to their table at the restaurant just in time to look out the window and see Danny depart the marina. A man rushed down the dock and jumped onto the prow of the boat. Even though she was too far to see any details, she knew it was Josh. The person was the right height and shape. Who else could it be? But she convinced herself there was no need to worry.

If Danny weren't one hundred percent okay, she would always know it was her fault. After everything discussed during their dinner, alarm bells should have sounded loudly in her mind. If she had called her friends at the resort security office, they might have immediately sent out their patrol boat. There was still enough light. They could have intercepted the boat.

But she gave the situation the benefit of the doubt because a part of her wanted Danny to have a chance to work the relationship out. But once home she rethought her position, and tried calling Danny at the camp because she needed to be sure. No one answered. She phoned multiple times, allowing an extra half hour for transit in case he made a turn down the wrong channel, but after the fourth time of receiving no pickup, she realized night had fully descended and feared she had waited too long. At that point, giving in to her fear, she called both the tribal police and the resort security. Because she was who she was, they agreed to send out a search boat.

It was a dark night, and the flowage was immense. Decades earlier, when the Coeur de Lattigeaux River had been dammed for the generation of electricity, the spreading waters turned swamps into miles of open water that stitched together the small lakes that were left behind from the glacial period. The resulting footprint was immense and included miles of rugged, tangled shorelines. From year to year, the edges of the flowage ebbed and grew as water levels shifted. There were many indistinct boundaries, all lined with brush. Everyone searching knew there was little chance of finding a missing boat in the darkness, but no one wanted to tell that to the widowed wife of the dead tribal leader.

In the morning, authorities added a helicopter to the mix, and it didn't take long to spot a craft jammed into half-submerged trees along one shoreline. By the time the rescue boat arrived, the motor on Danny's boat had run out of fuel but through the night its continual attempt to move forward firmly lodged it into the mix of brush and crumbling shore. On the boat's floor, Danny was lying in a pool of blood, unconscious. A bloody folding utility knife rested near him.

There was no sign of Josh.

A knock on the door interrupted Cynthia's thoughts. An elderly man who looked a lot like Danny peered in.

"Mr. Lahti, come in," Cynthia said. She was surprised to see Danny's father. Even though he lived nearby in Thread, it hadn't occurred to her that she should notify him. Now she felt a bit foolish. She wondered how he discovered that Danny was in the hospital, but remembered that bad news traveled fast in small towns.

"I'm sure Danny will be glad to see you when he wakes up," she said. She wasn't sure that was the truth.

"Do you think so?" he asked. "We don't talk much but maybe I should be changing that. Are you sure it's okay to stay?"

She nodded yes, and he took the other chair. Cynthia remembered when Danny's dad would sometimes come into the café back when she and Danny worked there as teenagers. He never had much to say then either, but she always trusted that he loved his son, but just didn't know how to show it. Remembering those days, she smiled at him and said a silent prayer that Danny would also smile when he saw his father.

Then another visitor appeared, really two. An officer from the tribal police entered the room, along with Andrew, the comptroller from Lattigo Industries.

"Is he awake yet?" the policeman asked Cynthia, even though he already knew the answer. It was a way to start the conversation.

"No," she replied. Seeing the young man's face upset Cynthia; she realized how tired she was of cops and their uniforms. This was one of the men she had talked to when Chip first went missing, but that didn't mean she wanted to talk to him again. Life was too complex, and no one ever wanted to unite all the untidy pieces.

"We wanted to give you an update, ma'am," the police officer said. "We've towed the boat back into the marina here in Lattigo, and it'll be a joint investigation that will involve both the tribal police and the county sheriff. It's not clear whether the incident happened in tribal waters or on state land. But we're used to cooperating." Then he blushed. No doubt he recalled the earlier and unresolved incidents regarding Chip Grant and the suspected embezzlement.

Andrew spoke next, "The officials will want to speak to Mr. Lahti as soon as he wakes. But based on what you already told us as well as the evidence in the boat, it seems pretty clear what happened. Given your account of the marina last night, we believe Josh Gunderson jumped on the boat with Danny Lahti as it was departing. It appears some type of altercation occurred once they were out in the lake, and that Mr. Gunderson pulled a knife from the tackle box to attack Mr. Lahti. Based on scuff marks and damage to the side of the boat, it looks like Mr. Lahti fought back and that in the struggle Mr. Gunderson went overboard."

"We're dragging the bottom of the lake near where we found the boat," the officer added. "And we're bringing in divers. But we may just have to wait for the body to reappear. As far as we can tell the boat was moving during the fight, so we don't really know exactly where the fight happened. The flowage is a huge area to search, and the bottom is littered with dead trees that could snag a clothed body. It's possible the body will turn up today, float up in a few days as it decomposes, or even that it might never be found."

"I understand," Cynthia murmured.

"But the state sent in its investigators who are processing the boat as a crime scene. We got blood samples, fingerprints, the knife, and soon we should be able to get a statement from our victim. We will make sense of it."

Andrew looked closely at Cynthia as he asked his next question. "Do you know why the two of them might have fought?" The Lattigo Industries comptroller had seen all of the material from her private investigator. No doubt he had his own suspicions on Josh's role in the Lattigo embezzlement, but luckily he didn't know the latest details about Josh.

Before she could answer, the sounds of the medical equipment changed. Danny moved, opened his eyes, and asked, "What happened?"

Danny found it extremely comfortable to remain living in the guest room at Cynthia's home, although he knew it was time to move home. The challenge was to know which home that should be—remain in Thread at the camp or return to the mansion in Los Angeles. As long as she would have him, he was prepared to stay with Cynthia.

Nearly a month had passed since the police discovered his unconscious body lying in the wale of the boat. During that time, he neither ventured back to the camp nor stepped onto the boat, which with Cynthia's help, had been returned to storage at the boathouse. It might have been wiser to have simply sold it, but like many things he held on. Cynthia also hired people to close up the camp. Sooner or later, he would have to deal with the place. But at the moment, he didn't want to give it any thought.

Despite a thorough search, the authorities never found Josh's body, but forensics evidence clearly identified both his fingerprints and blood on the boat. When combined with Cynthia's eyewitness account of the man jumping in the boat and Danny's testimony, no one doubted that Josh attacked Danny that night, that Danny responded in self-defense, and, as far as Danny knew, everyone believed Josh drowned when he was knocked overboard.

That was Danny's belief as well. Even though his innate sense of ESP often failed him, he still believed it tuned him in to the universe of people who mattered. He felt no presence of another. He had killed Josh.

In a way, it didn't really matter whether Josh was dead or alive. The man had legally handed his life over to Danny before his disappearance. As a result, everyone found it easy to finalize the liquidation of Josh's scattered assets, and the funds from the sale were in accounts under the control of Danny. If Josh's body never floated up, eventually they could petition the court to declare him dead. In the meantime, it made little difference.

At least it didn't make much of a difference to cold and logical minds. In reality, it mattered greatly. Danny suffered from knowing he could never ask Josh the questions he really wanted to know. For the rest of his life, he would struggle with what drove Josh to discover in Danny's behavior the answers to his personal life questions. What did he really expect to learn from testing Danny? Danny would never forget the look on Josh's face right before he fell overboard. There was a knowing satisfaction in it as though Danny had finally said or done what Josh wanted to see all along. Was it that Danny finally fought back? Or was it something else?

Danny understood the itching pain of questions that could never be answered. His mother's suicide left him with that pain. In a way, Josh provided Danny one gift, although he was certain that was never Josh's intent. While disclosing his mother's checkered past made her death more mysterious, the new information freed Danny. At last, he realized that it was impossible to know any other person's motivations, thoughts, fears, or goals. One could only hope to know one's own.

When he woke up in the hospital bed and saw his father there, he was surprised to realize the man's presence made him happy. Eventually, he knew he would ask his dad about the woman who died in that bombing and more details about his mother. Perhaps he could learn what made his father love his mother. For far too long, they had avoided talking about the person who had been so central to each of them. But Danny felt no hurry. He was just happy that his father cared enough to show up at his bedside.

All in all, it was a time for new beginnings. That's what he decided. After meeting with a psychiatrist to talk about Josh, he realized that Josh displayed the classic symptoms of a sociopath—the man didn't care what the rest of the world thought of him, nor was he bound by any social mores. Josh felt superior and free to do what he wished. That diagnosis made it easier for Danny to let Josh go.

There was plenty of money. At least Josh had left him that. When Danny finally decided where he wanted to live and what he wanted to do in the days ahead, cash would not be a concern. Likely, he would sell both houses and use much of the proceeds to set up a foundation to do some good.

Cynthia said that after her baby was born, she would like to join him in creating a fund to support youth from the local tribe and promote a better northwoods environment. It was a good idea. Maybe he could lure Kenosha to the Midwest to manage the charity.

The days ahead were bright. They were good. And Danny was happy that Josh was at the bottom of a lake.

One Year Later

"**Think back.**" That's what the voice on the radio counseled. In his hotel room, Danny was up very early to catch a return flight to Los Angeles. The day before he had attended the first day of Barbara Linsky's annual BLINK conference in Boston.

"Close your eyes. Think back to the very last time you were truly happy. Be slow and think deeply. Imagine looking completely around you. Go three hundred and sixty degrees around the scene. What can you see? Try to remember every detail, and let the feeling of that moment reconnect."

It had been so long since Danny felt unfettered happiness. He thought that hearing someone from Actuades speak about the algorithms and models developed at Premios and brought into glory at the fully capitalized firm would somehow bring about a sense of closure. Linsky insisted on his attending her conference. "Focus on the good that Josh brought into the world," she counseled. But a year had not reduced the pain and betrayal that he felt from their years together.

Neither time nor dragging the flowage between Thread and Lattigo ever brought up Josh's body. But Danny had moved on. With the passage of a year, he came to realize exactly what it was he saw in Josh's face that night. It was Josh's recognition that Danny intended to kill him, and for some reason seeing Danny's fury pleased Josh. He wanted Danny to choose anger.

"Breathe deeply," the radio talk show guest went on, "and allow your mind to flow backward to that happy moment." Danny snapped his travel bag closed, and sat on the edge of the bed. He considered following this early morning radio pop psychiatrist's advice.

"Why not?" he thought to himself as he sought to locate some former happy moment. He landed on a point in January of 1994, and almost laughed aloud imagining how strange it would seem to someone else that this instant in time should remain in his memory as a good moment. But there it was.

Danny mentally returned to a morning in 1994. It was after the sun had risen on the day of the destructive Northridge earthquake in Los Angeles. By then, Josh and Danny were living together in a small duplex in the hills of Silverlake, just a few houses from where Wally and Stephen lived. That day they woke to the fierce jostling of the world beneath. The power failed and the buildings groaned. Dishes were thrown from their cupboard and cracked into shards when they hit the tile floor. But the two boys were okay, and they held each other in the doorframe and kissed as the earthquake rumbled on. Danny remembered thinking, "What if this is our last kiss?" and he didn't care because he was in the arms of the man he loved.

But the shaking soon stopped. The old frame building did not collapse around them. Danny remembered how Josh looked at him that day, and in that moment Danny believed the person in his arms was someone who would do anything for him. And he was overjoyed to have him in his life.

But Danny hadn't yet to reach that last happy moment of his memory. That instance came later after the winter sun had fully risen that same morning, and when they could look across the bowl of west Los Angeles toward the Hollywood Hills. Smoke was rising in pockets from a few burning buildings, or maybe the puffs were just signals of outside campfires. The city sounds had shifted. Sirens punctuated the air, but there was no roar of the normal rush of traffic. It was the dawn of a different world, one in which time stood still. In that suspended moment everything might still be possible if everyone could only reach across and touch one another.

Josh suggested they dress, walk to the home of Wally and Stephen, and make sure their friends were okay. By the time they arrived, Stephen had already pulled his gas grill into the driveway, lit a fire, and was boiling water for coffee while heating a pan to fry eggs. They spied Wally walking up the street.

Just as the radio voice commanded, Danny tried to recall each detail. As he mentally looked in that direction, he recalled how Wally was encouraging two homeless people from the neighborhood to come along. It was as though he had invited them to breakfast. At the time, Danny remembered thinking how much they reminded him of two crazy old coots back in Thread.

And when Wally reached the group, he talked about something that seemed so odd. What was it? Did he say he had been dreaming about being back in Thread? Something about when they all met at the original Loon Town Café?

Doing this exercise almost made Danny feel as though he had traveled back in time. He could recall the look of the old coffee pot on the grill . . . the smell of the coffee in the chilly air . . . the homeless woman who displayed tinfoil woven in her hair and muttered about being tracked by aliens . . . and Josh's smile. Even now, prompted by memory, he felt himself smile in return. Then Stephen lifted up the pot to offer fresh coffee. He said the Loon Town Café was open again. Maybe that was the moment his friends decided to restart the restaurant in Los Angeles.

The exercise relaxed Danny. Strange that such a moment would stay with him after all these years. But at that time he had friends. He had a lover. He was part of a community of experience he valued. And now it was gone.

A rap at his hotel room door broke him out of his reverie. It must be room service delivering the quick breakfast that he planned to eat before departing for Logan Airport. Danny walked over to let the server in. When he opened the door, he saw a breakfast tray on the floor that had apparently been delivered earlier. His eyes moved up to see a person standing outside the door, but it wasn't a hotel employee. It was Josh.

Josh walked in and closed the door. "I don't have much time," he said.

"What? How?" Danny stammered. There was no way this was happening. Josh was dead. He had killed him and left him to drown in the cold waters of Wisconsin.

Josh handed him a set of car keys and a Hertz envelope. "There's a rental car waiting with the valet. I want you to take your bag, go down to the lobby, get in that car, and drive back to Wisconsin. Now."

"Why would I do that?" There was no way Danny would listen to Josh. He had a non-stop flight to catch to Los Angeles.

"Just do it. Get on Interstate 90. Stay on it all the way to Rockford, Illinois. Then turn onto U.S. Highway 51 and drive north into Wisconsin until you can branch off on 17 to go back to Thread. You'll be safe in Thread."

"What are you talking about? What are you involved with now? Why are you even here? Why aren't you dead?"

Josh seemed different—calmer, sadder, and maybe even crazier. "I couldn't help myself. I can't let anything go, so when I saw that someone was talking about my old projects at BLINK, I had to sneak back and hear what was said. I wondered what survived and what didn't. Interesting, but so sad that the best parts were abandoned. By some. But not by me. I've kept track in my own way of everything and everyone from those days. And then I saw you in the audience. And I knew there was something I had to do.

"That's why I'm here now. To keep you alive.

Danny didn't know what to say, so he stood there silent.

"In my own way, and you have to believe this. I love you. Back at the lake, I found out what I wanted to know, so now I promise that I'm going to let you live your life however you want. But first you need to listen to me. You need to change your plans. Drive home. Whatever I've done in the past, forget it. Trust me when I tell you to take this car and leave Boston."

Danny eyed him. Perhaps his willingness to listen was due to a remnant of the flush of good memories churned up by the just completed exercise, or maybe he decided it was safer to escape by just following the commands of a person he considered crazy. In the years that would follow, Danny never understood exactly why he listened to Josh, or why he didn't demand answers to all the questions in his mind. He just did what he was told.

He called down to the front desk to check out of the hotel, picked up his bag, and walked with Josh to the elevator. They rode down in silence. As they approached the valet station, Josh stayed at his side until they reached the car, and then he held the door as Danny got in.

He handed over the rental agreement and keys, "Follow Fremont until you see entrance signs for the Massachusetts Turnpike. That's Interstate 90 and it heads straight west. Drive safe. And don't forget me."

With that, Josh turned and disappeared into the foot traffic of downtown Boston. The valet closed the door. Danny started the engine, pulled out into the street, and drove through the narrow streets until he reached the turnpike to head west, away from the East Coast, back toward Wisconsin, returning home.

It was a beautiful morning. The sky was deep blue. The clouds were picture perfect. It would have been a wonderful day for flying. He could see contrails of jets in the sky above. Maybe one of those was the plane he should have been on. Would he listen to Josh and drive as promised, or would he detour and head toward a city to buy a new ticket and catch a different flight to L.A.? He still didn't know.

He thought back to his memory of the morning of the earthquake. When he opened the door to the person who showed up this morning, he saw something of the Josh he recalled in that memory. Danny decided to honor his promise to that memory. He would drive to Thread.

Danny laughed. Josh thought he had forced Danny to change, but the man was wrong. He hadn't changed at all. Nothing that God could throw his way would ever alter who he was. He was his own man, and now he was free to chart his own course, wherever he wanted, to whatever might lie in his future.

When he entered the car, he had thrown his sports coat on the passenger seat and he noticed that the boarding pass had fallen out of his inner pocket. It was resting on the seat. American Airlines flight 11, leaving Boston just before 8:00 am, headed toward the City of Angels. Some frequent flyer probably got upgraded to first class when Danny didn't show up to claim his seat. September 11 was going to be that person's lucky day.

Danny didn't care. He was in a car driving, leaving Josh behind forever, about to return home. He was ready to live life again. Alone and unentangled. Free of Josh. Free to be whatever he cared to be.

Author's Notes

This book completes the trio of novels that make up my Thread series—three works that interweave a related cast of characters and their same small hometown in northern Wisconsin. While each is written in a different genre—*Tales From the Loon Town Cafe* is a humorous novel about an oddball set of characters; *The Finnish Girl* is a dark family saga; and *The Devil's Analyst* is a more traditional mystery thriller—together, I hope they create a believable and compelling set of characters.

I would like to thank several people who helped me complete this title. My thanks to Betty Cary who diligently provided a copy edit of the draft and made sure I was consistent with so many details. Tina Masiak and Chris Storey were equally assiduous in making certain that I kept my timeline and my geographical references accurate. I also appreciate an early reading by Dixie Walker who warned me so often when I got carried away. Thanks also to the many readers who have ever sent me a comment or posted a review. Above all, I would like to thank my husband Robert Tieman who has been my rock of support and best of critics ever since I decided to chuck corporate life early and pursue writing in my retirement.

Finally, I salute the talents of Dena Kuhn at AzureFire who has done a masterful job at designing the current covers for all three titles in the Thread series.

ABOUT THE AUTHOR

Dennis Frahmann grew up in Wisconsin, trained in journalism, and spent most of his adult life in New York, Minneapolis, and Los Angeles. Today he resides with his husband, Robert Tieman, in the seaside village of Cambria, California. This is his third novel.

To learn more, visit www.loontown.com or follow the author at www.facebook.com/loontowncafe

www.ingramcontent.com/pod-product-compliance
Lightning Source LLC
Chambersburg PA
CBHW051235260626
47162CB00002B/448